# DRAGONS LIVE FOREVER

---

Written and illustrated
By
Sandy Wright

# DRAGONS LIVE FOREVER

Copyright © 2016 by Sandy Wright

# DEDICATION

This book is dedicated to the people around me that constantly enrich my life. My husband Stewart, whose love and support, not to mention his computer skills made this book possible. Our little dog Ellie who makes me smile every day.

My Mum, who encouraged me to keep writing despite my appalling spelling. My sisters: Celia and Tina, whom I love and miss very much.

To all my friends and family in New Zealand and England, who, over the years have encouraged me to write and paint.

And of course a special mention for Peter, Paul and Mary, who released the song Puff (The Magic Dragon). The song that so upset me as a child, but set the seed that has been growing for many years and has now blossomed into this book

# TABLE OF CONTENTS

| | | |
|---|---|---|
| 1. | Introduction | 9 |
| 2. | Island of the lost | 11 |
| 3. | Stranger than fiction | 41 |
| 4. | Don't mess with the boss's wife | 60 |
| 5. | Drink me | 74 |
| 6. | Dragon song | 87 |
| 7. | Running out of time | 102 |
| 8. | On our way | 106 |
| 9. | Island of dreams | 115 |
| 10. | Precious gold | 127 |
| 11. | Going home | 161 |
| 12. | Goodbye can be the hardest word | 175 |
| 13. | Change isn't always a good thing | 193 |
| 14. | Another adventure | 202 |
| 15. | I spy | 216 |
| 16. | Seek and you shall find | 224 |
| 17. | Beauty and the beast | 246 |
| 18. | The best laid plans | 265 |
| 19. | Who's hunting who | 290 |
| 20. | The cavalry | 308 |
| 21. | Choices | 345 |
| 22. | A change of heart | 363 |
| 23. | Home at last | 382 |

# INTRODUCTION

This book is fiction. However there are people working very hard every day to preserve life for future generations. Sadly there are over 41,415 species on the IUCN red list and 16,306 are endangered species threatened with extinction. It is estimated that in the last 500 years human activity has forced over 800 species into extinction.

By working together we can find ways to protect and care for our world and all of the creatures we share it with.

We all need a sanctuary.

# ISLAND OF THE LOST

It rained in the night, the constant drumming on the canvas overhead kept me awake, and so had the many voices of creatures that emerged, as darkness fell. It occurred to me, that nature didn't just whisper, it shouted its existence, at the top of its voice, and there were some pretty strange voices here!

The sun was high in the sky, when I eventually dragged myself from my tent. Over the last few years, I'd gotten used to sleeping under canvas, and had known little else. The noise of the Island was almost deafening, with birds and insects, all excited to get on with the new day. Was it Monday - Wednesday? I had no idea. I wasn't even sure, what month it was. It was just another day.

\*\*\*

I'd spent most of the time since my accident, here on this Island. The job offer had come out of the blue, but at a junction where I'd needed some time to think, and recover from my injuries. This Island, in the middle of the ocean, had given me a new focus on life. In actual fact, I didn't have a clue where it was, but that had been part of the deal. Strange maybe, but at that point, I didn't much care where I went, as long as it was away from the whispers and smirks of the people around me. People I'd once called my friends. Funny how you see a different side of people when things start to fall apart - the backside of them, as they disappear into the distance at speed. I think maybe, I'd just always chosen to be around the wrong kind of people. My mother would be the first to agree with that.

I washed in the stream nearby, which was now overflowing with fresh water from the downpour. The water was refreshing and crystal clear, however looking up I spotted a small bird on a branch directly above my head. It sounded, for all the world, as if it were laughing at me. Maybe I'd choose another spot, next time.

Breakfast consisted of little cardboard flakes, from my supplies. God how I missed Bacon and Eggs! I'd been given the things I would need, when I was dropped off, but I suspected, someone had been less than honest. I told myself, it was better than nothing, but while I was eating my cardboard food, I imagined that somewhere, someone was tucking into a steak, bought with the money, left over from the food budget for my trip. I bet whoever packed this rubbish, was having a laugh at my expense.

It seemed everyone was laughing at me lately. Ironic really, the hunter had become an easy target!

After dressing, I grabbed my notebook and camera. My job here was to catalogue and photograph the wildlife on this isolated and uninhabited island. It had seemed strange, to be offered a complete turnaround in my career, but I needed to work, and this was as far away from everyone as I could get. So I'd jumped at the offer, without asking too many questions.

To my surprise I found I enjoyed working with my camera and I liked the fact that the animals and birds, I found living on the island would remain alive, long after I'd left.

I'd managed to catch the occasional fish - to supplement the cardboard. I had my riffle with me, but somehow I couldn't bring myself to point it, at the small wild pigs, I often saw nosing around my camp. They did treat me with suspicion, it was hard not to imagine them turning on a spit.

Instead I photographed them and laughed at their antics, they were very entertaining and company too. They seemed quite intelligent, too intelligent to eat my card board food.

I headed for the beach to photograph the birds visiting the island, to breed on the rocky cliff's edge. They crowded together, and clung to life on little ledges, high above the beach. Constantly screaming and cursing one another, at the tops of their voices, not unlike a lot of the human population I'd known over the years. They couldn't stand, to be together, but would struggle, to survive apart.

\*\*\*

The beach here was simply beautiful, the ocean looked calm, but today something in the translucent, turquoise waters caught my eye. A glint of light, as I watched the sparkle came closer.

My eyes focused but my brain struggled to catch up. This had to be a dream - for what was emerging slowly from the crystal waters, couldn't possibly be real. Could it, Could she?

I'd really been isolated far too long, I had after all, started to talk to pigs, lately! Maybe I'd had a little too much sun or cardboard poisoning?

In front of me a beautiful woman emerged from the waters. I was transfixed by this strange vision of loveliness.

13

There was no sign of a boat. We were miles from anywhere. Where had she come from, was I dreaming, did I even care?

She approached from the shallow water, her long blond hair hung loosely to her waist, a few strands, held back from her face with a pearl comb. She seemed to glisten, as small droplets of water cascaded down her slim body. And oh - what a body!

I did notice however that my vision of loveliness, had a fairly impressive knife, sheathed in a belt around her waist. She was wearing a white swimsuit, that was a little too sensible, to be from one of my dreams.

But - hey, I was in the middle of nowhere, wearing khaki shorts and a T-shirt with 'Too Hot to Handle' embossed on the front. I was beginning to regret that choice of outfit, although in my defence, when I'd put it on, this morning, I certainly hadn't been expecting company. Both T-shirt and shorts had seen better days, a bit like me.

As my Vision approached, I noticed how impossibly green her eyes were. They seemed to be looking into my head and reading my thoughts, and she definitely shouldn't know my thoughts at this moment. God, she was so beautiful.

I was in a trance until the vision in front of me shook her head, and cold water droplets splashed my face and brought me back, to what I assumed was reality.

"Where the hell did you come from? This island is private," I shouted and instantly hated myself. What the hell was that? I really had been alone too long. Thankfully, my vision ignored my outburst.

She smiled patiently and asked, "Is your camp nearby? I could really do with a drink."

My mind was working overtime now. Maybe she had been shipwrecked. Oh god- and I was giving her the third degree, hardly the knight in shining armour. At this rate, I was likely to be alone for a very, very long time.

I gathered my senses. "Look I'm sorry, can we start this again? My name is Alan. As far as I knew, I was here alone. I was just surprised to see someone, especially someone like..." my voice trailed off. I could feel myself going red all the way to my toes.

She continued, "My name's Natasha and I have been sent to find you Alan."

I found myself wanting to hear her say my name again, and at that moment I really didn't care why she was here, or how she got here - I just didn't want her to leave. Ever!

I led the way to my camp, which seemed a lot untidier then I remembered it this morning.

For the first time in what seemed like ages, I had company, real company. "I only have water," I said apologetically.

She took the plastic cup I offered, "That's fine," she said and drank it all. I refilled her cup. We sat on the log by my tent. Apart from my small bed, it was the only furniture in the camp. Just thinking about the bed made me blush again.

I quickly pulled a couple of pairs of pants (thankfully – clean-ish) from my makeshift washing line. I hoped she hadn't noticed, but the smile on her face told me otherwise and yet again I felt the rush of red to my face.

"I was sent to find you Alan, and offer you a job. I'm sorry if I took you by surprise." She glanced at the underwear I was trying - without much success, to stuff into my pockets. She smiled and continued, it would have proved difficult to get word to you, and Colin thought it would be best if someone talked to you in person.

I felt confused I have a job. I already work for Colin Jacobs. I presume we are talking about the same Colin. Millionaire - owns this and several other islands?

She smiled. Yes, he thought you might be ready for a new challenge.

Now I was suspicious. What sort of challenge? Although I'd heard a lot about the man, I'd never actually met him. The job offer, I had accepted, was sent to me by e-mail and arranged through an office in London. Of course it had seemed strange, but I was in a strange place at the time and had accepted the offer without too much thought. Now I was in an even stranger place and feeling a little unsure of my future.

Is Colin not happy with my work here? I already told his office I hadn't done this type of thing before. I was a hunter for many years, but he should know, that I have no intention of ever hunting again. If that's what this is all about, then you are wasting your time.

Natasha touched my arm. It was a good job I was sitting down, or my knees would have given way. Please don't be upset Alan, we know all about you and your former work.

I thought I heard a little hostility in the words 'former work' but if it was there, it was only for a second and she followed it with a compliment. When you did hunt Alan, you were one of the best. I was told you could find anything, and it is this skill, we require.

"The best," I added. I still had my pride. However, just to get my point across I added for emphasis, "I won't kill any more, nor will I help you kill."

Natasha seemed to soften a little. "We know that too, but we need your help to find something. We don't want to kill it and more importantly we don't want anyone else to kill it, in fact, quite the opposite. Will you help us Alan?"

I couldn't think straight, I was struggling with her proposal. "Look, I'm not sure I understand why you've chosen me for this task. Colin can afford to employ anyone, so I'm pretty sure, he could find whatever it is he's looking for, without my help."

She wasn't giving up, she hit me with another compliment.

"You said it yourself Alan, you are the best." Her smile lit up the camp, and I felt myself swell with pride. However, reality was at last beginning to kick in and I felt I needed to tell her that I had my doubts.

"I was the best, but I'm really not so sure anymore, you see - I had an accident, sometime ago."

She smiled, reassuringly. "We know about the accident, but your injuries have healed Alan, and you look well."

"I am fully recovered from my injuries, thank you. Unfortunately some people - well most people, think I'm stark raving mad. They say, I left my mind up in the mountains."

She seemed to be studying me. "Do you think you lost your mind Alan?"

Could I tell her, I wasn't sure anymore. Colin must have heard the stories, hell everyone had heard the stories - it had been all over the news. Perhaps no one had told her.

I felt I had to explain. "Look Natasha, on my last hunt I nearly died. I came back with a story that even I find hard to believe."

"I would like to hear it Alan," she said.

I shrugged. "Ok what the hell, there's no television on this island and the newspapers had certainly found it entertaining. I would like to say that you shouldn't believe everything you read, but in this case it was true! Well some of it. I believe in one local rag, there was proof that I'd been abducted by aliens. If nothing else - it will make you laugh."

She smiled. "Colin told me a little about you, but I think I would prefer to hear your version of events Alan, I can't imagine, it will contain anything but the truth."

Her lovely green eyes seemed full of genuine interest. How could I refuse, in fact it was strange, suddenly I felt I wanted to talk about it, for months I'd been trying so hard to forget. Perhaps I really was getting better. I tried to focus and recount my experience.

"A few months ago I was in the mountains, miles from the nearest town, hunting a mountain lion. There was a good price on its head. Stories abounded of a monster, three or four times bigger than normal. I'd become separated from my group. This didn't worry me, my senses always worked better without distractions. I suspected we were looking for a large male. We had followed its tracks for days. They were big tracks, but in the snow it's often difficult to judge accurately.

My senses told me I was close, so I took aim. I thought I was ready for anything, how wrong can you be. What eventually exploded from the tree's, took all the breath from me. I'd never seen a cat that big! I stared into huge green eyes and hesitated. I don't know whether it leapt at me, or was simply just trying to get past me. I got a shot off, but at the same time, I lost my footing on some loose stones and fell.

How far I fell I don't know. All I remember was the pain, and then I blacked out.

I should have been dead alone in the snow, but when I came too, I was in a cave. I drifted in and out of a dream. The large cat with beautiful green eyes licked and cleaned my wounds. It dripped water into my mouth with a huge paw, and lay down by myside at night to keep me warm against the freezing cold of the mountains."

I stopped and looked at Natasha, expecting laughter or at least a sign of sympathy for this poor mad man. Instead, she just looked back with those soul piercing eyes. It struck me that her eyes were the same colour as the mountain lions, and just as deep and mesmerizingly beautiful.

I continued, "I was found three days later, in a cave high in the mountains. My rescuers couldn't understand how, in my state, I'd made it to the cave high on the hillside. I had managed to tear off pieces of my clothing, to leave a trail they could follow. I'd somehow kept from freezing to death, although there was no trace of a fire.

It was over a week before I was strong enough to tell my story. A month later I was able to leave the hospital, but only after convincing them I wasn't a danger to the public.

They blamed my ramblings on a head injury. I should have kept quiet. Everyone thinks I went mad on that mountain. Hell, I think I went mad on that mountain! But no one can explain how I survived. I should have died - I would have died. Someone or something helped me, I am sure of that. I'm also pretty sure it didn't have anything to do with little green men. It's alright if you laugh, I'm used to it. "

Instead of laughing, she smiled her beautiful smile and reached out and placed her hand on mine. "Why would I laugh Alan?" Her reaction was unexpected. "Tell me more about what you remember." Her hand felt so warm on mine.

"You really believe me?" I could have kissed her, for more reasons than the obvious one! This woman was the most beautiful thing I'd ever laid eyes on, and she believed me.

Natasha squeezed my hand. "Of course I believe you. Why would you lie?"

It sounded so simple. I laughed, and immediately found myself relaxing. I began to talk, for the first time, about how safe I'd felt lying next to that big cat. I remembered no fear - just peace, and how her thick fur had warmed me. (I just knew it, was female). Even though I was in a lot of pain from my injuries, there was a part of me that would have loved to stay in that cave - high on the mountain - safe and warm. If the search party, hadn't found me, that's exactly where I'd be now.

To have someone listen to my story, and not only believe me but actually seem interested, was amazing. Here I was, on an island with the most beautiful woman I had ever seen, and she believed me - or at least she seemed to.

For the first time in a long while, I felt happy and almost sane.

Well - happy any way.

Natasha looked serious for a moment. "Alan, you need to come with me. I know you're not mad, but there are some things you couldn't possibly understand.

I'm not the one to explain, but if you come with me tomorrow, at day break - I'll take you to someone who will show you what you need to know. Perhaps then, you may begin to understand many things. For now however, I need you to just trust me Alan, can you do that?"

I considered this, "Is the, someone you're taking me to, Colin Jacobs? I don't understand what he has to do with all this."

Natasha just smiled that lovely smile again. "Be ready at dawn Alan, and you will find out."

Could I trust her, on the other hand, how could I refuse her? "Ok I'll come. I think I've been alone on this island for long enough. You had best take the tent, as it can get a little cold and wet at night."

She laughed. "Thanks, but I've made other arrangements. I'll see you in the morning, bright and early."

I was shocked. How could she just leave, and where would she go?

"We're on an island, alone in the middle of nowhere. Come on, my company can't be that bad. At least have some food with me - It's bloody awful, but there aren't that many restaurants around here."

She laughed again. "Thank you Alan, but I'll be fine." She turned and headed towards the beach.

I blamed the wild pigs. They'd probably warned her about the cardboard food! I waited a few minutes then followed. I felt sure, that once she realized there was little or no protection out there, she would change her mind. Besides, I didn't want to lose sight of her, just in case this really was a dream.

When I reached the beach, she had already vanished, it was deserted.

The light was beginning to fade, so I headed back to my camp. I should just pack up my things, and be ready to head off at dawn.

While I was getting my few possessions together, I began to doubt myself again. Had all this really happened? Maybe I really was just plain crazy. How could Colin Jacobs, give me the answers I'd been looking for. What answers? I wasn't even sure, of the questions. Natasha said he would show me, for some reason that sentence worried me. She did seem to believe me when I'd told her my story, but come to think of it, that was strange too.

\*\*\*

Sleep came in fits and starts, I drifted in and out of strange dreams, where large cats and beautiful women with green eyes, came and went. I saw huge mountains, deep forests and always the ocean. I could leap and dive through turquoise waters. I was searching for something, there was something always just out of sight, with the music of a half forgotten melody ringing in my ears, a strange but beautiful song, calling to me from so far away.

\*\*\*

Waking well before dawn, I washed and gathered my belongings.

I scattered the cardboard food around, just in case the pigs changed their minds. I'd miss them. I checked my notes. I was going to see my boss. I felt sure he would want an update on what I'd been doing the past few months. I hurried to the beach, hoping to see Natasha splashing through the waves and emerging from the sea again. Yes - definitely mad.

"Are you ready?" I nearly jumped out of my skin, as Natasha's voice had come from just behind my right ear. I spun around, nearly knocking her over with my rucksack.

"Sorry, you startled me! I thought – oh - never mind, what I thought." I felt my cheeks burning and tried to hide my embarrassment. "Did you sleep well?" I wanted to ask her where and how, but somehow knew I wouldn't get any answers.

Natasha smiled and led the way up the beach, I had to run to keep pace with her. She was still wearing the same white swimsuit. I noticed she had nothing on her feet, and her hair was dripping wet. Where the hell had she spent the night?

There were so many questions running around my head, but unfortunately the questions would have to wait, as it took all my energy just to keep up. I had a good idea where we would be heading, the only way on and off the island was a small airstrip. I'd been dropped there a few months ago with my tent and provisions.

When we arrived, it was obvious that the airstrip hadn't been used since then. The grass was quite long and I hoped a plane would be able to land safely. There was no time to dwell on this thought, as I could already hear the drone of the aircraft approaching.

Natasha stopped and turned to face me. "You are sure about this Alan? There's no going back once you get on that plane." She flashed those green eyes at me again, and although it seemed a little dramatic, I felt she was sincere. It didn't really matter at this point because I would have followed her pretty much, anywhere.

"I'm sure," I said, with as much confidence as I could muster. I pondered my immediate situation: I was leaving the island, with a mysterious and beautiful woman with flashing green eyes. To go who knew where and do who knew what, I had to admit, this was the best I'd felt in a long, long time.

The plane landed easily on the grass strip. Strangely I couldn't see anyone in the cockpit. I turned to Natasha to comment but she was already on the move. The plane came to a stop a short distance away, and Natasha headed for the steps.

Once inside, she put on an oversized shirt that had been placed on one of the empty seats. She indicated for me to sit. The door that led to the cockpit was closed and remained so. Everything seemed to have been pre-arranged. I had been expected.

I wondered if I'd ever really had a choice. After all, it was Colin Jacob's island.

Natasha handed me a glass of what tasted like fruit juice, but was hard to identify. It tasted a little strange, but I didn't like to complain. She sat down in a seat across the aisle from me, and I tried to find out a little more about my beautiful companion. However she was not in a talkative mood. Natasha reclined her seat, and pointedly closed her eyes.

I focused my attention outside the small window, it would be useful to try to work out where we were heading. However, geography was never my strong point. Put me down in a forest or jungle and tell me what you wanted and I could find just about anything. I've always had a knack for finding things. Gran called it a gift, but I'm pretty sure the animals I've hunted over the years wouldn't see it that way.

I tried to focus, but suddenly, I just couldn't seem to keep my eyes open. I tried to think, but my head felt fuzzy and I desperately needed to sleep. I would just close my eyes for a second.

\*\*\*

The next thing, I was aware of, was the change in the engine noise. We were coming in to land. My mouth was dry and my head still felt a little fuzzy. Well so much for finding out my location. I didn't even know how long I'd slept. My watch gave up on me a long time ago - a little like most of the people I knew. The watch was a gift from my father, although broken I still wore it. I could depend on it being right twice a day, that gave me one thing I could still rely on.

Looking through the window, I could see that we seemed to be coming down in the middle of a dense jungle, where a large air strip had been cleared. It was obviously capable of handling larger planes than this one. I suddenly remembered my lovely companion, and looked around. Natasha was watching me from across the aisle. Oh god, I bet I'd been snoring or dribbling or both! Once again I felt my cheeks burn - she had a way of making me feel like an awkward sixteen year old again, spots an all.

"We're here," she said, breaking the awkward silence, "Are you alright Alan?"

I shook my head trying to clear it. "Yes - sorry - I don't know what came over me. I don't usually sleep much on planes." Natasha seemed a little embarrassed but she just smiled and looked away. I had a funny feeling I knew exactly what had come over me - the strange tasting juice.

Still avoiding my gaze, she continued, "Colin sends his apology's Alan, but he has business to attend to. I will escort you to the house and he will see you at dinner."

"That's great," I said. I was more than happy to have extra time alone with Natasha, even if she had spiked my drink. No woman had ever gone to such lengths to avoid talking to me before. We left the plane, having neither seen nor heard a pilot, but my mind was on Natasha. I was looking forward to the next part of the journey, and hopefully I could keep myself awake.

\*\*\*

A small buggy was waiting a short distance from the plane, and we climbed in. Natasha drove us along a well-made road, through the thick vegetation. It was hard to see anything but trees, however the noise told me that the island must be home to a multitude of birds and animals, and I found myself imagining what might lurk beyond the tree line.

"How long have you worked for Mr. Jacobs?" I ventured.

"Colin and I have known each other a long time."

I got the feeling again that I wasn't going to find out much, so I tried a different tact. "It looks like a beautiful island - is there much wildlife here?" This seemed to work, it was obvious that Natasha had a passion for the island and its inhabitants.

She talked about the many rare and endangered plants, birds, and other species that lived here. As if on cue, a huge bird stepped out in front of us, Natasha had to break hard to avoid hitting it - although I had little doubt, that we would have been the ones that came off badly.

"What the hell is that?" I half whispered, it resembled an ostrich on steroids, and was far bigger than any bird I'd ever seen. It eyed us with suspicion, but showed no fear. Natasha didn't seem at all alarmed.

"It's alright," she said softly - More to the bird than to me, I think. "Isn't she fabulous? They've been here a long time, before any of us, they tend to treat the place like their own. That's a female. She will be fine as long as we don't upset her. They're very powerful birds. Sadly, I believe there are none left in their native home of New Zealand. "

"I wouldn't dream of upsetting her," I said nervously. In my memory something stirred. "It looks a bit like a moa! Did you say it was originally from New Zealand?"

"Yes I believe so," she said with a smile, as if this was nothing out of the ordinary.

I tried again, "Natasha, they have been extinct for hundreds of years."

She shrugged. "Yes, sad isn't it. We'll go around her."

She manoeuvred the buggy carefully around the huge bird, and from where I was sitting it didn't seem to be very extinct, or come to think of it, even slightly endangered.

I just stared speechless, until it disappeared into the bush. "But they don't exist, anymore," I said, half to myself. This didn't make any sense.

Natasha laughed. "I wouldn't want to be the one to tell her that, would you Alan?"

I found myself laughing too. I shook my head. "No, but I don't understand - how did she get here? I'm guessing she didn't fly."

Natasha laughed again. "You're very funny Alan."

She explained that Colin was interested in the preservation of many creatures, big and small and that this, and several other islands, had become a sort of last stand.

I listened, still not sure if what I'd seen could possibly have been real – although the truth was, that at this moment, even if Elvis himself walked out of the woods, I really wouldn't care. I was sitting next to the most beautiful woman I had ever met, and she thought I was funny. That would do for now.

The house appeared to be part of the bush - a sort of huge tree house supported by massive poles. We pulled up in front of several garages. I supposed these held the more prestigious vehicles owned by this millionaire. I felt a little hurt, that a golf buggy had been seen as the right thing to collect me in, although, Colin had sent an Angel and a private plane. Previously the most anyone had bothered with was a second class plane ticket and a Taxi fare.

Natasha was already out of the buggy. "I have things I must attend to," she said, leading the way up the large wooden staircase, so I will have Jack show you to your quarters."

I wanted to ask her more questions, just to get her to stay even for a few more moments, but the sound of barking startled me. I looked along the corridor that stretched out in front of us. I'd had a bad experience with dogs: in fact I'd had four bad experiences. I've been bitten four times, each by a different dog. It wasn't that any of them were serious bites, just a few stitches - that was all. But I was well aware that I had a sort of chemistry with dogs, and it was all bad!

I automatically took a step back.

Natasha looked concerned. "Are you ok Alan? You don't have allergies do you?"

I shook my head, "No, it's just - I have a thing about dogs. They don't usually like me much," I confessed.

She laughed. "Oh spike is fine, he loves everyone. Its Jack you will need to watch."

I didn't understand what she meant.

Spike appeared at high speed. A small terrier cross, flew down the corridor towards us, skidded past us on the tiled floor, and collided with a small table sending it flying. I had to smile. Undeterred, he gained control and made a bee line for Natasha. With one impossible leap he was soon in her arms and licking her face with enthusiasm. I couldn't help thinking, lucky dog.

Natasha managed to get Spike under control and said "Hello Jack, this is the guest we have been expecting."

I swung around. I hadn't heard anyone approaching, yet standing just behind us was a tall athletic looking guy, with piecing blue eyes. What was it with these people and the eyes? Jack was a good few inches taller than my six foot, with long dark hair.

For just a moment, I thought Natasha hadn't been joking about Jack. Of course I must have imagined it, but for a split second I thought he actually - growled at me. It made the hairs on the back of my neck stand up, but I put it down to my over active imagination. Natasha left me with Jack. He made me nervous. It didn't help much, when before Natasha left she lent close to Jack and I heard her whisper, "Be nice Jack - please."

Spike however was a different matter. He had decided to make me feel at home by leaping into my arms, and giving my face the same close attention he had given Natasha. I would not normally have been comfortable with this, but somehow I couldn't help but like the little fellow.

I had taken an instant dislike however to Jack, and the feeling seemed mutual. He led the way to my room in silence. Three corridors and what seemed like a few miles later, we stopped outside a door, he pointed. "Your room," he growled.

"Thanks," I said, trying to sound as friendly as possible. As he turned and left, I felt relieved to see him disappear down the corridor.

It was left to Spike to show me my room - or at least he tore around chasing his tail, and jumping on and off the bed. I didn't know if this was allowed, but after all I was the visitor here, so I let him have his fun. After a while he tired of this and scratched at the door. I let him out and he raced off down the corridor, getting paw spin on the tiled floor.

*\*\**

The first thing I did was shower. I looked in the mirror for the first time in a long while. I needed a shave. My thick light brown hair had been bleached almost blond by the sun, and now reached my shoulders. Pale blue almost-grey eyes, looked back at me. I looked older than my 26 years, but I felt older too. I shrugged, maybe the beard. That definitely had to go. Anyway - this was pure luxury: hot water and fluffy clean towels. It had been a long time since I'd had these simple pleasures, and I hadn't realized how much I'd missed them.

I lay back on the huge bed, and tried to think over all the things that had happened in the last couple of days. So many strange things, Jack was definitely strange, and the beautiful Natasha too. Where the hell, had that large bird come from? Could it really be a moa? You could fit what I knew about birds on the back of a postage stamp, but I remembered seeing one in a museum somewhere and it had definitely been placed in the: has been extinct for a long time category. There were definitely some strange things going on here.

Funny but the only one I felt completely at home with was Spike, and dogs were not usually my thing.

*\*\**

I needed some air, and I thought it would be a good idea to have a look around.

Leaving my room I headed in the direction I thought, should lead to the lobby, and the stairs down into the grounds. Not as easy as I expected, as it turned out this place was like a rabbit warren. I felt sure I must be going around in circles, but then I heard Spike barking and followed the sound. This took me through some double doors, down some stairs and into a small courtyard.

Spike had just managed to thrust the small tennis ball he'd been holding in his mouth, into the bush - a pretty impressive throw for a small dog. I was up for the game, so I walked towards the undergrowth to try and retrieve it for my new found friend.

The bush in front of me growled, I stopped, frozen to the spot. I knew Spike must have heard it too, but instead of running for cover he started to leap up and down, barking madly. For a few terrifying seconds, I had visions of us both being on the menu: me the main course, and Spike the appetizer or dessert.

Suddenly the tennis ball cannoned back past us. Spike barked with delight and chased it down. I breathed again. Whatever it was, had now gone. I got the feeling Spike had some very large playmates, that I would prefer not to meet. We played for a while, thankfully with no more support from the side-lines.

*\*\**

The sound of the door opening at the top of the stairs made both of us look up. "Hi, I'm Colin and you must be Alan. I am pleased to finally meet you."

Spike greeted Colin with his usual enthusiasm. Colin was a lot younger than I'd imagined. He was probably in his late thirties, tall with dark hair and I was pleased to see as he came down the stairs to shake my hand, that his eyes were a normal shade of brown.

"I see you've met Spike, he's a great little character isn't he?"

I agreed. "Yes we're getting along well. I'm not usually a dog person, but that doesn't seem to worry him. "

"My son Toby chose his name, he thought it made him seem more aggressive.

Jack and Spike have a little competition going between them, to see who can kill any unwanted little visitors who somehow make it onto the island. I'm not sure who is leading at present.

I guess Natasha will have introduced you to Jack. I hope he was polite - his social skills are sometimes a little lacking."

"He was fine," I lied. "So Jack's a trapper here?" That did make sense. I found it easy to imagine Jack as a bit of a killer.

Colin laughed. "I think it's safe to just say - he gets rid of other predators."

I tried to put the thought of hunting out of my mind. I changed the subject. "Natasha is an interesting woman. Has she been working for you long?"

Colin smiled. "Ah yes, the lovely Natasha. We have known each other since we were children, we had a mutual friend. Now, shall we go to dinner, I'm starving!"

Trying not to sound too desperate, I asked, "Will Natasha and Jack be joining us?" I was really hoping to see Natasha again. Jack - not so much.

He smiled, maybe reading my mind. "Yes Natasha will join us. Jack rarely eats with us he prefers to make his own arrangements.

I' m sure you have a lot of questions Alan and I will answer them all in good time, but if you will bear with me, I would prefer we wait until the morning. I have things I would like you to see, which I think will help to explain a lot, but for now let's eat."

Colin led the way to the dining room where a large round table was set for five. I was about to ask if he had other visitors, when Natasha appeared in the doorway and all other thoughts were swept from my mind.

A vision of loveliness dressed in a long red dress, which hugged every curve of that perfect body. Her long blonde hair flowed around her shoulders and a pearl comb held a few golden strands in place. She couldn't have been out of the shower long, as a droplet of water dripped from a strand of loose hair and onto her bare neck. My eyes followed it, transfixed, as it made its journey over her shoulder and down between the mounds of her breasts.

I suddenly realized where my gaze had wandered and feeling totally embarrassed, forced myself to look up - only to look straight into those beautiful green eyes.

She smiled. She had to be aware of the effect she was having on me.

I tried to focus. "It's good to see you again Natasha." I found myself wishing we were alone. Behind Natasha, a boy had just entered the room. He was about 13 or 14, with dark hair and a confident smile. It didn't take much to work out he must be Colin's son. My heart sank for an awful moment I had the thought that Natasha could be his mother. With relief I saw he was followed closely by an attractive woman with the most amazing head of long, curly auburn hair. Like Jack, she had those piercing blue eyes. Unlike Jack however, she had a warm smile and greeted me like a long lost friend. I instantly found myself liking her. She offered me her hand

"I'm Sophie, Colin's wife and this is our son Toby. We have so been looking forward to meeting you Alan, and hoping you would be joining the team. There aren't many visitors to the island - because it's a bit off the beaten track," she said and glanced at Colin.

"We are quite remote here, but it suits our purpose," Colin explained.

"Where exactly are we?" I asked, I noticed Sophie left the answers to Colin.

"The island is unnamed. We don't want to draw any attention to ourselves here, so no name means - no place on the maps. In the grand scheme of things we are very insignificant, and that's how we want to stay."

"Dad calls it 'The Island of the lost' Toby said with a wry smile.

Colin just laughed. I was pleased to see that I'd been seated next to Natasha.

Colin kissed his wife warmly, and gave his son a fatherly slap on the back. "And what's our only offspring been up to today - and don't say school work. I happened to look in on you when I got back. The Books were all there, but there was no sign of the scholar."

Toby grunted, "I joined Natasha for a swim with the dolphins in the bay."

Colin shook his head. "You're getting as attached to the water as she is. Just be careful how far out you go."

Toby scowled, "Oh Dad, I'm not a kid anymore."

Sophie laughed. "He's been working hard lately darling, so cut him some slack. As long as he's with Natasha you know he'll come to no harm in the water."

Natasha caught my eye - which wasn't difficult, and smiled. "We were fishing, and we lost track of time Colin, but you know he's safe with me." For my benefit she added, "The water is my second home Alan, I love the ocean and - I swim pretty well." There was a snigger from Toby across the table.

Sophie changed the subject. "Alan, I hope Natasha has taken care of you. You must have had time to talk on your way out here. I hope she had good things to say about us all."

"We didn't talk as much as I would have liked, but it was obvious that she has a passion for the island." I glanced at Natasha, she smiled back.

Colin nodded. "We all love the island - it's our home, and more importantly its home to many others. What we're doing here is very important, but I won't say too much tonight. Tomorrow I'll show you around and explain things as best I can."

"Thanks that would be great."

Toby had been watching me, he couldn't contain himself any longer, "Alan, you don't look anything like the pictures in the papers. We read your story and Dad said you were very lucky to be alive. The area of mountains where you were, is thick with forest, there are no paths up to the cave where you were found. Your rescuers did well, even with the trail she had laid for them."

I wasn't surprised they had read the papers. "Who is this she you speak of Toby? The papers said I must have laid the trail!"

I looked around the table. Suddenly everyone was looking everywhere but at me.

I'd agreed to wait till tomorrow, but Toby had started this. I wanted answers now, "Colin have you been there. How is it you seem to know more than the tabloids?"

Colin shot a look at Toby and sighed. "We went up there after we read your story. A mountain lion of the size you suggested is rare: some would say impossibly rare. As you already discovered, no one believed you Alan, but we did. We had to go and see for ourselves.

The team Sophie spoke of, has been put together to seek out and rescue animals in need of our help, and bring them to this and other islands, where we can protect them from people.. "

He stopped.

I sighed. "You were going to say 'people like me' weren't you?" There were awkward glances around the table. "It's alright. I know exactly what you mean, and you could say, I've seen the error of my ways." I laughed. It seemed to ease the tension. "You have your work cut out for you. There must be a lot of species close to extinction now."

Colin shook his head sadly. "Yes far too many, but these are very special animals - like your big cat. Someone should care."

"Did you see her?" I asked. I was surprised at how much I wanted to know if she was alright.

The question however was left unanswered, as a handsome dark skinned woman swept into the room. "Good evening everyone and welcome." She gave me a generous smile, as she bought in a trolley stacked with food.

Colin seemed happy with the interruption. "Ah, that smells delicious Meg. I'm starving."

The woman shot Colin a sharp look. "No you are not starving! Hungry perhaps, starving no - not after the breakfast you put away this morning. Now help yourselves before it gets cold."

Colin laughed and introduced her. "This is Meg and she has the task of looking after all of us here, and does a good job." He patted his stomach, "Maybe a little too good."

I felt frustrated that my questions remained unanswered. But the food looked fantastic, especially a large plate which contained a whole fish - covered with slices of lime and what looked like spices of some kind. I complimented her.

Meg's smile grew broader, if that was possible. "You have Natasha and Toby to thank for providing the main course. Natasha is unsurpassed at catching fish."

Natasha laughed and it sounded like music. I had an image in my head of Natasha and I, out on the ocean in a small boat - just the two of us. "I haven't been fishing for a while - perhaps you would take me out Natasha," I suggested hopefully.

"I'm not sure that you would be up to it Alan," she joked. Everyone laughed, a little too hard I thought, and I got the feeling, I'd missed something, however it didn't worry me for long. The food smelled fantastic, and I was hungrier than I'd realized. "You are lucky to have such a good cook out here on this island, so far from civilization," I commented.

Sophie looked up. "You will find most of us pretty civilized here Alan." She seemed amused rather than offended, but I felt I'd been rude.

"I'm sorry," I said quickly. "I didn't mean that the way it sounded."

She smiled. "That's ok Alan. I think we all have our own views on what is civilized."

Colin sensed my embarrassment and changed the subject "Meg, was Sophie's nanny in Africa, as a child. Her father is a well thought of witch doctor, and thankfully Meg has inherited much of his skills. There's not much she can't cure with the simplest of plants she gathers on the island. Most of us, owe her our lives."

This sounded a little dramatic, but Colin seemed sincere. "Ah, alternative medicine," I ventured, and knew instantly I'd put my foot in it. I had said the wrong thing yet again.

"There is no alternative to Meg's medicine. If Meg can't come up with a cure for it, the chances are, there isn't one." Colin seemed very serious.

In this day and age, it seemed to me those people had a lot of faith in herbs, but I wasn't going to make the mistake of saying that out loud. I made up my mind to think before I opened my big mouth again.

I felt there was a lot I didn't understand about this island and its occupants. Dinner was excellent however, and it had been a very long time since I'd had a good home cooked meal.

Meg kept disappearing into the kitchen and bringing back more plates of food, and we all dug in. Conversation was limited as everyone was busy enjoying the meal.

As the dishes were cleared away, I tried to find out more about my hosts. I went for what I thought might be the weakest link. "So Toby, what's it like living on an island? You must have heaps of adventures."

Toby sighed. "It's ok, but it would be a lot better if Dad would let me go on the expeditions."

Colin gave his son a stern look. "We've had this conversation Toby, and the answer hasn't changed - You're still too young. Don't wish your life away."

I felt I'd opened a can of worms, so I might as well see if any of them would wriggle out. "What expeditions?" I asked, hoping to find out more.

Colin seemed to relax a little. "I believe Natasha has told you that our aim is to save the most endangered species - if we can."

I nodded. "Where do you start? There are so many!" In my mind I was thinking -especially if you count the one's which have been extinct for a few hundred years, but this time I kept my mouth shut.

Colin continued, "It probably wouldn't surprise you that in most cases we start with newspapers. We listen to stories and study myths and legends, and maybe even something as simple as a song can often offer up a clue."

Everyone laughed but I wasn't sure why. A private joke I suspected. I was beginning to think I was missing an awful lot here, when, suddenly my brain caught up. "Of course, it was the story of my accident. That's why you contacted me out of the blue like that."

"Yes, that and your legendary hunting skills," Colin confessed.

"I don't hunt anymore." I put in quickly.

"We know, and as you have already heard, we're not in the business of killing," Colin reassured me.

I shook my head. "Then why am I here? What is it you want from me?"

Natasha put her hand on mine and my arm tingled. "We feel you have a skill which would be very helpful to us Alan."

I tried to focus which was difficult with Natasha's hand still resting on mine. "You believed my story about the mountain lion. You think she exists." For some reason, instead of feeling reassured - this worried me. There was another snigger from Toby at the other end of the table. His father shot him a glance that obviously said a thousand words, and Toby suddenly found the table cloth fascinating.

Sophie smiled. "We all believe you here Alan." She got up from the table and announced "Toby and I will excuse ourselves now and leave you to talk. Toby has some work to finish, and I have some things to discuss with Meg. It's lovely to have you here Alan, and I hope you decide to stay and help us."

With that, Sophie led a complaining Toby away, as he shot me a glance that said, "Mothers!"

We left the table and moved into a large lounge that looked over the trees. There was a bright nearly full moon, lighting a path across the ocean in the distance.

Colin handed me a brandy. "I can see why you love this place. It's beautiful here, even at night it seems magical."

Natasha smiled, and kissed Colin lightly on the cheek as she said good night.

I watched her go, and realized Colin was watching me with a slight smile on his face.

He sat in one of the large leather arm chairs and waited till Natasha had closed the door behind her. "She is quite something isn't she?"

I nodded, "Yes she is. I don't think I've ever met anyone quite like her." I sat in the chair opposite Colin and tried to stifle a yawn.

He laughed. "I can almost guarantee that you haven't," he said, finishing his drink. "You look all in Alan. It's been a long day. I'll have Spike fetch you for breakfast as he's taken quite a shine to you. Tomorrow I will answer a lot of your questions."

Much as I wanted to talk and find out more, I had to admit it had been a long day and I was grateful when Colin left me at my bedroom door. He was already half way down the corridor when I opened the door to my room. Through the open window, I heard something that sounded out of place here.

I called after Colin - "Are there wolves on the Island?"

He didn't turn, but before he disappeared from view at the far end of the corridor, I just caught his answer.

Once inside my room I undressed and slid into bed. I tried to think about all the things that had been said over dinner, piecing them together and trying to get a picture of this place in my mind. And of course there was Colin's parting answer.

He'd said 'sometimes.'

\*\*\*

I really was tired, and the bed was pure heaven - especially after the sleeping bag on the camp bed I'd been used to. Sleep overtook my thoughts and dreams crept in, mostly of a beautiful woman with long blonde hair and flashing green eyes.

In my dreams I felt I was never far from the ocean - in fact at times I imagined I was far below the waves, darting easily through the warm waters. There was something else always there in the distance - an island surrounded by strange rock formations, and in its heart a mountain covered by forest. I felt strangely drawn towards it, but the harder I tried to reach it, the further away it seemed. I could feel someone or something watching me, something waiting silently, waiting patiently. Waiting for me!

I awoke to the sound of yapping at my door. I had to smile as, true to his word - Colin had sent Spike to fetch me for breakfast.

I let him in and endured the wash he gave me, he licked my face and ears enthusiastically, after I had given him what was obviously an acceptable amount of ear scratching. He then waited patiently, while I washed myself again. The look he gave me said he thought this was over kill - but I was a human, and this meant he had to make allowances for his new friend's strange habits.

Spike led the way down the corridor and into a large kitchen. Meg greeted me with a cup of steaming hot coffee.

She didn't seem old enough to be Sophie's nanny. I guessed she was in her late thirties - maybe early forties. It was hard to tell. She was a tall woman with jet black hair, and her bright smile was made even brighter by her dark complexion.

"Good morning Alan. Did you sleep well?" she asked.

"Yes - my room is very comfortable, and the meal you made for us last night was fantastic." She greeted this compliment with another warm smile. I liked her.

Spike waited patiently by a large bowl on the floor at the end of the table.

I laughed. "He obviously enjoys your cooking too."

Meg emptied some food into Spikes bowl.

Spike looked up from his bowl, and gave a little yap as Colin came in.

"Good morning. I trust you slept well. You looked all in last night! Spike had instructions to leave you until 9, and he's usually pretty accurate." Colin bent down to scratch behind Spikes ears.

"I hadn't realized I'd slept so late. Sorry - have I kept everyone waiting?" I wondered what they would think of me. My first day and I'd slept late!

Colin slapped me on the back. "Not at all, you take your time and eat. Meg does a great omelette and you can come find me and Jack when you're ready. Meg will point you in the right direction."

With that, he left me to enjoy my breakfast. Meg did indeed do a great omelette and the kitchen was warm and welcoming, just like Meg. After I'd eaten my fill Meg showed me out to the front steps. I could hear voices coming from one of the garages. I turned to thank Meg again, but she'd already disappeared back into the house. Spike had chosen to join her, no doubt hoping for some more leftovers. I could really relate to this little dog. I headed down the stairs toward the voices.

Colin was changing a wheel on a jeep, and it looked as if Jack was holding the front of the vehicle up at least three feet into the air. As I approached, the jeep was slowly lowered.

"Good breakfast?" Colin asked brightly.

"Yes, fantastic thanks. He's very strong," I said, gesturing to Jack.

Colin laughed. "Jack has many talents. Now, are you ready for a trek?"

I nodded, "Yes I could do with the exercise - I haven't eaten this much in a long time. Is it safe around the island on foot, especially if there are wolves?"

Colin laughed again. "We will take Jack with us, we will be just fine."

I could believe Jack had hidden talents. He still wouldn't win any awards for Mr. Personality though.

We set off into the bush, and Jack almost bounded out of the garage past us and into the undergrowth. He seemed suddenly full of the joys of spring. Colin saw my expression, he shrugged. "Jack loves his walks and prefers to be outside."

We followed Jack and headed along a fairly well used path. There was a lot of rustling from the trees and bushes around us, but not much to see apart from a few birds. Thankfully these were normal sized ones - singing or calling out a warning as we approached. Jack appeared every now and then sniffing the air. He hardly made a sound, one minute he was there, the next gone - he was so fast. I was trying to think of a polite way to ask Colin about Jack's strange behaviour, but as it happened, I didn't have to.

Colin stopped and turned to me. "It's time to let you in on a few secrets we have on this island. Now would be the perfect time to back out, and I would think no less of you. We'll drop you wherever you want to be, and you will never be bothered by any of us again. It's your choice Alan, but soon it will be difficult to go back."

I thought about this for a second but I was already hooked. "I'm not sure I have much to go back to Colin, no, I want to stay."

I tried to sound confident, but I was thinking here it comes - Eco Warrior or Green Peace activists.

Colin shrugged. "Ok then. You may find this hard to watch as it can seem a bit unsettling. To be honest, you do get used to it! Well sort of." He called Jack, who bounded out of the trees. "Ok Jack, I think it's time to get some proper exercise!"

Jack seemed pleased as he proceeded to remove his clothes, and fold them into a neat pile. He did have an impressive body. I wasn't sure if I felt jealous or just uncomfortable, either way I couldn't help but admire the way he looked. I was starting to think I was wrong about the Green Peace thing. Maybe I had joined a nudist colony? This was all getting very weird, but it was about to get a lot weirder.

Jack stretched and dropped to his knees. His breathing quickened, then he threw back his head and howled a blood curdling sound - the stuff of horror movies! I'm not sure if I actually watched all of what happened next, I may have shut my eyes a couple of times. What I did see was that Jack's body began to contort in impossible ways. I looked across at Colin, but he didn't seem at all bothered by any of this, by the time I looked back - dark hair was sprouting from every part of Jacks body, except his nose which was now black and slightly damp looking. At the other end of his body there was now an impressive tail, wagging enthusiastically. The newly changed Jack bounded off happily into the bush.

I felt sick. Colin came over and stood next to me. He was watching me carefully.

The whole thing had only taken a moment or two, but those two minutes had changed my world forever.

Just like after seeing the moa yesterday, my mind was telling me, this was impossible.    My eyes however, were convinced they had just seen it happen.

"Impossible!" I managed to stammer."

"If you say so," Colin said calmly. " Alan, before you call this impossible consider this: have you never watched a caterpillar change into a chrysalis, and then waited three weeks to see it open up its wings, and fly up into the sky to explore a new world? Mother Nature can do amazing and sometimes seemingly impossible things. After all, she is a woman and you should never underestimate them.

Jack will have a bit of a run then catch up with us later. Are you ok?"

I had to think about this question for a moment. For one of the few times in my life - I was completely lost for words!

Colin continued, "Come on, we have a short walk to the cave, there is someone there I would like you to see."

I forced my legs to walk "What is he - Some sort of werewolf," I managed to stammer.

"Wolf man would be a better term. He's actually part man - part wolf and incidentally, he can change when he has a mind to and any bullet could kill him, it doesn't have to be silver.

A light came on in my brain.

"Sometimes," I said remembering Colin's words the previous night.

Colin laughed. "Yes Jack is helpful in any form. He has a great sense of smell and the strength of about four strong men - useful at times as you saw with the jeep, but he's as loyal as Spike. Oh and no he won't eat you."

Colin looked at me and laughed. "Alan, if you could see your face!"

I found myself laughing too. This did explain a lot, but I didn't understand any of it. "How is this even possible?" I asked

Colin sighed. "Jack is one of the last of his kind, and that's one of the reasons he's here."

"Wait, I saw a huge bird yesterday and it looked like something I'd seen in a museum."

"Yes there are a few moa's on the island. Eggs were bought here many years ago and they've done well."

I considered this for a moment. "Wait, that must have been hundreds of years ago," I exclaimed. "How could that be, unless you have some sort of time machine."

Colin laughed. "No - no time machine. They were rescued by a friend of mine a long, long time ago." He seemed unwilling to explain further.

A thought struck me like a blow to the head. "You said Jack was one of the last of his kind. That means - he's not the last."

"Yes Alan, well done, in fact Sophie is also like Jack. Sophie and I have been through a lot together. I won't say it has always been easy, but I love her dearly and it's amazing what love can overcome." Colin's confident shield faded just for a second. I couldn't even begin to imagine what living with someone like Jack could be like.

"But Sophie, she looks so. . ." I struggled to find the words.

"Human." Colin finished the statement for me. "It's alright - believe me, I know how hard all this is to take in. Sophie and I have had our difficult times.

Sophie is not comfortable in her wolf form. Her real father was killed when she was very young. Her step father and mother were afraid of what she could become, so she was forbidden to change. They moved to Africa, as far from the city as they could and consulted a famous witch doctor. The witch doctor's daughter became Sophie's nanny and her best friend.

Meg helped Sophie come to terms with who she is, and is helping her control the animal within- but Sophie still doesn't have the control Jack has, and therefore doesn't change too often.

Jack on the other hand was bought up in a pack of wolves, and only discovered his human form by accident. When you get to know Jack I 'm sure you'll also get to like him."

I found it easy to imagine Jack at home in a wolf pack.

"What about Toby?" I immediately knew I'd hit a nerve. The question hung in the air.

Colin seemed to think for a while before answering. "We are not sure what talents he may have inherited yet, but we're keeping a close eye on him."

I was stunned. "You think he may turn into something other than a wolf?" I asked incredulously.

Colin considered this. "Well it's possible he may have inherited my gift for languages, all languages even some animals.

I was starting to realize I was in well over my head here. "Of course" My mind was spinning. I hadn't thought I was this crazy! "Can I just try to get this straight?" I said. "You are Doctor Do - little. This island is full of wolf men and women, and long extinct animals and birds that to the rest of the world, only exist in museums and Michael Jason videos."

Colin laughed. "That seems to sum things up nicely. Anyway we're nearly there. Jack will have told her we are on our way."

"Told who?" I was beginning to feel a bit light headed. Maybe Meg had slipped me a potion at breakfast - drugs might explain everything.

The bush opened up into a slight clearing in front of us was a cave.

Jack - or what Jack had become, lay at the mouth of the cave licking himself. He was reaching places he definitely hadn't been able to reach as his former self!

There was a gentle rhythmic sound coming from within the cave. I recognized it. This sound was etched deep in my memory, one I would never forget - the purr of the mountain lion I had hunted months ago. She strode from the cave, and sat a few metres away on the grass. My legs felt like jelly and Colin reached out to steady me.

"It's a lot to take in I know," he said as he gently led me closer. "She's pleased to see you Alan and glad you are recovered."

I looked once more into those gentle green eyes, sank to my knees, and wept.

\*\*\*

It took me a little while to recover. Colin seemed to be talking with this beautiful animal.

Jack continued the task in hand as if nothing was going on. I ventured closer. "She is more beautiful than I remember. Colin if she understands you, can you ask her if she can ever forgive me?"

Colin turned to me. "There is nothing to forgive Alan. You have been her salvation - man was closing in on her, and she would soon have had nowhere to hide. Now she is at peace and . . . she is no longer alone." Colin nodded towards the cave. There was a low growl on cue from deep inside.

A large black cat appeared just inside the entrance, and to my relief it seemed reluctant to come any closer. That suited me just fine. Still mesmerized by the creature I believed had been a dream. I reached out and touched her thick soft fur and I heard again that rhythmical purr. I was transported once more to the caves, were a few months earlier this beautiful animal had saved my life. She was real and very much alive.

I turned to Colin, "She saved my life. I tried to kill her, yet she saved my life - why?"

Colin knelt by her side. The purring seemed to change, Colin smiled "She says you are a good person at heart and you have changed. She senses this in you and is pleased." Colin got up and bowed his head to the magnificent animal before us, then turned. "Sorry to rush this reunion but we must go, we have another appointment and I will be in deep shit if I'm late for this one. We're going to see George."

At the sound of the name Jack leapt to his paws and headed off at speed, into the bush.

The mountain lion rose and licked my hand gently, then turned and retreated into the cave. Her companion greeted her affectionately. They made a hansom pair.

"Where did you find him?" I said as they returned to their cave.

Colin shrugged. "The male cat has been here a couple of years, so we were over the moon when we read your story. We couldn't believe our luck when your mountain lion turned out to be about the same age as the male we rescued from a place in England. We nick named him Bod.

I think we got him out just in time, there had already been a few news stories and the odd photo. It was only going to be a matter of time before someone got off a lucky shot - or unlucky for Bod!   We have high hopes. They have been inseparable since they met, and who knows, we might one day hear the pitter-patter of tiny paws!

Now we really must hurry.  I told George we would be there by eleven, and it's ten to now.  God knows how, but he always knows what time it is - to the minute. Jack will go on ahead and tell him we are on our way. George hates to be kept waiting."

***

We followed Jack into the bush. There were several paths leading in different directions, and I began to wonder how many strange animals lay at the end of each path. There was so much I wanted to ask, but I found myself hurrying along in silence. I slowed a little, and turned to see Colin with that now familiar smile on his face.

"What?"  I said feeling slightly annoyed. He looked so smug - as if he knew something I didn't.  Of course he knew loads of things I didn't, but that wasn't the point.

"'What is it now?" I asked.

"It's true then," Colin said smiling.

"What's true," I said cautiously.

"You are a seeker Alan."

I'd been called some strange things in my time this was a new one on me. "A what?"

Colin smiled patiently. "A Seeker. That's what they used to call people who had the power to find things."

"Find what things? I don't even know what we're looking for."

He had that smug look again. "Never the less Alan, you have been leading the way since we left the cave."

I felt even more annoyed. "I've just been following you," I said reproachfully.

Colin laughed. "Yeah right, from in front!"

I had to admit, I was in front and I had been for a while. How did I know where we were going. Where was I heading? I didn't know. It was my usual instinct that took over.

"Look," I said. "I was just following the path." I knew that didn't sound convincing - not even to me, but it was the best I had.

Colin nodded. "And yet, without being told, you have chosen the right path, each time we have reached an intersection," he pointed out, patiently.

God he was annoying. "So what, I have a good sense of direction."

Colin smiled. "An uncanny sense of direction I would say. George was right - I think you will be able to help us."

I was at the end of my tether. "Who is George?" I cried.

We came to a halt at the edge of a clearing. "Alan," he said simply, "I would like you to meet George."

I turned very slowly. I had a sense of something very, very large breathing down the back of my neck. Even after jack and the wolf thing, and being reunited with the mountain lion –

nothing could have prepared me for this. I looked up and then further up - at George!

George was the size of a large double decker bus. Eyes like dinner plates, blinked down at me from an alligator-like head. He had a long neck covered in red, green and gold iridescent scales, that seemed to shimmer in the sunlight and a huge body with what looked like two large wings folded along his flanks. Curling around the huge body was a large, very long tail with a sharp arrow like point on its end.

This was turning out to be, one hell of a day.

I think maybe I let out a little yelp. I certainly took a couple of steps back, and promptly fell over some rocks just behind me. Colin reached down to help me up. Suddenly instead of fear, I exploded with anger "What the hell is this place," I half screamed at Colin, who was now standing next to George. "And George! What sort of name is that for a dragon?"

I had absolutely no doubt that the beast that towered above me, was indeed a dragon. Of course I knew they didn't exist, just like the moa, just like werewolves. But somehow they were all still here.

Colin was annoyingly calm. "I'm sorry Alan. There didn't seem any point in trying to explain any of this. You simply wouldn't have believed me. You had to see these things for yourself. As for the name, well I was only six when I first met our friend here, I wanted to call him Puff, because of a song I loved then, he preferred George, in hindsight I think he was probably right!"

I was beginning to calm down a little and realizing that Colin was right about one thing. I would never have believed any of this, if I hadn't seen it with my own eyes. I was still struggling to make sense of it even now, but I had to admit, for some strange reason the name George did suit the creature that stood before me. Calming down, I was able to look closer at George, and he seemed to be smiling at me. That didn't exactly make me feel any more at ease - for it showed off a mouth full of shining white teeth.

"Where did he come from?" I asked.

Colin shook his head. "That's a good question, one I'm not sure I can answer. I met him in Scotland but who knows where he was born. Dragons live for a long, long time, and I don't think even he would remember now."

A thought struck me. "This is your time machine. It was George who saved the moa eggs. I think I need to sit." I stumbled to some rocks nearby, and sat down.

I noticed Jack had gone to the edge of a large lake, and was lapping at the water noisily. He seemed totally at ease in his wolf form, he finished his drink, found a comfortable spot, circled it a couple of times and settled down. I had to laugh.

Looking on the bright side, I had to admit that Jack, in either of his characters, seemed far less intimidating now.

"Ok, I'm perfectly calm know," I lied. "I think I would like to know what's going on, and what you and George, need from me."

Colin came and sat next to me on the rock, to make matters worse, George followed his lead. The mighty dragon, flicked a few boulders out of his way as if they were pebbles on a beach. When he was happy he settled his huge body down, with his large head rested on a rock little more than a foot from me. He was so close I could feel his breath on my face. He seemed to be studying me with interest.

Colin spoke carefully, "We need you to find something for us Alan, well mostly for George really."

"Ok, let's say I buy it. What the hell could a millionaire and a bloody great dragon the size of a double decker bus, think I could find for them that they couldn't find for themselves?"

"We need you to find another dragon," Colin said conversationally, as if it was a normal request. Either they were off their heads, or I was.

"Oh, of course - another dragon." My mind was racing. "Are you mad? Where the hell am I going to find another dragon? Up until a few seconds ago I wouldn't have imagined I could have found one, and now you want me to find you another. How many dragons do you need?"

My head hurt. "What in god's name makes you think, I could possibly know where another dragon is. A moment ago dragons didn't exist to me, in fact even sitting here looking at George, I'm still finding it hard to believe my own eyes." I was ranting, but I needed desperately to let off steam. My outburst didn't seem to worry either of them.

Colin smiled. "We think that your, unusually good tracking skills will come in very useful," he said calmly.

I tried to get my head around this last statement. However you looked at it, this was one hell of a job offer! "But I wouldn't know where to start." Somehow I knew already that I was going to lose this argument, but I wasn't going to give up without a fight.

Colin just shrugged. "We can talk about the how later, but right now, George would like to talk with you."

I shook my head. "I don't have your skills Colin. For some strange reason, they neglected to teach me dragon at school."

Colin laughed. "You don't need any skill for this one, George has enough power for the both of you. It's not difficult Alan, just open your mind. He will understand and if you listen, you will hear his answer. Don't be afraid, he wouldn't hurt you."

I tried to think of something to ask George. The first thing that came into my mind was, "Have you ever eaten people?" Instantly I wanted to cancel the question. It was too late however, as a reply was already coming into my mind. The voice I heard was unexpectedly gentle.

"Funny you should ask that Alan. In my early days people used to bring me others of their kind, and chain them to rocks outside my cave. I have never had a taste for human flesh, as it gives me indigestion. I did not wish to offend, so I would take what they offered me."

I felt a little sick. "You would eat them to be polite?"

There was a sound like music, I realized George was laughing.

" Oh no Alan. I would take these offerings far away across the sea to another island, and leave them there. For reasons I did not understand, they were usually young and rather attractive maidens of your species. I must say, I found it hard to comprehend why they would want to get rid of them in this way, but humans have always confused me.

My arrival with the maidens was always greeted with great enthusiasm by the young men of the island. They appeared to look forward to my visits, and left me fish and fruit in return for my gift. The maidens were happy to be alive and were made very welcome in their new homes. They were worshipped as a gift from the gods. The arrangement seemed to work out well for everyone."

I had to smile, instead of a blood thirsty killer I was talking to a match maker! Something still worried me. How did George know humans gave him indigestion?

I just had to ask. "George what do you eat?"

The reply was instant. "On this island many things: fruit, vegetables, fish and I'm very partial to Meg's blueberry pancakes. The lake here leads to an underwater pool, which eventually goes into the ocean. I often meet Natasha in the water. Natasha is excellent at fishing you know."

"So I've been told," I said dryly.

There were definitely a couple of questions I needed to ask Natasha.

Instead I asked, "How old are you George?"

"I have no idea Alan. I have seen many changes in my lifetime. Once I felt the presence of many dragons but of late, I have felt only one. She calls to me, and she is afraid. She senses something is going to happen soon. She needs my help.

Alan I need to bring her to me here, but Colin will not let me go. He is afraid that others would see me, and would not be kind. Also, that the islands we protect would be discovered. He believes that people would hunt us down, and through lack of understanding and fear, there would be bloodshed, much bloodshed."

I wanted desperately to speak up for the human race and protest, but I knew he was right so instead, I listened.

"I understand I must remain hidden, but her fear grows and with it, mine. I need to find her and bring her here to safety and to me."

I didn't understand. "Why does she not come herself?"

"That is another good question Alan, and I do not have the answer. She seems to be trapped in a mountain and unable to release herself."

I shook my head to try and clear my thoughts. "This is all very weird" I said out loud, "And I don't see how I can help with any of it. I wouldn't know where to start looking and even if I could find her, how would I be able to release a fifteen foot dragon if she cannot get out herself, and then bring her here unnoticed? I would love to help, but I'm sorry I wouldn't know where to start."

Colin slapped me on the back. "You can let us worry about the little details," Colin joked. "After all, we have done this sort of thing before."

He looked up at George. "George has been my best friend for as long as I can remember. I can't fail him in this. The island, my fortune, all of this - is because of him. We must not fail." Colin spoke with such intensity that I could feel the strong bond between man and dragon, and I envied him.

Colin touched my shoulder. "Alan we must return to the house, it will take us an hour or so through the bush. We can talk on the way and I will try to answer some of your questions. We haven't worked out all the details of our quest, but between us we will. We're running out of time, but as yet we don't know why."

I found it hard to say goodbye to George. I felt sorry to leave him, there was so much I wanted to ask. As soon as we got to our feet, Jack disappeared into the bush ahead.

I tried to get my head around what I'd just seen. "I don't know where to start Colin - this is all so strange, I feel like I must be in a dream and I'll wake up at any moment."

Colin laughed.

I was surprised at his reaction. "What's so funny?"

He slapped me on the back. "The fact that you said, a dream and not a night mare! It's a good start."

I hesitated, finding it hard to put what I felt into words. "It's odd, I have this feeling. It's like I somehow knew they were all out there, as though I've been searching for this place all my life. That sounds a bit mad, doesn't it?"

Colin laughed. "Honestly – yes, but in a good way. I know you're going to be very important to us Alan. We all have special talents. We just have to work together."

I felt more relaxed, I liked the idea of being part of a team and wanted to find out more. "How did you meet George, and how does Natasha fit in to all this. Does she have special talents too?" I asked.

Colin smiled. "Ah Natasha, I can see you think a lot of her already. I can tell you she is special, but you already know that Alan. Talk with her.

As for George - this all started when I was six years old. After my parents were killed in a plane crash, I was sent to an aunt's place in a remote and beautiful part of Scotland. I couldn't understand what had happened. I spent a lot of time in my room alone. My aunt gave me some space. Then she insisted I take walks with her around the lock, and up into the hills and caves around her home.

One day she said I was ready and she left me sitting alone on the rocks, at the entrance to one of these caves. I don't know how long I sat, but after a while I was aware of someone watching me. I should have been scared but I wasn't. George spoke to me, and he seemed lonely, just like me. It was then that our strange friendship started. We spent long days exploring. Many caves went for miles underground. George could swim through the locks with me on his back.

Days turned into weeks, and weeks turned into years. I soon discovered I had a gift with languages even some animals, just like you could hear George in your head, I can hear animals and birds. The forests and jungles can be a bit overpowering, but George has taught me how to isolate the sounds I hear, and give them meaning. We would talk for hours about the things he had witnessed, and the many strange and unusual people and animals he had encountered during his long life.

Under cover of darkness, we would fly over towns and castles. I had to attend school but every weekend my world would become an adventure. How I looked forward to the holidays. It was during one of these holidays, that George took me to see another of his friends.

We went down to the ocean, and there on the beach was Natasha. She was a few years younger than me, but we had many things in common. She had lost both her parents to the sea. She lived with her grandmother in a small cottage near the beach. She would join us now and then on our adventures-George could carry both of us with ease.

Sometimes we would play hide and seek in giant corn fields, and it was only many years later we found out we had made the news. The strange crop circles we had created had been attributed to aliens. I realized then that sometimes, the truth can be stranger than fiction.

Natasha helped me improve my swimming, and understand some of the languages of the sea. Natasha loves the water." I felt he was about to say more, but stopped himself. We were close to the house now and Jack disappeared into the bush.

"I can't imagine how Natasha can still have a love of the ocean, especially after losing her parents that way." Colin hesitated then shrugged. "Maybe she feels closer to them in the water. I think these are questions you should ask her. In fact, I will leave you in Natasha's safe hands whilst I go find my offspring. I promised I would go through some of his homework with him. He will of course be hoping I'd forgotten, but his mother will have my head if he hasn't got his assignment finished, ready for his school visit on Monday. We'll talk more after dinner."

Jack strode purposefully from the bush on two legs, buttoning his shirt. I wondered how many stashes of cloths he had around the place. He nodded at me as he walked past. I smiled back. I had seen a different side to Jack, a relaxed and almost playful side.

He was, still as scary as hell though!

Natasha smiled. "Hello Alan, how has your day been? I did tell you there would be lots to see here." She wore a long shirt open to reveal a bathing suit, and my heart went into overdrive. Of all the things I'd seen today, she was the one that really took my breath away.

" I feel like I'm in some sort of dream. This place is amazing, you're amazing. I mean - you are all amazing," I added hastily. I could feel myself going red, yet again. "I'm not convinced I'm going to be much help, but I certainly will try to help, if I can."

Natasha smiled. "Good, it's great to have you with us Alan, we need all the help we can get. Colin makes light of the difficulties we face, but you must already understand the importance of keeping this island out of the public eye, and its inhabitants a secret. You met George?"

I tried to concentrate, it was weird, today, I had seen a werewolf and a dragon, and yet it was being close to Natasha that made my pulse race, and my brain feel like spaghetti! "Oh Yes, he's amazing. I can't understand how he's managed to stay a secret for so long."

Natasha laughed. "He has a very effective disappearing act. His iridescent scales can change colour to suit his background, a bit like a chameleon. You could be standing right in front of him and not know he was there. Most of the creatures here have some way of disguising themselves, or they wouldn't have been the ones to survive."

I couldn't resist, "And what disguise do you have Natasha?" I watched her carefully.

She seemed to consider this question, before giving her answer, "I am as you see, I have no disguise, but I think you have guessed I am a little different! Like Colin, I owe a lot to

George. Without him, I 'm not sure I would have survived, there have been some difficult times."

"Yes," I said. "I'm sorry about your parents. Colin told me they drowned when you were very young. It must have been hard growing up on your own."

Natasha looked down at her hands. "I don't know if they are dead or alive," she said. She seemed a little uncomfortable. "How much did Colin tell you Alan?"

I felt I had upset her. "I'm sorry, I must have misunderstood. Colin just said that you had lost your parents to the sea, so I just assumed. . ." I hesitated. The look on her face was so sad. I wanted her to smile again, and I wanted it to all be ok. What I really - wanted was to hold her close. Instead I waited awkwardly, not knowing what to say or do.

Natasha continued, "That's true in part. My mother chose the ocean over my father and me. The pull of the sea was too much for her. My father moved us closer to the sea, and every day he would stand and watch the waves. My grandmother looked after me most of the time. Then, one day he just walked out into the ocean and kept on going. He didn't come back. My grandmother and I waited in the little cottage for many years, but we never saw either of them again. I would sit all night on the beach - hoping they might walk out, or that I might catch a glimpse of them in the waves. Sometimes I would swim out, daring myself to go further but I would always turn back.

I still have this romantic notion that my mother was waiting for my father in the waves, and she took him somewhere safe, where they could be together."

I walked in silence, listening but not really understanding what I was being told. It had after all, been that sort of day. Eventually I had to say something. "I'm sorry Natasha, I 'm not sure I understand." We had reached the beach and we stood together on the sand.

Natasha looked at me, her eyes full of sadness. "There is no reason why you should understand, all this is very new to you. I like you and I already feel I can talk to you, but I need you to know we should just be friends. What happened to my father could easily happen again. I have inherited my mother's genes."

Somehow, I just knew she didn't mean the denim kind. She held up her hands. "The ocean is not only my second home, it could one day, become my only home."

For the first time I looked closely at her hands. The fingers all had a type of webbing joining them together, I couldn't think of anything to say.

Natasha went on, "I was born to swim - it runs in my family. My grandmother is the same, but she has always chosen to stay on the land. There comes a time when we must choose. I love the sea Alan, I just don't know how much."

"But you look ..." I hesitated.

She shrugged. "You were going to say - normal."

Damn - she was right. "I'm so sorry Natasha. I'm finding all of this a little hard to understand. You're a mermaid. That sounds like something from Walt Disney."

This seemed to amuse her. "That is probably the closest term you would understand. I don't have a tail, and unlike Jack and Sophie - I don't undergo metamorphosis into some other form. However, because of my webbed feet and hands I can swim like a fish and…"

She seemed to hesitate.

"I have gills," she said, almost apologetically.

It sounded like a confession and I felt my heart go out to her. She pulled back her long blonde hair and there, behind her ears - were what looked like slits in her skin. I tried to get things straight in my head. "Your mother was the same but your father was.." Again I stopped myself.

She looked away. "Normal," she said, half to herself.

I reached out and took her hand in mine, "I'm sorry, I didn't mean – oh I don't know what I mean. I'm sorry."

She smiled. "It's alright Alan, I know how difficult it is, but you need to understand what this means. Yes, my mother met my father on land and for many years she was happy, but she always heard the call of the ocean and one day, it was just too much. Although she loved us both, she left us. I have searched for them, but found no trace. I still hang on to the hope that she found somewhere they could be together, and one day I may find them again."

I didn't know what to say. "I'm so sorry." It was all I could come up with, but it sounded weak. She shrugged and changed the subject.

"Come on lets go for a swim. I promised Meg I'd get some scallops for dinner. How well do you swim Alan?"

Bugger! "Oh - I'm a pretty strong swimmer," I lied. It suddenly seemed important. Some of the comments made last night at dinner were now making sense.

Natasha had already removed her shirt and strapped a belt round her waist, with a large knife sheathed in a holster and a net bag. She must have seen my look of surprise at the knife.

"It's just for the scallops." She laughed. "You'll be ok, I'll look after you, I promise." She headed towards the waves, I followed suit, and took off my shirt and shoes.

How well could I swim? It had been ages since I tried.. I was in so far over my head already and now I might literally be in over my head! I was out of my depth in more ways than one. Natasha swam close by my side, and I felt I could swim for England at this point. Of course I was wrong.

Natasha looked across at me. "Are you ok to reach those rocks over there Alan? That's where I need to dive for the scallops." She seemed so at ease in the water - not a splash. It was as if the water just parted around her.

So far I was doing alright. "Oh I'm fine," I spluttered.

The rocks seemed a long way off, but I would rather drown than admit I couldn't get there. Of course at this point, drowning didn't seem much of a possibility. Suddenly Natasha was away through the waves.

I was alone.

My mind was wandering all over the place, sadly so was I! Everything that had happened over the last few days, seemed to be running around the inside of my head. Perhaps this was what they meant by your life passing before your eyes!

I was starting to tread water and the rocks still seemed a long way off. I went under and gulped, the salt burning my throat as I struggled to the surface, only to be hit by a wave. I went under again and started to panic. Flailing around, my arms touched something solid and I grasped at it. A muscular form lifted me bodily to the top of the water. Still hanging on I spluttered and coughed, but now I was being propelled through the waves at an increasing rate of knots.

The Grey muscular form I was hanging on to for dear life, sped through the waves and before I knew it I was next to the rocks. Natasha sprung from the water on to the rocks and clasped my hand, pulling me to safety beside her.

"I thought you said you could swim. Not the best time to exaggerate your skills Alan!" she scolded. She started to laugh. It was so good to see her happy again and in spite of myself, I found I was laughing too, in between coughing up sea water.

"What just happened?" I managed to splutter.

"You just met Hector. He's a friend of mine, we fish together sometimes. He's a dolphin," she added, seeing my expression. Natasha sighed. "You thought it was me, didn't you? I did tell you I didn't change."

I felt foolish, she was right. "I'm sorry I lied about the swimming. It was stupid. You would have realized my exaggeration, when you were giving me the kiss of life!" I realized what I had just said and felt my face turning red yet again.

Natasha just smiled. "You were never in any real danger. I knew that even if I wasn't close, Hector and his friends would be keeping an eye on us. I'm fast in the water, but nowhere near as fast as them."

Before I could stop, I heard myself asking. "How long have you known Hector?" ye gods, I was jealous of a dolphin - and not just any dolphin. This one had quite possibly just saved my life. Could this day get any stranger!

"You're jealous," Natasha teased.

"I'm not," I lied. She was laughing at me again, but I really didn't mind. I just loved to see her happy. In that moment I knew I loved her. "Ok just a little bit," I admitted.

"Well he does swim better than you," Natasha teased.

We sat on the rocks, enjoying the show. The dolphins jumped and twirled in the air, so alive, yet Natasha pointed out that both species we were watching, Hector's and Maui's Dolphins, were both so close to extinction now, that we may in fact be watching the last of their kind.

One thing was becoming as clear as the crystal waters all around me. The world needed more sanctuaries. We all needed a place where we could feel safe.

"I must thank Hector and get tea," Natasha said, unstrapping the net at her waist.

"I think it would be better for all of us if you wait here. I won't be long."

I wasn't going to argue. She dived into the water and although it was crystal clear, she quickly darted out of sight.

The dolphins continued to play in the late afternoon sun. Every now and then I fancied I saw Natasha, leaping from the waves with the dolphins. I envied Hector and his friends. I lay back on the rocks, the heat from them warming my body. I thought of George searching for his soul mate, knowing she was out there somewhere but not being able to fly off and find her. I wanted very much to believe, that I might be able to help. My thoughts were interrupted as Natasha burst out of the water, and soaked me. We laughed. She was so beautiful. Sadly though she said the words I was dreading to hear.

"We must get back now Alan. It will be getting dark soon. I wouldn't want you to catch cold, walking back to the lodge from the beach."

I felt like saying that catching cold seemed the least of my worries! Looking back across the expanse of water to the beach, it seemed a very long way off, and Hector and his buddies seemed to have disappeared.

Natasha pushed her wet hair out of her eyes. "Right, are you ready for the swim back Alan?"

It was time for a bit of honesty, before it was too late "Look Natasha I'm not sure if I can make it. My mother always said I could swim like a brick, and I think she may have been exaggerating my skill level!"

Natasha placed her hand on mine. "It'll be alright Alan, I'll be with you and this time the waves will push us towards the shore. You know, if you had been honest with me before, we wouldn't be out here."

I looked into those beautiful green eyes. "I wouldn't have missed this for the world. After all, if I hadn't come, I wouldn't have met Hector." I steeled myself for the return swim.

She laughed and held my hand as we plunged into the water. It seemed a lot colder now, but I struck out with determination towards the shore. Natasha kept close by my side and it really did seem a little easier. I was just getting my confidence when a wave swept over us, and suddenly I was fighting for breath again. Before I could start to panic, Natasha was underneath me in the water - her body supporting me and lifting me to the surface. She was completely submerged beneath the waves. Her body felt warm against mine.

A few metres out, Natasha left me and I struggled the last little way under my own steam.

I felt suddenly cold without her. By the time I dragged my tired body onto the beach, she was waiting on the sand. I sat next to her, wanting to feel again the warmth of her body against mine. I found it hard to breath, and that wasn't just because of the swim. We were close enough for me to feel her breath on my face, and for a wonderful moment I thought we would kiss.

I ruined it by coughing up sea water. Ha! So - romantic.

She slapped me on the back. "See Alan, already I'm not good for you." She laughed, but her eyes looked sad.

I got my breath back. "I'm a big boy, I can look after myself," I said, catching her hand in mine. "None of us know what the future holds, but I know I would like mine a lot better if you were in it."

She pulled her hand away. "It's time to go. The house is that way." She pointed towards a path leading into the bush. "You go ahead and I'll fetch the scallops, I'll catch you up in a moment. Keep to the path Alan."

I watched her go then gathered my senses, and headed towards the house. The path was well trodden and although my legs felt tired, it was good to be on dry land again. The sun was

67

going down, and I could feel every muscle in my body beginning to seize up.

I'd only gone a few metres when I stopped abruptly. Blocking the path in front of me was a large wolf. At first glance I thought it was Jack however this one was slightly smaller, with a shaggy reddish brown coat of thick fur. Its lips were curled back, to reveal impossibly large gleaming white teeth.

Its growl was low and menacing and it watched my every move. I felt that at any moment, it would pounce and tear me apart. My heart was pounding in my chest. Although my blood felt frozen in my veins, I could feel the sweat of fear on my face.

"Don't make any sudden movements," Natasha whispered – now at my side again.

"What the hell is that?" I said out of the corner of my mouth.

"Not what," she said, "who? That's Sophie!"

This statement took a moment to soak in. "You have got to be kidding me," I hissed.

"No, trust me Alan, now would not be a good time to joke. Be very careful. Sophie is still working on controlling her animal side. Don't make any sudden movements. Let her smell you, she should recognize the scent and hopefully back off."

This didn't fill me with confidence. "Hopefully! What do you mean - hopefully?" I felt sick to my stomach.

Natasha's voice was calm. "Just stand still and try not to look afraid."

"I'm not afraid, I'm petrified," I hissed. "Doesn't she recognize me? We only met last night. I thought she liked me!"

Natasha shrugged. "Sophie depends on different senses in this form, and the water will be masking some of the scent. Maybe if you offer her your hand," Natasha suggested.

"What! You must be joking. I 'm very fond of both my hands, thank you." In spite of my fear, I could feel the warmth of Natasha's body as she stood close by my side. She spoke calmly but urgently now. "Please Alan trust me. Hold out your hand towards her, but carefully. Don't make her feel threatened."

I shot her a glance. "Oh, come on! She feels threatened!" I swallowed hard. I held my breath as the huge animal moved a step closer, and began to sniff. Drool dripped from its jaws. Could this really be Sophie? This beast was nothing like the playful and helpful Jack I'd met this afternoon. I'd actually liked Jack more in his wolf form.

I felt like turning and running back into the ocean. I'd rather take my chances with the water than this animal, that could at any second ripe my throat out. So close now that I could feel it's breath on my skin, I closed my eyes and prayed. When I opened them again, to my immense relief Natasha had been right. It – or - she seemed to be satisfied that I wasn't a threat, or dinner!

Turning swiftly she disappeared into the bush and we were left alone, standing side by side. I couldn't move. "She is nothing like Jack," I stammered, still shocked. "What would she have done if she hadn't recognized me?" I really didn't need to ask - I'd seen the horror films.

Natasha put her arm around me. "It's best not to worry about that now, she's gone. Sophie and Jack check the island every now and then, just in case we have any uninvited guests. It's unusual for Sophie to be out alone."

I still felt weak at the knees, but this time it may have had more to do with Natasha's close proximity. Natasha seemed suddenly to realize she had her arm around me, removing it quickly she walked on briskly, I ran to catch up. I didn't want to be left out here alone!

"I don't understand - Jack was kind of funny!" I knew that wasn't the right word, but the contrast was amazing.

She smiled. "I know what you mean, Sophie and Jack had different upbringings. Jack was raised by wolves so he is more comfortable in that form. Although don't let him fool you - he is a powerful animal when roused, so try not to cross him in either form.

Sophie is different. She was raised by her mother and stepfather. Sophie's father was killed tragically when she was very young, and her mother was terrified at what might happen to Sophie if people knew. So she was forbidden to change. That may be easy to say but not so easy to do, and if it hadn't been for Meg something terrible might have happened. But I'm sure they will tell you their stories in their own time."

I tried to pull myself together and focus. "Colin said Sophie's father died on a hunting trip."

Natasha nodded. "Sort of. Sophie's father was killed whilst he was hunting! He had trouble controlling his love of lamb."

The penny dropped. "Oh god, you mean someone shot him." It hadn't crossed my mind, but of course it made sense.

Natasha sighed. "Well they shot a wolf. No one was to know, that the wolf was also a loving husband and father."

I felt a little calmer now, and I couldn't help but feel sorry for Sophie. "No wonder her mother was afraid for her. Sophie seems such a sweet person. I can hardly believe she can become something like – that." I could still feel my heart thumping in my chest.

Natasha shrugged. "We should get back, I'd like to shower before dinner. I think you've met nearly all of the team now!"

I stopped. "What do you mean, nearly all! There's more? I really couldn't handle any more surprises today."

Natasha laughed. "Oh there's just Ben and I think you'll like him, he flew us here yesterday."

I had forgotten all about the flight. "I didn't see the pilot and I'd wondered who had been in the cockpit. He must have made a fast exit. I haven't seen him around the house or on our travels."

Natasha's playful smile had returned. "Oh Ben wasn't on the plane, he is always in his lab."

I felt perplexed again. "But you said he flew us back from the island."

She nodded, "Yes he did, but he wasn't anywhere near the plane.

Ben is what I think you would call a high tech wizard.

I'm sure you'll meet him tonight, although Colin practically has to drag Ben out of his Lab. He's always working on something new.

Ben does love Meg's cooking, so no doubt you will meet him at one of the meals when he realizes he's hungry." Natasha laughed again.

God I loved to hear her laugh. I thought about what she'd, said and it sunk in.

"Let me just get this clear. There was no one flying the plane?"

She laughed again. "Surely Alan after all you've seen and heard today, that can't possibly seem so strange." I shook my head - Natasha was right.

She laughed. "You will learn to trust us in time Alan, most of the time, we really do know what we're doing."

I took her hand. "How about you, could you learn to trust me? I would be the first to admit, most of the time I really don't know what I'm doing!"

I looked into those deep green eyes and for a second, I thought I connected. There was something there - I could feel it. She pulled her hand away quickly, however she couldn't hide a smile. She greeted Spike, who rushed to meet us from the house.

"Spike will show you back to your room and I'll see you at dinner."

She turned briskly and walked away - the moment was lost.

\*\*\*

Spike launched himself into my arms, licking my face and wagging his tail with so much enthusiasm, we both almost hit the deck.

Well at least there was no doubt I had made one definite friend here.

After what was obviously the appropriate amount of fuss, Spike allowed me to put him down. He put his head to one side as if waiting for my instruction. "Well Spike it looks like it's just you and me again. Natasha seemed to think you would show me back to my room, and I really don't want to get lost in this place. What do you say?" With a bark that obviously passed for 'no worries mate' in dog speak - Spike trotted back up the stairs. He waited at the top to check that I was following. Surely he couldn't possibly have understood what I'd said, but sure enough - within a few moments, we were standing outside my room. I bent down and gave Spike a scratch behind his ears.

"You're amazing, thanks Spike," I said. He seemed pleased with himself and with a couple of short barks, the little dog turned and trotted back down the corridor.

Everything in this place was a little remarkable, even Spike. It was odd after everything I had experienced today. Surely I should be running for the hills or at the very least radioing for help, but instead I felt excited. Of course there was Natasha, but it wasn't just that. I wanted to stay, I needed to stay, and in some odd way this place was starting to feel like home. This was like a dream, a fantasy, something people only write about. But this was true and this was happening to me.

Putting aside the fact I had almost drowned, and my new boss's wife had nearly torn me to bits. There was a dragon, called George. A real, living, breathing dragon, could he breathe fire I wondered? I should have asked. Jesus! what a day.

Of course there was no question I would have to improve my swimming. I laughed at that thought. It was totally mad, that after everything that had happened today, the thing I thought I needed most at this important time in my life, was a swimming lesson. Maybe Hector would give me a few tips! After all there shouldn't be a problem. I could get my new boss to translate!

I showered and collapsed on my bed, feeling drained. I must have dozed off. The next thing I heard was Spike barking outside the door, and I knew it must be time to dress and go to dinner.

As I opened the door Spike fell in, carrying his tennis ball, he placed it carefully at my feet, it was a precious object. Obviously he felt he'd earned a reward for his time and effort. I picked up the ball and we were instantly in a game of tug of war. We played for a short while, almost taking out a bedside lamp. I thought it best to stop before we wrecked the place. "Ok Spike, I'm getting hungry. Let's go to dinner," I suggested. He understood the word 'dinner', although, that's probably not that unusual for a dog.

As we headed out the bedroom door, I almost bowled over a small framed man with very large framed glasses, walking past my door. I made my apologies, "Sorry, we weren't looking where we were going. I don't think we've met." I held out my hand. "I'm Alan.

"Oh yes," he smiled back. "Our man Crusoe!" He shook my hand, enthusiastically.

On closer inspection, he looked a lot younger than I'd first thought. His comment went right over my head. "I'm sorry?"

He laughed. "All alone on a desert island. Robinson Crusoe," he explained. "I'm Ben, and I was your pilot yesterday. I do hope you enjoyed your flight."

So, this was Ben. "Ah yes, the hands off pilot," I joked.

He bent and scratched Spike behind his ear. "I see Spike is showing you around. I can also smell Meg's cooking drifting down the corridor so let's follow our noses. We can walk and talk."

Spike led the way and Ben and I followed. I would guess Ben to be in his late or mid-twenties but it was hard to tell. As well as the impossible glasses, he had a thick head of curly blonde hair. Ben was right, something really did smell good, and it had been a long time since breakfast. As usual I was the one trying to make conversation. "Natasha said you are a high tech wizard. I'm sorry I don't really know what that means, apart from the fact that you can fly a plane from a long way off. Is that legal by the way?"

Ben laughed. "I've been doing a lot of work with radio control, amongst other things..."

"That must be interesting," I said, uncertainly. "But I don't really see how that fits into things here."

Ben laughed again. " Colin has been very generous. My lab here is fantastic. Tina and I research data from around the world, looking for anything out of the ordinary. Tina found you."

"Tina?" I said doubtfully. "Natasha had mentioned that you were the only person, left to meet."

Ben looked a little uncomfortable. "Ah well - Tina - isn't really anyone. What I mean is she isn't actually a person, she's a compute. My computer, I designed her." he said proudly.

I gave him a sideways look. "You called your computer Tina! That seems a little unusual."

This comment made him laugh. "You have been on this island how long? And you, think that's unusual, besides, there is a reason for that particular name. I can give Tina practically everything, apart from a heart, so I named her after my sister. She has the biggest heart of anyone I know. I figure, it's the next best thing. I'll introduce you to her later if you would like."

"Would this be your computer or your sister?" I joked.

He laughed. "I like you Alan. Tina-the computer, is in the lab, beneath your feet."

I couldn't help looking down. " You said Tina found me - Tina the computer that is." For the first time since I arrived here, I'd found someone who actually wanted to talk about what they did. Ben was obviously very proud of his work.

Ben explained, "Yes, I have programmed Tina to search out special words in the media, anything unusual like you Alan. Tina found many references to you in TV programs, newspapers and magazines. She found you very - interesting, and definitely worth investigating."

"Fantastic." At least I was interesting. "Have you known Colin long?" I asked.

Ben shook his head, "Just a few years. He's a great guy."

When we arrived at the dining room, Colin and Natasha were already at the table and deep in conversation. Colin looked concerned about something. I imagined Natasha had been telling him about our run-in with Sophie earlier. I felt uncomfortable and didn't know what to say. However, the awkwardness was swept away as Meg entered the room pushing a trolley piled high with great smelling food. We took our seats. I was about to ask where everyone was, when Sophie entered.

We all stood, Colin greeted her warmly and kissed her lightly on the cheek.

She apologized, "Sorry I'm a little late, I had to take Toby his dinner. His father has confined him to his room, so he is feeling sorry for himself." Sophie avoided looking my way.

Colin sighed. "Toby was supposed to be completing his project today. Instead, he has spent most of the day with George. What was I supposed to do?"

Sophie bent over and kissed his cheek. "I suppose you were right dear, but it's not as if Toby is the first boy to choose to spend the day with a dragon, rather than doing his homework."

We laughed and the awkwardness seemed to ease a little.

I found myself looking at Sophie in a different light, her lovely auburn hair, the only thing that linked this beautiful woman - to the beast that blocked my path, and threatened my life earlier that day. I tried to concentrate on Ben. He seemed very young, but at least I could understand his motives. Colin was funding his research and in return Ben used his talents and Tina, to find gossip on the airwaves. This was obviously how they found out about unusual sightings around the world, and how I came to be here in the first place.

Again Meg didn't join us. I found that strange, knowing her close relationship with Sophie and the obvious respect everyone had for her. Perhaps, like Jack she chose to eat alone.

***

We finished dinner and moved to the next room. Meg joined us with fresh coffee. She sat down next to Sophie on the couch. Colin handed round the mugs, and for a few moments, we just sat looking out over the island in silence. It was breath-taking, and hard to believe the secrets this island paradise, kept from the rest of the world. Colin was the first to speak. "Ok, we all know what we have to do."

I was tempted to say I don't.

Colin continued, "Meg, we need you to give us some direction. Do you think you can find her?"

Everyone's attention turned to Meg. She nodded. "I have felt her through George. I think with Alan's help, we should be able to at least identify the island, and perhaps get a picture of the surroundings."

I couldn't keep quiet any longer. "I still don't understand what I can do? I really would like to help believe me - but I haven't felt anything apart from confused, since all this started."

Colin smiled reassuringly. "It's all right Alan. Meg will help you channel your power."

"I have a power?" I said doubtfully.

Colin laughed. "You have power Alan. You just don't know how to use it yet. Meg will help you."

That sounded reasonable. "Ok, what do I have to do to find this power?" I said, still not entirely convinced.

Natasha smiled. "Just trust us Alan."

At this point I really had no choice. Meg came and sat by my side, took out a small bottle from her apron pocket, and offered it to me. "Drink this Alan, it will help you block out your surroundings here, and focus on what you need to find. You have a gift Alan, one you have used many times without realizing it. You just have to learn some control."

Now that sounded just like my mother.

I hesitated. I'd never been into drugs, and this was not what I'd imagined I would be doing this evening. Natasha came and sat on the other side of me and took my hand. I looked into those deep green eyes. "It's alright Alan, there is nothing to be afraid of, Meg would never do anything to harm you, and I'll be here with you all the time."

Her voice was gentle and reassuring, and her hand felt so right in mine. Besides I did want to help George, but I just wasn't so sure about what was in the bottle. I was reminded of Alice in wonderland. Maybe I should check the room for rabbit holes! But what the hell, I was in up to my neck now, so what harm could it do? I took the bottle and without further hesitation drank the contents.

I was surprised when nothing seemed to happen - the boat I was sitting in bobbed gently in the middle of the ocean, drifting slowly towards...?

Hang on a minute, I was on a boat. My mind seemed dull and my thoughts drifted past slowly with the waves. There was an island, and I was moving towards it. The sand was soft between my toes, and now I was walking through trees, thick trees - a jungle. The trees had gone, and it was cold and damp. I could hear the sound of water dripping. I closed my eyes, but instead of darkness I could see a light. I headed towards the light. Well you're supposed to, aren't you? Unless you happen to be a moth! There weren't any moths in the cave, in fact there wasn't anything in the cave. It opened out into a huge cavern, and at the end of the cavern was a wall of stones.

Movement caught my eye as I tried hard to focus. Whatever it was, it was coming out of a small hole in the wall. Maybe it was a rabbit from a rabbit hole! It grew larger as it approached, and I could see it wasn't a rabbit, but a small child. She ran past me, as if I wasn't there! Was I there?

I drifted towards the small hole that was high up in the wall of rocks. I could just see through to another cavern beyond, which was bright - almost too bright, I blinked trying to focus. I could just make out something moving within. Maybe it had seen me too, because it was coming towards me - closer – closer, I couldn't quite see, closer still. I could nearly make it out now. Just a little closer and I should be able to …! "Shit!" I gasped and fell backwards – down – down, I fell further and further, an impossible distance, then backwards, rushing back out of the cavern. Not running but flying back through the jungle, out into the ocean through the rock formations.

From a distance now, I could just make out the mountain in the heart of the island. It looked like a fork with three prongs, reaching high into the blue sky and all around it, a jungle of lettuce on an island sand plate. Was it me shaking, or the world? The earth trembled and the sea boiled. Everything was falling apart coming down around me, and I was screaming. I was afraid - drowning!

Suddenly someone had my hand, lifting me up, pulling me back. I came too with a start, my heart pounding in my chest. I blinked, as Sweat was dripping into my eyes. My hands were shaking but true to her word, Natasha was there next to me, holding my hand tightly in hers and calling my name. I focused with all my strength, on that beautiful face and lovely green eyes. I pulled myself up and gently kissed those lovely lips.

The nightmare was over. Natasha helped me sit up, but she looked slightly embarrassed. Now that I was aware of the rest of the party in the room looking down at us, I understood why! Ben was smiling and even Colin looked a little amused.

I shook my head. "What just happened," I stammered, trying to gather my thoughts.

"You tell us Alan," Meg said calmly. She was still sitting on the other side of me, watching me carefully. "What did you see Alan? You were talking about an island and something coming towards you. You saw something, something that terrified you. We need to know everything, every detail is important."

I sat for a moment trying to put things together. The room was silent, and I felt everyone waiting. I tried to recall everything I'd just experienced. It seemed so jumbled, like awakening from a dream or nightmare. I closed my eyes. "Oh god." I opened them quickly. It was still there. "It saw me. It was looking right at me."

Natasha still held onto my hand. "What was it Alan, what saw you?"

I took a deep breath. "I'm not sure, all I could make out was a huge eye, but I know it saw me. I felt as if it looked into my very soul."

Colin handed me a brandy, and I drank it in one. They waited patiently while I gathered my senses. I told them about the strange rock formations in the water and the jungle, the three pronged mountain that reminded me of a fork, the vast damp caves, and the wall of fallen rock. I even described the small child, who had walked past me as if I hadn't been there. I'd felt like a ghost, drifting through this strange mixed up world. I could see Ben taking notes, and writing down every detail.

Slowly I recalled everything, but what I couldn't put into words was the fear. Not fear of the sea, not of the island, not even from the giant eye - although that had scared the hell out of me. It was the fear that the world as I knew it was falling apart - breaking up all around me. As the memory of that feeling came back, I felt my body start to shake. Here in the relative safety of the lounge I could make myself believe it was just a dream, but I had felt real fear and not just my own!

Natasha reached out and took my hand again and smiled. "You've done well Alan. Ben will give Tina all the information you have given us, and she will find a match I'm sure." Natasha squeezed my hand.

Calmer now, I remembered the kiss. Natasha's hand was still in mine. That's where I felt it belonged. This world at least, felt safe again. I turned to Meg. "Do you really think what I saw was real? I don't understand, how, could I see those things. What was in that bottle?"

Meg shrugged. "I could tell you Alan, but then I'd have to kill you." She smiled sweetly, but something in her voice told me this wasn't a joke.

"What you saw was real, whether you understand it or not. You have a gift Alan. You were asked to find something - it just happened to be a dragon! Now you have a link to this dragon, albeit an unconscious one. You have found her Alan. You saw her I'm sure and yes, she could probably see you - or at least sense you." Meg smiled. "Natasha was right, you did very well."

Although I didn't know Meg very well, I recognized that those few words were praise indeed. Now my head was beginning to clear, and I remembered I'd seen this island before in another dream. It was a long way off, but I was sure it was the same island. I told the others, and they didn't seem at all surprised. Colin slapped me on the back. "Well done Alan!" He joined Sophie, putting his arm around her as they stood together. They made a handsome and seemingly normal couple.

"We had every faith in you," Sophie said smiling sweetly.

I found this hard to believe. "How could you possibly know about me, when I had no idea?"

Colin smiled. "A little bird told us, well a large mountain lion! Anyway she knew you were special. She told me, I told George, mystery solved. George senses your power. He believes you are a seeker Alan, and tonight you have proved him right. In time you will not need Meg's help, as you will learn to channel your thoughts and focus on your search. With what we have learned tonight, hopefully we should be able to start looking. What do you think Ben?"

Ben was already gathering up the notes and drawings he'd been making, while I'd been recalling my dreams. He looked up. "We have enough I think. If this island exists, Tina will be able to find it. I can't say how long it will take, but we'll get on to it straight away. Alan, perhaps you would join me. You may remember some more stuff as we update Tina, besides I would like you to meet her. If she comes up with some pictures, you may recognize something that will speed things along."

At that moment I would really have preferred to stay hand in hand with Natasha, but I could feel the urgency in the room and I agreed to go with Ben to help in any way I could.

We left the others talking and making plans. I overheard talk about a ship, before we were out of earshot, Ben lead the way down the stairs and along a corridor. He stopped at a heavy looking door and entered a code in a key pad. The door beeped and slid open to let us pass.

As we entered the room, the lights came on and large screens around the room began to show images of the island. A soft female voice greeted us.

"Hello Ben, this must be Alan. Hello Alan it's nice to finally meet you. I have read a lot about you."

"Hello Tina." I was a little unsure of how to make small talk with a computer, but this was unlike any computer I had seen before - she filled the whole room.

Ben was pushing buttons, and feeding his sketches into a slot. He indicated a chair. "Take a seat Alan, we've a lot to get through. I'll give Tina all the info we have and she will start a search. As she finds images that might match our information, Tina will put them on the screens around the room. If anything looks familiar, yell out and we'll see if we can find this island of yours."

Tina spoke, "Alan, do you have any idea where in the world the island might be?"

I shook my head, "I don't Tina. Sorry, but my geography has never been very good."

Lights blinked around the room. "That's alright Alan. I will do a worldwide search.

Incidentally I teach Toby Geography three times a week, may I suggest you join our lessons. I'm sure with the right teacher you would soon improve."

Could a computer sound smug? This one did. "Thank you Tina, I will certainly bare that in mind."

Ben laughed. "I just knew you two would get along. Now play nice. I'll organize us some coffee, it will be along night."

As I watched, images started to flash up on the screens around the room.

Ben headed for the door. "It will take a little time for Tina to sort out the most appropriate images, so relax for a while."

For the first time, I had time to take stock of what I'd seen. Had I really been there, could I have seen the rocks, the island - another dragon. Did she see me? Even without Meg's potion I had dreamed about the island, but could I really be a seeker? Perhaps it was all true. It could explain why I felt like I'd been searching for something my whole life, could I now be close, to finding it?

My thoughts turned not to dragons, but to Natasha. I caught a glimpse of her back on one of the screens as she headed towards the sea. Shit! Did she sleep in the ocean? That could make life difficult. I made a mental note to improve my swimming as soon as possible.

"You like her?"

I jumped, and looked around the room. Ben had gone to get the coffee and the screens were still sifting through images.

"I'm sorry," I said, to no one.

"You may well be in time Alan, but never the less you do like her."

The voice of Tina filled the room. It was a soft and gentle voice and it was beginning to seriously, creep me out.

She continued, "You are falling in love with Natasha and she is falling in love with you."

"She is!" For a second my heart leapt, and then I remembered I was talking to a machine. "How can you possibly know that?"

Tina sounded smug again. "I control security cameras all over the island and I have studied articles about love and relationships. I am interested in human emotions. I find you all fascinating."

I wanted to ask her more but stopped myself. This was crazy - it had to be a joke. Ben must be out there somewhere, watching me. Just at that moment the door beeped and slid open, to reveal Ben with the coffee. "Anything yet?" he asked. He certainly didn't look like someone who had just played a practical joke. He offered me a cup.

I hesitated. Should I say something about my conversation with Tina? I decided against it. "Nothing yet," I replied and took the coffee gratefully.

Tina spoke again, this time in more business-like tone. "Ben, I have isolated a few images that match your input."

"Thanks Tina. Start putting them on the front screens, but slow things down a bit to give Alan time to get a good look. How many so far?"

The lights flashed again. "Two thousand, three hundred and sixty two - so far."

I sighed. We both focused on the front six screens. Images started to appear - rock formations, jungle and mountains from all around the world. It had been a long day and it looked like it might be an even longer night. At 2 am, I was beginning to think I must have imagined the whole thing. There really couldn't be any more strange rock formations in the world! Then a picture caught my eye. Could it be?

"Tina, stop!" I hadn't realized how loud I'd shouted, Ben nearly fell off his chair. I think he'd been dozing. The screens froze. I found myself apologizing to a machine. "Sorry Tina, I didn't mean to shout."

"That is quite alright Alan. Did you see something?" Tina purred.

"Yes top row, screen two," I said excitedly. The image appeared again.

"Do you recognize it?" Ben was wide awake now.

I took a few moments. "I think so, it's a strange angle but it could be some of the rocks in front of the island. Tina, could you find some more shots of the same island for me please?"

Again, lights flashed. "Of course Alan, one moment please."

The screens went black for a second, then, they began to fill with images. I could hardly believe what I was seeing, but there was no doubt that this was it, this was the island of my dreams.

"That's it! We've found it." I said.

"Are you sure?" Ben already had the phone in his hand.

"I'm sure," I confirmed. The phone was answered almost immediately. No one was getting any sleep tonight.

Ben had come to life. "Colin is on his way down. Tina get us as much information as you can find, you know what we'll need." He turned to me, now totally awake. "This is where it really starts," he said, with genuine excitement. Colin entered a few seconds later and he and Ben started giving Tina instructions.

I felt at a loss, there was nothing further I could do. I was relieved when Colin suddenly remembered me. He turned and smiled. "Well done Alan. This could take the rest of the night, and you look all in. Why don't you go get some rest and we'll all meet for lunch later on. Hopefully we will be in a position to brief everyone then. "

I managed a smile. I felt exhausted. I was only too pleased to wish them luck and head for my room. It took me a few wrong turns to eventually stand in front of my door, without Spike this place was like a maze.

I made a note to myself to buy him a new ball when I got the chance, as a little thank you. I should have washed, I should have cleaned my teeth, I should have undressed and I certainly should have said a little prayer, but instead of all those things - I just collapsed onto my bed and instantly fell asleep.

In my head there was music, a gentle sweet sound, not words, or maybe they were words. I couldn't make them out, but I felt uplifted by the sound.  There was a light, so I headed over the rocks towards it. I climbed higher and higher until I reached a gap. It was small, too small to get through.  But I needed to get through - I needed to reach the music. Abruptly the sound stopped. Instantly I felt lost, cold and alone, so very alone.  I peered through into the cavern beyond.  It was lit by a bright light, a golden glow, a warming glow.

I knew it must be her. As my eyes became accustomed to the light I could see her below, in the cavern. She was beautiful - a shimmering golden dragon, slightly smaller than George. But she looked so sad and I felt over whelmed with her pain, her sadness. I needed to reach her, I needed to help her. I cried out to her. I needed for her to hear me - to know I was coming to help her - we were coming to help her... So much pain!!

A distant voice called my name. "Alan! Alan!"

I woke to find Natasha was sitting on the side of the bed. She looked concerned and I realized I was crying. The pain, the loneliness, the fear remained with me. Natasha put her arms around me and held me close.  I felt lost and confused. She stroked my hair. "It's alright Alan, it was just a dream, but you're safe now," she whispered. I should have enjoyed being this close to Natasha, but I felt like my heart had been wrenched from my body. I tried desperately to regain some control.

Eventually I managed to find the words. "It was so real, loneliness, emptiness." I forced myself to recall but I felt like a child relating a nightmare. Natasha didn't speak as she continued to stroke my hair, and slowly I relaxed.  "I remember music - lovely music in my head. I saw her Natasha, but she is so sad so lonely and I felt her pain." I swallowed hard to stop the tears from returning. "She has been alone for so long, so very long. Something is coming - it will end, she will end. Alone." The words rushed out and I couldn't stop them.

Natasha just listened. I felt like a fool. "I'm sorry Natasha. I don't know what is happening to me. You must think I'm an idiot." The images were fading and I was left feeling embarrassed. My world felt like it was falling in on my head. Just when I thought this whole thing had been a mistake, she kissed me - and the world stopped spinning.

Her voice soothed me. "It's ok Alan. What you heard was the dragon song, it can be very powerful. Not many people can say they have experienced it, but it is magical and truly beautiful."

The feeling of emptiness was wearing off now and I looked into those beautiful green eyes. "I don't understand. You've heard her too?"

Natasha smiled. "Not her Alan - George, many years ago."

I felt the bond between us growing. I wanted to pull her to me and kiss her again but I was afraid the magic would be gone. For now, it was enough to lie side by side on the bed with her hand in mine.

After a while Natasha sat up. "Are you feeling a little better?"

I would have liked to have said no so that she would lie beside me again, but instead I nodded. Natasha smiled, "Good, because Colin sent me to see if you had rested. They have found the location of the island you identified. A ship is on its way to pick us up, so we have a lot to do.

Colin thought you and I should go and tell George what's going on. Do you feel up to it Alan? I could go alone."

"I'm fine now, and I'd like to see George again. I hope he can explain a few of the visions I've been having. I still don't fully understand the images I've seen in my dreams, or the great fear and sadness I feel when I wake. However, I could do with a shower and a change of clothes. I'll only be a few moments."

"Of course Alan, I'll wait for you in the kitchen. I want to talk to Meg before we go," and with that she was gone. The room seemed empty without her.

After a hot shower and change of clothes, I felt a lot better. I was really looking forward to talking with George again. I had so many questions.

Natasha and Meg were talking as I entered the kitchen. Spike had obviously just had a snack. He looked up from his bowl to let out a couple of short yaps to greet me, and then went back to business.

"He likes you Alan," Meg said, as I stood watching the little dog dig in.

I smiled. "He seems to like everyone apart from Jack. What is it with them?"

Meg smiled. "Oh they like each other, but they both think they are top dog, on the island."

There was a fantastic smell of pancakes, and Meg pointed to a seat at the table. "You both have time for some blueberry pancakes. It will be a long day." Meg placed a large plate in the middle of the table. "Eat!" Meg's tone said we were not going anywhere till we had cleared the lot. Natasha sat opposite me and we both did as we were told.

"These are great thanks Meg," I said with my mouth full.

Meg was watching us enjoy the food with obvious pleasure. "You have had another dream Alan."

It wasn't a question. I wasn't sure how she knew, but presumed Natasha had told her. "Yes, every time I close my eyes now I seem to be able to see this golden dragon. It's hard to explain, but I feel so much loneliness and pain, and the feelings seem to be getting stronger. If what I'm seeing is real, then something is very wrong. Do you know what it all means Meg?"

Meg tried hard to disguise the worried look that came over her face. She turned away quickly, and spoke with her back to us. "I've made heaps of blueberry pancakes so take them with you to George, they are his favourite. Tell him I will be out to talk with him later." Meg gave Natasha a package and turned to face me. "Talk to George Alan. If anyone can understand your dreams, it will be him."

Natasha took the package and smiled. "You spoil all of us Meg. I'll tell George you'll see him later." Natasha turned and I was over the moon, when she took my hand. "Ok let's go - you can lead the way seeker," she teased.

I laughed. "I'm not sure if that's a good idea if we want to get there today."

She squeezed my hand. "You have got to start believing in yourself Alan."

Spike jumped up and gave a couple of little yaps. Meg laughed. "You are in luck Alan, Spike says he's going with you and he likes to lead." Spike trotted out in front of us. The rest of the house seemed oddly quiet, and I guessed everyone else was making plans. I couldn't help wondering what those plans would involve.

Spike led the way through the forest and we followed on. I thought it might be a good opportunity to try to find out more about Natasha. "Do you have memories of your mother?" I asked as we walked.

Natasha seemed to think for a moment. "I remember her smile, and the way she would sing to me at night before I went to sleep. For a long time after she'd gone I would imagine I could still hear her at night singing to me, but I also remember hearing my father crying when he thought I was a sleep," she said sadly.

I felt for her. "You must miss them very much."

She shrugged. "It was a long time ago, but what about your family Alan?"

My family history seemed tame, after Natasha's story, "My father was a journalist. I never saw much of him, he was always off somewhere, looking for the next story. It was just after my eighteenth birthday that he disappeared. I would like to say I missed him, but I never really got to know him. I suppose I blamed my mother for him always being away. She never tried to stop him. There was always just one more story to chase.

After he disappeared mother never seemed to want to talk about it. This made me angry too, I needed to know the truth, but my mother seemed to accept his disappearance too easily. We don't know what happened to him. Maybe she didn't care! I don't know. We don't talk much anymore. She never remarried. As far as I know she's still teaching. We've never been very close. No that's a lie, we were once, but something happened. Something changed. Perhaps they just stopped getting along. I don't know, I was packed off to a boarding school as soon as I was old enough, and holidays were always awkward affairs."

We walked on in silence for a few moments. For some reason I suddenly felt sad, even though I had always thought I didn't really care. Natasha seemed to sense the change in me and reached out and took my hand.

The bush opened up to reveal the edge of the lake, and the cave mouth where yesterday I had met George. From above our heads we heard a familiar yapping. We both looked up to see Spike seemingly suspended in mid-air.

Then like magic, George began to appear. One minute Spike was in the air, the next he was standing high up on George's neck - obviously very pleased with himself.

"I don't understand. How can you not see something the size of a dragon? It's as though he's invisible one minute and there the next."

Natasha was laughing. "I tried to explain. It's his scales, the light reflects off them. Now you see him, now you don't. How else do you think he could have stayed unseen for so long. I suppose it is magic - of a sort."

George looked down on us from on high. "Hello Alan, it is good to see you again, and Natasha, if my nose is not mistaken you have a gift from Meg for me - pancakes! Blueberry I hope."

Natasha held up the package. "Yes, Meg said to tell you she will be out to see you later."

I found myself staring up at this magnificent beast. I still found it hard to believe I could be in the company of a real dragon. Second time around however he didn't look half as threatening, especially when you took into consideration the small dog perched happily on his back. George ate. When he had finished, we sat on the rocks in front of the cave.

I was the first to speak. "I think I've seen her George."

George seemed anxious. "I thought as much. I too have seen her in my dreams. She is afraid and alone. Something approaches."

I tried hard to remember the details of my dream. I needed to make sense of it. "George I don't understand what I see. She's in some sort of cave, and I think she may be trapped." I hesitated - I couldn't find the words to describe the feelings I'd experienced.

"It is all going to end." The words just came out, and suddenly I realized that had been what I'd been feeling. It was all coming to an end. But what was ending? What did that mean? I looked up into Georges face, and saw the sadness I had seen in the golden dragons eyes. "What does it mean George? What is it?" He slowly lowered his head, and Spike jumped to the ground.

He looked sad. "I wish I knew Alan, I have seen what you have seen and felt what you have felt. She is a golden dragon."

I felt angry. I had expected George to have all the answers. "Yes, I've seen her, she shines like the sun. But what does that mean? Is she special?" I felt stupid. Of course she was special - she was a bloody dragon!

George was silent - deep in thought.

Natasha reached out and stroked his nose. "Please George - you know something more you're not telling us."

George looked into the distance and seemed to be recalling something from a long distant past. "She is a golden dragon. It is told in the book of truths that she has the power to foretell the end."

I went over this a couple of times in my head. It was such a simple sentence, but what did it mean? Finally I had to ask, "The end of what?" The silence was deafening, so I tried again "The end of what George?" Spike had now settled himself on Natasha's lap.

I couldn't stand it - I needed to know. "What is it George. The end of her, the world, what?" George seemed to consider this for a second, a second that seemed like a lifetime. When he spoke, it was almost a whisper.

"I am not sure Alan. All I know is, that it is said the golden dragon has the power to foretell the end of the world!"

We all sat in silence for a while, watching the dragonflies hovering over the lake, dipping and dancing, rushing busily here and there. The noise of the island all around us, sounded even louder as if confirming that life was going on as usual.

I shook my head, "No. That can't be it!" I said, almost to reassure myself.

George stood up to his full height and for the first time, looked angry. "Alan, for many years I have watched humans fight and kill over what they think is their piece of the world, but whether you live in the penthouse or the basement flat - when the great wrecking ball comes, the result is just the same." He seemed to calm a little. "Whatever it is we will find out soon, and then I will come with you to find her and bring her back. If it is the end, I must be with her and we will face it together."

Natasha gasped. "No George, Colin was afraid of this! You must not leave the safety of the island."

George seemed determined, "I must go with you. If what we suspect is true, it will only matter for a very short time. If the end is to come, I want to be by her side - I must be with her at the end," he insisted.

I had remained silent - processing all of this in my mind, but now it was suddenly clear. I stood slowly and faced them both. "No! This is not the end," I said emphatically. "I don't know exactly what is happening, but it is not going to end like this." I tried to sound as confident as I could. "George, you must stay here. The safety of everything depends on your patience and trust! We will go and find the golden dragon and bring her home to you, and you will have time together I promise. You must trust us."

George lowered his head and looked into my eyes. "What if you are wrong Alan?" he said softly. He was so big, yet suddenly he reminded me of a small child. Those large sad eyes studying me carefully, expecting me to put things right- Me!

I pulled myself up to my full height. "I'm not wrong in this. I too have felt that something terrible will happen, but I'm sure it's not the end of the world, the end of that Island perhaps. But not the end of everything, there is still time - there has to be time.

If the golden dragon can see the future, she would know if there was no point to all this - yet she is still trying to reach us. She wants us to find her. There must still be time to make a difference. You must give us a chance to try George. You have waited so long. Wait just a little longer Please." In that moment I believed every word I was saying and I hoped to god I was right.

Natasha placed her hand gently on his shoulder. "Please George, you have to leave this to us. Alan is right. She wants him to find her. She is reaching out to him - to you. There has to be a reason. There has to be a chance."

We sat in silence, and even Spike seemed to understand the enormity of what was going on here. I had to be right - I couldn't bear to think of the alternative. For the first time in my life I felt I had a purpose, something to fight for, someone to fight for. I wanted to belong here with these strange people, strange creatures. Fate could not be so cruel as to take it all away, not like this.

George bowed his head toward me and spoke.

"You are right Alan, she is reaching out to you for a reason. I will trust you to bring her home to me. You have five days - I can wait that long, and then, we will see!"

Natasha took my hand. "She kissed George gently on the end of his snout. "Thank you George, it will be alright. Come on Alan, we have a lot to do."

We headed back towards the house. I glanced over my shoulder once but could no longer see George. We walked, lost in our own thoughts, Spike trotted along beside us. Suddenly Natasha stopped and turned to face me. "Do you really believe what you said back there?"

I took both her hands in mine. "Yes, I have to. I have just made the most important discovery of my entire life, and I'm not going to lose it now."

She laughed. "You're mad!"

"I believe I told you that when we first met, so you can't say I didn't warn you." I pulled her close and we kissed. This time she didn't pull away, and for just a few moments, nothing else mattered. We held each other close, and even the future of the world, could wait, just a little longer.

I think we would have both liked to remain like that for some time, but Spike broke the spell with a couple of polite little barks. Natasha looked down at him. "You're right of course Spike. He says we should be getting back."

"How do you do that?" I asked.

She looked puzzled. "What."

"How, does everyone understand what Spike is saying. It just sounds like barking to me."

She smiled patiently. "You will learn to understand him Alan - you just need to open your mind. Come, we must hurry there is a lot to do. We will need to tell Colin what George has agreed - I think he'll be relieved."

I hesitated. "You think George will keep his word and wait?"

Natasha nodded, "Yes I do, but we still only have five days. George would not lie to us."

We increased our pace. "Let's hope it's a fast boat. It will have to be big too, if it's going to have a dragon as cargo."

Natasha laughed again and it was nice to hear her relaxing once more. "Oh, it's big and fast. It's one of Colin's fleet but Ben has done a few modifications! We have used it before."

This fact didn't fill me with confidence. "Should I be worried about this - Ben seems a bit like a mad scientist to me."

This comment bought another smile to her face. "You two should get along just fine then," she teased. "Seriously though Ben is a genius, and if anyone can get us to and from an island with a dragon on board, Ben is the man to do it. The difficult bit is not attracting attention. You understand now how important secrecy is."

"Surely people would be pleased that these animals had survived..." Before I'd finished the sentence, I knew that it wasn't that simple. There would always be someone out there who saw them all as a threat, and would hunt them down, or worse, experiment on them to find out how they ticked. At best they would all be in some sort of zoo, at worst on a lab table. I shuddered.

Natasha was watching me agonize. I knew she could work out the thoughts that were going through my head.

"I 'm sorry." I suddenly felt I needed to apologize.

She smiled. "There is no need to be sorry. You are one of us now Alan, and the past is just that. We help each other survive as best we can. Now, let's get back and see how the plans are going."

As we approached the house, peace had been shattered. There were several vehicles being loaded with boxes. Jack was doing a lot of the lifting and Ben was doing a lot of the instructing. He turned to greet us as we approached.

"About time you three got back, we were beginning to think you got lost. Most of the heavy stuff is done!"

Natasha laughed. "Maybe, but not done by you Ben." She slapped Jack on the back. "Well done Jack, but you should let Ben do some of the lifting, it would be good exercise for him!"

Jack just smiled and grunted, but he seemed happy to be the muscle of the team.

Ben pretended to look hurt. "That is so unfair. You know I do the thinking."

Natasha winked at me. "Come on Ben, we know Tina does all the thinking. Only a woman could do so many tasks at once!"

I hadn't noticed Sophie at the top of the stairs, accompanied by a very sullen looking Toby. "We're off Natasha. Toby has an appointment with some exams. I hope he has been honest with us about keeping up with his studies." Sophie shot a glance at her son, who kicked at a stone on the ground. "I'll try to be back before you have to leave, but if I'm not - look after the boys will you. Make sure Colin keeps in touch."

Toby was obviously not happy, and was muttering under his breath the whole time. "It's not fair. I could help," he protested as his mother led him away.

Sophie laughed. "If you were old enough Toby, you would already know that the world isn't fair, now the plane is waiting, say good bye."

Toby grumbled his good byes, and his mother whisked him away.

Natasha turned back to Ben, "where is the boss?"

Ben laughed. "I see you're both going to sneak off and leave us to do all the hard stuff. Colin said for you to meet him in the lab, he will want to know how it went with George."

They all seemed close - like an extended family. I still wasn't sure of my role in all this, but I knew I wanted, and even needed to have a part to play.

As usual, Natasha seemed to read my mind. In fact it was starting to worry me - could she actually do that - She took my hand. "Don't take any notice of Ben. Come on, let's leave the guys to it - they obviously have all this under control."

We found Colin in the lab talking to a small round metal ball. After all that had gone on in the last two days this didn't seem unusual.

He stopped as we came in. "How did George take it?" he asked with obvious concern.

Natasha reassured him. "If you mean is he going to stay - I think so. Alan persuaded him to give us a chance, and he said he will wait five days."

Colin seemed a little relieved. "That doesn't give us much time, but I must say I'm surprised you managed to stop him coming with us. Thank you Alan - you did well. He must have a lot of faith in you. Did he tell you his concerns?"

I sensed Colin was waiting to see how I would respond.

I nodded, "Yes, but he has got it wrong - it's not the end." The words came out a lot louder than I'd meant them to, and they both looked at me. "I'm sorry," I said quickly. "I didn't mean to shout, but she needs us for a reason - she expects us to be able to do something. I'm not sure what yet, but if it was the end of the world - really the end of everything - there would be nothing we could do, right?"

Colin nodded. "Actually Alan that makes a lot of sense, in fact, Tina2 was just trying to work out some possible reasons for the golden dragon's concerns." Colin directed his attentions back to the small silver ball. "Tina2, would you repeat your findings for Natasha and Alan please."

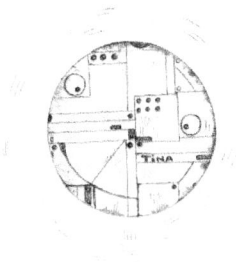

The little sphere bobbed. "Certainly Colin. Hello Alan."

"Hello Tina, you seem a little more compact today."

"Yes Alan. I will be accompanying you on your journey, so Ben and I have devised a form in which I can be of more use. A portable me! I am still fully functional but I can move freely. I am also completely water proof and of course - armed."

"Of course," I said, a little dubiously. Colin saw my expression.

"I'm sure we won't need to use violence for any reason," he reassured me. "But Ben likes to think of everything, and he wouldn't want to send Tina out into the world, without her own protection."

I suppose I could understand that. "I can see why we shouldn't leave home without you Tina, but aren't you needed here?"

The lights flashed. "You are right to be concerned Alan. However I will also be here! I have no problem operating in several places at once, and Ben and I can still keep the island safe for your return."

I was surprised. "Ben won't be coming with us?"

Colin laughed. "It's ok Alan, I can captain it perfectly well without Ben."

I had hit a nerve. "Sorry, I didn't mean that the way it sounded. It's just that Natasha said it was a big ship, and there doesn't seem that many of us to do whatever it takes to make a big ship - go!" It was obvious I had no idea what I was talking about.

Several lights flashed along the sides of the small sphere. "I can see you know a lot about modern ships Alan. I could give you lessons in that as well." Tina observed. If I didn't know better, I would have sworn Tina was laughing at me.

Colin tried, but failed to hide his amusement. "What Tina is trying to say is that most of the ship's functions are automated. I'll just point us in the right direction, which of course has already been plotted. If needs be I can hand things over to Ben and Tina here. If the need arises, they can override the systems so we can keep our hands free," Colin explained. "Anyway Alan, you can rest assured that we know what we are doing up to a point."

I thought about this for a second. "Ok that's reassuring," I said. "However, at what point - do we no longer know what we're doing?"

Colin considered his reply. "Yes on that notion, Tina thinks the Island may be only days away from an eruption that will probably send it to the bottom of the ocean. Things may get interesting!"

I couldn't just let that one slide. "If I heard you right, you have a strange idea of what's interesting. Up till now I had thought all I had to worry about was a huge dragon or the end of the world. Now it seems there could also be a volcano involved." Things were just getting better and better.

Colin smiled. "I did tell you we had been working on other possibilities. Tina has detected some activity below the island, and we think this could be the disaster the dragon has seen. It could indeed be the end - the end of the island and her, if we can't get her out.

There is also a small population of about 30 people to consider."

"Do we know how long we have?" I asked. Everyone seemed so calm. Had they faced these sorts of problems before?

Colin shrugged. "Tina can you give us any idea yet?"

"I am sorry Colin, all I can tell you is the activity is increasing. I will keep monitoring it, and may be able to give you a few hours warning before it erupts."

I shrugged. "Great! I'm beginning to realize what I've gotten myself into."

Natasha looked directly at me. "So you're still sure you don't want out Alan?"

I didn't need time to think, "I won't pretend all this doesn't scare the hell out of me, but this is something I need to do, so I'm in this all the way. Besides, I promised a pretty large friend I would do something for him and I'm not going to break that promise."

Colin nodded and smiled. "Alright then team - let's get this show on the road."

The lights flashed and there was a strange whirring noise from Tina, she seemed to be considering this, then she said, "Colin, I feel I must point out that you will have to go by sea."

Colin laughed. "Sorry Tina, it was just a figure of speech.

I returned to my room. It was a pleasant surprise to find that Meg had taken my dirty things and returned them all washed, aired, and folded neatly on the bed. For the first time in a long while I felt like I belonged. I had a purpose. Of course, I still wasn't completely sure what that was.

We had all agreed to meet back in the dining room later. Natasha had said she would see me at dinner and had headed out towards the ocean. I had a suspicion that she would be talking to Hector, and although it seemed totally mad - I felt jealousy.

It didn't take me long to pack. I only had a few belongings with me. The rest of my stuff had been placed in storage many years ago. I'd always promised myself one day I would buy a place and put down some roots. Somehow, I'd never been able to find a place I wanted to call home. Perhaps I'd been looking for the place, when I should have been looking for the person.

I'd fallen in love - really in love, maybe for the first time in my life. Now, I didn't care where home was as long as Natasha was there too. Of course I knew there would be difficulties to overcome, but she would be worth it. Colin and Sophie seemed to manage reasonably well. They even had a son who, at least for now seemed pretty normal. God I really had to stop saying that word. Who the hell was I to decide what was normal - on this island nothing could be considered normal.

I lay back on the bed and let my mind drift, I could hear music, singing, beautiful but sad, so sad. It was the golden dragon. She had crept quietly into my dreams again. The cavern must have been huge, she seemed small. She looked lost and alone in the middle of this cold, damp place - but wait, she wasn't alone - the child was there too, sitting on some rocks so that she was level with the dragons head. They seemed to be talking but I could not hear the words. I reminded myself that of course they would be in my head, not in my ears. I had to open my mind.

I concentrated hard and yes - there it was - the dragon was speaking gently but insistently to the child.

"You must leave me, you must leave this place."

The child was crying but she was defiant, "I won't leave you."

"Maya, you must go. You must make your people leave this place."

The child sounded angry now. "They will not hear me, they are not my people."

The dragon sighed. "Maya you know you can make them listen, you have been given a gift. You have to go and use this gift to help others, this is your destiny."

The child Maya, reached out and stroked the dragon's snout. "What about your destiny. You said this was not your time, you said you could see things."

The dragon seemed to be thinking, and finally she said softly, "I'm sorry Maya, I don't know. I can no longer see. Perhaps it is my time - I have lived for many, many years."

Maya's voice was only a whisper now. "I don't care, I will never leave you."

The images faded, and as I opened my eyes a feeling of hopelessness engulfed me. I had a sudden need to be with the others, especially Natasha.

In the dining room everyone listened as I tried to relay every word, every image I had seen in my dream. When I'd finished, the room was silent for a few moments.

Colin was the first to speak. "Right, let's eat and then we will get the rest of our things together and get underway. Ben, you and Tina will stay here and keep an eye on things, and monitor the island. Give us as much warning as you can. Sophie will be back soon to help you.

Jack, Natasha, Alan and I, and of course Tina mark II, will get into position as fast as we can. We can use the exceptional speed of our craft to cover the distance, but it will still take us around 30 hours to reach the island."

Meg spoke, "What about the people Colin?" She had joined us for the meal, and to my surprise Jack was here too.

"We will do what we can Meg but we can't force these people to leave their homes. We must concentrate on the golden dragon, she is our priority. First things first, let's find our dragon. If we can do that, and help these people while keeping a low profile then we will."

Meg tapped her knife on the table. "Ok people let's eat! I have not spent the last three hours in the kitchen for this food to be stone cold. Things will work themselves out, they always do."

Colin apologized, "Sorry Meg, as usual you're right. Let's eat now and talk later. We will have plenty of time to make plans once we get on the ship."

We all enjoyed the meal, and I just hoped it wouldn't be our last together. The rest of the meal was eaten in comparative silence. When we had finished we all helped clear the table and take things to the kitchen. Spike was patiently waiting for his turn to be fed.

Meg uncovered a dish that was on the breakfast bar. It didn't look like left overs to me. Spike was one of the family after all and Meg looked after us all very well. As soon as the dish was placed on the floor Spike tucked in, his tail wagging like mad.

I found myself alone with Meg in the kitchen. She took my hand and spoke in almost a whisper.

"Alan it's not hard to see you have fallen for our beautiful Natasha, but take some advice from someone with more years of experience than you could possibly guess. Go slowly. The best things in life are worth waiting for. Don't rush her or yourself."

I nodded. "I know she's frightened because of what happened to her father."

Meg patted my hand. "Yes and you should be too. Take care Alan, that's all I will say." Meg turned back to the dishes.

Colin poked his head around the door. "Ok we will all meet downstairs in 1 hour. Gather your things and say a prayer if you've a mind to - we could probably all use one."

I would have liked to stay and talk to Meg some more. She seemed to have so many years of knowledge and experience, yet she still seemed so young. I got the feeling there was a lot more to Meg than I already knew, but now was not the time. Instead I thanked her for the advice and for doing my laundry. Meg looked up from the dishes with that now familiar broad smile. "You are part of a family now Alan, we look after each other."

I headed back to my room to collect my things. Spike trotted along with me and I was grateful for the distraction. I still felt like everyone knew what they were doing, but me.

When we reached my room I sat on the bed. Spike jumped up next to me, and pushed his head under my hand. I stroked him. Things felt a little better, after all the golden dragon had come to me, and hopefully she would be able to guide me. This was a different type of hunt and this time my aim would be to preserve life not to take it. I liked that thought.

Suddenly I felt as though I could sleep for a week, and when this was all over I probably would and maybe, just maybe, I wouldn't be alone.

I was the first one down to the vehicles with Spike. We played with his treasured tennis ball.

Natasha's voice made me jump. "You just can't help but love him can you?"

She was standing above me on the stairs. I looked up into those amazingly green eyes, and nodded in agreement. "Sometimes you just can't help yourself." Our eyes met and again the world stood still, and I could feel my heart beating in my chest.

Ben interrupted the moment. "You two love birds can get a room when we get back. Come on Alan, a little help here." Without ceremony Ben thrust a couple of bags at me. I was surprised to see Tina2 hovering by his side about five feet above the ground. She must have noticed my expression.

"Hello Alan," she said, in her silky voice. "I would not be of much use in the field if I couldn't manage stairs now, would I?"

I always felt like she was teasing me. I still found it hard to think that this was just a machine, although I got the feeling that if I tried calling her just a machine, I could end up exterminated!

Meg came to say goodbye. Colin kissed her on the cheek. "Take care of them Meg. Get Sophie to contact us when she gets back, I would like to know how Toby did in his exams."

He reached down and gave Spike a good scratch behind the ears, "You look after everything for us boy." Spike replied with a couple of short barks.

We loaded the rest of the bags and headed towards the air strip. I was with Natasha and Colin. I was a little surprised. "I thought we were going by boat?" I said.

Natasha smiled. "We are Alan, but this island has no deep water moorings - in fact because of the reef, it's almost impossible to land a boat here. That's actually what makes it so perfect for us. We will fly to a larger island just south of here, where Colin's ship is moored, and waiting for us. All the arrangements have been made. We have used this ship to transport George once before, it is a large cargo ship - specially fitted out for our purpose. As far as the world in general knows, we are doing a survey on endangered marine life!"

"God knows there's a lot of that," Colin added, with no humour. "Most people ignore us. One of the good things, about having lots of money, is that people tend to expect you to be eccentric. We are more than happy to let them believe just that."

Eccentric! The world thought Michael Jackson was eccentric for having a chimp for a best friend. What would they make of a man, who kept a dragon in his back yard, and had a wolf as a handyman? I think that probably goes well beyond eccentric!

\*\*\*

The plane was already waiting on the run way, and it didn't take us long to load up and board. I was pleased to see that Ben took the pilots seat. "I thought he didn't like to fly?"

Colin agreed, "Yes but we have got to keep up appearances. When we land there will be more of my people there to help us load this stuff on the ship, and get us underway as quickly as possible. Ben will fly the plane back home and leave Tina2 with us. The ship has already been loaded with most of the things we need. Once Tina is on board she will link into the computers, and be able to input all the data for our destination.

You look tired Alan, get some sleep. The flight will take us about 45 minutes. In fact it would be a good idea if we all got a bit of shut-eye." Colin lay back in his seat and closed his eyes.

Natasha was in the seat just a cross from mine. She pushed her recline button.

I tried to relax. Even Tina seemed to have switched off. Every now and then, a subdued green light would flash just for a second, as if to check she wasn't missing anything. I reclined my seat and closed my eyes.

It felt like I had only closed my eyes for a few seconds, before Natasha was shaking my arm. "Come on sleepyhead, we're here," she said.

I forced myself awake; I must have been tired after all. Suddenly a thought hit me like a fist in my stomach, and I felt close to panic. "I didn't see her!" The panic in my voice made everyone turn to look at me. I lowered my voice. "For the first time since all this started, she wasn't in my dream. I'd slept and she wasn't there! What does that mean? Could we be too late?"

I felt a sense of great loss. I realized I'd become accustomed to the dragon in my dreams. The idea, she may have been taken from me, was suddenly too much to bear. I felt a sudden wave of helplessness overcome me.

Natasha glanced over at Colin with a look of uncertainty on her face.

Surprisingly it was Tina2 who offered reassurance. "I have been monitoring activity on and around the island Alan, and there has been no major change in the current situation. Perhaps your dragon is busy!"

Natasha touched my hand. "You were only asleep for a short time Alan, and we are all very tired. Let's just keep focused on the job in front of us."

She was right of course. I felt a sense of relief flowing back.

Ben stuck his head through the door, "Less talking you lot and a little more help. It's all right for you lot, off cruising, but I would like to get back home sometime this side of morning."

Colin laughed. "Ben's right! Let's get this stuff into the vehicles - it's only a 5 minute drive to the wharf, but we want to get underway within the hour."

The two men who had bought the vehicles out, greeted Colin and he shook their hands. They helped us load up. As I grabbed the last couple of bags I noticed Ben holding Tina. He was talking to her as one would a child.

"Now you keep out of trouble, and let me know everything as it happens. Sorry Tina, but I will have to cover you for your trip to the ship, it's best, if you're not seen."

The little lights flashed on and off. "Yes Ben I understand, I will keep you updated. You should not worry - you have made me well!"

He gently wrapped her in cloth, and placed her in a leather box. I felt honoured but a little worried, when he handed the box over to me. "Take good care of her Alan." I felt Ben hesitate just slightly before he let go of the box.

I found it hard to understand how much he felt for this computer, but there was no doubt in my mind that he loved her on some level. I assured him that I would guard her with my life. It was a bit melodramatic, but it seemed to help.

Ben said his good byes to the others, and as we headed to the wharf I saw the plane take to the sky's again for the return trip.

I sat the box down carefully on the seat beside me. Natasha was in front with Colin, who drove at speed over the bumpy grass. I picked up the box and put it on my lap to try to soften the journey for Tina. The box seemed very light for something of such great importance, and I had to laugh. Knowing Ben, he had probably designed Tina2 to survive a nuclear explosion, and here I was trying to protect her from a few bumps.

Jack was in the jeep behind, with the two men. I couldn't help noticing they'd both automatically jumped into the back seat to let Jack drive.

As we neared the wharf, I was amazed at the size of the ship in front of us. One thing though, there would be plenty of room for an average size dragon - or two!

The two men helped us get the gear on board, but after a short conversation with Colin they left. Natasha saw me standing on the deck, still carefully holding on to the box.

She smiled. "You can give Tina to Jack now. He'll take good care of her, and I'll show you where everything is. Grab your stuff and we'll put it in one of the cabins. You can have the one next to mine - so I can keep an eye on you!"

I liked the sound of this so I quickly handed over my charge, and grabbed my bag to follow Natasha below deck. The cabins were small but very comfortable, each one with its own shower and toilet. I was pleased to find I even had a small window, when I looked out I could see we had already started to move away from the wharf.

Natasha appeared in the doorway. "Well what do you think? Will Sir be comfortable here?"

I nodded, "Definitely," and added "I like the thought of you just next door." I was pleasantly surprised to see her blush.

She changed the subject quickly. "I'll give you a tour of the ship, so you can find your way around. She looks huge, but most of the room is taken up with the storage areas and engine rooms below deck. The kitchen and all the cabins are on this level, and above us is the bridge. The ship will be well stocked, so if you get hungry just help yourself."

We did a whistle stop tour, when we reached the bridge, Colin was on the radio informing the powers that be that we were on our way out of port. He gave our heading and general direction, and when he'd signed off he turned to greet us.

"Hi Guys. Alan, did Natasha show you round?"

I nodded.

He laughed. "Not impressed eh! Well once I'm sure no one is watching, we can open her up and then you'll see what she can really do. Tina2 have you sorted yourself out yet?"

The small silver sphere was seated in a special slot for her - on the panel in front of us. Different coloured lights flashed on and off, and there was the now familiar soft whirring sound, that I assumed meant that Tina was thinking!

Tina sounded a little disgruntled. "I was not unsorted Colin, however I have made all the necessary connections and I am now online and ready."

Colin didn't seem to notice. "Great, you keep us on this course and let me know when we are clear to really get this thing moving."

Jack was sitting in front of another bank of lights, I was surprised, he seemed at home on the ship. He shouted to Colin, "There's a call from home coming in. Should I put it on speaker?"

"Yes. Thanks Jack." The radio crackled into life and Colin adjusted the microphone. It was Sophie. "Hi honey, how is everything going?"

"Hi babe, everything is good here. Did you manage to get our wayward son, to concentrate on his school work for more than two seconds? He can't have done his exams yet, but has he at least got his thinking cap on?" Colin joked.

I couldn't help noticing the slight hesitation, before Sophie spoke again, "Now honey, I don't want you to get upset but there was a bit of an incident."

Colin looked instantly concerned. "Sophie what sort of incident?"

Sophie sounded calm. "It really wasn't too bad. Toby lost his temper and - well, he bit someone."

Colin looked as though he was going to explode. "What! Explain to me Sophie, how that can possibly be described as 'not be too bad'?"

"Calm down dear, he got into a fight. Both boys apparently lost it, and when they were separated - the other boy had a nasty bite on his arm that needed just a few stitches." The headmaster has been great. He felt that both boys were to blame, and has put it down to them both being anxious about their exams. Honestly, I agree with him. Everything's ok, but I've bought Toby straight home with me. We will talk when you get back."

Colin had gone pale. "I should come home."

Ben's voice interrupted. "Sorry Colin, there really isn't going to be time. If you want to get to this island before the eruption, you are going to have to go right now. Tina has just picked up more movement, so it really is now or never mate, sorry."

Sophie came on the radio again. "It's ok, really. Meg is with Toby now, and you know how good she is under these circumstances. Neither of us would be able to do any more than her and besides we all know if Toby had actually – changed, he could have taken the boys arm off. He would have needed a lot more than a couple of stitches."

I thought I heard Jack snigger, but Colin on the other hand was definitely not amused. "Oh thanks darling, that makes me feel so much better!"

Natasha laughed. "You know Sophie's right Colin. Let Meg handle this one. If you were there now, you would only end up in a shouting match with Toby. He'll be upset enough. Things will have settled when we get back and you can talk to him calmly."

Colin sighed. "You girls are right as usual. I'll put my faith in Meg. If she can't manage this situation, I 'm dammed sure I couldn't."

Sophie laughed. "Of course we're right honey, you lot get some sleep, you have a busy day tomorrow. Take care my love and don't worry, the problem will still be here when you get back."

Colin laughed." Thanks for that, I feel a lot better now."

The radio went silent, and Natasha put her arm around Colin's shoulders. "It will be ok he's in good hands."

He shrugged. "I hope so, but Sophie was right about one thing at least - we should get some rest, we don't know what tomorrow will bring. Jack and I will take turns on deck, although I have no doubt that Tina2 will have everything under control."

Perhaps I had been wrong. Colin had noticed that Tina had been upset by his last comment, and this certainly seemed to put things right. I know it's impossible, but I'm sure there was more than a little pride in Tina's voice when she replied. "Of course Colin, I have checked our course and if you would like I can now put the ship into over drive. I am sure we are no longer under surveillance."

"Thank you Tina, make it so," Colin said as he winked at me.

I was a big Star Trek fan myself. I understood the joke. There was a slight feeling of motion, and the ship seemed to speed up. Natasha ruffled Jacks hair. "You make sure the boss gets some sleep Jack. I know you can stay up all night, but Colin will be much more use to us tomorrow, if he gets some rest."

Jack pretended to be annoyed but smiled at Natasha. "I will do my best Nat, but you know what he's like."

Natasha laughed. "Thanks Jack. Come on Alan let's get some sleep, everything is under control here." I followed her back to the cabins, and she stopped at her door. I wanted nothing

113

more than to lie next to her again. Well that's not strictly true, but Natasha kissed me lightly on the cheek and entered her cabin. I would have loved to follow her, but instead I entered my own room. It seemed smaller and emptier than before. The bed however was very comfortable and I lay down to rest, actually hoping that if I slept, I would dream.

***

The cavern at least was still here, although it seemed darker than before. I stumbled over the rocks that seemed to cover the floor. I could still see a light high up in the cavern wall and relief flooded over me. It was her.

As I headed towards the light, my foot dislodged one of the rocks and it tumbled down the slope. There was something strange about the sound it made, it sounded hollow as it bounced away. Something wasn't right. It was too dark to see properly, so I picked up one of the many rocks I'd been stumbling over. I found it harder to climb with the rock in my hand, however luckily this one seemed to have a handy hole that my fingers fitted.

Closer to the opening now there was enough light and I stared down in horror at the rock in my hand. My fingers were slotted neatly into its eye sockets! I let the skull fall. The sound it made, echoed through the cavern, it tumbled down to join the many others littering the cavern floor. I woke in a cold sweat.

I lay on my bed. Part of me felt relieved after all, the dragon was alright - but I may just have stumbled over another slight problem. Light filtered through the thin curtain drawn across my window, it was morning. I washed and left my room. My head was spinning with what I'd just seen in my dream and how that could impact our mission. I knocked lightly on Natasha's door. She answered straight away.

"It's not locked Alan, you can come in."

I opened the door. Her cabin was exactly the same as mine, only much tidier.

Natasha lay on her bed, still fully clothed. Part of me was slightly disappointed and part of me, was relieved. I wasn't sure I could control my feelings under extreme circumstances. She patted the bed. "Come lie by me Alan."

I did as she said and lay next to her. I had enough courage to slip my hand into hers.

She didn't pull it away but squeezed it gently. "Did you sleep?" she asked.

"Yes," I said. I knew I sounded tense. Was it the dream, or the strain of being so close to her and not being able to take her in my arms for fear she might push me away?

She smiled. "You saw her - but something's wrong! What is it Alan?"

God she could read me like a book. Was that a good thing? I tried to sound matter of fact. "Yes, she is still ok. However, we may have another - small problem."

Natasha sat up. "What is it Alan? What did you see?"

How could I put this? "I saw the golden dragon, and she seems to be alright." I was pleased that sounded very positive.

Natasha wasn't fooled. "Yes and?"

I shrugged. "I think it would be fair to say, I got the distinct impression that our golden dragon - may not be strictly vegetarian!" I was about to explain when there was a polite cough. Colin stood just outside the open door, I couldn't read his expression. I felt like a teenager caught in his girlfriend's bedroom. I almost sprang from the bed. I could feel my face burning.

"Oh hi Colin," I stammered, "We were just - talking."

Natasha smiled. "Come in Colin, Alan was just telling me about another dream. He thinks we may have another problem."

Colin nodded again, no real expression on his face. "That may have to wait. We've made excellent time, and are approaching the island. Tina is picking up increased activity underground. She says we need to act fast. As well as a possible dragon, it appears we were right about the people. Around thirty of them are left on the island. Tina says they will not survive if the volcano erupts, and she says, it will erupt." He didn't wait for us.

We both followed Colin quickly up to the bridge. I could hardly believe my eyes. The view that met us, mirrored my dream. I could see the rock formations and the strange mountain, we were really here.

"Shit!"... I nearly jumped out of my skin. Jack had come up behind us and brushed past me. In defence of my reaction, he was at least waist height. As a wolf, he was a huge son of a bitch! I smiled to myself, thinking that this was one of the few occasions when 'son of a bitch' was a fairly apt expression and not offensive at all.

Colin was now very much in charge. He had recovered from the shock of Toby's incident and decided that the sooner we got finished here, the sooner we would be home. He ran his hand over Jack's shaggy shoulders. "Jack is going to circle the island and check if there are any animals left. Tina seems to

116

think everything that can leave, has already gone. Animals and birds have a sixth sense for this sort of thing, but we should check all the same. It's a shame people don't always have the same insight. We're going to try to find the people and get them off the island. God only knows why they're still here.

Don't ask me how yet. This is a plan in the making, and I'm afraid it will just have to work itself out as we go along. Natasha, you take to the water. There may be another way into the caverns that Alan has seen. If the dragon is anything like George she may have a way to the ocean to feed, but for god's sake be careful - things are going to get rough."

At this point I interrupted Colin. I had to make him listen. This could be important. "Look I really need to tell you what I saw in my dream."

Colin seemed distracted. "Ok Alan, but make it short. We may not have a lot of time. Tina thinks things are moving far quicker than we could have anticipated."

I hesitated, somehow what I'd seen went against everything I'd felt about the dragon, but I had to tell them. "The golden dragon may not be eating just fish and vegetables. There may be a good reason why there aren't many people still alive on the island!"

Colin turned to face me. At least I had his full attention. "And you think this why?" he said carefully.

There was no going back now. "I saw that the cavern was littered with bones and human skulls. I picked one up - by accident," I added quickly. Colin hesitated for no more than a second.

"Alright Alan, we will all keep that in mind. Thank you."

I had to stop myself from shouting 'But you don't seem to understand, we could be lunch'. He obviously saw the expression on my face.

"Look Alan, we're all here to do a job. We have both promised someone very special that we would bring this dragon home. I don't know about you, but that's what I intend to do, so let's get on with the task at hand and worry about the rest later, alright?"

I nodded agreement. I knew that he was right. Besides, my whole being told me what I'd seen was wrong, but nevertheless we could be trying to rescue a Man-eater.

Colin continued, "Tina you're in charge here, keep the ship steady and keep us informed about any changes. As I said, Jack will scout the island but it's important that no one sees him change, so he will remain in wolf form until we are safely back on board ship. Alan, you are with me. Your job is to locate the golden dragon and then we will figure out a way to get everyone out of here, before that mountain over there erupts and sends everything back to the bottom of the sea. Alright! I do hope no one has any questions, because I sure as hell haven't got any answers. Let's go."

Colin handed us all small headsets. "Keep these on at all times, so we can keep in contact with each other. Tina will update us constantly. When she says move out, we get out of there - no matter what! Is that understood?"

Natasha and I nodded. It was starting to sink in, just how dangerous this could be for all of us. If that mountain erupted, we could all be dead within minutes.

Colin continued, "Tina, we are counting on you to call us back if things get bad. Get ready to get underway the minute we're all on board, and get us out of here fast. I don't care who sees us."

As we headed to the back of the ship, I managed to grab Natasha's hand and held her back for a moment. "Natasha, please be careful." I wanted to say so much more but now was not the time, and I found myself beginning to doubt there would ever be time.

She squeezed my hand and kissed me lightly on the cheek. "Try not to fall out of the boat Alan. We both know swimming, isn't your strong point!"

At the rear of the cargo hold, a strange looking vehicle was waiting for us. It was large, and seemed to be a combination between boat and truck. Colin saw me looking at it.

"It's one of Ben's creations and will go practically anywhere."

He pressed a button and a section of the ship began to lower. I could see the waves lapping gently. Everything seemed so calm. In fact it was a beautiful day. It was hard to think of what might happen here shortly. Jack leapt easily onto the boat and Colin followed him. I turned to watch Natasha who had already slipped easily out of her dress. She wore the now familiar white swimsuit. She stood on the edge of the platform, turned and gave me a smile, then dived effortlessly into the sea and instantly vanished beneath the waves.

Colin saw my uncertainty. "Just get in Alan and Tina will raise the hatch when we are clear." He was obviously feeling the pressure of the situation, but he still managed to read my thoughts. "She'll be alright. Natasha can look after herself pretty well. I need you to concentrate."

I pulled myself together and got into the boat. It didn't seem possible the thing could float, but it did far more than that. As soon as we were clear of the ramp, we sped away from the ship and headed towards the island. The strange rock formations I'd seen in my dreams were even more impressive up close. Some of them had small trees and plants growing on them and looked like small islands, themselves.

As we got closer to the main land we had a reality check. The peace was broken by a loud rumbling sound, and the boat was suddenly hit by several big waves that came out of nowhere.

Colin shouted over the noise. "Tina, give us an update, what's happening?"

Tina's voice sounded in my ear piece. "That was the largest disturbance I have monitored up to this point Colin. You don't have long. I am sorry I cannot be more precise at this time, but I will try to be more accurate, once I have analysed the data."

Colin glanced at me and shrugged. "Ok, thanks Tina. Keep us informed."

Colin had to shout over the noise of the engine and the waves hitting the front of the boat. "We will drive up onto the beach as high as we can into the undergrowth. It will hide the boat from any unwanted attention. Jack will scout around the island to check there are no stragglers, and you and I will head for the centre. Hopefully your uncanny sense of direction won't fail us now. Try to concentrate on the golden dragon. Don't let your mind wonder. Natasha will contact us, when she can."

We left the boat hidden in the undergrowth at the edge of the beach. There was another deep rumble that seemed to come from right under our feet, and for a few seconds the earth trembled and shook. Colin and I just looked at each other, trying to steady ourselves. Jack started to whine. Tina's voice came over the ear piece.

"I cannot be exact, but I think you have a little over two hours, so you will have to hurry. Oh! And Colin, Sophie sends her love."

Colin looked concerned. "Tina, you didn't tell Sophie exactly how bad things were getting here did you?"

The reply was instant. "My instructions are clear Colin. I am to update you. I see no reason to alarm anyone else at this time."

Colin looked relieved. "Thank you Tina, Alan and I are heading into the heart of the island now, and Jack will scout around to see what he can find."

I felt I had to comment. "Tina is a very unusual computer, almost human at times."

Colin laughed. "Yes, she is – unusual. Although I'm not sure she would take kindly to being called human." He rested his hand on Jack's head to reassure him. "It's alright Jack, you head off and we'll meet you back here as soon as we can." He placed a collar around Jack's neck that had a small radio attached to it. He bent down slightly so that he was looking into the large animal's eyes. "If we are not back here, when Tina says 'get back to the ship', you just go. You will have no problem reaching it. You can change back if you like, at that point, I don't think it will matter - but you must get out of here fast."

Jack hesitated for a second then bounded off into the trees. As I watched him go, I said to Colin, "Won't he scare the hell out of anything, if they see him?"

Colin smiled. "More than an earthquake you mean. Seriously, unless Jack wants to be seen, you don't see him. Trust me on that."

He was right, anything left on this Island, would be a little preoccupied at present.

I closed my eyes for a second, and tried to feel the golden dragon. It was hard to focus and I wasn't sure if it was working, but I led the way along a well-trodden pathway. It wasn't long before we came into a small village. It was just a few huts built around a larger central structure, as we approached the larger hut, we could hear singing. The sound stopped abruptly as we stood in the entrance, and around thirty faces turned towards us.

Colin said something in a language I didn't recognize, and I stared at him.

He shrugged. "What can, I say it's a gift."

A very elderly man approached us. The others parted to let him through with obvious respect. They bowed their heads as he passed. He stopped in front of Colin, completely ignoring me. He and Colin spoke. I couldn't understand what they were saying so I looked around the room where the others gathered. I realized they were old, a mix of men and women. Some holding hands, others looked as though they had been crying. I didn't need to understand the language to know that these people had gathered here to await death.

Someone caught my eye, a small child. She seemed totally out of place here in this room of old people, but I recognized her. It was Maya, the small child I had seen talking with the golden dragon. I made my way over to her and knelt down so as not to scare her. I told her my name, but she just looked at me, perhaps not understanding. She was looking past me, and I looked up to see that Colin had come over, and was standing behind us.

I turned to face him. "Can you ask her what her name is Colin? She'll understand you."

The old man had followed Colin, he spoke and Colin translated.

Colin nodded. "This is Manu, and he is the elder of the village. He said the child cannot speak. She was found on the beach when she was just a baby. He says she was a gift from the sea."

"This is Maya. This is the child I saw in my dream."

At the sound of her name Maya reached out and took my hand. Almost instantly I could hear her voice in my head, and suddenly I understood. I had heard her talk with the dragon just as we had talked to George. I concentrated, if a small child could do it so could I.

Colin broke my concentration. "Alan we must get these people off the island now. The old man says they have chosen to stay and die, so they can be with the elders."

This confused me. "I don't understand. Who are the elders?" I couldn't imagine there could be many people older than them.

Colin related the story Manu had told him. "For many years they have taken their dead to a cave at the foot of the great mountain. There, the dragon spirit watches over and protects them, and in return they take offerings of food to the cave."

He stopped and smiled. "I think we have identified the bones you saw."

I felt relieved. "So the dragon wasn't killing the islanders, she was watching over them. But why are all these people still here? They must realize the danger they're in."

Colin nodded. "Many have left but these people believe that the dragon spirit is still here, and they will not leave her to die alone. For that reason they have chosen to stay and die with her."

I looked around with a new sense of respect for these people. "What about Maya? Surely she should have been made to leave with the others."

Colin spoke again with the old man. "He says. When the time came to go they looked and looked, but she was nowhere to be found, the others could wait no longer."

Maya squeezed my hand and I looked down into her small face. I heard her voice in my head. "Please, I can take you to her but we must hurry. She said you would come but you have taken so long." Suddenly I knew what had to be done. "Colin, you take these people to the boat and get them back to the ship. Maya will show me where the dragon is, and as soon as I find her I'll report to you."

Colin looked unsure. Natasha's voice came over the intercom. "I've found an underwater entrance that looks promising. The tunnels look as though they have been blocked, but there's been a lot of rock falls and things have opened up. I can get through easily so I'm going in. I will contact you again if I find her."

Colin seemed to come to a decision. "Ok Natasha, but be careful, the tremors could bring down more rocks at any time, and you don't want to get trapped down there."

He turned to me. "Alan, take Maya with you but keep in contact. I will get these people out of here and come back as quickly as I can. Listen to Tina, if she says get out, you move! Is that clear?"

I nodded. "Crystal!" I took Maya's hand again.

Colin turned back to the old man. I couldn't understand what was being said, but I could tell he was having trouble convincing them to leave. I used my mind to talk to Maya. "Maya, how can we make them leave?" Her voice sounded clear in my head. "Tell them you are here to rescue the dragon spirit, and tell them she will be safe. Tell them they must leave, or the dragon spirit will stay because of them and be lost to the world forever."

In a smaller less confident voice she said, "You can save her can't you? That is why you have come. You won't let her die."

I told Colin what to say, and although the people still looked unsure they began to pick up their few possessions and help each other towards the door.

I turned back to face Maya again. "We are here to try Maya, but you should go with the others. We are running out of time, and I can't be sure we will get off the island before the mountain erupts."

She just smiled and began to pull me towards the door. "Then we must hurry - she isn't far."

I heard Colin shout after us. "Be careful."

We raced through the trees. Maya could move surprisingly fast for a young child. I tried to work out how old she would be, maybe seven or eight years, it was hard to tell.

More than once I stumbled, around us huge trees crashed and fell, one missed us by inches.

Maya had disappeared ahead, breaking through some bushes, I almost fell straight into a huge mountain of fallen rock.

I looked up, and saw the rocks were blocking what had once been a very large entrance to a huge cave. I followed Maya as she scrambled up the slope. It wasn't easy, but I could tell the child had done this many times before. Near to the top there was a small gap and Maya fitted through easily, but I had to move some stones and make the gap a little larger.

It was a good job I hadn't been around Meg's cooking for too long, or I would never have managed to squeeze myself through. I saw Maya scrambling down the other side, and into the depths of a huge cave. I knew this cave. It was the one I'd seen many times in my dreams. The floor would be littered with bones, human bones. At least now I understood why, however, understanding it didn't make it any easier to cross.

Maya had already disappeared across the cave floor and into the gloom beyond. I thought I could see a faint light up ahead. I found myself rooted to the spot. My dreams had not prepared me for the smell! It wasn't a smell of rotting flesh, thank god, but a sort of sweet musty smell. The villagers obviously treated the bodies of their dead in some way. How long ago was the last body placed here? I found myself imagining my feet breaking through the outer shell of the human body, to the soft squishiness inside, and I shuddered. Sometimes my imagination was just too vivid! Scrambling over bones was one thing, but over fresh corpses - that was a whole different matter.

Another rumble made the cave floor tremble and rocks began to fall all around me. If I didn't move now I could be joining the bodies on the cave floor. I forced myself on, and over the uneven surface beneath my feet. Thankfully it was too dark to see clearly, and I focused on the light I could see gradually getting stronger up ahead. I reached another steep bank of rocks.

Looking up, I glimpsed Maya beckoning me from what looked like an even smaller gap, but the light was much stronger here, and it was easier to climb, when I could see where to put my hands and feet.

I was soon able to put my head and shoulders through the gap and look into the cave beyond.

# PRECIOUS GOLD

After the gloom of the previous cave I was blinded for a few seconds. As my eyes began to adjust, I tried to take in this new space. The cave was slightly smaller but bright - so bright it was like looking into the sun.

I was trying to decide if it was safe ... well as safe as anywhere could be when you are looking for a dragon, on an island that might well explode at any given moment! Another tremor hit, and it shook me and a load of rocks came free from the wall. I tumbled head over heels, landing in a heap of rubble on the cavern floor.

I picked myself up. Maya was sitting on what looked like a heap of golden stones, she was smiling. Something in the way she smiled made me look a little closer, and the golden stones flexed!

Now my eyes were more accustomed to the light, I could see she was sitting on large golden claws. Above the claws a scaly leg shone, bathed in a strange inner light. Slowly, very slowly as if someone altered the lens of a camera, the whole image shifted just slightly and came into focus. There was no doubt - this was the golden dragon in all her shining splendour.

Maya was perched happily on one of her huge feet. It was easy to see why the islanders thought she was some sort of spirit, as light danced over her scales and made it hard to focus. Her whole body shimmered as if in a heat haze.

I didn't feel fear, just awe. I had never seen anything as impressively beautiful as the beast that stood before me now. She was glorious!

The dragon lowered her head and I realized she was indeed similar to George, only maybe a little smaller. She seemed to be made out of pure gold. We had found her. Now what?

The radio in my ear made me jump. It was Colin's voice.

"Alan, Natasha, come in. Can either of you hear me?"

I tried to get my head together. "Yes Colin." I tried to sound calm, difficult under the circumstances.

Colin continued, "I've managed to get everyone off the island, but no sign of Jack. I'm bringing the boat back, so where are you? Have you found her?"

My heart leapt when Natasha joined the conversation.

"Yes Colin, and god - she's more beautiful than you could possibly imagine."

Desperately I scanned the area. If Natasha was seeing what I was seeing, she had to be close by. A moment later I spotted her emerging from a pool of water behind the dragon. I couldn't help myself, ignoring the beast between us, I ran over and pulled her close. To my pleasure and slight surprise, Natasha didn't resist me, in fact quite the opposite!

Colin interrupted the reunion, "What the hell is going on, will someone talk to me, have you found the dragon or not?"

Natasha pulled away but still held my hand. "Sorry Colin, just getting my breath back," she said and winked.

We both turned to look at the dragon, who shimmered back. She seemed huge in this restricted space, and I was thinking - how the hell were we going to get her out of here? We must have both been thinking the same thing, but Natasha spoke first. "Colin, we have found her. Give us a minute to assess the situation and we'll get back to you."

She squeezed my hand. "What was it like coming in your way?"

My elation at being reunited with Natasha was wearing off fast, things didn't look good. "There was hardly room for me to get through, and there must have been tons of rubble. It would take days to shift it, and the rest of the mountain could quite easily come down on top of us if we tried. What about you?"

Natasha shook her head. "I think it might be possible." She didn't seem all that confident.

"That doesn't sound good, do you really think you could get her out? That's one big dragon." I already knew we had no other choice and Natasha confirmed this.

She shrugged. "If you can't get her out that way, then it appears we have no choice - it's the only other way out. We have to try. The tunnels have cleared a bit. The last big shock moved some rocks that had been blocking the entrance to this cave system, otherwise I wouldn't have found you. I think I could help the dragon through and out into the ocean. It would then only be a short swim to the ship."

She was right, it was the only option. "I'll come with you then, perhaps I could help."

Natasha laughed and shook her head. "No Alan. You couldn't possibly hold your breath long enough, and as for the swim to the ship..."

She didn't have to spell it out, I knew she was right. Natasha notice Maya for the first time. "Who is the child Alan?"

I had forgotten all about Maya. "This is Maya," I said, and added, "She doesn't speak. I have a feeling it was Maya that bought us here. She is the child from my dreams."

Natasha approached Maya and the dragon carefully. "Hello Maya, I think you can understand me. Am I right? Nod your head if you can."

To my surprise Maya nodded. I was bemused. "I don't get it, how come she can understand us? The islanders seemed to speak a different language."

Natasha shrugged. Now was not the time for questions.

She continued, "Maya can you talk to the dragon and tell her we can help, but she has to trust us. She has to come with me now. Do you understand?"

I heard Maya's voice in my head again, only clearer this time. I was getting the hang of this. "I cannot get the dragon to leave her home and her charges," she said sadly.

I concentrated my thoughts. "Maya our friend has taken the rest of the people off the island, they are safe. When the mountain erupts who knows what will be left, she will no longer have a home. Tell her we have a new home for her."

I glanced at Natasha and I could tell she was impressed with my communication skills. I felt very pleased with myself. With this new feeling of importance I decided to go for gold quite literally! I carefully approached the golden dragon and she lowered her head slightly. I heard Maya's voice saying, "It's all right he is a friend." A hardly noticeable puff of smoke escaped from the dragon's nostrils, and I couldn't help but wonder if I had narrowly escaped being incinerated. I carefully placed my hand on the dragon's huge golden leg, and was surprised at how warm and smooth it felt. I pictured George in my mind. This had to work.

Out here in this cave, I found it hard to think of George, he seemed so far away, then slowly I began to feel him in my head, in my thoughts and taking over my mind. I could feel myself flying through the air, speeding across the ocean to the island and to George.

Once the connection was made, I felt his mind and from the trembling of the scales beneath my hand, I knew the Golden dragon felt his presents too. Even with the distance between them I could feel the chemistry and a sudden feeling of renewed hope.

I pulled away and dropped to the floor exhausted.

After a moment to clear my mind, I looked up and saw the difference it had made to the golden dragon. I felt maybe now we had a chance. She no longer looked sad and lost, she held her head high and seemed to sparkle even brighter than before.

Natasha helped me up. "I knew you could do it Alan," she said, "And without Meg's potions. You're getting stronger all the time."

Maya ran over and tugged at my shirt. As I reached down she wrapped her arms around my neck, and I heard her voice in my head. "Thank you, I knew you were the one."

Natasha smiled obviously amused. "I see I have competition!"

We were brought back to the problems we still had to face, when Colin's voice came over the radios. "I have the boat back on the beach, so should I head to the caves. I don't think we have much time?"

Natasha was quick to respond. "No Colin, I'm going to lead the golden dragon out through the underwater caverns. The tremors have opened up some passages and I think we will be able to get out that way."

Colin sounded worried. "I don't like the sound of that! Are you sure you can get her out that way Nat? Can you both make it out safely?"

Natasha glanced at me and I reluctantly nodded - we had no choice.

She continued, "I know we can make it, besides I think it's the only chance we have of getting the golden dragon out of here Colin. Alan and Maya are on their way back to you, wait for them on the beach. We'll all meet back on the ship. Are the islanders all safely on board?"

"Yes, they were reluctant to leave without the dragon spirit but I managed to convince them she would leave as soon as she knew they were safe. Tina is explaining to them all about Volcano's and eruptions. I asked her to try to keep the people entertained, to help take their minds off things. I'm not sure she understood the concept!

Alan, get yourselves back here as soon as you can. I'll keep the boat as close as I can in the water just off shore, we will need to get away fast. I've not seen Jack so if you spot him, tell him, he needs to get his furry butt back here right now!"

As if to remind us of the situation the ground began to shake and a number of rocks were dislodged from the walls and fell around our ears. I tried my best to shelter Natasha and Maya and was surprised when the rocks seemed to bounce everywhere but on our heads. When the rumbling had passed, I looked up to see that the golden dragon had spread her wings out above our heads, protecting us from the worst of the deluge.

I gave Natasha a hug, there was so much I wanted to say, but all I could manage was, "Be safe."

I tried to pull Maya away but she ran over to the golden dragon, who lowered her head so that the child could wrap her arms around the dragons golden neck. It was a strange and touching sight and I knew how she felt, but time was running out. Risking the dragon's wrath I pulled Maya away, and knelt down and looked into the child's tear stained face. "We must let them go Maya, it's their only chance. We will see them again on the ship. I promise." I tried to sound more confident than I felt. Maya nodded and allowed me to help her up the mound of rocks. I was secretly saying my own prayer that we could still get out the way we'd come. I couldn't help one last look behind. The cave we had just occupied was now in darkness, the dragon and Natasha had disappeared into the water.

I followed Maya, diving head first through the gap at the top of the rock wall. The light from the golden dragon had gone, but it was actually a relief, not to be able to see much. I made a point of not looking down as we crunched across the floor. Maya had already reached the exit high up on the far wall of fallen rocks, and to my relief disappeared through the hole. Thank God it was still there.

I followed her out and into the daylight. It seemed to have clouded over and when we were a little way from the mountains looking up and back, it was easy to see why as a thick cloud of black smoke billowing from the summit, and a red glow marked the top peak. In my imagination, I could already feel the heat that would shortly follow. We ran on as fast as we could. The island seemed completely void of life now and a strange hush had settled all around us. There wasn't even a wisp of wind - the island was waiting, holding its breath.

I didn't dare look behind me again, until we reached the beach. Once there, we both fell onto the sand. I struggled to get my breath back but Maya recovered first and sat up. The fear I saw reflected in her eyes, made me follow her gaze.

The top of the mountain was now gushing red lava. It looked like a deadly firework show, as red hot rocks were shooting out onto the surrounding island and everywhere they hit flames were erupting. In a deadly way, it was mesmerizing and strangely beautiful.

Colin shouted at us to move. I grabbed Maya and carried her out into the shallows, towards the boat. Suddenly she started to struggle to get free, frantically pointing at something back towards the shore. I looked in the direction she was indicating, and there on the beach was a small shaggy dog. It just stood there watching us.

Colin had grabbed Maya, but I could see he had read my mind. "We don't have time Alan, we have to go. Have you seen Jack?"

I had completely forgotten about Jack, assuming he was already safely on board the ship. That helped me make up my mind. "I'll go back and shout out for him from the beach. I'll just take a minute Colin, I promise."

Colin looked torn. "Alright, you have two minutes and then we have to be out of here."

I made my way back to the beach. The little dog stayed put, watching me nervously, I was only inches away, so close, I could almost reach down and grab it.

Suddenly the little dog let out a couple of frightened barks and turning on its heels ran back into the undergrowth and disappeared.

I'd lost it "Shit!" I turned to see Jack slinking out of the bushes, carrying something in his mouth. I was filled with anger and emotion, this was just too much! How could he hunt, at a time like this, he was a monster. I ran towards him, wanting to hurt him. Just in time, I heard, the supposed-meal, dangling from Jack's mouth, give a pathetic mew. I stopped just short of self-destruction. I was close enough to see properly now. Jack was carrying two tiny Kittens, with great care in his huge jaws. One looked almost lifeless but the other was mewing constantly.

Jack took no notice of my outburst as he brushed past me and headed into the water. With one leap, he was back in the boat next to Colin. The relief on Colin's face was obvious.

Turning back I frantically searched for the little dog, as the realization was fast dawning on me that I'd run out of time. I had no choice but to leave it here, to certain death. I could no longer endanger the others. With a heavy heart I swam as quickly as I could out to the boat.

Colin helped me on board. "I'm sorry Alan," he said, "But we really have to go. I haven't heard from Natasha yet, and she might need our help."

I knew he was right, as we headed away from the island I thought I saw the little dog far behind us struggling in the water, I could no longer hold back the tears.

Maya sat huddled in the bottom of the boat, I couldn't look at her.

We travelled back in silence. Jack had carefully settled the two kittens on a blanket on the floor, but it looked as though one of them might already be dead.

As we moved away from the island I began to ask myself some disturbing questions. How could I have let myself believe so easily, that Jack was a monster! The same way I had ignored my instincts and believed the golden dragon was eating the islanders. If I was ever going to be able to trust my senses, they were going to have to improve.

It only took moments to reach the ship but it seemed like a lifetime. Tina had bought it as close as she could, and the back was lowered ready for us. Colin manoeuvred the boat easily back on board, I helped Maya out and wrapped her in a blanket.

Jack very gently picked up his new found charges, and took them to a small box under the stairs. I couldn't believe how delicately he placed one of the blankets in the box and gentle dropped each kitten onto it. This task completed, he came and stood next to Colin. We all looked out at the ocean, waiting. There was nothing else we could do. It was up to Natasha now.

Colin strode up and down. "Where the hell is she? We have to leave now. Tina, get us ready. As soon as I give the word, get us out of here as fast as this thing will go."

There seemed to be a moment's hesitation before Tina answered. "Colin you told me to tell you when we had run out of time. Colin we have run out of time."

We stood in silence. No one wanted to think about leaving without Natasha, or the Golden dragon. Then when all hope seemed lost, one golden claw grasped at the metal, then another. There was a terrible scrapping sound like chalk on a black board, as more claws scrabbled for a hold and the golden dragon slowly hauled herself up and onto the ramp. She stood in all her glory, water droplets, sparkling like diamonds as they cascaded down her body in the dwindling sunlight.

I scanned the ocean. Where the hell was Natasha, I walked past the dragon to the edge of the ramp. Tina's voice was insistent. "We have to leave now Colin!"

I felt sick to my stomach. "Where the hell is she," I shouted at the ocean. As if in answer to my plea, a webbed hand appeared over the edge of the ramp. I rushed forward to help her, my heart pounding in my chest. Natasha smiled up at me with those beautiful green eyes of hers and thrust something towards me.

The soggy missile landed in my arms and shook itself vigorously. I wiped salt water from my eyes, as the little shaggy dog yapped and licked my face.

Natasha laughed. "Sorry I'm late. I had to make a small detour. I believe you lost something Alan."

Natasha put her arm around me and smiled at Colin. "Thanks for waiting for us, but I really think we should go now."

I realized I was crying but luckily the little dog was licking my tears as they fell. I wasn't the only emotional one - Colin had turned away and Maya rushed over and hugged Natasha, tears streaming down her pretty face.

"How the hell did you manage to find him," I said, trying to hold the squirming, wet dog away from me.

Natasha smiled. "She - I saw her struggling in the water swimming towards the ship, so I just gave her a hand. I remembered you saying how much you liked dogs Alan, so I thought she must be yours!" She laughed. It was the most beautiful sound I'd ever heard in my whole life.

"Get us out of here Tina - Fast!" Colin shouted.

I got the feeling Tina hadn't waited for the order once she knew everyone was accounted for, we were already underway.

Jack had withdrawn to the shadows, and from the now familiar sounds I guessed he was changing back.

\*\*\*

We were all beginning to relax a little when the ship lurched sharply a couple of times, sending us all sprawling across the floor. I looked up to see the metal hull of the amphibious craft bearing down on me. In the excitement there hadn't been time to secure it. I couldn't move and as I closed my eyes, a thought struck me - after all I'd been through in the last few days, I was going to die in a stupid accident. Somewhere in the distance I heard Natasha cry out. After a couple of seconds, that seemed like the rest of my life – and so easily could have been, I dared to open my eyes. I still felt firmly attached to the land of the living.

Looking around, somewhat relieved, I saw that Jack was now in human form and standing over me holding back the boat. He'd obviously only had time to put on his trousers, his upper body rippled with muscle. Jack hadn't even broken a sweat. I on the other hand was sweating like mad, my heart pounded in my ears. I felt rooted to the spot. Natasha grabbed my arm and pulled me clear.

Colin helped Jack push the craft back into position and secured it in place.

Natasha threw her arms around me. "Are you alright Alan? That was too close for comfort." I had to agree, but was enjoying being in Natasha's arms. It took me a few moments to regain my faculties. My legs felt like they had decided they would no longer be needed. I forced myself to leave Natasha's arms.

For the second time today I strode over to Jack. I held out my hand. "You saved my life, if it hadn't been for your strength and speed I'd be wearing that boat! Thanks Jack."

Jack looked slowly down at my hand and seemed to consider it carefully, then he reached out and I felt his strong grip. I think for the first time I dared to look into his pale blue eyes, and what I saw there, was so different from the monster I'd once imagined.

\*\*\*

Colin appeared to be talking with the golden dragon. She had seemed a little on edge and rightly so. She had just left what had been her home for goodness knows how many years, and she was in a ship with strangers. Colin's words seemed to put her more at ease and she lowered her head as he gently stroked her nose. After a few moments more she curled herself into a ball and started to snore loudly.

"Right everyone, we have a lot to sort out. Alan if you've finished playing with boats, I will need you with me! We'll have to reassure the islanders and work out what to do with them. Natasha and Maya, you break out some stores and try to do your best for our new guests down here."

I noticed he had glanced at the box, and it seemed that he too was unsure how long the kittens would survive. Still better they were here than left behind.

He turned to Jack. "Well done Jack, but for now I will need you on the bridge. Contact Ben and Sophie, tell them what has happened and that we'll be making a detour. I will join you as soon as we've made our older guests comfortable, oh and Jack, put your shirt on will you - you put me and Alan to shame."

We all laughed, Jack looked puzzled but did as he was told.

I couldn't believe I'd forgotten about the islander's plight, in all the panic I hadn't given them a second thought. I followed Colin up the steps and along a couple of corridors, as we opened a door, I could hear worried voices.

The room was well furnished with comfortable sofas and chairs, and a table in the middle. However the elderly islanders were huddled together in one corner, looking out of a small window.

The island was now some distance away, you could see dense smoke filling the sky, the mountain that towered over the island had all but disappeared. Hot lava flowed into the sea and steam spat and spluttered all around. The lush vegetation that had covered much of the island had been destroyed.

I'd been on a high, but looking around at these frightened worried faces I realized they had lost everything. That island had been their home, and the home of their fathers and forefathers before them. Where would they go now?.

Colin spoke to them and he translated for me. "They say most of their people went to an island to the north of here. I'll get Tina to check it out and hopefully we will be able to drop them there, and reunite them with the family members who left before the trouble."

Colin placed his hand on my shoulder. "We have done all we can Alan."

I nodded agreement. "I know - it just doesn't seem like the happy ending I was hoping for."

Colin smiled. "It very rarely is. This is real life Alan. Can I leave you to look after things here. You'll find provisions in the cupboards over there, so get them anything they need. I've told them I'll get back to them, once we have located the rest of their people."

As Colin left the room all eyes turned to me. I opened cupboards and some of the ladies helped me pass out crisps and biscuits. At least we didn't have to worry about their appetite.

I stood back and watched them picking out all the chocolate biscuits from the variety packs. One of the women came over to me and touched my arm. She looked eighty if she was a day. She spoke in the strange language and the only word I could make out was Maya. I realized she must be worried about the child. I tried to speak slowly so that she would understand. "Maya is safe." I was surprised when she took my arm and steered me away from the rest of the group.

When we were clear of the others she spoke in a whisper, and I was amazed that I could understood what she was saying. "You will look after her and her secret," she whispered.

I wasn't sure I understood what she meant by secret. "You know about Maya's secret?" I ventured. The old lady laughed and continued, "My name is Teano and when I was just a girl about Maya's age I too had a golden friend. In time I grew too old for make-believe and my father forbade me to go into the mountains. I missed my friend but all too soon I had a husband

140

and a family, and no time to play." She sighed and looked into the distance. "Time goes so fast," she added sadly.

As she turned back, for a brief moment I saw the sparkle in her eyes - the sparkle of the child she once was, and I could only imagine the adventures her and the golden dragon must have had. I began to realize how hard it must be to outlive the ones you loved. How many times had the dragon lost her friends, simply through the natural progression of time?

I wanted to tell Teano about George but I knew I couldn't. Instead I reassured her that Maya and her golden secret would be taken somewhere safe. Teano smiled and removed something carefully from around her neck. "I want you to have this. It was given to me by a good friend," she said as she placed what looked like a flat shell on a leather cord, in to my hand.

I shook my head, "I can't accept this," I said trying to give it back.

She was insistent. "Please you must. When you wear it close to your heart she will be able to speak with you."

I looked closer and as I turned the shell this way and that, it seemed at times to sparkle and then to almost disappear. "It's beautiful," I said, "But what is it?"

Teano's eyes sparkled like the shell. "It is a small part of her - wear it and you will understand. You must take Maya with you. She needs to be with people who can manage her. Protect them well, they are both very special."

I remembered the little dog. "Teano we found a little scruffy dog, she was left on the island. Do you know who she belongs to?"

Teano smiled. "I would say she knows where she belongs, now."

I wasn't sure the old lady had understood. "She must have belonged to someone once."

Teano seemed to consider this for a moment before she replied. There was no show of emotion in her voice. "Whatever you found on the Island - had been left there."

I tried to take this in. "I don't understand."

She smiled. "These things were no longer needed. The people have moved on to start a new life. Take good care of your little dog and she will be a loyal friend."

With that she re-joined the others. They were obviously more resilient than I'd thought, but I suppose the first rule of survival was - when you find food you eat, as you never knew where or when your next meal would appear.

I thought about Teano's words. I studied the gift she had given me. "Part of her," she had said! She had to have meant the dragon, and I guessed she wanted Maya to be with people who understood her.

Watching it shimmer around my neck, I realized it had to be one of the dragon's scales. It had obviously been something of great importance to the old lady. I didn't understand how it would help me with the dragon, but none the less I would treasure it.

I left the old folks, relatively happy now, raiding the cupboards. I made my way back along the corridors and down into the hold. Natasha greeted me as I descended the steps. "Is everything alright up there? How are they coping?"

I laughed. "They have discovered chocolate biscuits. What about our guests down here?"

"See for yourself," she said taking my hand and leading me further into the hold.

It would be easy to miss the dragon, she had settled herself at the far end of the room. What I'd thought was the sound of the engines was her breathing deeply. She had tucked her head under one of her front legs, and the end of her nose poked out from under a foot. It looked strangely familiar, like a large dog settled by the fire. As she breathed in and out her shape seemed to almost disappear. I turned to Natasha. "It's as though her light has been switched off - are you sure she's ok?"

Natasha smiled. "Yes at least, I think so. The swim has taken the last of her energy, she just needs to rest. I think her light dims for her own protection while she sleeps."

I was impressed. "So she can turn it on and off to save power. That must be useful." I looked around the room, and spotted Maya on the floor next to the box that held the kittens.

Natasha took my hand, "Come and see how the youngest members of the family are doing," I knew from her smile, that thankfully my fears had been unfounded. Maya had both kittens in her lap, and to my relief they were both sucking noisily from two small bottles. It was hard to tell the kittens apart as they looked like little tortoise shell twins, with their tiny paws trying to grip the bottles and milk dripping from their little chins. We both laughed, they looked so comical.

"They look great, I could have sworn one of them was already,"... I stopped myself.

"Are they going to be ok?" I whispered.

Natasha nodded. "I think so, Maya is a natural. It was her who managed to get them to start feeding and from then on, they haven't wanted to stop."

I noticed the little scruffy dog tucking into a bowl of food at Maya's side. "She looks to be doing well after her swim. You can't imagine how pleased I was to see you with her, it was amazing. How did you manage to find her?"

Natasha took my hand again and led me across the room to some seats. "Coffee?" she said offering me a mug.

I took it gratefully. "Thanks, this place is well stocked".

She laughed. "This isn't the first time we've done this sort of thing you know."

The little dog had finished her meal and came rushing over. With one leap she was in my lap and I fussed her happily, scratching behind her ears. I even let her lick my face, even though she smelt strongly of fish. She was a little bundle of energy. I noticed the look Natasha was giving me. "What," I said defensively.

She just grinned back at me.

I sighed looking down at the small bundle of happiness in my lap. "I thought I'd left her to die," I said, forcing back the lump in my throat. The pain of watching the little dog struggle in the water, and the thought of having to leave her was still very fresh in my mind. I looked away.

Natasha took my hand and squeezed it. "Sometimes doing what you know is right, can be hard. You had no choice Alan." She lowered her voice to a whisper. "That's sort of what I wanted to talk to you about."

The little dog had curled up in my lap and I continued to stroke her gently and could feel the warmth of her little body against my legs. I felt comforted and relaxed, with my coffee in one hand and Natasha by my side. All seemed right with the world again.

Natasha continued in a whisper, something seemed to be bothering her. "Alan you said in the cave that you felt Maya had been the one who bought us here, not the dragon! What made you say that?"

I shrugged. "It was just a feeling I had when she was in my head. It seemed familiar, somehow I can't really explain. Why? It hardly seems to matter now."

Natasha nodded. "Maybe, but I think you're right about Maya. I think she sent me to get the little dog." Natasha stopped and looked over at Maya. The child seemed totally engrossed and happy feeding the little kittens. She continued, "I think she has some sort of power Alan, it's not something I can explain."

I laughed. "She's just a child, I don't understand. You're not really worried, are you?"

She shook her head. "It's hard to explain. Alan, it was as though I had no choice. I had an image in my mind of the little dog floundering in the water. I knew I should stay with the dragon and get back to the ship, but I couldn't help myself. I had to go after the dog!" Natasha stopped and stroked the little dog on my lap.

I wasn't sure I understood.

Natasha tried to explain, "What I'm saying is - I felt as though I had no choice! It was as if someone invaded my mind and I had to go back for the dog. I couldn't have left her even if I'd wanted too. Alan if I'm right, she could be dangerous!"

I found it hard to think of the small child sitting on the other side of the room gently rocking the kittens back and forth in her lap - as dangerous, but I had a feeling Natasha could be right. There was something, going on here that neither of us understood. "What do you want to do," I said, hoping she didn't mean to lock Maya up.

Natasha shrugged. "Nothing - at the moment. We'll have to talk to Colin, but for now we need to watch her. We don't know what she could be capable of. Let's just concentrate on getting home - Meg will know what to do."

I had to agree, I couldn't believe how much I was looking forward to getting back to the island.

Natasha smiled again. "Do you want something to eat? I'm making sandwiches. We'll all feel better once we've had something to eat and a rest. It should be plain sailing from here on in."

"Please, I'm feeling pretty hungry after watching the old folk eat." I made my way over to Maya. Scruffy followed me. I'd decided that was the little dog's name.

The kittens had at last finished feeding and Maya offered me one small bundle to hold. It mewed softly and curled up contentedly on my lap. I stroked the tiny body and marvelled at how this tiny thing could have survived. It was mainly thanks to Jack. Scruffy didn't seem to mind the kittens. She lay down between us and tucked her nose under her paw, and like the dragon was instantly fast asleep.

"Maya," I used my mind to talk to her. I felt I was beginning to get the hang of this form of contact now. "One of the old women gave me something and I was wondering if you know what it is?" I fished inside my shirt and found the pendant, which seemed to be much brighter here even though there was less light. Maya smiled, and produced a similar looking pendant from around her own neck.

"The lady's name is Teano," she said, her voice soft and gentle in my mind. "She was once a dragon companion like me, but she grew too old."

I nodded to show I understood. "The dragon gave this to you Maya? Teano said it was special. Do you know why?" I tried to find out more as carefully as I could.

She looked confused. "All gifts are special," she said simply.

I knew she was avoiding the question, so I tried to be more precise. "What does it do Maya? You called me for help and I came, so I need you to be honest with me now please." She seemed to consider this for a moment.

Finally she nodded. "You are right, I'm sorry, you should have the pendant. With it you'll be able to talk with the golden one."

At least now Maya was talking, however things were still as clear as mud. "I don't understand Maya, how does it work?"

She looked down at the kitten in her arms. She seemed to be thinking then spoke quietly in my mind. "You now wear one of the golden dragon's scales around your neck and when you hold it close, you will be able to talk with her. That is the magic of the gift." She smiled.

I found it hard to see this small lost child as a threat. But if she could somehow find her way into your mind -well,

Natasha could be right- but that problem could wait. I looked over at the dragon still sleeping peacefully at the back of the room. The sooner we got back to the island and to George, the better. Natasha came over and put a plate of sandwiches down beside us.

She smiled. "You two put the kittens back in their box to sleep and eat something. I'm going up top to see what's going on and take up some food. Watch that dog doesn't eat any more she'll explode."

"Scruffy?" I said as sternly as I could as the little dog's nose came very close to the sandwich plate.

Natasha laughed. "Scruffy! Yes that suits her, it looks like she has adopted you Alan."

I hadn't thought of what was going to happen to the dog or Maya, come to think of it. It was a responsibility I hadn't expected. I watched Natasha until she had disappeared from view then looked down at the little dog. All her attention focused on me and my sandwich. When she saw me looking she wagged her tail happily. I did feel a sense of responsibility, it was a strange feeling. For most of my life I'd managed to avoid such a bond, was I ready for one now? It would seem as though I had no choice. As if reading my mind Scruffy yapped and handed me a paw, I shook it gently and gave her a small bit of sandwich. She took it happily.

A few minutes later Jack came down to check on the kittens. His relief was obvious, he actually laughed when he saw them. It was the first time I'd heard him laugh, it was a great sound. I still had one of the kittens in my lap, so I picked it up carefully and tried to put it into Jacks huge hands. He backed away quickly, and seemed almost afraid to touch the tiny bundle.

The kitten woke up and mewed. I pretended to fumble and almost drop the kitten, my plan worked, with lightning reflexes Jack caught the kitten and cradled it carefully in his arms.

I couldn't help remembering the image of Jack in wolf form carrying the two tiny kittens carefully in his mouth, the kitten purred gently. The look on Jack's face was magical.

My opinion of him had changed so many times since our meeting a few days ago. Scruffy still wasn't sure and remained a little suspicious of Jack, watching him closely and hiding behind me. Secretly I felt a little flattered that she thought I could protect her from him. Thankfully now, I had no worries about Jack. The dragon still slumbered in the back of the room and I found it amazing how easily you could forget she was there.

"Alan," Colin's voice sounded over the intercom.

"Yes Colin, what's up?"

"We could do with you up on the bridge. Jack can keep an eye on things down there for a while."

"Ok Colin, I'm on my way." I headed for the stairs. I turned to Jack. "Take good care of the new family Jack," I joked, and before I could stop myself - automatically slapped him on the back. I held my breath for a second realizing what I'd just done and expecting to be decked, but to my huge relief and surprise Jack simply grunted and continued to stroke the kitten.

On a high, I headed up the stairs. Scruffy however was not happy at being left and tried to scramble up the metal steps. I had to stop and scoop her up, worried that she would hurt herself. She rewarded me by licking my ear enthusiastically. As soon as we'd climbed the stairs I set her down, and between us we managed eventually to find the others. Natasha smiled when she saw scruffy in my arms - well, I'd had to pick her up again to negotiate the steps leading up to the bridge.

Tina was hovering above the console, lights flashing and behind her was a large screen showing the lab and Ben. "I see you have picked up a new friend Alan," he joked.

Sophie joined Ben on the screen. "Hi Alan, we hear you've done very well on your first outing. Who's your new companion?"

"Thanks. This is scruffy." I felt a little embarrassed and put the little dog down. She seemed happy to explore the bridge, so I turned my attention back to the screen.

Ben looked more serious. "There's not much left of the island. You were all cutting it a bit fine, I was beginning to get worried and Sophie here was having kittens..."

Ben went red in the face and there it was - that embarrassed silence again. I had to say I felt secretly pleased, that someone else could put their foot in it as well as me. If Sophie was upset by the comment, she didn't let on.

"Yes, talking of kittens, I hear Jack has adopted a couple. And what's this I hear about a child," Sophie said quickly, "We just sent you out for a dragon." She laughed, and we all relaxed again.

Colin pulled a face. "Hey don't look at me. I just waited in the boat, it was the others who bought back the strays. How's George? Have you told him we'll be heading home soon, with his - gold shipment?"

Sophie laughed. "Yes he's over the moon, and Alan I don't know how you did it, but he said you connected him with the golden dragon - Just for a moment, but in that moment he said the part of his life that had always been empty, was filled with light and warmth. It meant a lot. He's waiting patiently now but don't be too long, we all miss you here."

I picked up a note of worry in her voice and Colin obviously caught it too.

"Where's Toby? I'd have thought he'd have wanted to say hi to his old man. Is everything ok?" Colin couldn't hide the concern in his voice. In all the excitement, I'd completely forgotten what had happened with Toby at the college and what the implications of that could be.

"He's still sulking, but I don't think there's anything to worry about. He sends his love." Sophie sounded convincing.

"Meg is keeping an eye on him," she added, "he'll be fine honey. How are your passengers?"

Colin shrugged. "Tina has located the island where we believe the relatives of our elderly passengers have made their home. We've sent a message and we're heading there now. It will take about Four hours, but I'll let you know the minute we have off-loaded our cargo and are on our way home.

"We miss you honey, hey try not to worry and get some rest. You look all in." Sophie blew Colin a kiss and the screen went blank.

Natasha put her arm around Colin. "Sophie is right. We could all do with some rest. Tina can watch things for a couple of hours and Alan and I will check in on the old folk, and make sure all is well below deck. I'm sure Jack has things under control. You go get a couple of hour's rest. Is that ok with you Alan?" Natasha looked my way and smiled.

I'd thought we were going to tell Colin of the suspicions we had about Maya, but Colin had enough on his plate. It would wait.

Colin laughed. "The women in my life are right as usual. Tina, call me if you need me. Thanks you two, I'll be in my cabin, so first sign of trouble call me - promise Natasha?"

Without waiting for a reply Colin headed for the door, leaving Natasha and I alone in the control room.

"Don't you think we should have said something about Maya," I said when I was sure Colin had gone.

Natasha shook her head. "It can wait, anyway they're just suspicions. We have no real proof, and for all we know it could just have been the dragon's power rubbing off. You and I have got pretty close in the last few days, so it's possible I may just have picked up on your fears for the dog. Let's give Maya the benefit of the doubt for now.

You go check on the islanders. I'll check below and we'll meet back in your cabin."

150

Natasha squeezed my hand and followed Colin out the door.

Scruffy was looking decidedly sheepish for a dog, and it didn't take long to work out why. I couldn't be cross, after all we were on a boat, so where was a dog to go. I hoped she was house trained, although she quite clearly wasn't boat trained.

"It's ok girl," I reassured her, "I'll soon clear this up."

"Tina, we have a small problem!" The now familiar lights flashed.

"I believe you have the problem Alan. What you need is in the cupboard on your right. There should be some wipes, and the next door is a rubbish shoot. Sorry you are on your own with this one," Tina's lights dimmed.

I cleared up Scruffy's little indiscretion and picked her up to reassure her. "It's ok girl, just don't do this when we get home." It was then it really dawned on me... Scruffy was my dog.

\*\*\*

The Islanders had made themselves comfortable with cushions and blankets; they were all asleep, snoring loudly. I had to admire the way they were making the best of things.

I shut the door quietly and made my way back to my Cabin, or should I say - our Cabin. As soon as I opened the door Scruffy trotted in, took one look around and jumped onto the chair in the corner. Turning a couple of times, she managed to push one of the cushions on to the floor to make herself more comfortable. She soon settled down and was almost instantly asleep.

I lay back on my bed to wait for Natasha and closed my eyes for a second.

\*\*\*

Swimming easily through the water I was keeping pace with Natasha. We were laughing and playing, leaving Hector in our wake. After a while we leapt from the water onto the sand, where we lay side by side. I could feel the heat of the sun warming my body.

Natasha began to whisper, then, she started to lick my ear enthusiastically and - bark! I opened my eyes, Scruffy barked again.

She had both paws on the bed and could just reach me at full stretch. I scratched between her ears. "How long were we asleep girl," I asked.

"Only an hour or so."

I starred at Scruffy, and for a second I thought I was either still dreaming or I had a talking dog. Then I noticed Natasha at the door. She was smiling. "I left you to sleep. You looked to be having a good dream, anything you would like to share."

I felt my face colour. "I don't remember," I lied. "Is everything ok," I tried to cover my embarrassment.

She shrugged. "I'm not sure. Colin has called for us. It sounded urgent."

We hurried back up to the bridge. It was getting easier to find my way around now, and I automatically picked Scruffy up to climb the steps. Colin and Jack were waiting for us.

"What's happened Colin? Is there a problem, it sounded urgent," Natasha asked

Colin looked worried. "Yes. We've heard back from the port we contacted about the islanders. They're very grateful for our intervention, but I fear a little suspicious about why we were there in the first place. They are sending a naval ship out to greet us and respectfully but insistently asked if they can send a small party to board us. They want to meet the elderly folk and escort them safely back to their ship, but I suspect they also want to check us out!" Colin couldn't hide his concern.

My heart began to race "What the hell do we do? They're bound to want to search the ship. How in God's name do we hide a dragon?"

Colin paced up and down a couple of times. "The first thing is not to panic. We have no choice. We have to let them come on board, so we're all going to have to be on the ball.

Jack, I want you with me. Alan and Natasha, you go below. Natasha, hide Maya and the Kittens as best you can. Alan, do your best to communicate to the dragon that she needs to keep her camouflage up, and her head down! If we all keep our heads we still have a good chance of pulling this off." Colin did his best to sound confident and no one questioned him.

We all set about our given tasks. I picked Scruffy up and followed Natasha down to the hold. Instinctively I moved Scruffy's make shift bed and food bowl, to the back of the hold with the dragon. Natasha moved the kittens and their box, under the stairs.

Maya came and joined me in front of the dragon. "She seems to be asleep Maya. I need to ask her to keep hidden. We may be getting some unwanted visitors very soon."

Maya smiled. "You can talk to her yourself now."

I remembered the pendant I held it close and tried to concentrate. It was a little disconcerting when the dragon opened her eyes and the room was suddenly filled with light. I steadied my nerves and explained that a man in uniform may come looking for her, and for all our sakes it would be best if he didn't find her, so she needed to keep herself hidden.

Although the dragon didn't speak, she lowered her head slightly and closed her eyes again. The light went out. I looked at Maya. "Did she understand?" The pendant didn't seem to have helped much.

Maya's answer was in my head. "She understood, Scruffy and I will stay with her. She'll keep us all safe."

Maya took Scruffy from me, and settled herself and the dog between the front legs of the dragon. It amazed me that the little dog didn't seem afraid of the dragon at all.

I left them and went back to join Natasha, who had just finished putting things back in cupboards. We looked around and sure enough the place looked empty. Only if you looked really hard, could you see that some of the shadows looked a little too - shadowy!

We joined Colin and Jack out on the deck. A short distance away a large war ship was following us, and a small craft had pulled up alongside.

Colin's confidence seemed to have waned a little. "I hope we're ready - we are ready - right?" He looked for reassurance from Natasha and I.

Suddenly it dawned on me, that I had no idea what the hell we would do if these guys found the dragon. They could take her and we couldn't do a thing to stop them. I wondered if there was a law against being in possession of a myth!

I could see the guns trained on us, in a friendly sort of way of course - for now! There were probably thirty men and women waiting for the order to board us. The four men who climbed the steps to join us on deck, made no attempt at looking friendly.

"Which of you is Colin Jacob's?" One of the men said, stepping forward and saluting. They all wore soldier's uniform and I noticed they were all armed. Friendly weapons I presumed, although I'd never really understood the expression 'friendly fire.'

The man, who by his manner was obviously in charge, spoke reasonably good English. To give him credit, he did at least try to look and sound friendly, but I have to say he failed miserably on both counts.

Colin stepped forward. "I am Colin Jacob's. You're welcome aboard my ship. If you will accompany me, I will gladly take you to the islanders we rescued. I'm sure they will be honoured, if not a little surprised to have such a large and impressive escort to their new home."

"Thank you Mr. Jacob's, we are of course in your dept. My name is Captain Hapi."

It was difficult to suppress a smile, as this man was the opposite of his name sake.

"It was very fortunate for the islanders that you were so close at hand. Can you tell me what exactly you and your team were actually doing – so close at hand? Mr. Jacobs," Hapi spat the word – Mr - as if it were an insult.

Colin led the way along the corridors to the rooms the old folk had made their own. He smiled politely. "We were monitoring the volcano, and I'm afraid we misjudged the speed at which things progressed. Unfortunately we do not have your superior technology. You had obviously worked out it might be too late to save these people, or you would of course have sent your own ship to get them out." Colin's tone was innocent and friendly and he was managing to keep his calm.

It was like watching a game of cat and mouse.

One of Hapi's men came with us, the other two stayed on deck. I noticed Colin glance at Jack who stayed behind to keep an eye on them.

Hapi was not happy at Colin's comments. "We had been misinformed Mr. Jacob's. We had been told the island had been evacuated, but if we had been in possession of the true facts we would of course have removed the remaining people from danger. We had not been informed of your operation. You could have put yourself and your crew in great danger." He could have given Jack a run for his money in the bad attitude stakes.

The islanders had gathered together in the centre of the room. I couldn't help but feel a little protective of them, even though I'd seen how they seemed to adapt to whatever came their way. I somehow knew they would be ok but I hoped for his sake, Hapi had a well-stocked larder on his ship. I could hear Colin had doubts too. "Will they be alright? Have you informed their family members? Will someone from the Island be there to meet them?"

Hapi nodded. "Of course family members have been informed and will meet us on our return. They will be well cared for. As you quite rightly pointed out, we have great technology at our finger tips. Everything has been arranged, and these people are no longer your concern Mr. Jacobs. As soon as the islanders have been safely transferred to our ship, with your permission of course, I would like to have a look around. Do you have a problem with that?"

It was obvious we had no choice in the matter.

Colin nodded politely. "Of course I would be honoured to show you the ship, we have nothing to hide. I'm not sure what would be of interest to you. My staff however have more pressing things to do, so if it's alright with you I will have them go about their duties." Colin indicated we should carry on.

Natasha caught my eye and I followed her below deck. We left Colin to deal with captain Hapi and his remaining men.

Natasha sighed. "We have a problem - Captain Hapi is a shit! He's going to search the ship from top to bottom and he's looking for trouble."

I'd not heard Natasha swear before, but I had to agree. They would be here shortly, and if it was trouble Hapi was looking for, we had a boat load. We checked around making sure we couldn't see anything out of the ordinary, then we got a small boat down from its fastenings and made like we were doing some repair work. It wasn't long before we heard voices at the top of the stairs.

I heard Colin say, "The hold is empty. We have no cargo at present."

Captain Hapi replied, "I would still like to see that for myself, if I may."

He reminded me of a snake. I hardly knew the man, but I hated him with vengeance. As they reached the bottom step, Colin stood to one side. "See, just routine maintenance."

Captain Hapi eyed what we were doing with interest, but made no comment. He headed over towards the back of the hold. I held my breath, a few feet more and surely he would see something. He stopped a horrible smirk on his face. "What have we here?" he hissed. My heart was in my mouth. We all followed his line of vision, and it was almost a relief to see he had spotted the Kittens in their box.

Hapi was enjoying this. "If I'm not mistaken and I rarely am, these kittens are quite unique to the island you have just left. Perhaps you would like to explain why you have not handed them over to us, surely you did not mean to steal them Mr. Jacobs?"

He was so smug. For a moment I thought Colin was going to blow it all and hit the bastard, but to his credit, he managed to keep his calm. "We were unsure if the kittens would live, they are still very sick. We have the capability to care for them and I feel if you take them now, they will probably die. We will happily return them to your government when they are fully recovered." Colin forced a smile.

Hapi grinned from ear to ear. "We of course appreciate your consideration. However, it is not my concern weather they live or die. My orders are to return anything you may have stol... may have acquired from the islands. Is there anything else you are keeping from us? You are in serious trouble already and I would hate things to get worse for you." His tone said just the opposite. He bent down to pick up the box containing the sleeping kittens.

I heard Natasha gasp. Maya had appeared from out of the shadows.

I held my breath - what the hell was she doing?

Hapi saw the child, and I thought he was going to wet himself with the excitement of this new discovery. "Ah, what have we here? it seems we have another stow away Mr. Jacobs. I find it amazing how a small child could find her way onto your big ship without being noticed."

I couldn't take my eyes from Maya. There was something about the child's expression. As Maya drew close to Captain Hapi, she reached out for his hand. Hapi was too busy gloating to notice. He took Maya's hand automatically - and his expression suddenly went blank. For a few seconds the scene seemed to freeze. I realized I was still holding my breath and let it out. It was the only sound in the room.

After what seemed like an age, Colin spoke. "Are you alright Captain?" he said, with what I thought to his credit, sounded like genuine concern.

The captain very slowly looked down at Maya. He seemed to see her properly for the first time and he actually smiled. Not the crocodile smile he had used earlier, but a warm genuine smile. He turned towards me and still holding Maya's hand, walked over. Out of the corner of my eye I could just see the look of amazement on Colin's face.

Captain Hapi placed Maya's hand in mine and smiled at me. It was like looking at a reformed man. I thought - any moment he's going to take my head off, but there was something different about the man now. Somehow, something had changed. Hapi slapped me on the shoulder and it was all I could do not to run for cover. This was too weird.

He actually winked at me as he said, "You're a lucky man to have such a beautiful wife and child. You must take very good care of them. Family is so important."

I nodded weakly and avoided looking Natasha's way - or my newly appointed wife's way! What was going on? The Captain turned his attentions back to Colin. "Thank you for your time Mr. Jacobs. You have a great ship here, it was good of you to show us around but now with your leave, we really must be getting the old folk back to their relatives. It has been quite an ordeal for them." Captain Hapi smiled and waved at us all as he headed back up the steps.

Colin watched the figure disappear then in an urgent whisper, said, "Would someone like to explain to me what the hell just happened here?"

I looked at Natasha and we all looked down at Maya.

Colin looked flustered. "Never mind ... It will have to wait. I'm going to make sure our Captain Hapi, gets off my ship, while he's still in his newly found good mood. Tina I've no doubt you've been listening," Colin said with a hint of sarcasm. "As soon as our guests are clear, get us out of here and head for home. I want to get as far from here as possible, just in case our Captain changes his mind."

Tina replied instantly, "Yes Colin."

Colin turned his attention to Natasha and me. "I want to see you two on the bridge in ten minute. I'll send Jack down here to keep an eye on," - he hesitated just for a second, "things," he said looking at Maya.

Maya had gone back to sit by the kittens with a look of total innocence on her face. As soon as Colin had disappeared up the steps, Scruffy came bounding out and jumped up and down to get my attention. I picked her up and scratched behind her ears. "Yes, you were a very good girl." She seemed as relieved as the rest of us.

The dragon still slumbered in the back of the hold as if nothing had happened.

I put Scruffy down next to Maya and the kittens, and followed Natasha over to the boat to help her tidy away the tools we'd been pretending to use. I spoke in a whisper. "Did you see that?" Instantly I felt like an idiot of course she had seen it! "She changed him completely. Do you think he'll be ok?" It was another stupid question. Neither of us knew, and if the truth were told we didn't care much either. The only important thing was that our Mr. Hapi had seemed a lot more human when he'd left than when he had arrived. If anything, it seemed Maya had done the man - and the world a favour, but I didn't share this thought with Natasha.

"She worries me Alan." Natasha seemed really concerned.

I tried to reassure her. "Look Maya just saved our skins and quite possibly Hapi's too. Can you imagine what Jack would have done to him if he'd tried to take the kittens?"

Natasha nodded, "Yes, we'd have seen yet another side to Captain Hapi - his insides!"

I laughed but deep down I knew that probably wasn't a joke.

Jack came down the stairs and at the same time the ship lurched slightly. I could feel we were moving and picking up speed. The Captain and his crew had let us go. I wondered if he would remember anything and hoped if he did, we would be far away. Scruffy had curled up and was sleeping, so I managed to climb the stairs with Natasha and leave without any fuss.

We found Colin on the bridge. "Alright what's going on? That little girl put right in seconds, what years of therapy had obviously failed to do for our Captain Hapi. How is that possible?" Colin sounded pretty calm but it was obvious he wanted answers. The trouble was I wasn't sure we had any.

To my surprise Natasha spoke up for Maya. "Come on Colin, however you look at it the child saved our skins. We don't know what she's capable of but up till now she's only tried to help, so we should give her the benefit of the doubt, at least until we can find out more."

Colin turned to me. "What do you think Alan? You've had more to do with her than any one."

I thought about this for a moment. "Natasha's right Maya did save the day, but I do think she's a little odd! So that probably means she should fit in well."

They both laughed. Colin looked relieved. "Alright let's get home. We can find out more there, just so long as in the meantime the child keeps herself out of our heads."

I glanced at Natasha and she just shrugged. Without a word we agreed not to mention anything else, it could wait.

Colin seemed happy to be heading for home. "Tina, get Ben and Sophie up on screen and work out how long it'll take us to get back. We'll get the ship as close to the island as we dare. Let's not forget - we have a dragon to deliver safely."

Coin turned to Natasha. "Will the dragon be strong enough to swim, she looked all in last time I saw her?"

Natasha shrugged. "She's resting now but to tell the truth I don't know, she used all her energy to get to the ship and my guess is she hasn't eaten much for weeks. It'll probably be a good idea to have George come out to meet us just in case."

Colin agreed. "I'll get Sophie to talk to George. I think he'll be only too pleased to come meet his new companion. God I hope they hit it off."

It hadn't occurred to me that they might not actually get along. Of course they'd never met, well not properly. What the hell would happen if they didn't like each other? It was obvious from the silence that none of us were prepared to go there. We were all deep in thought when the screen came to life, and Ben greeted us. "Hello wayward travellers, you on your way home yet?"

Colin tried to hide his concern, but didn't manage very well. "Oh hi Ben, Yes we're on our way. Where's Sophie? Is everything alright?"

Ben shook his head. "It's ok Colin, chill. I sent her to get some rest. Everything's good here. What's the plan? What do you want us to do?" Ben seemed totally at ease.

Colin relaxed a little. "We have a very, very tired dragon on board, and somehow we need to get her onto the island. We may need George's help, as she's no reason to trust us, but she should trust him. Talk to him, and see what he thinks would be the best way to tackle this, after all this is his territory not ours. The last thing we want is to upset her."

I felt sorry for the dragon. Because of her size, it was easy to forget how lost and alone she must feel. Her world had been literally torn apart and turned upside down. The people she'd lived to protect had gone and her home of many years had been destroyed. Now she was in the belly of a strange ship, taking her far away from the things she knew. How must she be feeling? I decided I should go and try to talk to her and perhaps reassure her, if I could. I left the others making plans for our return and headed back down into the hold.

As I descended the stairs I noticed all was quiet. Jack had sorted out some cots and Maya was fast asleep in one, next to the box containing the kittens. Scruffy was asleep on his bed beneath her. Jack had settled himself on a blanket on the floor, with his back to the wall but in good sight of any possible approach route.

I couldn't help but smile, seeing Jack curled up with his head tucked under his arm. Even in man form he reminded me of a large dog, with his thick black shaggy head of hair partially covering his face. I noticed however, that as I approached he opened one eye. I knew full well that if I'd been perceived as any kind of threat, he would have cleared the distance between us in an instant and been at my throat.

I made my way to the back of the hold. I could hear the dragon breathing rhythmically and hesitated, I didn't want to disturb her. I was about to walk away when one large eye opened. Slowly the other followed and she raised her head slightly, and rested it on the beautiful golden claws of her front feet. The voice that sounded in my head was surprisingly soft and gentle.

"Hello Alan, you are not disturbing me. I would be pleased if you would stay a while and talk."

Now I was here in front of her it was hard to think of what to say, but there was something that had been worrying me for some time. So I asked, "There is something that I have been struggling to understand. Back there on the island - the cave was blocked. Forgive me if I'm wrong but with your power, surely you could have released yourself at any time, but you chose to stay. Why? You knew you would die."

There was a moments silence then she spoke. "Ah - you are right of course, I had decided that it was my time." She said this as if she were talking about taking lunch or going for a walk. I couldn't believe she was saying she wanted to die. "But you called me to you - I'm a seeker, I was to come and save you." This sounded stupid, even to me.

Again, the moment's hesitation, "Indeed, you are a seeker Alan and a good one. I helped Maya summon you, but I wanted you to save the islanders and her. In fact until you showed me 'The One,' I had no intention of leaving the island."

Her words both pleased and confused me. "I don't understand why you would want to die?" I was appalled at the thought of this beautiful creature being lost to the world forever. As I looked into her blue green eyes I saw such pain and sadness, it was all I could do to stop myself from turning away.

She spoke again with such emotion. "Alan, I have lived for hundreds of years. The world has changed so much, but alas, the people remain the same. In the early days we were many. Some abused their power and raided the land, others like my mother and I kept ourselves private and helped if we could.

Man killed each other to start with, then they began killing us. Seekers developed a skill, they could sense us. Some sort to be our friends and helpers, but others sort glory by killing us. Many dragons died. Dragons do not bond until we are over two hundred years old. The odds were always against us. When my mother was killed, protecting me - I thought I was the last! I have been alone for so many years. Many times I left my sanctuary to search, but each time I saw death and destruction, and wars, so many wars.

I could not believe the things I have seen you do to each other, and to the land and other creatures. You can be so cruel, yet you call us monsters and beasts. I'd had enough and decided that the island would serve as my tomb. I saw the destruction coming but I could not make the people leave. That is why I told Maya about seekers, and with my help to focus her skills, we found you.

But I did not know 'The One' was with you. When you showed me him, for the first time in too many years I had dared to have new hope." She stopped, and I sensed her emotion. Oh god! How many wars had she seen over the years, how much death and destruction had she lived through? Suddenly I felt so ashamed - I wanted to show her there was some good in the human race, that there could be a life for her and most of all that she would no longer be alone. I knew what it was like to be alone.

All I could say was, "I'm so sorry." I choked on the words. Somehow they just didn't seem enough. I wanted to ask who had killed her mother but I was afraid, it may well have been a seeker, like me.

The dragon's mood brightened. "Would you show me 'Him' again?" The sadness had eased and there was a hint of excitement in her voice. I smiled to myself, I wasn't worried any more about whether they would get along - they were quite simply made for each other. They were each other's last chance for happiness.

"I will try," I said, trying desperately to remember how I'd managed it before. "This is a little new to me, may I touch you?"

Even in the darkness of the hold, now that she was awake her whole body sparkled and shimmered. Even though I'd seen it before it was still breath-taking. She bowed her head once, and I gentle placed my hand on her shimmering scales. I concentrated hard, and this time the image of George came more easily into my mind. The familiar sound of the wind rushing in my ears, and the feeling of speed even though I knew I was standing still.

George was there in front of his cave, I saw him look up. He sniffed the wind. He arched his head towards us - I knew he sensed us. The lines on his weathered face seemed to soften, and in my mind I thought I heard him say very faintly, "I am here, waiting for you,"... the image faded and was gone. When I looked up into the face of the golden dragon, a small diamond sparkled and dropped to the floor, a single tear that twinkled like a falling star.

"That was George," I said and added, "The dragon." As if she might not have realized that fact – stupid.

She seemed puzzled. "The One, is called George?"

I remembered what Colin had told me about dragons not needing to name themselves and added, "It's a human thing, we like to give our friends names."

"Why?" she said.

This was a good question and I found myself having to think about it. "To be honest I'm not really sure, but it helps us recognize and contact our friends and just makes us feel better I think." That was the best I could come up with and I could see she was thinking.

After a moment she said, "What is my name Alan?"

I looked up at this magnificent creature with so much strength and power. All she really wanted was to belong, just like the rest of us. Without really thinking I said, "Goldie!" As soon as I'd said it I thought how stupid, she should have a name that says beauty or power or something magical, and I come up with 'Goldie'. How bloody imaginative!

"Goldie, Goldie, GOLDIE." The dragon repeated it a few times then to my surprise said, "Yes I would like very much to be known as Goldie."

I smiled thinking that Colin was really going to get a kick out of this. I'd really ribbed him about calling a dragon George and he'd been about eight at the time. I'd managed to come up with Goldie. Never mind, Goldie was happy and at this moment that was all that mattered. She seemed to glow with an inner light now, being happy suited her.

Suddenly I wanted to be with Natasha, so I left Goldie to get some rest.

Everyone else was still sleeping. As I headed back up the stairs I sensed Jack watching me go - not much if anything could get by him, but strangely now I felt reassured by this fact.

I headed straight for the cabins not the bridge. I would be of little - or no help with the planning. Ben and Colin would manage all that between them.

I found Natasha sitting on her bed, looking through some photographs. She looked sad.

I coughed politely. "Can I come in," I said from the doorway not wanting to intrude.

"Sorry Alan, I didn't see you there. Of course come in. I was just looking through some old photos I have of Gran and my parents." She indicated for me to sit next to her on the bed.

"This is Gran, outside the batch she had for as long as I can remember." Natasha handed me one of the pictures and I could see that although the woman might have been in her seventies, she still had an air of elegance and beauty about her that age had not taken. She stood on the porch of a small building, next to an equally old looking rocking chair.

Natasha smiled again. "I have such wonderful memories of those days, it was just before…" She stopped. She didn't have to say anymore.

I took the other photo from her outstretched hand.

"This is the only photo I have of my mother and father. It's of their wedding day. Father destroyed the others, he was so angry at first, when she left us. That wasn't so bad, but then he became sad, he missed her so much Alan."

Tears filled her eyes, and I held her close. I wanted to ease the pain but I didn't know what to say. Instead I simply held her as she cried, and finally she fell asleep.

I lay next to her as she slept and memories of my own father flooded back. I'd pushed them to the back of my mind for so long I felt I hardly knew the man, and yet I remembered the last time I'd seen him. It had been my eighteenth birthday and he'd actually been home on one of his - all too few and far too short visits.

He'd talked about one last story, something he had to do, answers he'd been searching for all his life. It was going to change things, and finally he would be able to spend more time with me and my mother. He didn't stay for the party but before he left he gave me the watch, the watch I'd worn every day since, the watch that had never seemed to work properly for me. It had long ago stopped working altogether but I still wore it, I couldn't bear to part with it. That was the last time I saw him.

I don't know how long we lay together on the bed. It was no good looking at my broken watch. There and then, I made a promise to myself that one day I would make it my business to find out what had happened to my father. I felt a little better.

Natasha began to stir in my arms. "Hello beautiful," I said.

She sat up. "I'm sorry Alan. That was silly of me."

I brushed a wayward strand of hair from her face. "There's nothing to be sorry for Natasha, you miss your parents and in fact, you made me admit to myself that I miss mine too. I'm grateful for that but I realized something else, I've fallen in love with you." The words just came out, and I suppose I'd hoped she would melt into my arms and tell me she loved me too, that we would live happily ever after.

Unfortunately that wasn't what happened.

Natasha sat up and moved away slightly. "I'm sorry Alan but I did try to warn you. It's my fault I've let us get too close. You should know that when we get back to the island I'll be going away." With that said and my bubble well and truly burst, she left the room.

I sat on the bed alone. For the first time in my life I'd said those three little words, and she'd walked out on me without looking back. I picked up the pictures of Natasha's family and studied them again. After a while it started to make sense, she was going to look for her family and like me, she needed to know the truth. I felt lost and empty again. For a little while I'd let myself believe that everything would be so simple, but I knew that life wasn't like that.

Well I wasn't going to give up, not without a fight! Natasha was worth fighting for.

All I had to do was persuade her that we were meant to be together. I knew it in my heart, in my very being. I just had to convince Natasha. I looked down again at her father's smiling face. He'd been so happy then. I wondered if he had paid, the ultimate price for his love?

I didn't care. I was willing to give up everything for Natasha. I simply wouldn't let her go.

I followed her upstairs. I knew she would be heading for the bridge, and I found her there talking to Colin.

Colin turned as I entered. "What's up with you? You look like you lost a dollar and found a nickel. We did it, but you wouldn't think it, looking at you two. We're going home!"

Colin looked from one to the other. "Oh - you two love birds have had a fight, it happens to the best of us. You'll make it up, trust me, it's the best part. Besides, anyone can see you two were made for each other."

Natasha didn't look amused. "I'm going to check on things below deck. I hope the dragon has got some of her strength back, it's going to be a bit of a swim to shore," she said as she headed for the stairs.

"Goldie," I said. "The dragon is called Goldie."

Natasha stopped and turned. Well at least that had made her smile. "The dragons name is Goldie? Who thought that one up?" Natasha said, then seeing the look on my face added not too unkindly, "Scruffy the dog and Goldie the dragon. Alan you're on a roll!"

I shrugged. "I know, but she put me on the spot and it was the first thing that came into my mind." I waited for the comment I knew would come from Colin.

I didn't have to wait long. "Goldie. Ha! And you thought George was bad." Colin laughed, and slapped me on the back. "Go down stairs with Natasha and you two make up, I can't handle the rest of this journey with you two looking like a wet week! We should be happy."

169

I didn't have to be told twice, so I followed Natasha down the stairs and caught up with her in the corridor. "Wait," I said catching hold of her arm.

She turned to face me and I could see that she had tears in her eyes. I pulled her too me and held her. "I know you're afraid for me Natasha but it's too late, I can't live without you. I won't let you leave, not like this. I do love you and nothing you can do or say will change that."

She didn't resist. "I love you too Alan, that's why I have to go," she whispered.

"I don't understand, if you love me then why," I said, my heart racing. She loved me!

She pulled away. "I have to know what happened to my mother, and if my father is dead or alive. If they are together somewhere perhaps they are happy, perhaps there is hope - but if he's dead,"... her voice trailed off.

I could understand her fear but it didn't matter. "It's different Natasha, we're different. That was them, this is now. We can make it work. There has to be a way, there is always a way," I said, maybe trying to convince myself as well as Natasha. I had to believe it, but more importantly I had to make her believe it. I couldn't lose her, not now. I pulled her back to me and held her tightly. I was afraid to let her go again and Natasha seemed happy to stay like that too, but Jack approached us from the other end of the corridor and we had to move to let him past.

"I thought you two had a room," he commented gruffly as he squeezed past us, but I noticed he had a smile on his face.

Natasha started down the corridor. "Come on, we must get things ready below. We can talk later."

I caught her arm again. "Promise me we will talk, you won't just go," I pleaded.

"Oh Alan," she protested.

"Promise me," I insisted.

170

She nodded, "Ok Alan. I promise."

Scruffy met us with enthusiasm - she really did remind me of Spike. It was going to be interesting to see who was boss when we got back home. I put Scruffy down after I'd fussed her and looked around for Maya. She was at the back of the hold. She had both kittens in her arms and had obviously taken them to show Goldie. To my amazement the dragon very carefully lowered her head, and oh so gently rubbed the end of her scaly nose over the kitten's backs, causing both kittens to purr loudly.

Natasha smiled, "She's so gentle, just like George. They are going to find happiness together," Natasha said, but she looked distant again.

I couldn't miss this opportunity. "We could be that happy too, if you would only give us a chance Natasha." She ignored my comment and continued, "Alan will you take some food to - Goldie." She smiled. "The name does fit her quite well. Tell her what we have planned, it won't be long now. Ask her to eat something. It will help her get her strength back. She must be strong enough to swim to the island and we can only get so close. George will be here to help soon. I'll feed scruffy and get the bottles ready for the kittens, as they still have a bit of a trip. Send Maya over when she is ready and she can give me a hand."

I took the bag of whole fish she handed me and headed over to Goldie and Maya.

Scruffy had heard food mentioned and sensibly stayed with Natasha.

I bowed to the dragon, and asked Maya to join Natasha to help get everyone fed. She stroked the dragon's snout with great affection, and left with the kittens carefully cradled in her arms. As I watched her go, I found myself wondering how Captain Hapi was now, and whether Maya had changed him forever or just short term. In any case Hapi would never admit to anyone that he had let his prey go, so I figured we were relatively safe.

I offered the food to Goldie but she didn't seem interested. "You must eat something. You will need all your strength to swim to shore. George will be able to help you but you must be able to help yourself." I held up one of the fish for her inspection. She took it delicately with one of her golden claws and with all the skill of a master chef, filleted it and handed me back the head and tail, still attached to the back bone. She carefully did this with all five fish I offered her.

When she had carefully stripped her last fish she lowered her head and I looked into those beautiful eyes, they had a new sparkle to them. I heard her voice inside my head.

"We are close, I can sense his presence. He comes for me now."

Tina's smooth voice came over the intercom. "Alan! Colin has asked me to inform you that we are in position, a quarter of a mile off shore. George is on his way, please prepare our guest."

"Thanks Tina, we will be ready," I said, hoping I was right.

Natasha came and stood next to me and gently stroked the dragon's head. "Is everything ok? Is she ready?"

I shrugged. "I think so. Goldie can feel George's presence, and I feel it too. The trouble is it's not an exact science. How will we know when to lower the back?"

Natasha didn't have to answer, as Colin chose this moment to join us. He seemed in good spirits. "I can answer that, Ben has attached a tracking device around George's neck. We will know exactly when he's at the door and Tina will lower the back. We'll also be able to track them back to base. Natasha will go along as an extra pair of eyes, and the rest of us will take the ship back to the main land. Sophie will pick us up in the plane. With luck we'll all meet up again for one of Meg's great meals."

Goldie moved forward and extended her long neck. She looked so much better now. In fact she was positively - glowing. I'd forgotten how big she was. Now in the open she towered above us, a shimmering, sparkling mass of muscle. Her tail swished gently from side to side as she carefully negotiated the narrow hold.

I caught Natasha's hand. "We will 'ALL' meet up for a meal?" I knew I sounded desperate but I didn't care.

She squeezed my hand. "Yes Alan, I will be waiting for you."

She had stripped down to the familiar swim suit and I was reminded of our first meeting. It seemed like a life time ago when she had emerged from the sea and into my life. Would I lose her back to the ocean? My thoughts were interrupted by the sound of the metal door slowly being lowered. It was now late afternoon and the sun was low over the sea, the waves were calm and blue. I thought it was the perfect picture.

Then through the waves, leaping and jumping, the dolphins came. I'd never seen so many. The water was alive with lithe grey forms, dancing and spinning and in the midst of this magnificent scene there was a glint of gold and red.

"George," I heard Natasha whisper.

And again in my head I could hear the haunting sound of the dragon song. This time the sound was all around us and I realized it was now a duet. The song was different - it bought feelings of hope and joy, life and love. The dolphins heard the song too and became even more animated. They jumped and spun. It was a celebration, of the sheer joy of life. I felt drawn towards the water. I wanted to share in the magic. Suddenly Natasha's hand was on my arm and I looked into those beautiful green eyes, seeing that, like mine they were full of tears. I glanced around to see that we were all in a kind of trance, listening to the sound in our heads and watching the dolphin's sheer exuberance.

The golden dragon moved forward towards the open doorway. There was just enough room to unfurl her sparkling wings, before she swooped out of the ship and into the sky. For a few seconds she climbed high, then folded back her wings and dived into the ocean to join the throng. For a brief moment a rainbow of colours twisted and entwined in the water, and the song in my head was almost too beautiful to bear.

Slowly the sound began to fade and the waters stopped churning as the last dolphins disappeared from view. Before I could gather my wits Natasha kissed my cheek. Running forward, she dived gracefully into the waves and was gone. I was just quick enough to grab Maya and hold her back. The child was sobbing and struggling in my arms. Instantly images started to flash through my mind, scenes of Maya's past, the villagers, the mountain, the dragon. Scenes and people I didn't recognize and then - I pulled away sharply.

Colin came over to console the child, and I stood lost in thought. Scruffy started to paw my leg. I bent down to pick her up, stroking the little dog made me feel better. At this moment I felt confused and suddenly lost. What I had seen bothered me, I needed to check something.

Colin had taken Maya over to the kittens and they were feeding them together, to take her mind off other things. I slipped away unnoticed and carried scruffy up the stairs. She started to whine and as soon as I put her down she headed for the top deck. Nature called, so maybe this was the poop deck! Well anyway it was now.

With Scruffy more comfortable we headed to the cabins. I felt bad going through Natasha's ruck sack, but there was something I had to check. There it was the picture of Natasha's mother. I was sure now - there was no doubt in my mind. One of the images I'd seen when I'd held Maya had been of Natasha's mother a little older yes, but unmistakable.

# GOODBYE CAN BE THE HARDEST WORD

I sat on my bunk deep in thought. Scruffy was snoring slightly, with her head tucked under her paw. Colin appeared at the door carrying Maya. "She's fast asleep. It has all been a bit much for her. I'll pop her into Natasha's bed next door. We may as well all get some rest. Ben reports 'the eagle has landed', so I guess everything is alright. Tina will keep us on course and let us know when we need to dock.

Are you ok? After a successful mission everyone is usually happy.  We have pulled off something pretty special here.  Did you patch things up with Natasha?"

I nodded. "Yes and sort of - I'm fine, just a little stunned I think. I don't believe I'll ever see anything as fantastic as that again, even if I live to be a hundred," I said, relaxing back on my bed.

Colin laughed. "In our line of work you just never know? But it was pretty spectacular, I have to agree. Try to get some rest Alan," he said, scratching Scruffy behind her ears before he left. I watched him go, thinking that I wanted to tell him about Natasha's plans to leave and maybe ask him to persuade her to stay. Somehow I couldn't bring myself to say she might be going.  I felt that actually saying it out loud might make it happen - stupid.

I lay on my bed thinking. After a while I got up and crept quietly into the next room. Maya was fast asleep on the bed and I could see her small hands clasping the blanket up to her neck. I crept as close as I dared, trying not to wake her. This close I could see clearly there was no webbing on her fingers. Carefully I pushed the hair back from her ear, and as far as I could tell there was no sign of gills. I went back to my room, leaving her to sleep.

What did the images mean? Maybe the memory had been stolen from Natasha, when Maya had put the thought in Natasha's mind to rescue Scruffy. But then why did Natasha's mother look older? I was positive it was the same woman. I couldn't work out the link, if indeed there was one. I was tired, I needed to sleep. I would talk to Natasha when at last we got home. Although this was a short trip it was going to seem like another endless journey.

I found it hard to sleep, even though I felt totally wiped out, my mind wouldn't switch off. If I told Natasha about what I'd seen in Maya's memories, it would make her even more determined to go. Could I pretend I hadn't seen Natasha's mother? She would know something was wrong. She could read me like a book. I tossed and turned, agonizing over the choices I had.

Suddenly I sat up - she had loved him! My mother had loved my father so much - she had let him go. Tears filled my eyes. I'd always blamed her for my father's absences. After his disappearance I'd shouted at her in a fit of temper, I said she didn't care! Only now did it become clear. Sometimes it was because you loved someone so very much that you had to let them go.

I lay back on my bed, I had no choice. I knew I had to tell Natasha the truth whatever that meant to our future, as there could be no future for us without the truth.

I would contact my mother when we got back. I needed to talk with her.

It seemed as though I had just closed my eyes, when Tina's smooth voice came over the intercom. "Alan, Colin would like me to wake you and tell you we are about 20 minutes out. Please prepare to leave the ship."

Scruffy was startled. She jumped down and ran around the cabin barking, searching for the intruder. I laughed. "It's alright Scruffy that's just Tina. Thanks Tina. Is Colin on the bridge?"

"Yes Alan. Your new little friend is very noisy."

I scooped Scruffy up to stop her from barking and laughed. "Scruffy will learn to appreciate having you around Tina, just as I have!"

"Thank you Alan. I will try not to startle your friend again."

Scruffy was still far from happy. "It's ok Scruffy, you'll get used to Tina always being around. She grows on you." I put her down and got my things together. Maya appeared in the doorway and Scruffy rushed to greet her, glad to have someone she could actually see.

Maya looked a little lost. I put my bags on the floor, and sat back on my bed. "Would you like to talk? What's the matter Maya?" I asked.

She came and sat by me. I noticed the dragon scale pendent in her hand, she was turning it around and around in her fingers. Maya suddenly looked so small, so I took her hand and spoke as kindly as I could. "It's going to be alright Maya, we're going home. You'll be welcome there I'm sure." I did my best to reassure her, but I would be the first to say that I'm not used to children.

Even in my head her voice sounded so sad. "She was my only friend and I've lost her. I have no one to talk to now. The golden one was the only one who cared or understood."

My heart went out to this small child, abandoned so many times in her short life. "You haven't lost her as a friend. You've just helped to make her happy and you'll make new friends, lots of new friends. I'd like to be your friend Maya, you can talk to me. I'll introduce you to George, you'll like him. There are many marvellous things on the island, so it's going to be a new adventure, a new life for all of us, you'll see." I squeezed her hand and hoped I was right.

177

Maya's smile returned and the small voice in my head asked. "Where are the kittens?" She jumped down from the bed.

I smiled, "I think they will be with Jack, they'll be safe. Come on let me get the gear together and then we'll head up to the bridge and find them." I grabbed my ruck sack and we headed next door to collect Natasha's bag.

Maya skipped along the corridors with Scruffy in hot pursuit, her mind back on the kittens. She seemed to have left her concerns behind. I thought to myself, children and old folk had something in common - their resilience. She would be fine.

The ship had already come to a stop when we met Colin and Jack on the bridge. As I'd thought, the Kittens were in their box at Jack's feet. Colin was placing Tina in her travel box and we were all set to go. The transfer to the airstrip went smoothly and the plane was already waiting for us. Sophie came down the steps to greet us and hugged Colin. "We missed you honey," she said and noticing Maya for the first time, came over and knelt down so that she was at her level. She gave her a hug. "You must be Maya. We've all been looking forward to meeting you and welcoming you to our home."

She turned back to the plane and shouted, "Toby, get yourself out here. Give your father a hug and say hi to Maya."

I noticed the look of relief on Colin's face at the sight of his son. Toby came down the steps and hugged his father. He looked fine. "Hi dad, great to have you back, we really missed you. Hi Maya." Toby greeted Maya with a light kiss on the cheek. Maya looked down at her feet but even so, I could still tell that she had gone red in the face. I knew that feeling. Something told me that Maya would be happy to have Toby as a friend.

"And who is this?" Sophie said seeing Scruffy.

I'd gotten so used to the little dog I'd even forgotten she was in my arms. "This is Scruffy," I said holding the little dog out so that she could get a better look.

"She's adorable. Spike is going to just love her.

Jack I believe you have rescued some kittens." Sophie looked into the box Jack was carrying, with care. "Meg is waiting to give them the once over. The rest of us can look forward to a fantastic meal, I hope everyone's hungry." Sophie took Maya's hand as we all headed for the plane, and Maya looked up at me and smiled.

By the time we'd landed and unloaded the plane, Ben had turned up in a jeep to pick us up. "Great job everyone. Things are going well here - if you know what I mean!" He winked. "The earth has been moving, oh and I really mean - moving!" He laughed and nudged me in the ribs.

"Ben, children present," Colin reprimanded.

As we had expected, the dragons were obviously hitting it off. "What about Natasha?" I asked trying not to sound to desperate."

Ben shrugged. "Oh she's about somewhere. I'm sure she will join us for dinner." He carefully took Tina's carry box from Colin.

"I hope you have taken good care of my little girl." Ben opened the box and took Tina out. She hovered at shoulder height and looked pleased to have her freedom. Scruffy barked at her and tried to jump up. Tina swooped, and Scruffy yelped and hid behind my legs. We all laughed.

It was a tight fit in the jeep but Sophie popped Maya on her lap, and Maya looked over-the-moon. I picked up a newspaper from the floor. "What's this Ben?"

"Ah yes, I thought you might like to look at the front cover. Tina came across the story while she was doing her usual checks."

The cover picture was of a smiling Captain Hapi surrounded by happy islanders, all hugging and kissing. I couldn't read the text.

"What does it say?" I asked, bemused by the look on the Captains smiling face.

"In a nutshell, it congratulated Captain Hapi for his brave rescue of the islanders. It goes on to say how he has vowed to see that the government helps to relocate and house them with their families, and give them any support they need. Didn't he do well?" Ben laughed.

I felt outraged. "He - rescued the islanders. That's a bloody cheek." I felt more than a little aggrieved.

Colin just asked, "Any mention of - us Ben?"

Ben sounded more serious. "Not a dicky-bird, and we've checked all the other papers and news reel - nothing!"

Colin sighed. "Great, then it was all a job well done." Colin relaxed back in his seat with his arm around Sophie.

I guessed I was going to have to get used to this. We could never get any credit for what we did. If there was just one story, then questions would be asked and that was the last thing we wanted. A secret society just like the comics I used to read.

*** 

There was still no sign of Natasha when we pulled up at the lodge.

Sophie helped Maya down from the jeep. "Toby can you take the kittens to Meg. They look pretty healthy now, but I think it would be a good idea to get her to look them over. Maya perhaps you would like to go too," Sophie said, and I saw her look at Colin.

"Yes that's a great idea," Colin agreed.

I knew they would want Meg to have a look at Maya too and this was a good way of doing it without alarming the child. Jack started to unload the jeep and Ben did the usual disappearing trick, which he managed every time there was heavy work to be done. I helped Jack with the bags. Suddenly

180

Spike appeared at the top of the stairs barking loudly, he bounded down the steps and into Colin's arms. Colin caught him. "Hello fella, you miss us too," Colin fussed him.

Scruffy was hidden behind my legs but let out an almost-polite yap at the sight of Spike.

Spike's ears pricked up. Colin put him down, and for a second the two little dogs stood looking at each other. Then as if an unspoken decision had been reached, they both bounded at each other tumbling and playing, like long lost friends. I have to say I was relieved.

Sophie smiled. "Well they look happy. Spike now that you and Scruffy have introduced yourselves, you can escort Scruffy to the kitchens. I think Meg has got your dinners ready." Spikes ears pricked up. Sophie had said the magic word. He scooted up the steps leaving Scruffy whimpering at the bottom. Spike stopped and seeing her distress came back down. I had to stop myself from rushing forward to help. Spike seemed to assess the situation. Then he jumped up onto the first step and waited. Scruffy seemed to realize what was expected of her and carefully she took the first step. Spike jumped up onto the next step and again waited for her to do the same. Slowly but surely the duo made their way to the top.

I felt so proud. My little girl had managed her first steps. Spike trotted off and Scruffy followed him. I volunteered to take Natasha's bag to her room. First I thought I'd dump mine. I was secretly hopeful that Natasha was in her room. We needed to talk.

As I opened my bedroom door, Natasha flew into my arms and kissed me. I dropped the bags.

"I missed you," she said between kisses.

"I missed you too. God you feel so good." My hands started to wander. She pulled away and I cursed myself for going too fast, but she didn't look angry.

"Now isn't the right time Alan," she said, but she didn't leave.

We sat together on the bed. I took her hands in mind "We need to talk,"

Natasha looked close to tears. "I'm sorry Alan, but you must understand this is something I have to do."

I stopped her, "I do understand, but that's not what I need to talk to you about. Don't get me wrong I would rather you didn't go, but I won't try to stop you. This is about Maya. I saw something – I'm not sure what it meant," I stopped. I didn't understand myself, so how could I explain it to Natasha. "We need to go and talk to Meg. I think she may be able to help me get something straight in my mind."

Natasha could see I was struggling with something. "What is it Alan? Talk to me."

I wasn't sure, I needed to be sure. "Natasha I'm confused. I've seen something I really can't explain and it involves Maya. Let's go see Meg."

Natasha agreed and we headed for the kitchens hand in hand. As we entered the room, we automatically parted.

Meg greeted us with a smile and a mug. "Hello you two, just in time for hot chocolate." We took them.

"Thanks Meg, how's everyone settling in?" I said, noticing Spike and Scruffy side by side tucking in.

I was surprised to see Jack standing with hot chocolate in hand. Maya was sitting at the table with Toby. She had a chocolate moustache and was swinging her feet happily.

Meg smiled. "Everyone is good, and it's great to have you all home. I was just going to ask Toby to show Maya her new room. Would you do that Toby?"

Toby jumped up from his chair. "Yeah, come on Maya." Toby Held out his hand, Maya hesitated then got down from her stool and went over to Meg.

Meg seemed to be listening and nodded. "You will have to ask Jack Maya."

Maya looked at Jack, seeming a little unsure. Meg encouraged her. "Go on, he won't bite." Meg looked my way daring me to say anything to contradict this.

Maya walked over to Jack and took his hand.

"Maya," Meg scolded, "You ask Jack properly. We don't use our gifts on our friends."

Maya looked guilty but Jack simply smiled and nodded.

Meg thanked Jack then looked down at Maya. "Ok honey, you may have the kittens in your room, and Toby will help you take a litter tray and water bowl. Off you go," Meg said ushering them out.

When I turned back, Jack had silently disappeared. All three of us sat at the table with our mugs of hot chocolate. "So what's up?" Meg asked. "Oh Just a minute," Meg looked down at the two dog's. They had finished their meal. "Spike take Scruffy out into the garden to play and Spike, be a gentleman!" She turned her attention back to us. "Sorry, now what's the problem Alan? You have something on your mind."

I thought for a moment - where to start? I was beginning to doubt what I had actually seen myself now. I tried to explain, "Something happened on the ship. When Maya was upset I put my arm around her to comfort her and - I saw images, lots of images all mixed up - of her past I think." I stopped, both women were waiting.

Meg nodded. "You must have tapped into her emotional state. You are beginning to unlock your power Alan but that's a good thing, it's nothing to worry about," Meg reassured me.

It hadn't felt good, but that was beside the point. "It's not just that, I saw," - I hesitated, but I'd gotten this far. "I saw Natasha's mother, at least I'm pretty sure it was her. She was older than she had been in the picture Natasha had shown me, but it was her." I stopped, noticing Meg patting Natasha's hand. I realized there were tears in Natasha's eyes.

"I'm sorry I didn't want to upset you Natasha. I knew I had to tell you. I don't understand how it could be, or what it means. I thought Meg could help us take Maya back or something." I stopped - both women were looking at me, not in a good way!.

Meg shook her head. "You want me to totally stress out an eight year old child, already traumatized by past events?"

I hadn't thought this through. "Ah! No - I mean yes - I thought you could use the herbs you used on me, to help her remember."

Meg looked a little guilty. "Ah yes - those' I'm afraid we couldn't risk the side effects on one so young."

This took a moment to register. "Wait a minute - what side effects? No one mentioned side effects to me."

Natasha had the decency at least, to apologize. "Sorry Alan but Meg was certain you were strong enough, or she wouldn't have allowed it."

Meg had been thinking. "Alan, it sounds as if you may have seen into Maya's mind. Maybe you saw the past, maybe things got a little muddled - either way, I think eventually Maya will speak again. She has suffered some trauma in her short life. When she is ready she will tell us, but it could take some time and I'm not sure what would happen if we tried to push her now." She turned to Natasha. "I'm sorry Natasha."

Natasha shrugged. "It's alright, really. Maya doesn't need reminding of the past when she has so much to look forward to in the future."

I felt out of my depth here. "'Sorry, I've not had much to do with children before," I admitted.

Meg smiled. "I'm sure, that will change when you two have children of your own."

Instantly I could feel my face burning, but this time I found some consolation in the fact that Natasha had turned crimson too.

Meg laughed. "What - you thought no one had noticed the way you two have been looking at each other. Oh Please."

We all laughed. Natasha touched my hand. "Thank you Alan, you could have kept this to yourself. I appreciate your honesty. If there is even a slim chance that Maya has seen my mother, then it gives me an area to start my search."

Natasha kissed my forehead and headed for the door. I knew she didn't want me to follow her. Had I done the right thing? I sat feeling miserable.

"More hot chocolate." It wasn't a question - Meg placed another steaming mug in front of me. I stared into its dark depths. "I'm losing her Meg, before I even get to know her properly."

I felt totally dejected. Meg put her hand on mine. "You're doing the right thing Alan. In your heart you know that, you must let her find her own way. She will return. You two were made for each other. Give it time, you'll see - There will be the happy ending you long for."

I left Meg busy in the kitchen and headed back to my room for a shower. A few steps down the corridor Scruffy caught up with me. I picked her up and stroked her soft fur, I had always avoided this sort of tie. Yet now I found so much comfort in having this little dog around.

Once in my room Scruffy found a chair to her liking and settled down. I showered and changed then lay on the bed and shut my eyes, just for a moment...

\*\*\*

I found myself surrounded by thick forest and I was walking uphill. The going was hard, but the terrain seemed somehow familiar. In the past I'd hunted many times through forest like this, but something worried me. It was quiet, far too quiet and I had the feeling I was being watched. A twig snapped behind me and I swung round sharply.

I sat up. Spike was barking at the door and Scruffy jumped down from her chair and joined in, so I got up and opened the door. They greeted each other and sped off down the corridor together.

I sighed and sat back on the bed. Another dream.

Out of habit I looked at my watch - I didn't know how long I'd slept but Spike had probably been sent to get me for dinner. My stomach was telling me that was true.

I followed the glorious smells to the kitchen and saw that Meg was busy with pots and pans. Spike and Scruffy took up positions, just in case anything might fall their way.

Meg looked up. "Good, you're here. The others are waiting in the dining room. You can take these in for me." She handed me some plates.

I was surprised. "Only five Meg?" I commented.

She smiled. "Yes, I had mine with Toby and Maya earlier. Maya is fast asleep, and Toby is busy saving the world – at least, the one on his computer. Jack has been away from home a while, he will be marking his territory. Now get yourself in there, everyone's hungry." She turned back to the saucepans.

I did as I was told and took the plates into the dining room. There was general chatter from around the table. I was pleased to see Ben had joined us. "Ah Alan at last - we are all skeletons!" He exclaimed dramatically.

I put the plates down and was relieved to see Natasha smiling at me. The seat next to her was empty so I sat down, and felt her hand squeeze my knee under the table. Just a small act but it sent shivers up and down my spine, and made it difficult to concentrate. "Sorry I kept you all waiting, I thought I'd only closed my eyes for a moment. I'll have to get this watch fixed." I leaned over and whispered into Natasha ear, "Are you alright?"

She seemed relaxed again, she smiled back. "Yes Alan, thank you."

That seemed to be the end of it. Meg started bringing in the food and everyone tucked in, conversation was limited. After a fantastic meal, we retired to the lounge. Meg joined us with a large pot of coffee.

Once we were all comfortably seated, Colin turned to Meg. "Well Meg what do you think of our little Maya then?" I sensed concern in his voice.

Meg took a moment to reply. "I have only had a short time with her Colin, so I can't be sure. It does seem however, that Maya has some abilities. Without the dragon's help she is inexperienced and unfocused. I am trying to assess how much of the power is hers, and how much has come from the golden dragon. Let's just say - she can help people make up their minds. I need to study her further and teach her how and when to use her gift."

Sophie sat casually on the arm of Colin's chair, and they seemed at ease with each other again. Whatever had gone on with Toby must have been sorted out.

Sophie summed up the situation. "Well that's settled then; Meg will be Maya's nanny. We dare not let her loose on the world, until we know what we are dealing with. Besides she has nowhere else to go and Toby likes having a little sister to boss around - although I think once Maya finds her feet, he may have the tables turned on him." Sophie laughed and stroked Colin's hair.

It did seem the perfect solution, I felt sure Maya would be happy. I suddenly remembered the reason for all this. "Has anyone checked in on our two favourite dragons lately," I asked?

Ben laughed. "If you ask me, George and his girlfriend, are making up for a lot of lost time, if you know what I mean."

Sophie sighed. "Yes Ben, we all know what you mean."

Colin nodded. "We're giving them time to settle in. Ben and Meg went out there to meet her earlier today... let's just say they didn't feel they should interrupt!" Colin went a shade of red, previously reserved for me.

We all laughed. It was really great to relax together again. It was a great evening. We told our own stories about the events of the last few days. I didn't want it to end, but eventually Sophie kissed Colin on the cheek and said, "Time for bed honey, I missed you." And the way she said it, no red blooded male would have ignored. Colin said goodnight and quickly followed her out.

Natasha and Meg started to clear the coffee things, so I collected some glasses and followed them into the kitchen. Scruffy and Spike were waiting for us.

Natasha kissed me lightly on the cheek. "You get off to bed Alan, I will stay and help Meg clean up. I want to talk with her." I was ushered out of the room. I tried to protest, but to no avail.

Scruffy caught up with me in the corridor, and trotted along happily beside me. I was glad of the company. After the warmth and comradery of the evening I felt a little lost, and really didn't want to be alone tonight.

As soon as I opened the bedroom door Scruffy jumped up into the chair she had chosen as her bed. It was close to the window and across from the door, so she could keep an eye on things from there. I got ready for bed.

I placed the dragon scale pendant in the bedside drawer. I didn't want to risk intruding on George and his mate, at this time. They had waited a couple of hundred years or more, they would have a lot of - catching up to do!!

My thoughts as usual turned to Natasha. Nothing had been mentioned about her leaving the island at dinner, and I hoped she had changed her mind. I switched off the light and tried to sleep. The moon was full, light filtered in through the open blinds. I couldn't sleep.

Scruffy lifted her head from her chair and began to growl. I looked to the door and saw it open slowly. Scruffy grumbled a little more, and then turned her back to the bed.

Natasha stood in the doorway, the moon highlighting her hair, making it shine like silver. She closed the door and the robe she was wearing slipped silently to the floor. I hardly dare breathe. If this was a dream, I didn't want it to end. I pulled back the sheets and she slid in beside me.

We didn't have to talk. There were no words for how she made me feel and how her body felt against mine. Our bodies seemed to fit together perfectly and I knew in this moment, I had at last found what I had been searching for.

We lay in each other's arms, both tired but neither wanting to lose a moment to sleep. Together we watched as too quickly, the moon traced its path across the sky. Soon the first light of day crept silently into the room. With it came the chill reality of dawn.

I held her close, and she said the words I had been dreading, "I'm sorry Alan. I know this is hard for you to understand."

I held her to me and said quietly, "You don't have to say sorry to me. I know you have to go and I understand, just promise me one thing Natasha - come back to me ... please." I had never loved or needed anything or anyone as much as Natasha at this moment. In fact - I loved her enough to let her go. I understood so many things now, because of her, because of this island.

She kissed me. "I love you Alan. I think I've known it since the first time I saw you in your fab T- shirt and shorts." She laughed.

Oh god, I remembered her as a goddess emerging from the beautiful blue waters. She on the other hand remembered me in a terrible T- shirt and scruffy shorts.

Natasha reached down and pulled something from her robe on the floor. "Ben over heard me telling Meg about my trip, so he and Tina came up with these."

She handed me a gold pendant on a chain, and looking closer I could see it was a dolphin.

"I have one too," she said, holding out a second pendant.

I wasn't really hot on jewellery. "Very nice," I said, a little uncertainly.

Natasha laughed. "You should give them some credit. You unscrew the tail and there's a tracking device! If either of us gets into trouble we can activate them. Tina will be able to find us wherever we are. They thought it would stop you from worrying. Pretty neat ha?"

I laughed. "I could get to love that computer," I said as I fastened the pendant round my neck.

"Careful Alan, I think Tina already has a soft spot for you."

I made a face. Natasha laughed. I helped her fasten the clasp round her slender neck. It looked great.

Natasha leaned closer. "See," she whispered seductively in my ear, "When we are this close the dolphins join together to form a heart." Her lips brushed mine and she kissed me - oh so gently.

I pulled her to me. "I like the look of them better when they're joined."

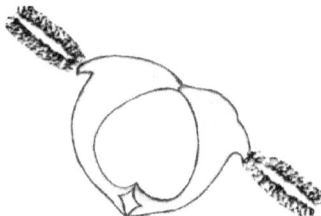

She was serious again now. "Alan, the sun is almost up, I must go. I want to say goodbye here. You're much better in bed than you are in the water."

In spite of the pain, I smiled. "Just a few moments more, I don't want to separate the dolphins just yet, they only just got together." She smiled and melted into my arms, and I understood for the first time in my life how important just a few moments could be. We savoured each precious second.

The time had come to let her go, and suddenly it didn't seem quite as easy as it had in my head. I kissed her and watched as she pulled on her robe.

Scruffy shuffled round in her chair to see what was going on, Natasha scratched her behind her ears, and she wagged her tail. "Scruffy you take good care of him until I return." As if in confirmation, Scruffy barked. Natasha smiled. "I will return Alan."

She closed the door and was gone. Scruffy whimpered, giving voice to my pain. Jumping down from her chair she joined me on the bed. As my tears fell, she licked them from my cheek. I stroked her and watched silently as the sun rose higher in the sky.

***

Scruffy and I walked out of the house and headed down to the beach. I just couldn't stay away. We stood on the sand for a long time watching the waves, listening to the strange sounds of the island all around. I wondered how many more heart stopping secrets this place held.

Scruffy bought me a stick and I threw it for her without much enthusiasm, but she persevered, and I found myself enjoying the game too.

She barked and headed back towards the house. "You're right of course girl. Let's go get breakfast." I followed her slowly thinking that as soon as I got the chance, I would explore this island paradise. This thought made me feel a little better. Spike ran out to meet us on our return and Scruffy greeted him, but she didn't leave my side.

"It's alright Scruffy I'm good, you go play with Spike. Hey but be good!"

I watched them play, happy in each other's company. I missed Natasha already. Spike ran up the stairs and with only a split seconds hesitation, Scruffy followed him. Who said 'you can't teach an old dog new tricks' - we were both, learning new things.

I sat down on the steps and looked out over the island. Who would guess it held so many secrets, and the key to all our futures.

Colin came and sat down beside me.

I sighed. "I miss her already."

He put his hand on my shoulder. "She'll be back. This is her home, your home now."

# CHANGE ISN'T ALWAYS A GOOD THING

I woke to the sensation of wet tongue in my ear, which under some circumstances might be a good way to start the day, however this little wet tongue belonged to Scruffy.

"You trying to tell me it's time to get up girl? Ok, just give me a minute."

Scruffy waited patiently while I got washed and dressed, then we made our way to the kitchen via the front steps. Scruffy needed to attend to her own call of nature. Whilst I waited for her at the top of the steps, I was startled by a scream from the woods. Maya ran towards me and all hell broke loose.

Scruffy started barking in alarm, which bought Spike rushing from the house to her rescue. It took me a moment to realize that it was Maya screaming. She wrapped her arms around me sobbing desperately. I held her and tried to comfort her, I could see scratches on her arm. Soon Colin and Sophie joined me at the foot of the steps, Meg wasn't far behind, and as usual Jack appeared silently out of nowhere.

Colin took in the scene. "What's happened, who screamed?" He was alarmed.

"It was Maya," I said still holding the sobbing child.

Meg was at my side. "Where's Toby? They went out together to gather some mushrooms for breakfast,"

She seemed concerned. It was the first time I'd seen a hint of panic in Meg's eyes, but just as soon as it appeared, it was gone and she took control again.

The look in Colin and Sophie's eye's made my stomach lurch. Meg had already taken Maya from my arms and was inspecting the scratches. In the same instant Colin glanced at Jack. "Go Jack, find him." The four words were said in almost a whisper, but the urgency was unmistakable. Before Colin finished the sentence, Jack's cloths were ripping from his body as he plunged forward. By the time he reached the trees he'd become the wolf, and noiselessly vanished into the bush.

The silence that remained was only interrupted by steady sobs from Maya. We were all stunned, even the two dogs stood frozen in time.

Colin seemed to wake from the spell first. "Sophie you look after Maya, tell Ben to get Tina searching the camera footage of the island. Find out what has happened, and see if they can locate Toby. Tell them what we suspect, so they know what to look for. Meg you're with me. We'll track Jack. He'll be able to retrace Maya's steps. Alan, contact George, he can pick you up from the beach." Colin hesitated for just a second adding, "Be very careful, if what we suspect is true, then this is not going to be the Toby we know. He will be confused and frightened. There is no telling, what he may do."

Sophie looked desperate. "I can help, I need to change. I could find him." Sophie pleaded, tears streaming down her face.

This time Meg spoke, not unkindly, but firmly, "No Sophie, you don't have the control yet, especially in an emotional state. Colin's right, the best thing you can do for Toby now is, take care of Maya."

My head was beginning to clear a little, "Maya screamed, I think I heard her say Toby's name!" In all the uproar, Maya had uttered her first words since we rescued her, and the moment had been lost in the commotion.

Meg nodded. "She's had a shock Alan. Let's deal with one thing, at a time."

She was right of course. Toby was out there somewhere. I concentrated on George knowing that if I could shut out everything around me, I could reach him. I focused. It was getting easier now and within seconds, I'd managed to communicate the urgency of the situation. I headed for the beach.

By the time I reached the sand, George was already circling above me. He swooped and landed just a few metres away, the force of his mighty wings sweeping up the sand, and blinding me for a moment. He lowered his great head and I realized, for the first time, that I was expected to climb on board. Stupid but it hadn't occurred to me, I would have to take to the air on the back of a dragon!

I'd ridden a horse once, not very successfully I might add, I hoped this wouldn't end the same way. But I'd no time to worry about lessons. I scrambled up the giant shoulder using his scales like steps, and threw myself down just in front of George's mighty wings. Instantly they started to beat - we were off.

All I could do was hang on. The wind stung my eyes. I could hear George's voice clearly in my mind. "Alan we must both try to focus on Toby. With our powers combined, we should be able to see him."

I tried to ignore the startled look on the faces of the birds as we swooped past, and I definitely tried hard not to look down. I closed my eyes. To start with all I could see was a sort of fog, then slowly this began to lift and I could see trees and rocks. I could see the mountain lions - they were both hunched and growling, shackles raised. They seemed to be looking right at me but no - not at me. It was Toby or whatever Toby was now. I knew where he was.

"That's it," I shouted against the wind, forgetting he could hear my thoughts. "George, he's outside the mountain lions cave. They're seeing him off, in no uncertain terms. We should hurry." There was no answer in my head - just a terrifying increase in speed. Suddenly we swooped making my stomach lurch, I was thankful I'd not had breakfast.

Soon we came in low over the cave. I knew Toby would have bitten off more than he could chew with the mountain lions. Whatever he'd become, would be no match for the mighty mountain lion and her mate. If they felt threatened, they may rip him to shreds. They could have no way of knowing who or what this strange thing was, that threatened them.

Suddenly I saw him. Slightly smaller than Jack and Sophie, but still pretty impressive, even from this height. George had seen him to. We swooped and landed on some rocks a few metres above him.

"There is no room for me to land down there," George said, lowering his head so that I could slide off.

I tried to steady myself, grateful to be back on the ground. "I'll go down and try to keep him here. I saw Jack a little way back, so the others won't be far behind. I'll keep him busy. If he moves off again, we could lose him in the dense jungle."

My mind was screaming at me, idiot! What the hell was I going to do?

George shared my concerns. "Be very careful Alan, there is little I can do from here."

" I'll go carefully, I may be able to get through to him, or at least stall him long enough, for the others to get here."

I made my way down the rocky slope, only a few feet from the bottom, I dislodged a couple of rocks. They betrayed me instantly, landing a few feet from Toby's crouching form.

He turned to face me. He was the size of a large Alsatian. His lips distorted back showing huge teeth, he growled and snarled. My legs felt like jelly, but, anyway there was no point in running, I didn't want to turn my back on him. I edged my way round and he began to circle me, but he seemed unsure of what to do. I wondered if maybe he thought I could be a threat to him, after all what idiot would come down to face him, without a plan!

Now he had his back to the rocks. I was thinking, if I could just keep him here - my foot caught on a tree root and I tripped. Either this startled him or it was the sign of weakness he'd been looking for. He cleared the ground between us in seconds. I automatically raised my hand in defence, and felt the searing pain as he bit into it. Just as suddenly, he let go.

I dropped to my knees. Behind me I heard a deep guttural growl. I could feel hot breath on the back of my neck. I didn't turn my head, I didn't have to - there was no mistaking that sound. Jack stalked carefully past me, Toby or what Toby had become, edged backwards. The change had not affected his wits, and he had the good sense to back away. Jack towered over him menacingly, but the wall of rock was behind him, he had no place to go. My plan had worked - not quite as well as I'd hoped. Toby was stuck up against the rocks. He still growled, but his tail was tucked between his back legs.

At this moment Colin and Meg burst through the trees at a run. Colin was out of breath, but I noticed Meg seemed strangely unstressed, as they moved in on either side of me, and behind Jack.

Colin held up his hand. "Keep down Alan, stay where you are," he whispered.

This was pretty lucky, because at this point, I didn't think my legs would have supported me anyway. I watched as Jack held his ground and Colin and Meg moved closer.

Colin spoke quietly to Jack who eased back slightly, but remained poised. I realized just how big Jack was in his wolf form. Toby had seemed impressive in a scary-large-dog sort of way, however Jack took fear to a whole new level. He was definitely horror movie material.

I had almost forgotten George until I heard his voice in my head, he wasn't talking to me.

"Sing to him Meg," he said gently. "Sing to him."

As the jungle held its breath around us, Meg began to sing, softly and hardly audible, but so soothing. I felt the pain easing in my hand, my body relaxed. The song was beautiful, not unlike the song I'd heard the dragons sing, so soft and light. I

197

felt my body drifting. I was finding it hard to keep my eyes open, and I could see that it was having an effect on the others too. Colin sat on a rock close by, even Jack had slumped back on his haunches. However, the effect on Toby was startling. He lay down and covering his black nose with his paws, almost instantly began to sleep, snoring gently.

Just as quickly, he began to change. His brown shaggy hair started to thin, his tail had gone and he was Toby again, lying naked, on the ground. I was fighting to keep my own eyes open. Abruptly the song stopped. Immediately the pain returned and my body tensed, as the thoughts began to race around my brain - unreasonable thoughts. Thoughts of the possible side effects, a bite might have.

I heard the beat of George's wings, as he took to the air again. Colin had wrapped Toby in his shirt and scooped him up easily, carrying him back the way they had come. Jack had already slipped away unheard, and only Meg seemed to have noticed me and my distress. "Alan, are you alright?" she said kneeling down next to me.

"He bit me," I managed to stammer, still lost in thoughts of old werewolf movies and horror films, fully expecting at any moment, to feel the urge to scratch behind my ear with my foot or sniff around trees.

Meg inspected the wound and smiled. "It's not so bad, just a couple of puncture wounds. I'll put some cream on when we get back. As for the thoughts that are rushing around that brain of yours, you can forget it! You have to inherit the genes, you cannot be turned. This isn't a scene from a movie, but if it were, you would be either a hero or a bloody idiot. I'm not sure which," she laughed. "Come on Alan, let's get back. We'll be needed at home."

She helped me up. I felt a bit foolish, but as we started the trek back I realized this was my chance to find out a little more about - the mysterious Meg. We followed a well-trodden pathway, and stopped outside the mountain lions cave. The female lion emerged and approached us. She lowered her head. Meg stroked her gently and spoke in a language I didn't understand, but the lioness seemed to be listening. I caught sight of the male lion just inside the cave. He watched us silently and after a few moments the lioness turned and walked back to join her mate.

Meg caught sight of my expression. "I thought I should explain what had happened, they would have been worried. Now we really must hurry, I want to be there when Toby wakes up." She led the way through the trees.

I tried to make conversation. "Do you still have family in Africa Meg?"

"Yes," she said without turning around.

Well that was a promising start. I tried for more, "Your father was a witch Doctor, was it he who taught you how to talk with the animals and the song that put Toby to sleep?" I ventured.

Without turning she answered, "My father is still a witch Doctor, the best witch Doctor in Africa, and yes Alan he taught me everything I know. He still gets great knowledge from my grandmother, and I, in turn, still learn from him. There is much that needs to be passed on." Meg spoke evenly. She was moving at speed through the trees, yet she didn't appear to be out of breath at all, she seemed unbelievably fit for a woman of her age. I was huffing and puffing, trying to keep pace with her.

Meg seemed to have so many years of experience and then other times she seemed so fit and youthful. The fact that her Grandmother was still passing on her knowledge to her father, could be a clue.

I tried another question, "How old is your Grandmother Meg?"

She glanced over her shoulder and smiled. "Grandmother is dead."

199

I felt embarrassed. "Oh I'm sorry, I misunderstood. I thought you said your father was still learning from your Grandmother."

Meg stopped. There was a glint in her eye. "You didn't misunderstand me Alan. Come, we are nearly at the house." She left me standing at the foot of the steps. Far from understanding more about Meg, she was becoming even more mysterious.

Ben met me. "I hear you're the hero of the day," he said slapping me on the back.

"I really didn't do much," I said honestly. "Where's Toby now?"

"Everyone's upstairs, although I think Maya is playing with the dogs out back."

I'd forgotten about Maya. "Is she ok? She seemed pretty upset before." Maya had actually uttered her first words and because of the panic, no one had really noticed.

Ben smiled. "She seems fine, go see for yourself. I'm heading back to the lab." Ben didn't seem fazed by the events of the morning. I guess these people were used to dealing with the extra ordinary. I made my way to the kitchen and out the back door, where sure enough, Maya was throwing the tennis ball for the dogs. She was laughing and apart from the bandage on her arm, she seemed fine. I sat and watched them play. I wondered what impact this new event would have on things. I didn't have time to wonder for long, Ben burst through the kitchen door, almost over shooting the balcony.

He was holding up a photograph. "Tina has found something," he shouted.

I couldn't make out what the picture was of, but Ben looked pleased. "I think you're going to enjoy this one Alan, its right up your alley." Without another word he turned, and rushed back into the house, with the dogs hot on his heels, barking enthusiastically. They didn't know what was going on, but they were enjoying the game anyway. Maya came and sat next to me on the steps. She looked up at me and smiled.

Well one thing was certain, there wasn't going to be much time to lick my wounds. I smiled back at Maya. This was my life now. I should be running for the hills but instead I was excited. Where were we going and what would we find? Well, there would be only one way to find out. The hunt was on.

# ANOTHER ADVENTURE

A couple of days had past, since the incident with Toby. I was passing my time exploring the Island. The others were making plans.

Pricilla eyed me with her usual suspicion. I un-wrapped the blueberry pancakes Meg had given me earlier. No one on the island, large or small, was immune to the seductive powers of Meg's blueberry pancakes, including me!

I had grown quite fond of this enormous bird. At over two meters high she was an impressive sight. Colin confirmed my initial suspicions, that she was indeed a moa - extinct for many years, from her home, New Zealand. Still here she was, alive and well.

She was one of many on the island. Despite, their large size the others managed to stay well out of the way. I suppose having been extinct once they were presumably keen not to go down that road again.

Pricilla bent her long neck and took the pancakes I offered one at a time, she was surprisingly gentle. In fact I had found out that moa's were not the only birds on the Island, that you would normally expect to find in a museum. 'Dead as a Dodo' was not an expression I would be using anymore!

***

Things had thankfully calmed down after the resent turn of events and I do mean turn. Life had returned to – normal, not a word that came easily to me anymore. Colin, Ben and Tina had locked themselves in the lab. They were busy researching the new job.

I left Priscilla, very disappointed that the pancake supply had run out, and walked back to my room - narrowly avoiding a couple of small bright green lizards with amazingly blue tongues, squabbling on the path. It would have been sad for them to have been saved from extinction, only to find themselves squashed on the sole of my shoe.

Scruffy stretched in her chair. She had been sunning herself. For a few seconds she seemed caught in a difficult dilemma - whether to be cross with me for leaving her behind, or to forgive me. The indecision didn't last for long. She bounded forwards wagging her tail, greeting me enthusiastically. All was forgiven.

*** 

There was a light knock at the door. Scruffy jumped down and rushed to meet Spike, who pushed his way in as the door opened. The two dogs leapt and tumbled out into the corridor, past Colin. "Hey you two watch it. Hi Alan Sorry! I didn't mean to disturb you."

Colin hesitated for a second in the door way. His usual confident smile had deserted him, for the moment. The past couple of days had been difficult, to say the least. His teenage son was going through the change and in this family that meant far more than acne and mood swings.

"It's alright Colin what's up?"

"Meg has lunch ready, but I wanted a word with you, in private before we join the others Alan."

I was slightly distracted, the smell of cooking drifted in from the corridor. "What did you want to talk to me about? It's not Toby?"

I heard both dog's heading off, and knew they would be making a bee line to the kitchen, where Meg would have a meal ready for them. I felt my mouth begin to water and my stomach rumble as the smell's drifted into the room.

"No Alan, Toby is doing just fine thank you."

Colin sat on the bed. I could see he had something on his mind. "You miss her?" he said.

It was a statement not a question, he already knew the answer. It was no secret, I felt lost since Natasha left.

Colin continued, "We're almost ready to go, are you going to be alright Alan? It can get tough out there. I need to know you can cope, our lives could depend on it. We would think no less of you if you wanted to sit this one out."

I shook my head. "I appreciate your concerns Colin, but this is just what I need to take my mind off things. We all miss Natasha, but she's got to find the truth. I know how important that is," - I thought of my father, missing presumed dead. It was a terrible word presumed, it didn't give closure, it didn't give anything.

"Do we have an idea of where we're going yet?"

Colin laughed. "As usual we're working on hearsay and rumours, but thanks to Tina we have a good idea of where to start, as for what we might find - well sort of. Have your dreams given you any clues?"

I shrugged. "Sorry Colin, not much really. I seem to be in a forest, it's cold, bloody cold and something is there, watching me. I can feel it - but that's all." I shuddered, I was still finding it hard to interpret the visions I got. Meg assured me that in time things should become clearer.

He shrugged. "Never mind, let's eat. We can review the information Tina and Ben have gathered, in the lab afterwards." His confident smile had returned.

"Ok Colin, give me a minute and I'll meet you in the dining room, the smell of Meg's cooking is working its magic on my stomach."

He laughed. "Great see you there, don't be too long though as Toby and Maya seem to be competing at the moment to see who has the largest appetite. They seem to have become even closer since......" He hesitated. "They have become good friends, who would have guessed it; Toby seems to enjoy having a younger sister to look after."

So we would soon be off - again on an adventure, it wouldn't be the same without Natasha. I reached for the dolphin pendant around my neck and closed my eyes, somehow knowing she wore the matching half made her seem closer.

I had to admit there was that mounting feeling of excitement and curiosity I had always experienced before the hunt. My work as a guide for hunting parties seemed like a life time ago now. I was happy to use my searching skills in a completely different way, to ensure the survival of the things we sort not their destruction.

The idea of bringing things back alive rather than as a trophy for someone's wall, seemed a more useful way to spend my life.

***

I left my room and headed off down the corridor, I could hear raised voices as I neared the dining room.

"Alan, can you tell dad I'm not a child any more. I bet your parents let you do loads of things when you were 14?" Toby pleaded.

I had obviously walked in on the eternal parental dilemma, how much protection can you give a growing boy? Too much and you alienate them, not enough and you could lose them forever. In Toby's case I could understand Colin not wanting to let him out of his sight, this boy had the ability to change into something - far more challenging than an awkward teenager.

"Sorry Toby, I spent my teens in a very strict boarding school not much room for adventure there." In fact that was a little white lie, it had been strict but teenage boys will always find a way to break the rules. I took my seat.

"Good evening Alan is everything alright?" Sophie seemed concerned. They had probably all been talking about how I was managing without Natasha. Was it that obvious that I had totally lost my heart to her? I gave them all - my best smile.

"Good evening all, yes I'm really good. I can't wait to find out where we're off to next."

Toby was still keen to make a point, "I could help. You'll be one short without Natasha."

It wasn't hard to see that Colin wasn't going to change his mind.

"Now that really is enough, let's eat." Colin's tone finished the argument.

Maya was seated next to Toby she seemed to be enjoying the entertainment, I smiled and winked at her, she returned my smile. Maya was growing in confidence daily, since her rescue. Even Toby changing into a werewolf before her very eyes had hardly set her back at all. Children could be so resilient. But like the rest of us Maya was a little out of the ordinary! Meg had taken on the role of nanny and teacher, whatever she was doing with the girl was working, she looked so much better.

"No Ben or Jack this evening," I ventured.

Colin smiled. "Jack is doing his usual turn around the island, and Ben, ha! there was no way I could get him out of the lab today. Meg took him a tray. We'll join him and Tina after we've eaten."

Everyone concentrated on the job of eating, Meg really was a fantastic cook. After the plates were cleared Meg took a smiling Maya and a grumbling Toby off to study.

Sophie kissed Colin lightly, "I'll see you later honey, I promised I'd help Maya with her reading."

Colin watched them go. You could tell he loved his family very much, despite their differences or maybe because of them their relationship seemed strong.

"Well, shall we go and find out what Ben and Tina have turned up?" Colin led the way down to the lab. On the way we passed the kitchen and two very happy dogs tucking into their dinner, across from them two happy cats at their bowls. Looking at them now it was hard to believe these were the same tiny kittens Jack had rescued, they were growing so fast.

The door to the lab opened and Tina's smooth voice greeted us.

"Hello Colin, hello Alan so nice to see you again, I had hoped to see a little more of you Alan, now that you are less – distracted."

Ben looked a little embarrassed. "Tina that's enough, concentrate on the job at hand please."

I always had an uncomfortable and unreasonable feeling that Tina was flirting with me; silly she was after all just - a machine!

We took up our seats in front of the monitors.

"Ok what have you two managed to dig up," Colin said, helping himself to a cup of coffee from the pot Meg must have left earlier. I did likewise, experience told me it could be a long night.

Ben cleared his throat, "Ok as usual a lot of the photographs and first-hand accounts can be dismissed as fabricated or the product of too much beer and an over active imagination. However in these three cases the subject is most definitely real and by doing a size comparison with back ground objects we can estimate the creature to be approximately two metres from tail to nose." Ben paused for effect.

I stared at the screen in front of me. "I can't really make out what we're looking at here, everything looks white to me."

Ben seemed deflated but then rallied, "Sorry I'll get Tina to isolate the subject, Tina. Do your best will you." Ben really enjoyed showing off Tina's skills.

"Of course Ben, the subject is always well camouflaged. In these photographs the subject is white on a background of snow, but if I change the colour of the snow slightly leaving the object in question white you should be able to make out an image on each of the three shots."

The screens altered slightly and yes there it was. "Oh my god!" I gasped, "That thing looks huge, is it what I think it is? It looks like some sort of pure white wolf."

Ben nodded. "The first hand reports of sightings that we feel could be trusted, seem to suggest a very large animal indeed, but perhaps more interestingly for us, they also suggest that whatever it is, does not always travel on all fours, but has more recently been seen upright!"

The room went silent for a moment as this latest revelation soaked in. This thing could be another Jack or Toby.

Colin nodded, "Where is it Tina? Do you have a location for us?"

The lights flashed around us. "I believe so Colin, it is in a remote mountainous area, until recently unheard of, however a new ski field is being developed and the area is likely to become more popular. The sightings are getting more regular, people are afraid. Rumours abound of a monster up in the mountains randomly killing men, women, and children. Demand is growing to hunt it down and kill it, for the sake of tourism - would you believe!"

Colin shook his head. "I take it, that as usual none of these reports are proven?" he said dryly.

"You are correct in your assumption. There no reports of missing humans. There have however been several reports of large deer and bear carcasses discovered half eaten, as if something has been disturbed. This tends to suggest that whatever it is, is avoiding human contact, rather than seeking it out. However, I would conclude that it is only a matter of time," Tina reported.

Ben helped himself to another coffee. "This sounds as if it's right up Jacks alley."

Colin nodded thoughtfully, "Maybe - but I want you and Tina2 on this one as well Ben, with Alan's help of course."

Ben nearly choked on his coffee, spilling it down his shirt. "What," he spluttered. "But it's cold up there. You know I hate the cold, besides who's going to keep an eye on things here?"

Colin simply smiled. "Mind you don't spill your coffee on Tina Ben. I understand your concerns; however, I think Sophie, Meg and two dragons will be able to handle things, besides it's time you got out of this lab and saw a bit of the world." It was obvious to me Colin had already made up his mind.

Ben wiped the coffee up with his sleeve. "Great, you could have picked somewhere warm at least," Ben grumbled.

This comment made Colin laugh. "Hey don't blame me. You and Tina do the research not me. It's going to take a couple of days to organize papers and flights, but I want you ready to leave with us Ben."

I felt a little uneasy, but unlike Ben I was in fact keen to get on with things, I'd seen parts of this forest in my dreams, so I felt confident that once we were there I would be able to get us close to the animal in the photos. The rest might have to be up to Jack.

Colin looked at his watch. "Right, it's getting late, let's call it a day. Thank you Tina." Colin headed for the door leaving Ben grumbling behind him. I said good bye to Ben and of course Tina.

I caught Colin up as he headed back upstairs. "Have you heard anything from Natasha?" I asked hopefully.

"No, sorry Alan and I don't really expect to. Natasha will return when she's found her answers, besides if she need's any help she'll activate the transmitter Ben put in the pendant, then and only then should we go looking for her. You have to trust me on this one Alan. I have known her since we were children, this is something she has to do, but she will come home."

I just nodded. I knew he was right again. I touched the dolphin pendant round my neck. As I passed the kitchen I picked up Scruffy who was asleep on a rug next to Spike.

"Say goodnight Scruffy." She gave a little yap to Spike as I carried her off to our room. I hadn't realized it was so late. I got myself ready for bed and Scruffy settled herself in her chair.

"Goodnight Scruffy," I said as I switched off the light.

I closed my eyes and tried to shut out the memory of the huge pure white wolf that, in a couple of days we would go in search of. Maybe it would be a good idea to take some of Meg's blueberry pancakes!

***

I woke to a polite but insistent bark from Scruffy. "You trying to tell me it's time to get up girl?"

Scruffy jumped up and down to indicate my training was going well. "Ok just give me a minute and we'll go get some breakfast."

Scruffy waited patiently whilst I got washed and dressed, then we made our way to the kitchen via the front steps so that Scruffy could attend to her usual call of nature. I made my way to the kitchen and out the back door.

Maya was throwing the tennis ball for Spike. Scruffy crashed the party. I laughed as the two dogs competed for the prize. Spike being the perfect gentleman let Scruffy win every now and then. I doubt she had ever seen a tennis ball before, yet she collected it like treasure presenting it triumphantly to Maya.

Maya heard my laugh and turned to greet me. "Ouch," she said indicating my hand, it still had a bandage from the bite I'd received from Toby.

I pointed to her arm, the scratches she had received that day had all but healed. "Ouch," I said in reply.

She touched my bandage, "Toby a naughty boy."

I smiled, "Yes a very naughty boy." After watching the dogs getting all the exercise I was ready for breakfast. Maya touched my hand, and almost instantly I knew what I needed - ice cream. I headed back inside but as I opened the freezer door the cold air hit me - Maya...!

I made my way back out to the yard, Maya tried her best to look innocently everywhere but at me. Both dogs now sat relaxing lazily in the early morning sun.

"Maya what have you been told about getting into people's minds without their permission?" I scolded.

Maya looked down at her hands, "But this time," I continued, "I think you're probably right, I think we all need ice cream for breakfast, chocolate and strawberry for me I think, what about you?" I watched as the smile crept back across her little face, even the dogs thought this was the perfect treat after all that running around. We all headed in for ice cream, of all things - for breakfast - it was fantastic!

The two cats appeared from nowhere as soon as I started dishing up, so it seemed only fair to put a little down for them too.

When we'd all but licked our dishes, apart from the dogs and cats, they'd licked their bowls so clean I was afraid the pattern would have faded, I suggested to Maya that we might go for a walk along the beach.

It was early and the house was still quiet. We made our way out of the house and down the small pathway cut through the thick jungle that engulfed the house. Both dogs had thought a walk sounded like the perfect way to work off their ice cream and had joined us, leading the way happily.

Once on the sand, Maya began to run and skip, enjoying the early morning sunshine, the dogs played the game of dodge the waves.

I found myself relaxing and laughing.

As we headed for home, I asked Maya if she remembered her parents.

"The sea took them," she said simply, with no real show of emotion.

I was surprised. "How do you know that Maya," I asked. I wanted to find out more about her past, I was sure she was in some way linked to Natasha, or at least Natasha's mother. I needed to find out the connection between Maya and Natasha's missing parents.

"Nana told me that when I was a baby, the lady of the sea saved me, and bought me to her, I don't remember." She laughed. " But Nana used to warn me, when I was naughty, that she would throw me back, if I didn't behave."

Maya ran ahead, chasing the dogs and laughing.

The Lady of the sea, could this have been Natasha's mother?

Perhaps the child had been on a boat with her parents, it may have hit bad weather and gone down, Natasha's mother could have taken pity on the baby, perhaps even missing and remembering her own child. There was of course no proof of any of this, but it did fit the few facts I had.

We'd reached the house, Meg came out to greet us. "I was beginning to wonder where you four had gotten to, I noticed you had made your own breakfasts," she said with a wry smile.

I felt like a bad uncle, "I thought we needed a treat this morning Meg. Sorry."

Meg laughed. "Just so long as it was your idea Alan," she gave Maya a sidelong glance. Somehow Meg always seemed to know what went on, even when she was busy somewhere else.

Maya didn't notice, or pretended not to understand. "Can I go see Toby now Meg - Pleeeese.."

They had become firm friends, the fact that Toby had turned into a wolf before her very eyes only a few days earlier, hadn't fazed her at all.

I looked at Meg. "How is Toby doing?"

She smiled. "Toby will be just fine, he will adapt well, the change his body is going through takes a lot of energy, besides he is a teenager they like to sleep in. I will keep an eye on him, and when he is strong enough he will learn control. We all need a little self-control Alan."

She laughed, "Ice cream for breakfast ha!"

\*\*\*

I made my way to the lab. As I entered I almost fell over Tina2, who was hovering just inside the door, the small silver sphere easily glided up and out of my way.

"Sorry Tina," I said automatically and caught sight of Ben's smirk out of the corner of my eye.

Lights flashed around the room. "It's quite alright Alan."

I turned my attention to Colin who was looking at the main console. "Hi Colin, how are we doing?"

He smiled and seemed pretty relaxed. I couldn't believe he was taking this thing with Toby's so well.

"Are you sure you can leave at the moment, perhaps you should let us handle this one," I said trying to sound confident, praying desperately that he wouldn't agree with me. What the hell was I saying!

"I appreciate the thought Alan, but honestly I'll be better out of the way, Meg and Sophie have this one covered, after all we have been expecting something like this to happen for a while. In a way it's something of a relief, besides Toby will be pleased."

This amazed me. "Pleased," I gasped. "I don't understand, your saying he was looking forward to this?" I found it hard to believe turning into a wolf was something you looked forward to, maybe like the prom or your first kiss.

Colin sighed. "Come off it Alan, you've seen Jack. In the eyes of a teenage boy, having that sort of power, body and good looks beats language skills hands down." Colin seemed a little hurt, I knew what he meant, you always felt slightly inadequate in the presents of Jack. But still - a wolf!

I tried to think of something helpful to say. "I think Toby loves you very much, I'm sure he will realize that physical strength isn't everything, without you and your strength of character this island and its inhabitants wouldn't survive for very long." I was fairly pleased with my speech, Colin just shrugged.

"Well let's see if my strength of character can bring another lost soul home shall we.

Tina, how are we doing for location?"

Like me Colin really needed to take his mind off of personal matters at the moment, and it looked like we had the perfect distraction.

Tina sounded pretty pleased with herself. "I have narrowed our search to a small range of mountains, however the area is around a hundred square miles. I would suggest you start in a small village at the foot of one of said mountains, where I can confirm a real sighting of our target. I believe Alan can put his seeker powers to good use and will be able to narrow the search, once in place."

Photographs and maps began to appear on the screens in front of us.

I felt nervous whenever anyone referred to my powers, up until a few weeks ago I'd no idea I was any different to everyone else. I knew I should be pleased to find out I had powers, but deep down I still had this feeling it was all a big mistake and I would let everyone down. When Natasha had been around I found it easier to believe in myself but without her, I felt the old doubts creeping in.

Colin's voice interrupted my troubled thoughts. "That's good work Tina, I'll put a flight plan together and we will be on our way tomorrow morning. We'll have to stop on the main land and pick up some supplies, but if I radio ahead to my people there, they can have everything we need at the airport and it will just be a matter of loading up. Right people, let's get some lunch. Some of us - didn't get ice cream for breakfast." He smiled.

Were there no secrets in this place? We headed upstairs leaving Ben and Tina making a list of the things we would need. Tina2 followed me to the door and for a moment I thought the little silver sphere wanted to come too, I must have imagined it but she seemed disappointed when Ben called her back.

# I SPY

Lunch was a quiet affair, only myself, Colin, Meg and Maya, and of course the two dogs. Who waited patiently, beneath the table for their turn to be fed. Meg had taken a tray to Sophie. Toby wasn't feeling himself (no pun intended) so she felt happier in Toby s room, where she could keep an eye on him. He seemed to want to sleep, most of the time, lately. In my experience, that seemed like pretty normal, teenage behaviour. Meg had reassured us all, that everything would be fine.

Now that Maya had found her voice, there seemed to be no stopping her, it was great that she seemed recovered, but her constant questions were beginning to wear us all down.

As usual Meg came to our rescue, and suggested that she and Maya should go into the play room, to make a card, or picture, for Toby, to help cheer him up when he awoke.

Colin headed off too. "I'm going to check on Toby, and see how Sophie's holding up, I'll see you at dinner Alan."

I decided to go see George and Goldie, to give them an update. Even though I knew they would probably already know what was going on. I looked for Scruffy and Spike and found them lazing in the back yard, a walk seemed to be furthest from their minds, so I didn't disturb them. In truth, I really wanted to walk alone.

I took the now familiar path through the thick trees and headed for the centre of the island, I relaxed and trusted my instinct, in my mind's eye I could picture the two dragons, Goldie just inside the cave entrance and George just by the lake. His huge tail trailing backwards and forwards lazily in the water, making little ripples. They seemed so comfortable in each other's company. After far too many years spent alone, now they had each other. With that thought my mind of course turned to

Natasha, why could I see the dragons but not her? God knows I wanted to so badly.

I entered the clearing at the edge of the lake and wasn't surprised to see the scene before me, as I'd envisioned.

"Good afternoon Alan, we have been expecting you." George's voice sounded in my head.

"You have." I wasn't sure why this surprised me, if I could see them it was obvious that they would be able to see me.

Goldie joined George on the edge of the lake, she swished her tail through the water splashing him playfully, there was a sound like music in my head, and it took me a moment to realize that they were laughing. I relaxed a little.

"You came to ask us something Alan?" George prompted.

"I came to tell you that Meg say's Toby will be fine," I lied.

"And......?" George said patiently.

"I need to see Natasha, I need to know she's alright." The words gushed out, "I thought you could help me, I've tried but I can't find her."

"Has it occurred to you Alan that the reason you cannot see Natasha is because she does not want to be found?" Goldie questioned.

That thought hadn't occurred to me and I pushed it aside without consideration. "Please I just have to know she's ok. If we combined our thoughts, I know we could find her," I pleaded. Even if Goldie was right, I had to see her, if only for a moment.

"Come sit with us," George said with a sigh. "We will try."

I almost tripped over, as I rushed to join the two dragons. "What do we do? How do we do this, do I have to drink something?" I rambled, remembering the potion Meg had made me drink once to help me focus.

George looked a little bemused. "Alan you may drink something, if that is what you want, but all you really need to do is try to be calm, focus your thoughts. Sit between us and place a hand on Goldie's shoulder and a hand on mine. Think of Natasha and let your mind picture her."

I settled myself between the two dragons, placing one hand on each. After just a few moments, my hands began to tingle.

It was totally idiotic, I couldn't focus my mind, for days I hadn't been able to think of anything else, yet now, when I needed to focus on Natasha, my mind kept drifting off. I could see mountains. I could even hear the sound of wolves, howling through an icy cold wind and the snow, lots of snow. I shivered.

"Alan, picture her face, feel her with your heart." George's voice was soft and patient, breaking through my thoughts. I tried again, this time I remembered our last night together and the emotions flooded back. I could almost feel the warmth of her body against mine, her warm breath against my cheek. Instantly I was under water - deep under water. It was the strangest feeling and a little unnerving, I moved easily through the water. Tiny fish darted here and there. They seemed to be cleaning the larger fish that floated by, lazily on the current. Like clients in a spa.

Ribbons of colourful fish moved as one, soaring and diving as if through the air, then - sudden darkness, but wait not totally dark. Looking up, I could make out tiny pin points of light overhead, like thousands of small stars in the night sky. I tried to make sense of what I was seeing, it took a moment to realize, I was in a cave, a sort of underwater tunnel, under the ocean. I began to feel the walls closing in on me. I tried to calm my thoughts. Panic was beginning to creep in. This felt so real. My mind was screaming at me, YOU DO KNOW, YOU CAN'T BREATH UNDER WATER! Just when I thought my lungs would burst, I broke through the surface, spluttering and gasping for air.

I looked around. I was in a large cave. Again on the ceiling, tiny pin points of light, some sort of glow worm or algae perhaps. It gave the scene an eerie half-light, casting strange shadows around the huge cavern.

The cave was divided into smaller areas, that looked a little like rooms or small houses, they were linked by pools of water. I drifted over to one of the houses, to take a closer look. It was a room, with a hole cut out of the rock, as I looked out through the window, my heart skipped a beat, it was Natasha. She sat with her back to me, but I would recognize her anywhere. She had a small box on her lap and she was studying something.

I drifted closer, straight through the wall. My mind was screaming at me again, "You can't do that!" However, it seemed that I could and had. I was close enough to look over Natasha's shoulder. The box on her lap was open, and full of photographs. Natasha had several spread out in front of her. One I recognized, it was a picture Natasha kept in a water proof pouch at her waist, next to the large knife that always worried me slightly. Two of the pictures from the box were very similar, images of Natasha as a small child, standing with her mother and father outside her Grandmother's house. They looked like any normal family.

I stood transfixed, a small drop of water splashed onto one of the pictures, maybe from the damp roof of the cave, or perhaps - Natasha was crying - oh god! I wanted so much to hold her to me, to tell her it would be alright. I reached out towards her- a sound made me glance back, as soon as I turned my head, the spell was broken. I was being pulled back at high speed. The last thing I saw was Natasha, looking right at me. Was it possible she could have seen me? Did she know I'd been spying on her?

The rest was a blur as I sped backwards retracing my path. Now the sound I could hear was the lake, splashing up against the shore, as Goldie's tail made waves in the otherwise still water in front of us.

The sound, now clear and close by. Scruffy and Spike were barking at us from the edge of the forest.

My head spun I felt a little sick and my heart ached, far from feeling better for seeing Natasha upset and suddenly very angry.

"Get away from me bad girl," I shouted, as Scruffy and Spike came towards us wagging their tails. Both dogs stopped short, the impact on Scruffy was instant and heart wrenching, she let out a pitiful whine and turned on her heels, running back into the trees her tail between her legs. Spike stood his ground but growled slightly under his breath.

What had I done? It was the first time I'd raised my voice to the little dog and all she'd done was try to find me and greet me the only way she knew how.

"Spike," I pleaded, tears now falling freely. "Go find her bring her back, tell her I'm so sorry." I knew Spike would understand every word I said. He turned and raced into the trees.

I slumped to the ground. I felt I'd betrayed my two closest friends, the anger had subsided leaving only the pain and a feeling of emptiness and loneliness.

George sighed. "We tried to tell you not to interfere."

"I know. She seemed so sad, did she see me? Could she have known I was watching her?" I asked in a whisper I felt guilty. Not only had I been spying on Natasha but I'd shouted at my best friend, suddenly I felt as though I'd lost everything.

"Alan!" Goldie's voice had lost its gentle tone. "Don't just sit there feeling sorry for yourself. You can put this right, go find your friend and make it right." Her tone mellowed a little as she added, "Then I will tell you all that I know of the Ocean People."

I pulled myself together, she was right. I followed Spike into the forest. I didn't have to go far Spike had already found Scruffy and was gently but firmly pushing her back towards the clearing and the lake.

I sat down and called to her. "Scruffy come here girl." She looked at me with those big brown eyes that until one stupid moment ago had been so loving and trusting, now there was a hint of doubt in them. Suddenly it was just too much to bear, I hung my head and cried.

Scruffy was at my side again, licking the tears from my face, her little tail wagging. I picked her up and held her to me, scratching behind her ears. Spike barked and jumped up and down. I think he was pleased that things had returned to normal.

We sat for a while just happy in each other's company, the simple act of stroking her scruffy fur made me feel so much better. I made a vow in my head not to take my anger or pain out on the ones who loved and trusted me.

Eventually I got up still holding the little dog close in my arms. We made our way back to the clearing. The two dragons still sat side by side on the edge of the lake. Spike had joined them and taken up his favourite position on George's shoulders, looking down on us and the world.

I carried Scruffy over to sit with the two dragons.

"Will you tell me what you know about the Ocean people Goldie?" I said making myself as comfortable as I could on the rocks.

"Yes Alan, although I fear it is not as much as you would like to know.

A long time ago there were many Ocean people and many under water cities, they swam the oceans of the world. They hunted, with the Dolphins, whom they had an affinity. Gradually the oceans got busier.

The Land People who had already taken over much of the world, began to hunt the sea's, not with a rod and line as in the past but with huge net's, dragging in and killing anything in their path. Dolphins and Ocean people were caught in the nets too, but the people of the ocean's always carried their knives to cut themselves free. They tried to hamper the slaughter in any way they could, cutting net's even luring ships onto the rock.

As you have noticed they are a beautiful people, the women would sit on the rock's calling to the men on the ship luring them into the dangerous waters. But sadly it was a battle they could not win, too many ships, too many men, so much killing......"

Goldie stopped I looked up into her huge eye's and saw the diamonds glisten in the sunlight. I could only imagine the things she had witnessed over the years. I felt ashamed, ashamed for the killing, for the wars of the past, for the wasted lives, not least for my past, for the animals I'd killed in the name of sport and the trophies I'd helped collect.

I wanted to say something but there were no words to make these things right.

George entwined his tail around her, to comfort her.

Goldie moved a little closer to him as if for reassurance and continued the story.

"Ocean people retreated to more isolated waters and built their cities deeper and deeper to try to avoid contact, but more and young woman and men decided to take their chances on the land. As you have seen they can live comfortably on the land as long as they are never too far from the Ocean.

However, they did not realize that too long out of the water and their bodies adapt so well to the land, they can never go back. Some tried to return to the Ocean, disenchanted with your world, missing their people. They walked out into the ocean and drowned in the water, that once had given them life."

"I don't understand," I interrupted. "Natasha seems to live on land and in the Ocean with ease."

Goldie sighed, "Yes but she walks a tight rope. She must live as much in the Ocean as out of it. It's a balance, too much land and she is trapped there, too much sea and she may not return to the land. Sooner or later she will be forced to choose."

I had known Natasha struggled with our relationship believing it was not meant to be, only now could I begin to understand why. I had to believe we would find a way, a way in which, we could both be ourselves.

Spike barked and Scruffy jumped down from my lap.

"You're right Spike. You must all be getting back," George said, translating dog speak for me. "Alan you must not dwell on things too much, there is work to be done. Love will find a way."

I saw the dragon's eyes meet and understood what he meant - they had found each other, against all the odds. If they could find happiness, then there had to be a chance for Natasha and I.

I said my goodbyes and Spike lead the way back to the house, Scruffy stayed close on the walk back.

Once back in the house, I headed for my room to shower and change. Scruffy seemed torn between following Spike to the kitchen - or staying with me. I was touched when her loyalty to me won over and she accompanied me to my room. She sat patiently on her chair, whilst I got ready for dinner. She didn't have to wait long. I made it a very quick shower. The smell of Meg's cooking was sneaking under the door and into the room.

Soon we were heading back along the corridor towards the kitchen. I was surprised to bump into Ben. "Hi Ben, I didn't expect to see you out of the lab this close to a mission - washed and changed too." I realized too late, that probably sounded very rude. I needn't have worried though, Ben didn't seem to notice the comment, he looked preoccupied.

He was muttering under his breath, "I think Colin has it in for me," he grumbled.

"He said I needed to mix more, he said I was missing out. I ask you, what could I possibly be missing out on, I have everything I need here."

I knew exactly what Colin meant, but thought it better not to get involved.

"Is everything ready for the trip?" I tried changing the subject hoping this would lift his mood. I was wrong.

"Yes, but why I have to come is a mystery to me. You, Colin and Jack would have it covered I'm sure. I'll just be in the way besides, I hate the cold," he moaned.

"Look Ben, I'm sure Colin has his reasons." I gave up. We were at the kitchen door now and Scruffy ran in to meet Spike, they took up their places under the kitchen table to wait for their dinner.

Ben and I headed on into the dining room, I was surprised but pleased to see Toby seated next to Maya, even Jack was here. He looked a little uncomfortable at the table. It was obvious the whole family was here to show support for Toby after his ordeal.

Colin nodded at Toby, who stood and approached me awkwardly. "I wanted to apologize for my behaviour and to say thank you Alan, I don't remember much about what happened but Dad said, that without your help things could have been – well – bad."

Toby looking down at my injured hand added "Oh and sorry I bit you."

I had to laugh it sounded so strange. "It's alright Toby, I've no doubt you will have the best teachers to help you make the most of the gift you have." We took our places at the table. Even Meg had joined us this evening.

It seemed like an ordinary family meal, but as we tucked into the delicious food it occurred to me that in actual fact the word ordinary could not be used to describe any one on this island, let alone at this table.

Maya made most of the conversation having found her voice; she was certainly not going to lose it again in a hurry. After a while Sophie asked Maya to help her and Meg with the dishes, Maya grumbled a little (Toby's attitude was rubbing off on her) but she helped just the same. The rest of us including Toby headed for the lounge.

There were a lot of questions I wanted to ask about Toby, and what happened now. I found it hard to believe he would be going back to the mainland on his own any more for school, at least not until he had a little self-control. There was no time for questions because Colin was straight into the job at hand.

"Right, everything is set for tomorrow." He handed out some pictures and a map. "This is where we're headed, it's going to be cold, but I have extra cloths and Ski gear ordered. It will be ready for us when we get to the main land. We fly out in the morning. We'll refuel and collect our papers there too.

The team will be Myself, Alan, Jack, Ben and Tina2."

I heard Toby groan beside me, Colin obviously heard it too. "Toby you will be in charge with the rest of us gone. I will need you to keep an eye on everything here, we'll need to be in constant contact."

This seemed to make Toby feel a little better, it certainly made me feel better. The thought of taking Toby with us, in his present state, would have made me very nervous. It was bad enough coming to terms with Jack, who turned into a wolf at the drop of a hat, but at least he could be relied upon and was not likely to take a chunk out of you, when you least expected it.

"I still don't see why you need me there," Ben groaned. He was still trying to get out of the trip.

"You're going to be flying the plane Ben, I know you can fly it remotely, but if we encounter bad weather up in the mountains it could get rough and although I hate to admit it you are a better pilot than me. I need you there Ben, and that's the end of it." Colin went over to talk to Toby.

Ben seemed to accept the situation at long last. Secretly I think he was flattered by Colin's comments. That made me smile, Colin was one smart cookie he knew how to get the best out of all of us.

Toby said goodnight and went off to bed. Ben muttered something about going to the lab, it was only then I noticed Jack had already slipped away. For someone so noticeable, Jack seemed to be able to appear and disappear with such ease. Colin handed me a brandy and we sat in silence both lost in our own thoughts.

"How were George and Goldie today," Colin said, warming his brandy glass in his hands. I felt guilty and embarrassed, but not surprised that Colin already knew what I'd been up to.

"George told you," I said sipping my brandy.

"He was worried about you, Natasha will be alright you know, she's a lot stronger than she seems, you really must let her find her own way Alan."

I sighed. "I just needed to see her."

We sat looking out over the island, in the distance a wolf howled, Jack was out there doing his rounds.

"Will Toby be alright? We could maybe put this trip off for a few days," I said remembering how he must be feeling.

Colin looked into his brandy perhaps looking for the answer there, "He'll be fine, he's young, Meg will teach him a little self-control and before you know it he'll be hunting the islands with Jack."

I couldn't help but notice a hint of sadness in Colin's voice. Toby would now have far more in common with Jack than with his own father. We finished the rest of our brandy in silence.

Colin sighed and stood to leave. "Tomorrow will be a long day, we should get a good night's sleep." He hesitated at the doorway.

"Thanks for what you did Alan, George told me how determined you were to help Toby. It was very brave going in after him alone, we're all grateful that you decided to join us and make this your home."

I smiled. "It's me that should be grateful, it's hard to put into words, but for the first time in my life I feel like I'm in the right place at the right time. Does that sound daft?"

"No Alan, let's hope you can help us find, the right place tomorrow. Good night."

I sat for a few moments more, watching the stars, wondering if Natasha was out there looking up at the same stars.

Then I headed for my room via the kitchen of course to pick up a very tired little dog.

I was finding it hard to sleep. What was making it worse was the constant sound of Scruffy snoring loudly, how could a small dog make so much noise. Occasionally she let out a little whimper or wagged her tail. What do dogs dream of I wonder.

I found my mind drifting back to Natasha, hunched over the photographs in the cave beneath the ocean, had she been crying? How I wished I could be with her.

I must have drifted off to sleep because I was no longer in the cave but in a forest. Snow was falling all around me, I found it hard to see, but I was aware of something - it took me a few moments to work out that it wasn't what I could see, but what I couldn't see, which had drawn my attention. Some of the snowflakes were stopping before they hit the ground, landing on something, a large shape in the snow, a shape with large blue eyes!

A sound behind me made me turn sharply. I could make out a dark figure through the trees, the figure was pointing a gun directly at me. In slow motion I saw fire explode from the barrel, the noise split through the air and echoed around the trees.

I woke with a start, clutching my stomach expecting to feel warm sticky blood flowing through my fingers. Scruffy jumped up on the bed and licked my face, she seemed concerned, I had obviously woken her. I stroked her and reassured her that everything was alright, it didn't feel alright at all, images had been so real. The bullet couldn't have been aimed at me, but it had seemed to pass straight through me. Had the man's aim been true? Was our search over before it had begun?

I settled down again to try to return to the forest and find out more, but as usual I found it hard to focus and no matter how I tried. I couldn't return to the woods. Eventually I must have dozed off.

I woke to a light but determined scratching at the door.

"Spike, hang on a minute," I whispered. He'd come to collect Scruffy for a morning constitutional before breakfast, it was becoming a bit of a routine. Scruffy jumped down from the bed and stood patiently at the door. As I opened it Spike almost bowled her over in his excitement. She grumbled at him playfully, then glancing up at me for the ok. She joined him in a joyful rough and tumble along the corridor.

I closed the door and climbed back into bed for a few moments to get my head together. I didn't worry about Scruffy, Spike always took good care of her, and I knew I would find them in the kitchen later - at breakfast.

After a few moments I got up, showered and packed a few things into my ruck sack and then I too headed for the kitchen. I knew I would find everyone gathered there for one of Meg's hearty breakfasts.

I was feeling a little unsettled about leaving Scruffy, not that she wouldn't be well looked after in my absence, but it was the first time I'd had to leave her.

*** 

The kitchen was buzzing, although the room was large, the population of the island was packed into it, making it seem a little – well – cosy.

Scruffy barked and greeted me from under the large table.

Meg shouted above the general din, "Good morning Alan, it's a bit of a free for all this morning, I'm just going to put everything on the table and you can all tuck in."

"That's fine by me Meg thanks." I gave Scruffy a fuss and took a seat at the end of the table.

"Good morning Alan," Maya said, flashing me a smile. She was seated next to Toby, the bond between them seemed to be strengthening. Maya looked at Toby with obvious admiration. Sophie sat next to Colin watching Toby playfully tease Maya, with a slight smile on her face. For now at least, they seemed like a normal family.

Jack sat at the other end of the table. He nodded at me as I helped myself to the enormous stake of pancakes that had been placed in the centre.

"No Ben this morning," I said, between mouthfuls.

Colin laughed. "You must be joking, I'm making him leave his beloved computer. He'll spend as much time as he possibly can with Tina before we drag him away kicking and screaming and believe me, I'm not joking."

"But he's taking Tina2 with him, isn't he? I would have thought that would make him feel better."

Sophie smiled kindly. "You have to understand Alan, Ben lives and breathes for that computer. Tina2 is like a child, Tina is his first real love. It will be hard for Ben to leave her, but Colin is right, you may need him on this one and it will do him good to get away for a while."

Colin laughed. "I'm pretty sure Ben won't see it that way honey.

Alan are you all packed and ready for the off? I'd like to make a move after breakfast."

Colin pushed the maple syrup my way. I thanked him.

"Yes I'm ready, I haven't got much in the way of warm clothing though. I can do layering as long as that means three or four layers of T-shirts."

"That won't be a problem. A plane will pick us up in about an hour, it will have all the supplies we'll need including warm clothing. The pilot is one of my trusted staff. All he knows is that this Island is a sanctuary. I like to keep private for my family. I will send Jack out to scout the air field, there always seems to be one particular moa who loves to frequent the air strip. I don't think even I could explain away something that big to the pilot, even if he was a fan of Sesame Street.

Once we're air born Ben will take over from the pilot and we'll drop him back on the main land. We'll then head off for our skiing and hunting holiday in the mountains."

It was easy to forget that Colin was probably one of the richest men in the world. He had several large and very successful companies, and a network of people at his beck and call.

I was beginning to realize you would be a fool to underestimate this man, he had a way of commanding loyalty and respect from the people around him and I was proud to be one of those people.

We all ate until we were fit to burst and plates were wiped clean. Colin was first to get up from the table.

"Alright let's make a move, Toby you can take us out to the airfield and bring the jeep back." Colin kissed Sophie as he headed for the door.

Toby seemed pleased to be part of the team, if only as the driver. He collected the keys proudly from a hook near the door and followed his father.

I looked down at Scruffy, I really hated to leave her. She obviously felt the same way, and she looked up at me and whined, it was breaking my heart. Spike came to the rescue. The little dog came over and sat next to Scruffy and gave a couple of little yaps, I knew he would take care of her. I thanked him and gave Scruffy a cuddle. "I'll be back soon, Spike will look after you, be good."

I put her back next to Spike on the kitchen floor.

Meg came over. "She'll be fine with us Alan, don't worry."

She placed her hand on my shoulder. "You take care of yourself, I have an idea that when you return someone else may be in need of your shoulder."

Colin shouted, "Let's get going, we have a plane to catch."

I gave Scruffy a last fuss and grabbing my rucksack headed out the door and down the steps to the jeep.

The team plus Toby headed for the air strip, it only took a few moments, the plane was already on the tarmac and a stout man greeted us.

After placing the box that contained Tina2 on a seat next to me, and giving me one of those 'keep your hands to yourself' looks, Ben joined the man in the cockpit. The rest of us settled ourselves in the main cabin, there was plenty of room.

Colin said goodbye to Toby. Jack seated himself at the back of the plane where he could see everything. Colin sat at the front. I was pleased, but not surprised, to see that we had our own headphones and movies and games for the trip. Scrolling through the menu I picked out an old black and white Dracula movie. Come to think of it, about the only thing I hadn't come across in the last few weeks were vampires, and the little voice in my head said don't tempt fate. How I laughed at the thought.

***

Minutes turned quickly into hours and soon we were landing. Colin thanked the Pilot and we refuelled the plane.

We took off with Ben in the pilot's seat. Next stop the mountains.

I relaxed back in my seat and closed my eyes. Almost instantly the dark forest engulfed me, the wind howled in my ears; at least I thought it was the wind. There was a large moon high in the sky above the trees. It sent strange shadows dancing amongst the branches. But there was something else dancing in

232

the shadows. Maybe it was just the shadows themselves or maybe a woman; tall and slender, with long flowing hair that looked almost silver in the moon light. It cascaded around her shoulders and down over her body. Her silver hair was in fact the only thing she was wearing, as she weaved and danced amidst the trees.

"We're almost there."

The voice woke me. I pulled myself upright in my seat, it was Colin.

"Sorry to disturb you Alan? You seemed to be dreaming, did you see anything useful?"

I could feel myself going red, I felt like a school boy caught looking through the girls changing room window. I gathered my wits.

"Yes! I mean no, I don't think it was anything – important." I should have told Colin what I'd seen, however naked women in the woods were not high on our search list.

Colin shrugged. "We need to get ready. We'll be landing soon, there are clothes and equipment in the back, just pick out what you need."

I nodded. "Ok." A thought struck me, "What exactly do I need?"

Colin smiled. "A good pair of boots for starters, some warm clothing and ski's, poles and Ski boots, just in case. I think I got the sizes right but there should be plenty of choice. Just help yourself."

I headed to the back of the plane. Jack had already sorted out what he would need, it didn't seem like much but considering he could produce his own thick fur coat I supposed it would suffice.

I was surprised to see Ben. "Aren't you flying the plane? I asked with obvious concern.

Ben laughed. "Don't panic, Tina2 is in control at the moment. Unlike most women she doesn't need a new wardrobe.

I on the other hand, will need some warm cloths, if I'm going to survive out there in the wilderness."

Drama queen I thought, but I picked up an extra jumper just in case.

Not long after I'd returned to my seat, the seat belt signs came on and the plane started to descend. I couldn't see much out of the window apart from snow; it seemed to be a white out. I could feel the wind buffeting the plane. I prayed Colin hadn't been exaggerating Ben's piloting skills. It wasn't the smoothest landings I'd ever had, but as Colin opened the door to the outside world the howling wind and snow made me realize that Ben had done a pretty good job.

***

You couldn't see much outside, partly because of the storm, but also because there wasn't much to see.

We made our way to a low building and piled in with our gear. The room was light and welcoming.

A couple of people looked up from a desk along the back wall. Despite the reasonably warm room, they were well wrapped up in hats, scarves and woollen coats. The two woollen clad figures spoke to Colin, in a language I didn't recognize. Colin knew what they wanted and responded with presumably an appropriate greeting. He handed over our papers and passports, the officials seemed to warm to us a little, surprised at Colin's masterful grasp of their language.

I looked around, it was obvious that they weren't used to mass tourism here. In the corner of the room was a small stove giving out a fair amount of heat, grouped closely round it was a couple of chairs and a small table. On the table, two mugs, a kettle and some biscuits – custard cream I noted, so must be first class.

As Colin came back with our passports, the door at the other end of the building blew open and a large coat, boots and hat tumbled in, accompanied by an icy blast of cold air.

As the mountain of cloths approached, it removed a hat and I could see that wearing them was a larger than life character with thick black hair and a beard white with snow.

"You must be the Thompson party," he bellowed.

Colin stepped forwards.

"Yes, and you must be Mr. Adams. I'm Colin Thompson and this is my party of three Ben, Alan and that's Jack.

"That's me, Grizzly Adams to my friends," he bellowed.

The giant shook my hand, crushing my fingers and laughing loudly. I couldn't help noticing the two officials shaking their heads - they had obviously heard this many times before. I got the distinct impression that they would like us to leave, so they could get on with their usual duties, I suspected they would involve sitting by the fire in the first class lounge, with a brew and a custard cream or two.

"You picked the middle of the worst storm we've had for months to come here, I wasn't sure you'd get through.

Well, best get you to your lodge, the roads are pretty bad but I've got the chains on the truck. You city boys look like you could do with a bit of excitement! " He laughed.

I wasn't sure how many friends Grizzly had, but I was pretty sure they would all be deaf.

We loaded all the gear into the monster truck. It was just like its owner, with huge tyres wrapped in heavy chains, as if to subdue the beast. It growled into life. We all piled in and set off. How Grizzly knew which way to go was a mystery, I couldn't see a dammed thing. I wondered what his real name was. Probably a Kevin or a Keith, I decided on Keith.

Keith shouted above the noise of the storm and the growl of the engine. "We got the Lodge ready for you, all the things you requested, fires set and there's plenty of wood. Fridge is stocked so you won't starve. You won't be able to hunt for a day or two, not till the weather settles at any rate."

I was beginning to feel a bit truck sick, I normally travelled ok, however this could not be called normal in any stretch of the imagination. The truck bounced and skidded all over the place (I would normally say all over the road but calling what we were on a road, would be pushing it a bit). Snow built up on the windows and what little you could see through the gaps was - well, just more snow!!

Just when I was beginning to think I would rather take my chances with the skis, we skidded to a stop outside of a large wooden building. The welcoming light from the windows seemed to promise warmth, stability and just maybe something, other than snow.

"Thank god that's over," Ben groaned. To say he didn't like the cold he was the first out of the truck clutching the precious box containing Tina2.

Keith helped us unload the truck and opened the door to the lodge. It was impressive, a large wood fire crackled and roared, comfortable leather sofas and thick fur rugs filled the large room. Ben headed for the chair nearest the fire and collapsed into it with a sigh.

"Thank you Mr. Adams, this will do us nicely, if you would kindly show me where the brandy is I'll ask you to join us in a drink." Colin dumped his bags and removing his coat and scarf.

"The name is Kevin, and brandy is in the Kitchen just through here, I'll give you a quick tour."

"Bugger," I said, and realized I'd said it out loud. All eyes turned to me. "I stubbed my toe," I said, feeling more than the heat of the fire on my face. Not Keith then, I thought.

Kevin took Colin on a tour. Jack had already started sniffing around - in a very real way, the problem was obvious. There were stuffed animal bits all over the place. Trophies on the walls and rug's on the floors, even the bloody lamp seemed to be a stuffed bird of some description. The place just smelled a bit musty to me, but Jack's senses had to be in overload.

I joined Ben by the fire and sat in the chair opposite. Ben was looking down in what could only be described as sheer horror; he had partially wrapped his feet in a rug on the floor. I followed his gaze. At the other end of the rug, the problem was only too evident. The rug at Ben's feet had a head attached to the other end. This was bad enough, but this head was that of a large wolf, mouth wide, teeth bared in a frozen snarl.

"Shit!" Our eyes met in panic, we both looked around the room for Jack, and luckily he had disappeared for the moment. I gathered the thing up and stuffed it unceremoniously into the large wood basket by the fire, then stuffed some logs on top.

"He's bound to smell it," Ben whispered, trying to tuck his feet as far as possible under his chair. He was right; I grabbed a small oil lamp from the mantel piece and sprinkled some of the contents into the basket, it smelled pretty strong. I placed the lamp back and sat down.

"First chance one of us gets - we bury that thing outside." Ben nodded agreement.

Colin and ...Kei....Kevin emerged from the kitchen carrying a tray of hot coffee and brandy. We gathered around the fire, if Kevin noticed the missing rug he didn't mention it.

"Where is your other friend, will he not join us for a drink to toast the hunt? It will bring good luck," Kevin said raising his glass.

Colin raised his glass. "Jack tends not to need luck when he hunts, just instinct, and he doesn't drink. Perhaps we should drink to better weather."

I was in need of a drink myself, it had been one hell of a day. The storm still raged outside, I didn't envy Kevin his drive home, where ever home was. In fact Kevin didn't seem keen to make the trip either, uninvited he poured himself another brandy.

"You can't beat a successful hunt, nothing like pitting your wits against an animal. I bagged most of these." Kevin indicated the various heads adorning the walls. "Magnificent eh" he said proudly.

Pitting your wits plus a double barrelled riffle, I thought as I looked around. Sadly there would have been a day, not so long ago, when I would have agreed with Kevin. But now it made me feel sick to my stomach, seeing such magnificent animals stuffed and nailed to the walls.

Kevin didn't seem to notice the lack of enthusiasm from the rest of us. "You'll have to come down to the main Hotel. I have my best trophies there, and the restaurant is one of the finest in these parts. If you can shoot it, we'll cook it for you.

The wolves here are clever buggers and make for particularly good sport." Kevin downed his second brandy and looked set on a third. I noticed Jack, had silently appeared behind him, very, very close behind him. His eyes were wild his nostrils flared and the almost inaudible sound of a growl was building in the back of his throat.

Colin leapt forward grabbing Kevin's arm and skilfully placing himself between Kevin and Jack, he quickly guided Kevin to the door, taking the glass from his hand and grabbing his coat and hat on the way. He glanced back at me, "Alan I think Jack's allergies are kicking in, he needs his medicine, take him into the kitchen."

Ben helped me push a snarling Jack into the kitchen. Colin explained to Kevin, as he gently pushed him out the door that Jack was allergic to animal hair. So we might have to remove and store a few of the trophy's, for his comfort. We would of course, take great care and replace them before we left.

As the door closed on Kevin, still trying to put his coat on Colin said in his friendliest voice, "Thank you so much, we'll find our way to the hotel tomorrow. We look forward to talking some more then." Colin shut the door and leaned heavily on it with a sigh.

I had to smile, boy that man could think on his feet.

In the kitchen Jack paced up and down, I'd never seen him this agitated. Thankfully Colin joined us as soon as he was sure Kevin had gone. "Right you two, get out there and get rid of that – stuff!"

"What do we do with it" Ben asked Colin, as we headed for the lounge.

"To be perfectly honest I don't give a dam. I saw a shed outside, dump it all in there. Jack and I will take the bags to the rooms." Colin half pushed half guided Jack out of the kitchen.

"Jack pick up the bags and take them to the rooms." Colin made it an order not a request and Jack responded automatically. Colin grabbed the rest of the bags and followed him out turning once. He indicated for us to get a move on.

I started by getting the wolf skin out of the basket and we gathered everything up even the bird lamp. Ben moaned like hell at having to go out into the storm, but even he'd been shaken by Jacks appearance. The idea of Jack losing control in a confined space, well in any space, really didn't bare thinking about. It only took a couple of trips to rid the place of the ghosts of animals past. I had to admit it seemed a lot better without the decor.

Job done we helped ourselves to more brandy, Ben carefully unloaded Tina2 from her case and set her down on the table. Lights started to flash and the small silver sphere started to hover a few inches above the table top. "Good evening Ben, good evening Alan, I note from my internal navigational device that we have arrived at our desired destination. Did we have a good journey?"

"I don't know about you, but I have had the journey from hell, next time I agree to come on one of these assignments, lock me in the lab and throw away the key Tina," Ben moaned.

Tina seemed to think for a moment before responding, "I have noted your request Ben. But I feel I should point out that – one, we do not have a key to the lab, two you would not survive without sustenance and three we have not in fact travelled from hell. I fear you may be in need of rest."

Colin appeared in the doorway, "I think you've hit on the problem Tina, we're all in need of a good night's sleep. I've got Jack cutting more wood for the fire; work should exhaust some of the adrenaline that's pumping around his body. This place looks a lot better guys! Good job."

Without asking I poured Colin another brandy, "Will Jack be alright? He looked pretty wired."

He took the glass and came and joined us by the fire. "He'll be fine. I don't want him changing, not just yet. He wants to get out into the mountains and have a good sniff around, but it's too dangerous even for Jack. I want to talk to some of the locals and have a look around in day light before we go rushing out, especially in this storm.

Tina can you give me a weather report for the area?"

"Good evening Colin. Yes. The storm will blow itself out over the next few hours. Tomorrow will be clear in the morning with a few snow showers coming in late afternoon. You have a call coming in. Would you like me to put it on visual?"

"Yes thank you Tina."

Tina made a few clicking noises and produced a small screen, Toby's face appeared.

"Hi Dad, what's it like there? Mum checked the forecast and you flew through one hell of a storm, she was worried. I knew you'd be ok."

I could just make out Maya trying to push her way into the picture.

240

"We're all good. Ben had everything under control. How are things back home, I hope you're taking care of everything Toby?"

Toby smiled back at us. "All good here Dad. Meg and Mum have started giving me lessons, so that I can develop more control. When you get back I'll show you, it's so cool." Toby almost fell over and out of shot. He reappeared grumbling, "Alright just wait a minute," and added, "Maya wants Scruffy to say hello to Alan."

Maya appeared in the screen holding Scruffy up and waving a paw at me. "Scruffy wanted to say hello Alan, she misses you but we are looking after her for you." Scruffy yapped as if to confirm this. I had to admit, it was good to see the little dog and Maya looking so well.

"Thank you Maya, I know I can trust you, not too much ice cream for breakfast mind." I laughed.

Toby managed to gain control of the screen again, only to be ushered away by his mother.

"Alright you two take the dogs out to play." There seemed to be a bit of a discussion going on, Sophie sighed. "Alright let Spike say hello too." She moved over again this time to allow Toby to hold up Spike. Spike barked and wagged his tail enthusiastically.

"Hi Spike. I know you're looking after everything too," Colin said laughing.

"Alright now take the dogs outside to play. I want to talk to Dad."

Sophie shooed the children and dogs out and finally had the screen to herself.

Colin laughed. "You have your hands full honey. Toby seems well."

She laughed. "Oh he's going to be just fine, Meg is great with him, I wish I'd had her help when I first.............." Sophie stopped.

I knew life had been hard for Sophie. She had grown up in fear of what she could do, and what others might do to her if they found out. Life should be easier for Toby at least.

Sophie continued, "Maya is doing so well, she follows Toby around all the time, they're quite a little team; Toby, Maya and the two dogs. Anyway how are things at your end? I have been doing a bit of research on your hosts. Kevin owns most of the mountain, and as well as trying to get the Ski resort up and running. He is trying to get permission to organize regular hunting trips into the most remote areas. Sadly there are still a lot of people who will pay good money to hunt. Kevin Adams has been an enthusiastic hunter since he could walk. He was bought up in Africa with his father, a renowned hunter. He made a fortune helping the rich and famous bag themselves trophies.

Lately he seems to have made it his business to hunt down and kill the dangerous beast that has been spotted high in the mountains, above the ski fields. He wants to make the area safe for would be punters. Incidentally, Tina tells me there was a report of a sighting two days ago. She will send the information to Tina2, it might help with location. Tina also says that she has found some information on Sally Adams, although not under that name.

Jess Vandenberg was a very well thought of Doctor until about ten years ago when she simply vanished, not to be seen again until pictures of her wedding to Kevin Adams appear in a local rag, a year ago.

Tina is certain that they are one and the same person, even though Sally doesn't look a day over 35 in either of them - Bitch! Anyway, she's been helping to run the Mountain Lodge Hotel ever since. It seems a bit of a waste of her skills in my opinion, but each to their own.

Tina has analysed the area for the most likely places you could start looking for our illusive quarry, we've sent this information through to Tina2. We'll keep searching for any more useful data. Good luck, and be careful. Oh and how is Ben coping?" This last comment Sophie said with a smile on her face. I think she already knew the answer.

Colin groaned and pulled a face. "We have already met Grizzly Adams - as he likes to be called, he's quite a Character. I just hope we find our target before he does, we have already seen what Mr. Adams likes to do with his trophies. As for Ben, if he ever stops moaning, I'll ask him. I'm more worried about Jack at the moment, this place doesn't smell right and he wants to get out into the mountains, but it's too dangerous. We need to know what's going on here first." Colin stopped.

Jack had appeared carrying the logs he looked a little more relaxed, at least his face did, in spite of the cold Jack had stripped down to his T- shirt and jeans. The thin fabric of the shirt appeared to be fighting a losing battle to keep his bulging muscles contained. Small rips had appeared in the fabric around the sleeves.

Colin looked up and smiled. "That's great work Jack. Dump it all in the basket by the fire."

He turned back to the screen. "Everything is going to plan, such as it is. Let us know if there are any more sightings. We'll have a good look around tomorrow and perhaps get some gossip from the locals here. We all send our love," he blew a kiss and Sophie responded.

"Bye guys, bye love."

The screen went blank and Tina2 settled back onto the table, just a couple of lights blinked on and off to show she was still activated.

Jack filled the wood basket and we settled down in front of the fire. After a while Colin stood. "Alright guys, before we turn in I think we should sort out a few things:

1. We are here to hunt, I am well aware, of how we all feel about Mr. Adams, however we don't want Mr. Adams to be

aware. He needs to think that we're all keen hunters. Understood?" We nodded.

2. "This place is dangerous. Alan in the past, you have led hunts in mountains and terrain similar to this. I want you to advise us." I couldn't help remembering the last time I'd been knee deep in snow in the mountains. I'd spent months in hospital recovering. Hardly a great example. Colin continued,

3. "We're not here to change the way these people think, God knows I'd love to but, it's just not going to happen. We get in and out, quickly, hopefully having found what we're looking for.

4. Jack, you are an asset here but you are also in the most danger. In wolf form these people would shoot you as soon as look at you. I don't want you changing, not unless someone is near to watch your back." Colin looked at Jack, who was looking into the flames. "Jack is that understood?" he repeated. Jack nodded and mumbled without looking up.

"Alright then people let's get some sleep. Tomorrow Alan, you're with me. We'll go down to the hotel and meet the locals and have another chat with our Mr. Adams. Ben, you Jack and Tina2 can have a look around, if the weather permits. All the hunters on these mountains have to carry radio's with them for safety reasons, soTina2 should be able to pick up any signals that are close, you should know if you're not on your own out there.

We will talk more at Breakfast. I'm all in so I will say goodnight." Colin finished his brandy in one and headed out the back, he turned at the door. "By the way I'm in room one the first down the hallway, Jack is next to me in two, we put your stuff in room three Ben and that leaves you in four Alan, it's at the end of the corridor. Everything you need should be there gentlemen, if not tough, we can sort it out in the morning. Sleep well."

Ben hauled himself from his chair. "Well I think I've had enough excitement for one day, I'm off to bed, see you in the morning Alan." He headed for the bedrooms, as he passed Tina2 on the table, lights flashed on and she rose almost silently and followed him.

Alone with just the sound of the wind still howling around the lodge and the crackling of the fire, I helped myself to another small brandy and watched the flames swirl and dance over the surface of the wood. Even though Ben's relationship was a little strange, to say the least, I envied the fact that he had company tonight. I closed my eyes the fire crackled in the hearth the storm had died down a little. I finished my brandy and headed for bed.

I lay listening to the wind, it was gentler now, but still whistled and howled around the lodge, as if lost, and lonely out there in the cold mountains - that was, the wind - Wasn't it?

Ben stuck his head around the door, "Morning sleeping beauty. We have to fend for ourselves, so you and I are on breakfast duty this morning. Colin and Jack have gone to take a look around outside. I have managed to put the coffee on, but kitchens really aren't my forte and Tina2 isn't being much help, we could really do with a hand or two." Ben pleaded.

I opened one eye reluctantly. "Ok I'll be out in a minute, just give me chance to get dressed." He shut the door behind him. I dragged myself out of bed and drew the curtains. The storm had passed. The view outside the window reminded me of a Christmas card.

Icicles hung like Christmas tree decorations and everywhere pure white snow glittered and glistened in the morning sun. Very pretty, however, the realist inside me said 'Bloody cold!' I shuddered and speedily dressed putting on one of my new woollen jumpers provided for the trip. I pulled on a pair of extra thick woolly socks and struggled into my ski pants. Feeling warmer, if a little larger, I headed to the kitchen, just in time to see Ben trying to fish egg shells out of a large bowl. He looked harassed.

"You definitely said just put the eggs into the bowl and whisk briskly," Ben moaned as he flicked bits of shell onto the floor.

"I am sorry Ben, I thought with your I Q, you would have worked out that you had to open the eggs, before you placed them into the bowl," Tina2 replied smoothly.

Now I knew Tina2 was a computer, and therefore had no sense of humour, however I could have sworn, underneath that metal exterior, she was, at this moment, laughing her components off!

I managed to keep a straight face. "Why don't I take over and do breakfast this morning Ben. You two finish the coffee and lay the table." I tried to pick the bits of egg shell from the bottom of my new woolly socks. Ben looked a little aggrieved, but agreed with out argument and between us we had things under control when Colin came in.

"That smells good." He said, taking off his snow covered boots and hanging up his coat.

"How's Jack this morning," I ventured.

"Oh he's much better, he's had a run. Jack hates to be cooped up. He caught himself some breakfast this morning, so I've left him to enjoy it in peace. When he's finished eating I've asked him to put the snow chains on the jeep. You and I will need to go down to the hotel later this morning." Colin laughed and added, "Alan, I do hope you've been in charge of the cooking, the only thing Ben cooks that is edible, is packet soup."

"That's so unfair," Ben protested. "When I was at University, my peanut butter and cheese pizzas were the talk of the campus."

Colin slapped him on the back. "I'm sure they were Ben. Alan, please tell me that's not what we're having for breakfast this morning, that walk and the mountain air has given me an appetite."

Ben poured the coffee and I dished up bacon, scrambled eggs (which I had freshly made) and toast. I tried without much luck, to push out of my mind the thought of Jack, just outside tucking into whatever hapless creature he'd caught for his breakfast this morning.

Colin must have read my expression. "Rabbit," he said, between mouthfuls, without looking up. I concentrated on eating my meal, feeling embarrassed and a little ashamed, after all I was tucking into the rear end of some hapless pig. At least Jack had done his own dirty work.

If Colin noticed my embarrassment, he didn't show it. He continued, "Jack and I have had a bit of a look around this morning.  Jack picked up a scent along the top track.

Ben, after breakfast, you can take one of the rifles and Tina2 and follow Jack up there a little way, to see where it leads. Not too far mind. I don't want either of you far from the Lodge yet, but Jack needs to be kept occupied, it should be pretty quiet out there mid-morning.

Alan and I will take the Jeep and head down to have a chat with Kevin and some of the folks at the Hotel. We need to find out where they are hunting at present. It makes sense that if this animal we are looking for has any intelligence at all, we are likely to find it as far away from them as possible. It's a big mountain, and if you could go anywhere wouldn't you want to be as far away from Kevin, and his gun happy chums, as you could!"

Ben asked, "Which rifle do you want me to take?"

I was a little surprised. I hadn't imagined us actually going out there with the capacity to kill. I realized that had been, a bit naive.

Again Colin read my mind (he had an uncanny way of doing that). "Alan, I can see you're a little concerned with the armoury we have at our disposal. We do have a more traditional riffle with us just in case, however Ben very cleverly has adapted the other two weapons so that although they look and feel like a traditional riffle, they do in fact, shoot darts. These in themselves need to be handled with care. The dose they deliver would bring down a large bear. Said bear, would recover in a couple of hours, but I would make myself scarce, because this really would be a Bear, with a sore head. There is a subtle difference in the weapons. Get Ben to familiarize you with his version.

Take the real gun Ben, if you need to use it a warning shot should be enough to scare anything off, but be careful. You'll need your snow shoes."

Ben groaned. "It looks bloody cold out there. I could just get Tina to run a few scans and see what she comes up with."

Colin shook his head. "It will do you good to get out of the lodge Ben, besides you know as well as I do that Tina2 would only pic up radio transmitters and general heat source. That's not going to be very useful is it?"

"I wish people would stop telling me what I need," Ben muttered.

We finished breakfast and tidied things away. Jack came in wearing just his usual jeans and a shirt. He didn't seem to feel the cold like we did, and the mountain air did seem to suit him. He was somehow, taller and more animated, probably still exhilarated by the hunt for breakfast.

Colin and I left Jack waiting patiently outside for Ben, who was taking an age to sort out his snow shoes and boots. Jack always seemed more at ease outside even back home. But here, he seemed to come alive. I wondered if his original home had been similar to this. After all, he had been raised by Wolves and mountains and woods like these would have been a good habitat.

We headed down the road; it was fairly easy to follow the tracks left from the previous evening. At a crossroads a sign pointed out that the only options were, the Airport one way and the Hotel the other. In my mind, I thanked the person that had invented the snow chain over and over again. The countryside was probably quite beautiful but the blanket of snow that covered every inch, meant that we could only imagine what lay beneath the humps and mounds. The trees too had a shroud of snow, making them look like snow cones, perched on the mountain side.

It was about a fifteen minute drive to the Hotel which meant in these conditions it took us about thirty. As Hotels go, it was fairly modest but considering where we were, it had to be said, Kevin had done alright for himself. The front of the place was cleared and there were several large vehicles parked outside. We parked up and went in.

Kevin hadn't been kidding about the Trophies. The walls were covered. Everywhere you looked, glassy unseeing eyes stared back at you. If the souls of these animals haunted this place, they would have to get on really well, because there would be no room to move!

The entrance way was large and opened into a huge sitting room. The centre piece was an impressive log fire. The welcome heat hit you as you entered, from the cold mountain air; the next thing that hit you was the noise, raised voices. An argument was going on at the bar. Several men stood drinks in hand (even though it was only ten thirty in the morning).

"Ah. Colin and - your friend." Kevin greeted us, holding out his hand. "Welcome to my humble home." He shook our hands warmly. "Come join us. I'll introduce you." He led us over to the bar, to join three men. I noticed a photograph, on the bar in front of them.

"This is Mike and the two Dave's. They've come up to hunt from the village. We've been looking at a photograph supposedly of our mystery beast." Kevin indicated the picture on the bar.

"Can I get you guys a drink, the bar is always open?"

"A coffee would be good thanks," Colin said picking up the picture casually.

"City boys." Kevin sighed dramatically and shouted at the top of his lungs, "SALLY! Two coffees out here."

"It's hard to make out what it is! It just looks white!" Colin said, handing the photo to me. I took it realizing I had already seen a similar shot, back in the lab.

"What is it supposed to be," I said, tossing it across the bar.

"It's the beast," Dave said excitedly. "One of the villagers took it, whilst they were in the upper pastures feeding stock."

Dave two laughed. "Ghosts and shadows, you shouldn't encourage them Dave, they'll be seeing Yeti's next." We all laughed.

"Well, I can see something," Dave said sulkily.

Kevin poured them all another drink. "Well if it's up here, it's only a matter of time before we get it in our sights. Ay boys. We have a place set aside for her." He pointed to a noticeable gap on the wall, above the bar.

I was surprised. "You said her, I thought no one really knew what it was."

He laughed. "Oh some of the villagers say they've seen a – naked woman, dancing in the woods high in the mountains during the spring thaw. Too much homemade Schnapps I would say, but it's a great story to keep you warm, on a winter's night. If you know what I mean!" Kevin winked.

A tall, attractive woman appeared with a tray.

"Coffee gentlemen," she said, placing the tray on the bar.

"Thank you..... Sally wasn't it?" Colin said with a warm smile, offering his hand.

The woman smiled. She had an elegance that seemed out of place here. She took Collins hand gently and held it for a few seconds longer than I would have expected, she seemed to be watching him intensely, almost as if she were trying to read his mind.

Kevin introduced us. "This is my wife, Sally. She hates hunting but makes a mean stew and descent coffee too."

Sally smiled. "You will join us for lunch gentlemen. We don't get many civilized visitors from the city, during the winter time."

I noticed Sally exaggerated the word civilized and looked pointedly at Kevin. He didn't seem to notice.

"That's going to change once we get the ski field up and running, all the city folk will be flocking here for their holidays," he added, proudly.

Colin seized an opportunity. "Yes we'd heard about the planned ski resort, that's what caught our eye, we thought we'd kill two birds with one stone and maybe next time we come it will be for the skiing. I'd have thought that would be taking up all your time, more lucrative than the hunting, putting the chair lifts in you could have walking in the summer and skiing in the winter. People would pay good money to see the wild life - alive!!!"

Sally at least seemed keen on the idea. "I like walking and I would certainly prefer to have pictures on the walls rather than the inhabitants themselves!" she said dryly.

Kevin wasn't going to be swayed. He shook his head "You would, you're a city slicker just like these boys. There's good money in hunting, my father 'god rest his soul' made his fortune hunting. I intend to make that fortune grow. Don't you need to be getting food ready or something?" he growled at Sally. She just smiled back at him and with another smile directed at Colin, she disappeared in the direction of the dining room.

Dave snatched the picture back. "Well I still think there's something there." He tucked it carefully back into his jacket pocket.

Mike winked at us. "Course there is Dave." We all laughed and Dave seemed to give up. Kevin had obviously had enough. "Come on I need food, the weather forecast is good for tomorrow, your party is more than welcome to join us on the hunt in the morning. We would be happy to show you how it's done." He led the way towards the dining room.

Colin declined. "Thanks' but no, we would probably slow you down. Lunch would be good, thank you. Perhaps you can tell us a bit about the history of this place, whilst we eat."

The dining room had far less dead things hung on the walls; it resembled a French cafe rather than a hunting lodge. Sally's influence, I supposed.

A young and very attractive woman bought us some warm homemade bread, her effect on the two Dave's and Mike made it obvious they were either single, or they could be forgetful if the chance arose. Sally bought out the stew, it was excellent.

"We thought we heard wolves fairly close to the lodge last night," Colin said, trying to sound concerned.

"Oh they're out there alright, but you don't have to worry, they keep their distance, crafty buggers when they want to be," Mike said, peering past us towards the kitchens.

"What about this beast, everyone seems to be talking about. Is it out there, I mean really? It seems hard to imagine that people have lived here for years and never come across it before," Colin asked.

Dave 1 was obviously the expert. "Oh there's been a lot of talk over the years, but hardly anyone had any reason to come up this high into the mountains before, just the odd goat herder. The wolves had the place to themselves. It is out there alright."

Kevin laughed. "Well it won't be out there for much longer."

Suddenly I felt strange. The voices around me seemed to become muffled and distant, the room seemed to spin, I closed my eyes....

Growling and snarling filled the air, two huge bodies collided and clashed together rolling over and over, hair flying, bright red blood splattering the pure white snow, as the mass of teeth and claws cut and slashed - a shot rang out.....

"Alan, are you alright?" Colin had his hand on my shoulder. I looked around lost and disorientated, my head still spinning.

"You've gone white as a sheet man, are you ill?" Kevin said, and then bellowed towards the kitchen, "SALLY."

Sally appeared almost immediately and seemed to assess the situation quickly. She guided me over to an arm chair and put her hand on my forehead. "Bring him some water, please," she said, taking my pulse. I tried to get my head together, "I'm alright now. Thank you," I lied. The vision I'd had, could have only lasted for a few seconds, but for those few seconds, it had felt like I'd been transported to hell.

Colin was at my side handing me some water. "Here Alan drink this. What is it, what did you see?" I looked from him to Sally, her hand still on my arm. Her eyes seemed to be searching my very soul, but it was a two way highway, for a split second I saw something dark and dangerous. Something told me, we should be talking too Sally, but not here, and certainly not now.

She took her hand away quickly and looked unsettled.

I knew we had to go. "Sorry, it's just a migraine," I said. "I'll be alright. I just need to get back to the Lodge - to get my tablets."

Sally helped me up and again our eyes met. "You need to get back," she said. "Everything will be alright, I'm sure."

As Colin helped me towards the door I heard Kevin's voice behind us. "It can't be healthy, living in the city. Look at these guys, one has allergies that make him sound like, some sort of mad dog, the other has migraines, that turn him white as a ghost, as if the hounds of hell themselves were after him. Worse than that, the other one thinks we should be walking and taking pretty pictures, next he'll have us pressing wild flowers."

As the door closed behind us, I could hear them laughing.

Once out in the fresh air I felt a little better. Colin looked worried. "Alright we're on our own. What the hell, happened. What did you see?"

I headed for the jeep. "We have to get back up to the lodge," was all I could say. We climbed in, Colin caught my urgency and started the engine, and we set off at speed.

When I shut my eyes again, all I could hear was that shot echoing around the mountains.

Colin was on the radio. "Ben can you hear me? Report." There was no answer.

"I think they found it," I managed at last.

Colin almost crashed the jeep.

"Shit." He slowed down a bit.

I tried the radio. "Ben can you hear us?"

After what seemed like an age Tina2 answered. "Colin we are at the lodge. Everything is alright. However, Ben would like you to return as soon as possible please."

"Tina can you put Ben on," Colin said calming down a little.

"I am sorry Colin. Ben is rather busy. He is trying to remember his first aid. I am required to help, so I will sign off for the moment. I see from my tracking device that you are already on your way back, I suggest caution, the roads are dangerous and your speed is excessive." Tina was gone and the radio was silent.

"Alan what did you see?" Colin's voice was calm, but insistent.

I tried to recall. "It was a fight – teeth, fur and blood -a wolf fight. There was a shot..." How could I describe what I'd witnessed, those few seconds imprinted on my mind, a mass of teeth, nails hair and blood, and the sounds, those terrible sounds. Yes, it had been the sound of the hounds from hell and they were having the devil of a fight!

We travelled the rest of the way in silence. It seemed to take a lot longer to get back. Eventually we pulled up outside the lodge. The door was open...

We both hesitated, not sure of what we were going to find. The relief for both of us was obvious, far from being a scene from a horror film, it looked a little like a comedy sketch. Ben was fussing around Jack, who lay on the coach, covered in a blanket. This in its self wasn't too bad, but the sight of Ben with an apron on and a pair of rubber gloves, trying to administer to Jack, who growled and kept trying to bat him away. Tina2 hovered just out of harm's way, attempting to give instructions. The scene was hilarious especially as it came as a relief from what we had both been imagining.

"What the hell happened?" Colin shouted, above the confusion.

"It was an accident," Ben groaned, I didn't mean to hit him.

"You shot him!" Colin was suddenly more concerned and rushed over to Jack.

"I have inspected the damage Colin and the bullet has grazed Jacks arm, however some of the scratches are quite deep and may need stitches," Tina2 reported, hovering sensibly just out of Jack's reach.

"You scratched him too?" Colin turned on Ben.

"Not me, the wolf. She scratched him. I just shot him," Ben cried. Then added miserably, "It was an accident, it all happened so fast. I thought it was going to kill him," Ben wailed, collapsing into one of the chairs and trying in vain to remove his pink rubber gloves.

Colin bent down next to Jack. "I need to take a look Jack, Just relax. Everything will be alright." He spoke softly but firmly. Jack allowed him to pull back the blanket. At first glance there did seem to be an awful lot of blood, however on closer inspection most of the scratches where superficial, but the wound on his shoulder, looked pretty deep.

Colin looked back at Ben. "What part of shoot high did you not understand?"

"I did shoot high, just not high enough," Ben moaned. "You weren't there, it all happened so fast."

Colin shook his head. "Alright we need to get Jack cleaned up, Tina's right, he's going to need some stiches."

"Perhaps I can help." The voice came from the open doorway, we all jumped. Tina2 dropped instantly on to the nearby coach and her lights blinked out.

Sally stood in the doorway, carrying a bag. "I'm trained as a nurse, Alan didn't look too good. I thought you might need some help, however it looks like I may have another patient. Sorry, I didn't mean to startle you, if you would prefer me to go?" She waited, hovering just outside the door.

Colin glanced at me, I shrugged. "I don't know about you but my needle work isn't too hot." How much she had heard or seen was unclear.

Colin made up his mind. "Yes Sally, thank you, please come in, we would be grateful if you would take a look at our companion Jack here. There seems to have been an accident."

Sally hesitated for a second then crossed the thresh hold.

For some strange reason, I was reminded of the old vampire movie I had watched on the plane, there was something about this woman that made the hairs stand up on the back of my neck.

Sally didn't look like a vampire, but then Sophie didn't look like a wolf.

Vampire or not Sally was a godsend (if that wasn't a contradiction in terms). She inspected Jack's wounds with just a hint of admiration for the body they adorned, and preceded to clean and dress the patterns etched across his chest.

"I'll need to stitch some of these. Can someone get me some boiling water and clean cloths." She looked down at Jack. "You were lucky, she seems to have been playing. She likes you."

I questioned this remark, "You know what did this."

"Do you?" she said without looking up from her work.

Colin interrupted. "Alan you heard the lady, hot water and clean towels from the kitchen please."

When I returned Colin was helping bandage the graze on Jacks arm, Sally was holding a needle and thread.

"Are you going to do that without anaesthetic," I said feeling a little sick.

"Just a local anaesthetic, although I think your boy here is pretty tough. It's alright I do quite a lot of body repair work around here."

Seeing my expression Sally laughed.

"The nearest hospital is about five hours away on a good day, on a bad day well there would be no point setting out."

I didn't have the stomach to watch. "I'll go and put some coffee on, perhaps it's the blood or the stitching but I'm feeling a bit queasy." I headed for the kitchen, Sally looked up and smiled. "Blood is good, it's lack of blood that kills you," she added.

She had the most unusual pale green eyes. Strange how I hadn't noticed them before and did she just lick her lips. Oh dear, I really was letting my imagination run away with me; this vampire thing was getting to me. Still I thought Tina had probably been right about her being a Doctor, she certainly seemed to know what she was doing.

As I made coffee in the kitchen, taking deep breaths to keep my stomach contents in place, I could hear Colin asking Sally more about the area and the plans her husband had for the mountain.

Jack hadn't said a word since we came back, he didn't say much normally, but under the circumstances you would have thought he would have had some comment. A wolf that could leave this sort of impression on Jack had to be big, or mean, or both.

I took the tray in and placed it on the table near the fire.

Sally had finished her needlework and was packing up her bag.

Jack didn't look to worse for wear now that the blood had been cleaned away and his wounds dressed.

Sally picked up her bag. "Make him rest for a while, he's a very strong boy he'll be fine."

Colin smiled. "We can't thank you enough Sally. Stay and have some coffee." He poured the coffee and offering her a mug.

"No need to thank me, and I don't drink coffee, but you could answer me a question!"

"Of course," Colin said without hesitation, taking a sip from his mug.

"Why are you here? You're not hunters!"

She looked at Jack. "Well he might be and maybe...." She looked at me but seemed to change her mind, "But the rest of you, no."

Colin looked thoughtfully into his coffee mug.

I helped myself and passed a mug to Ben who had been keeping very quiet. He raised his eye brows, we both waited to see what Colin would say.

He seemed to come to a decision. "Honestly we may need more of your help," he said simply.

Sally smiled. "And what is it you city boy's think I can help you with here?"

"I think you know why we have come." Colin seemed relaxed, he was good at this cat and mouse game. He sat in one of the arm chairs and indicated the chair opposite for Sally to join him.

"She needs your help," he said quietly.

"Why should I trust you? You could be after a trophy, just like all the others," Sally whispered.

"You said it yourself; we're not hunters, well not in that sense. You know it's only a matter of time, if it isn't your husband, it will be one of the others and sooner or later she may be forced to kill. Then it would be open season."

"She wouldn't kill one of them, she's clever," Sally said. Her beautiful eyes seemed to have changed colour with her mood and now seemed hazel and very sad.

At this point Jack decided to get up and go find himself some clothes, his chest, arms and cheek showed clearly the vivid gashes. He turned his other cheeks to us, as he sauntered casually from the room.

Jack never seemed embarrassed by his nakedness, mind you with a body like that he had nothing to be embarrassed about. I supposed it was the animal in him, after all, as the wolf he never wore cloths, to him naked was natural.

Probably for very different reasons we all watched him go.

Sally with some effort managed to turn her attention back to us, for the first time she looked a little embarrassed.

"She didn't really hurt him. She could have torn him to shreds. She was attracted by his scent and I would guess she liked the look of him too, well she would wouldn't she? Even I'm drawn to him and he isn't my type. He's like her isn't he?" Sally stopped; she obviously thought she'd said too much.

"I should go, I have the evening meal to prepare"

Colin stopped her. "Alright Sally, we'll tell you why we're here, if you will tell us how you know so much about this beast of the woods." Colin quoted from one of the articles, we had read.

She shrugged. "I really do have to go. Kevin will have a fit if I haven't prepared this evenings meal, but I will come back in the morning, after I've finished breakfast. To be honest, I can't wait to hear how you lot fit together, you don't smell right. And why do you have a small metal space ship?" She glanced at Tina2.

260

Somehow I felt that even though Tina2 remained motionless on the couch, she still managed to look slightly embarrassed at having been spotted.

Sally had reached the door but turned. "By the way, I like what you've done with the place, its better without the wild life, strange, that even with all the animals gone I still smell wolf!!!" She was laughing as she closed the door behind her.

Ben sighed. "What the hell did she mean space ship, Tina looks nothing like a space ship, and I don't smell....do I?"

Colin sounded thoughtful, "I don't think she was referring to you Ben. I think we have to trust her. I get the feeling our Sally, or Jess, knows a lot more about everything than she's letting on. She certainly knows her medicine, Tina was right. The way I see it we have no choice but to try to get her on our side, but we can cross that bridge in the morning." Colin turned and gave his full attention to Ben. "All right Ben. What the hell happened out there?"

"It wasn't my fault. Jack got scent of something not far from the house. He changed and charged off into the woods. By the time Tina and I caught up with him all I could see was flying fur and claws. It looked like a black and white horror movie. It was definitely a wolf the size of Jack or maybe a little smaller but not by much and white, white as snow. Tina will have some images. Tina," Ben called.

The little silver sphere rolled over on the couch and blinked a couple of times. "Yes Ben."

"You took some pictures out in the woods, can we see them please."

"Of course Ben, in fact I took some film, I thought that might be of more assistance to us under the circumstances." Tina rose and turned to look at Colin. Well when I say look - she directed her lights towards him, no wait let's be honest about this, she looked at him - she definitely looked at him.

"Colin, would you like me to play the sound with the film, the quality is a little poor because of the many expletives expressed by Ben, who happened to be rather close to my microphone." At this point Jack reappeared from the bedrooms wearing jeans and a shirt he seemed distant, but none the worse for his ordeal.

Tina raised a screen and showed the images she had recorded. The scenes were a little less dramatic; they were accompanied by Ben's constant cursing.

Jack and the white wolf tumbled and clawed their way across the snow, leaving bright red streaks painted on the pristine canvas. The white wolf seemed slightly smaller than Jack, but could obviously hold its own. Suddenly a tree filled the screen. At the same time a shot rang out accompanied by a very loud, "Oh shit," from Ben.

Tina explained, "I am sorry Colin, but at this point it was necessary to take cover, a bullet would not have damaged me, however I calculated the possibility of a ricochet from my metal jacket could have injured someone!"

Ben groaned. "I aimed high, they must have jumped just at that moment. They were all over the place. I thought that thing was trying to kill Jack, how was I to know she was just playing with him. If that was a bloody game, I'd hate to see them at war."

I felt sorry for him, in all honesty I'm not sure I'd have handled the situation any better.

"You had the whole sky to aim at Ben, next time, when I tell you to aim high I mean aim really, really high," Colin scolded.

"She was magnificent." We all turned to look at Jack. He'd been watching the screen intensely, it was the first thing he'd said since his ordeal with the white wolf and far from being upset by his impromptu meeting, he seemed, positively - euphoric.

262

On the screen Tina had focused on the action again. Jack had changed and lay naked in the snow bleeding from a wound in his shoulder as well as several deep scratches across his chest. The white wolf was disappearing into the trees but she turned and seemed to hesitate for a few seconds, starring intensely, fascinated. Then she was gone.

Tina2 lowered her screen.

"Magnificent," Jack repeated.

"Jack is she like you?" Colin asked, as Jack sat on the couch looking into space dreamily.

"I think so," he said and seemed to come too. "If some idiot hadn't shot me, I'd have been able to find out. Everything was going fine till then. She won't let me near again." Jack bought down his fist hard on the table knocking one of the mugs to the floor, the mug was empty but it smashed and bits flew everywhere.

Colin put his hand on Jack's shoulder. "That's enough Jack. Ben was just trying to help, admittedly not very well."

"Oh thanks," Ben mumbled.

"I would have done the same....well, maybe not exactly the same," Colin admitted.

"You shouldn't have gone off on your own. From now on we stick together. Hopefully tomorrow we'll find out more about your wolf friend from Sally, I'm sure she will be able to help us, perhaps even give us a proper introduction. Till then let's get this place tidied up and have something to eat. There's a pretty good bottle of wine in the fridge, I think we could all do with a drink.

Jack, the Doctor said you should rest and that's what you're going to do. The rest of us can handle the chores." Colin glanced at Ben, "Isn't that right Ben, you can be in charge of cutting the wood. Just be careful with that bloody axe!!

Tina, will you send that film home to the others, I think they would like to take a look at Jack's new friend, I want to see what Sophie, makes of her."

Ben must have been feeling pretty bad about what had happened because without a word he fetched the wood and cleaned up the mess the mug had made. I ended up in the kitchen again, I didn't mind, even I couldn't go wrong with the four massive steaks in the fridge, one of which I knew wouldn't need much, if any cooking. Thankfully I found oven chips in the freezer. That invention must have saved a lot of kitchens, over the years. Steak and chips it was then.

After dinner we settled down in front of the big roaring fire. The day's events had taken their toll on Jack, who had turned in early after falling asleep a couple of times on the couch. For the rest of us, coffee and large brandies were the order of the evening

"What did you make of Sally?" I asked lying back in my chair and pushing my feet closer to the fire. Ben shrugged, "she said some strange things, what was all that about smells? More importantly she saw Tina2. Do you really think she thought we had an alien with us?"

He obviously hadn't shared my silly concerns about the vampire thing. In fact he was more upset that someone would mistake Tina2 for an alien.

Colin looked relaxed again. "Luckily, I think Sally, or Jess, has some secrets of her own, more importantly for us I think she has a soft spot for Jack's wolf friend. She will help us I'm sure. We just have to find some way of keeping Kevin and his buddies out of the equation. They think we're a bunch of city wimps and that's just the way we want it to stay."

"Sally was a bit odd though, didn't you think? And why, if she is a skilled doctor, would she hide herself out here with a man she obviously has little in common with!" I wanted to mention the suspicions I had but felt too stupid.

"Most of us have skeletons in the closet Alan. You should know that by now. This is probably as good a place as any to make a new life. As for Kevin, well he's probably a really nice guy, if we could just get him into skiing and walking rather than hunting." Colin finished his brandy just as Tina announced that a call was coming in from Sophie.

We all turned so that we could see Tina's screen clearly, although in my mind's eye, I saw Sally's closet with several fresh skeletons entombed within.

Sophie was obviously upset. "Good god Colin what happened. What was Jack doing out there on his own? Tina assures us he's alright, but he could have been killed. Who shot him?"

I smiled. Tina hadn't told her who had fired the shot. Her loyalty after all, was ultimately with Ben!

Ben looked a little sheepish. "It was a bloody accident, how many times am I going to have to say it."

"Ben shot at them. In god's name why?" Sophie turned her wrath on Ben, who even with the distance between them had the good sense to move a couple of steps back from the screen.

"I thought the thing was going to kill him," Ben groaned.

"So you thought you would get in first," Sophie scolded.

Ben hung his head. "It all happened so fast."

Colin interrupted, "It was an accident honey, you know Ben, he wouldn't hurt a fly.

You have to admit it looked and sounded pretty dramatic, what do you think? Has Meg seen it?"

Sophie's mood changed, she smiled. "They were playing, testing each other out. If you want a woman's opinion 'she likes him', if you want a wolf's view 'they are well matched'. What did Jack say about it?"

Colin laughed. "He thinks and I quote 'she is magnificent', is she like you? Do you think she can change?"

"It's hard to say, she's no ordinary wolf that's for sure. If we are to believe the pictures, maybe she is discovering herself. She maybe like Jack, the wolf life might be the only one she knows." Sophie moved out of shot and Meg appeared.

"If she is like Jack, she may have been oblivious of her ability for years, then something might have triggered her to change, or at least try to change. The process is not always a smooth one. You need to proceed with care. She is a wolf first and wolves basic instinct is flight or fight, kill or be killed, and Colin, take care of Jack; if he loses his heart, he may well lose his head," Meg added.

Sally had been right about the fight, although I had to side with Ben; in wolf terms they may have just been playing with each other, to everyone else they looked for all the world like they were trying to rip each other's heads off.

Privately I thought, there were lessons to be learned here;

1)    Don't play with Wolves.
2)    Keep Ben in front of you, at all times.
3)    Carry some garlic! Just in case!


I bought myself back to the conversation. Sophie was talking about George being a little worried. "Who has been acting strangely," I asked, realizing too late that I was rudely interrupting Sophie.

She just smiled. "As I said, George is a little worried about Goldie. Meg has been out to see her and she reports that everything is normal. What is considered normal, for a dragon, is a little out of my league, so we'll just have to take Megs word for it.

Sorry Alan there has been no news from Natasha, but I'm sure if there was a problem she would have been in touch. Scruffy misses you.

Oh and Darling, Toby sends his love. He's been doing so well. We've been going out for regular walks in the evenings. I have had to put him in his place a couple of times, but he learns quickly."

267

I remembered my first encounter with Sophie in her wolf form and shuddered, it was easy to understand why Toby would be a fast learner.

Sophie continued, "We'll let you get some sleep now. Is there anything else you would like us to do, from this end?" Colin nodded. "One thing honey, could you have another look at Kevin's wife Sally, I think Tina is right about the Doctor thing, it might be useful to know a little more about her?"

"Anything in particular?" Tina asked.

Colin shrugged. "Just see if anything jumps out at you."

There were a few seconds of confused silence at the other end of the line. Then Sophie said, "It's alright Tina, I will explain in a moment. Goodnight boys, take care and Ben – for pity sake, no more guns." The screen went blank.

I could just imagine Sophie trying her best to explain to Tina, what Colin had meant. When you analysed it, we do say the strangest things.

Tina2 hovered over to Ben and Colin. "If there is nothing more you require from me tonight gentlemen, I will shut down, there are some updates I would like to do."

"That's fine Tina2. Thank you," both men said, at the same time.

Colin got up. "Alright, well I'm ready for my bed. It's been another - interesting day. I'll see you in the morning gentlemen."

I was left starring into the flames with Ben. A few moments passed.

"I thought I'd killed him," Ben said quietly, into his brandy. "For a split second, I thought I'd bloody killed him."

He looked close to tears. "But you didn't Ben, that's all that really matters. Take the teasing, it could have been a lot worse."

We sat for a while both lost in our own thoughts, watching the flames dance and listening to the crackle and hiss of the logs.

Ben broke the spell. "Alan, you don't think Tina2 looks like an alien, do you?"

I laughed. "No Ben. Get some sleep, everything will be forgotten tomorrow. I'm pretty sure you'll have the chance to redeem yourself, before this assignment is over." I said goodnight and still chuckling to myself, I left Ben to finish his brandy.

I hurriedly got myself ready for bed. Away from the heat of the fire it was cold. I snuggled down under my blankets. I guessed it could only be around 9.30pm – early, even for me. It was too cold to sit and read, so I lay trying to focus my thoughts, first on Natasha. As usual when I tried to think of her, my thoughts were muddled and confused.

My mind seemed to drift off, of its own accord. I could see Sally. She walked easily through the deep snow, perhaps - not even through it, but over it. She was dressed in black and she moved quickly.

Outside of a lodge that looked a little like ours she stopped and seemed to be waiting. I watched as slowly the door opened. The lodge was in darkness, but by the light of the nearly full moon, I could make out the figure of a man. He seemed almost to be sleep-walking.

For several minutes the man seemed to be struggling with himself, he would start to shut the door, then open it again - as if he couldn't make up his mind.

Sally remained motionless at the door.

I felt a shiver go down my spine.

Finally the man's face relaxed, his lips moved. I couldn't make out the words he said, but Sally was swiftly over the thresh hold, and as she closed the door behind her I caught the flash of her pale green eyes, staring at me and .......did she just wink at me?

I woke with the blankets pulled up tightly around my neck. 'That was a nightmare' I told myself, that was just the product of wine, brandy and an over active imagination. Still, I reminded myself to look for that garlic in the morning.

I had a restless night. A few times I drifted off, only to wake with a start at the sound of a creaking floor board or the rustle of the wind through the trees. At last it was almost light and I must have dozed off, feeling more secure in the cool light of dawn.

The next thing I knew, Ben was shaking me. "What the hell Ben," I cursed

"It's Jack, he's gone! Colin is mad as hell. You need to get dressed now. We're all going out to look for him. You need to hurry Alan."

Ben rushed out and I forced myself into action. I didn't have much time to think. I just threw some clothes on and joined the others in the kitchen.

Colin looked more worried than mad. "Sorry Alan, but we need to find Jack before someone else does. I don't know what's gotten into him lately, he knows the dangers here, yet he seems bent on ignoring them."

"It's fine, I was a wake anyway," I lied. "I think Meg may have been right about Jack losing his head, we've all been there right. This girl – wolf – whatever, may have gotten a lot deeper than those scratches, in fact, she may have touched his heart."

Both men nodded thoughtfully. Oddly enough we were all in - shall we say - challenging relationships. You could probably call what Ben had with Tina – a relationship of sorts.

It took us a few minutes to wrap ourselves up against the cold; in spite of the warm clothing, the rush of freezing air that hit us when we opened the door took our breath away.

Ben had packed Tina2 into a carry case that could hang around his neck.

It was just light enough to see our way across the driveway, and up behind the garage there was a pathway that had been walked recently, large paw marks and boots. "This is the way we took yesterday," Ben confirmed. We followed the path, it wasn't easy to walk. The snow was compacted in places but in others quite deep and soft.

Tina2 spoke from her box, "I feel I should tell you that I am not picking up any radio signals in this area Ben."

"That's good. We have the mountain to ourselves then." Ben seemed relieved.

"Not exactly, Ben," Tina2 added.

"What do you mean, not exactly? Are we alone up here or not?" There was a hint of panic in Ben's voice. Colin had stopped short up ahead and I had that prickly feeling you get on the back of my neck.

"I am picking up heat sources Ben, lots of heat sources. Moving fast and heading this way," Tina concluded.

We stood with our backs together in a small circle watching the tree's, it was so quiet you could have heard the snow fall. Colin had the only riffle, I wanted to ask if it was the real one or the dart gun, but as it turned out, it wouldn't have made much difference either way.

Suddenly, silently, in every direction you looked there were wolves, large and small, grey and white. All of them crouching, watching, waiting, their breath rising like smoke through the trees, their eye's fixed on us. As a group, we held our breath.

I sensed Colin was trying to talk with them, I hoped to god he spoke fluent mountain wolf. Hours passed, well probably a couple of minutes. Standing in the snow waiting to be breakfast to around ten hungry wolves, it felt like hours.

Then just as suddenly something changed, the wolves began to fidget, their focus no longer on us. They seemed suddenly nervous, looking around and sniffing the air.

From out of the woods, clearing four startled wolves, Jack leapt into the ever decreasing circle to stand at Colin's side. The fur on his back was standing up and making him seem even larger than usual. Growling menacingly he advanced towards the closest wolves, forcing them to take a couple of nervous steps back, but the rest held their ground.

I couldn't help thinking, if they can count they are probably working out the odds now, Colin might take care of one of them, Jack could take out a few, but not even he could take on ten or more. If this came to a fight, it was going to end badly.

Then just when it seemed like there was going to be a bloody mess on the fresh white snow, a howl went up from the woods behind the pack.

Jack stopped growling and sniffed the air as if tasting the breeze that blew around us from the mountains. Gradually the wolves took up the cry, one after the other, howling, until I thought my ears would burst.

"She's here and she's not happy," Colin whispered.

That's great I thought, neither am I.

Higher up the path stood the white wolf, the other wolves fell silent and then slowly, very slowly - reluctantly it seemed, they left one by one, until only she remained standing in the clearing.

She showed no sign of fear, in fact she seemed to be studying us. Her focus was mainly on Jack. I noticed even Tina had appeared above the top of her box to get a better look.

I had to admit Jack had been right, she was magnificent.

After the last wolf had disappeared into the tree's, she turned to follow, then stopped to look back at Jack, she seemed to be waiting for him, almost willing him to come with her.

"Jack No," Colin said sternly, seeing Jack start in her direction. "Now is not the time, we'll find her again or she will find us." He put his hand gently on Jack's thick main.

When I looked back the white wolf had gone, just the wind howling through the trees. I felt chilled to the bone and suddenly very hungry!

We stood for a few moments. Ben broke the spell. "I think I peed myself, if we don't get back to the lodge soon I'll probably never be able to get out of these trousers."

"Thanks for that reality check Ben, but you're right let's get back, it's cold and we could all do with something to warm us up." Colin knelt down in front of Jack who was still looking longingly after the white wolf. "We'll help her Jack, but you know we need to take care, let's get you back and changed into something more human and we can make plans alright?" Colin patted Jack on the back of his great shaggy neck.

Jack obediently turned and trotted back in the direction of the lodge. "All right let's move guys," Colin said, following Jack back down the path.

As I caught up with Ben he was muttering to himself or Tina2, it was hard to tell. "That's it I am never leaving my lab again, he can't make me. I will lock myself in and throw away the bloody key. I'm not cut out for this shit. My feet are freezing."

I passed Ben and caught up with Colin who wasn't letting Jack out of his sight. "Well what did you make of that, did you manage to talk to them, could you understand them?" I said almost jogging to keep up.

"I'm not sure if they understood me, I am sure they didn't want to listen. What was interesting was the control she had over them, if she hadn't turned up when she did - well let's just say things could have been bad."

"You think she leads them?"

"They listen to her, but not all of them wanted to. I get the feeling something has changed more recently and she may be losing some of her control. Speaking of control it was touch and go with Jack back there, we must watch him carefully. Alan, would you follow him into the barn, he'll have left his clothes there, wait while he changes will you. I don't want him left alone, especially whilst he's in wolf form."

I groaned, the last thing I wanted to do this morning was watch Jack change back, you really only had to see that once to realize it was something you never wanted to see again, but I agreed.

As we neared the lodge Colin called Jack back and I could see why, there was a truck parked outside, it seemed to be empty.

"Shit Sally, I'd forgotten about her, it looks like she's let herself in! Alan you wait here with Jack, Ben and I will go down and keep her busy. You two join us when you are both – presentable. Give us a few minutes to check that she's in the house." Colin left me standing next to Jack.

Well if Sally had let herself in, out went the vampire theory - unless if you invited them in once, they had a free pass?

Back in the real world I started to wonder what I should do if Jack decided to head off after his girlfriend, how the hell would I stop him. I needn't have worried, we watched Ben and Colin disappear into the lodge, waited a few moments, then made our way to the barn. I shut the door behind us and turned the other way whilst Jack did what seemed to come naturally to him. What had Colin compared it to, a chrysalis turning into a butterfly – hardly.

It always amazed me how fast the whole process was, when I picked up the courage to turn back, Jack was already wearing his jeans and putting on his shirt.

I headed for the door, all I could think of was warmth and food in that order. Jack said nothing, but picked up an arm full of logs. Of course, we needed an excuse for being out here in the barn. Tall, dark, handsome and clever too, god sometimes I hated this guy. We loaded up with logs and headed for the lodge.

Colin was right, it was Sally, and by the time we entered the living room with the logs, they were all seated around the large table. Sally turned and watched us, or more precisely she watched Jack.

"Your boy is pretty tough, no need for me to ask how he is after yesterday's ordeal. Not many people would be out in the snow fetching logs in minus twenty degree temperatures with nothing on their feet!" she said smiling.

We all looked down at Jacks feet. Of course, he hadn't bothered with shoes when he had crept out this morning. Colin laughed. "Old habits die hard. Jack is from a poor background, none of his family possessed shoes, I bought him his first pair." I had a feeling that was probably true.

275

Sally looked thoughtful for a moment. "As you say," she agreed, "Old habits do indeed die hard. Well, now we're all here I believe you owe me an explanation Colin."

Sally took a sip of her drink. I almost dropped the logs. A bright red droplet oozed from the corner of her mouth. She caught it and wiped it away with the back of her hand.

"It's early but you look like you need a drink Alan, you're white as a sheet, Bloody Mary?" Colin offered. "Sally has taken hers without the Vodka, Ben and I felt we needed a shot to warm us up after our bracing walk. What about you?"

I shook my head. I had to get a hold on my imagination. "Thanks, but I think I'll put the kettle on for a coffee, a nip of brandy in it wouldn't go astray though." I headed for the kitchen. Tomato juice! Of course, what the hell was wrong with me? I had to get a grip.

When I returned with the coffee the fire was roaring and the warmth was returning to my extremities, I felt a lot better, but seeing Sally with blood red on her lips reminded me of my concerns. I couldn't shake the image in my head, of Sally, closing that door and winking at me. It had been a hell of a dream.

To my surprise Colin was showing Sally Tina2. They were discussing the little sphere. Sally was turning Tina2 over in her hands. "And you say it will pick up any station?" she said. Colin had obviously gone for the radio idea.

"Marvellous, a radio that can fly, how - useful," Sally said. There was no attempt to hide the sarcasm in her voice.

"She doesn't fly, she hovers," Ben said defensively.

Sally smiled, "she? – well, it doesn't matter. I would like to know what you're really here for, what is the real purpose for your visit. And don't try the hunting thing. I wasn't born yesterday, in fact, quite the opposite."

"We're here for the white wolf," Colin said simply. Sally nodded. "I gathered as much. Why?"

"She's different, but you already know that. How different? Well, we hoped you might be able to tell help us with that question."

"And if I help you, what do you intend to do with her?" Sally snapped.

"We would like to take her with us. I have an Island where she would be safe, at least a lot safer than she is here. You must know it's only a matter of time before she is discovered." Sally seemed to consider this for a moment. "You all live there?"

Colin nodded.

Sally pointed to Jack. "He lives on this island too?"

Jack had curled up in a chair, near the fire. Colin glanced at Jack and smiled. "Yes, and others. We make it our business to seek out the unusual, the misfits of this world, the things that for some reason don't fit into the new order of things, whether they're animal, human or........." Colin left the sentence unfinished.

Sally sipped her drink. Jack growled and twitched in his sleep. She smiled. "Alright, I will tell you, what I know.

I'm often out in the woods at night - walking! At first, I sensed something watching me. I didn't take much notice, there are often creatures of the night, watching, keeping an eye on the forest. A few nights later I glimpsed the white wolf, I knew she was following me. Night after night was the same, she kept her distance.

We enjoyed each other's company. I bought music with me into the woods. She seemed to love the music. Months passed like this. Then one night instead of on all fours she stood and as I watched, she began to dance and twirl. As she danced, slowly, her legs and arms lengthened and straightened, her hair grew long, her nose short, and the wolf looked more like a woman.

She must have seen my expression, she looked down at her arms and a look of terror filled her eyes. Instantly she was the wolf again. I tried to calm her, but she took off.

This was a couple of weeks ago. I haven't been able to find her since."

Sally's story more or less told us what we needed to know, although we had suspected it, this confirmed that the white wolf was in fact like Sophie, Jack and now of course Toby.

After some time Colin spoke, "You understand Sally. We need to find her, we can help her. Here she doesn't fit any more, not with the wolves, not with the humans. She will be lost and lonely. The wolves already sense that there is something wrong, sooner or later they will reject her. Then where would she go? Like it or not Sally, we are her best and probably only hope. Some of us know exactly what she's going through!"

"He's like her, isn't he?" Sally said, looking at Jack.

"Yes and he isn't the only one, it - kind of runs in the family." Colin looked a little awkward but Sally hardly seemed to notice.

"Look I must get back. I told Kevin I was coming out here to ask all of you over for lunch. Kevin's buddies left this morning, so it will just be us. Alan, will you keep me company in the jeep, the others can follow us."

I hesitated. She laughed. "It's alright Alan, I won't bite."

Colin smiled and slapped me on the back. "Yes Alan you keep Sally company and Ben, Jack and I will follow on."

I reluctantly did as I was asked and followed Sally outside. I hoped she was telling the truth. I still hadn't found the garlic. We left the others and headed out into the crisp late morning air, it was a beautiful day it seemed strangely peaceful, after the morning's events. I got in the Jeep next to Sally and we headed for the lodge.

"Well?" Sally said, without taking her eyes from the road.

"Well what," I said, unsure of what she expected from me and not wanting to make any silly accusations, especially in a confined space.

"It was you last night, I sensed you watching me. I 'm not sure how. But it was you, Alan."

My mind was in turmoil, she had seen me. How could that be? It had been a dream - it had to have been a dream. The alternative would mean............oh shit!

I tried to unravel what was going through my mind "Your name is really, Jess. You were a Doctor in the city. How did you end up here?" I asked, trying to keep my voice level and stop the panic that threatened to overcome me.

She sighed. "Yes, my father chose the name. He was always a little disappointed."

"He wanted a boy?" I ventured.

"He wanted a wolf."

I laughed, until I realized she hadn't been joking.

"I don't understand." This conversation, had taken too many turns, just like the road. My head was spinning and I was feeling sick. Sally or Jess glanced at me and shrugged. "Mixed blood, he was hoping I would take after him, but instead I took after my mother. I was born in these mountains many years ago. My father built the lodge. I've come home Alan."

I wanted to find out more, but it struck me that finding out too much could be dangerous to your health. My curiosity got the better of me, "Your father is one of the wolves?"

She laughed. "Clever boy! No - maybe there might be a distant relation or two, but father died along while ago. My mother left us when I was very young, like me she couldn't stay in one place too long."

I'd thought I was beginning to find my way, but she'd lost me again. "I'm sorry I don't understand. Why did she have to leave?"

Sally sighed. "We grow old very slowly - our kind. If you stay in one place too long, people start to talk, fearful, jealous people!" She glanced my way, and I shifted uneasily in my seat.

"But rumours take on a life of their own, it's best to just move on. What about you Alan, you have mixed blood too. I sense it, but there's something there I'm not familiar with. I sensed you watching me the other night, but I would have smelt you and heard your heart beat if you had been within half a mile of the place. How could that be?"

The thought of this woman being able to hear a heartbeat from half a mile away didn't surprise me. I tried to think, how much could I say?

"I'm a seeker, I'm not too sure yet how that works, but I have visions, like dreams. Part of me is transported and able to observe things." It was the best answer I could give her.

She didn't seem surprised. "From your mother's side I would guess."

I felt secretly pleased that she was wrong. She seemed to know far too much already.

"No, I think it was my father. I didn't know him that well. He was a reporter, he travelled the world. I hardly saw him at all, after I was sent to boarding school. He went missing when I was 18 - presumed dead."

Jess smiled. A slightly unsettling sight, not only did it show off an extraordinary large incisor, but it left me with the feeling she knew something that I didn't.

"Your father disappeared, could I hazard a guess that your mother seemed older than your father at the time?"

Suddenly I felt even more uncomfortable. Without waiting for my answer she continued, "Your mother has re-married?"

"No," I snapped.

That smile again. "I thought not," she added.

I was beginning to feel angry now, without really understanding why. "I don't think she's ever accepted that he's really gone. I don't understand, how could you know that my mother was older than my father? I'd never really thought of it before. What is it you're getting at?" The rising tone of my voice betrayed my anger "My father's dead, he loved us. He wouldn't just up and leave us."

She shrugged. "My mother loved us Alan, that's why she left, to let us live in peace. Sometimes the greatest love of all can be to let that someone go. We're here - the others won't be far behind."

Sally stopped the jeep and started to get out. "Wait," I grabbed her arm. "What were you getting at? I know I have mixed blood, human and seeker. I'm not a bloody vampire." I spat the words out, regretting them instantly.

Jess looked down at my hand on her arm. I quickly pulled it away. Her eyes shone with that pale green glow I'd seen before. She suddenly looked terrifying and angry, very angry. "A bloody - vampire, how dare you call me – bloody." She seemed larger than life now and far, far too close for comfort. She didn't raise her voice, she didn't need to. Her fury was obvious. "It's your species that rape the earth, you cruelly cage your pray, then with little or no mercy, kill it. What a waste of life! Tell me Alan, how many of your meals have gotten up the next day feeling happy and alive? Bloody vampires as you call us - rarely kill. In fact we preserve life. It is important to us."

My anger was easily trumped by hers. I sort to defend myself. "But you create more vampires by sucking people dry," I shouted, desperately trying to hang on to the monster card, although little shafts of doubt were creeping in. This wasn't a movie, I had been wrong about so many things lately.

Sally's mood seemed to change, her features softened a little, she seemed more sad than angry. She sighed. "We create, as you put it, the same as everyone else. A higher power than you, or I, decides how you are born Alan. What you make of your life after that is up to you! My people have subtle differences, yes, our diet of course and our longevity, but sunlight isn't a problem, nor is garlic or holy water. This isn't the movies Alan."

No point looking for the garlic then, there would be no help there.

Sally smiled again. "I didn't mean to upset you Alan. I would suggest you speak with your mother, that's all, and try to keep an open mind." And with that, thankfully she left the Jeep, heading into the Lodge.

I sat for a moment, trying to calm my nerves and unravel my thoughts. My father always looked the same in all the photographs I'd seen, had my mother aged more than him? I'd never thought about it before.

Colin opened the Jeep door. "You alright Alan?"

"I don't know," I said honestly. Colin indicated for the others to go into the lodge and joined me in the front of the jeep. "Ok what's wrong, you look bloody awful."

"Strange you should use that turn of phrase," I said bitterly, I couldn't begin to talk about the thoughts I was having about my family, instead I gave voice to the other fear that had been creeping silently around in my head, made stronger by Sally's words.

"Is she coming back Colin?" I felt close to tears.

"Did she leave because of me?" I could hardly speak. Natasha had given my life meaning. I didn't want to think of facing it, without her.

Colin put his hand on my shoulder. "Look Alan if that's - all that's bothering you, you can rest assured that Natasha will come back. She's not the type to cut and run without letting her friends know what's going on. We're her family and she's like a sister to me. She will come back. What happens after that, I think is between you two. That's all, that's bothering you?"

Colin suspected more, I knew. He always seemed to read my mind, but I just needed to get some thoughts straight in my head before I talked to anyone else. I was relieved, when Colin didn't push for more.

"Look, we'd best get in. I don't remember if there were any wolves heads on those walls, but if there are, we'd better get between Jack and Kevin before Kevin's head finds its way into the décor too."

I followed Colin quickly into the Lodge; Jack had been a little unstable lately and if Kevin started boasting about hunting down the beast of the mountains, I think we would all have a job to restrain him.

We needn't have worried. Sally had taken Jack and Ben straight through into the dining room. Kevin greeted us from behind the bar, "Red, white or a beer."

"Beer would be good," Colin said. I agreed. Kevin seemed to approve.

"Glasses are on the table. Sally has rushed the other boy's through, probably the big guy's allergies. How's the migraine?"

Colin thumped me in the back. I'd forgotten the excuse I had used last time we were here. "Ah - Much better now, thanks." A thought struck me, "I was wondering Kevin, did you build the Lodge."

He laughed. "God no, this place is about two hundred years old, we did it up and added bits, but the original building was built by a local guy. A bit of a hunter himself, by all accounts. Sally managed to dig up an old picture of him and his family, very attractive wife and a little girl, it's around here somewhere."

As we made our way to the dinner table I did some quick sums in my head. However you looked at it, Sally was wearing exceptionally well.

We joined Ben and Jack. This side of the lodge was positioned so that you could see out over the trees and up to the mountains beyond, I noticed with a smile that Ben had the camera case that housed Tina2 over his shoulder, it would have been unthinkable for Ben to have left her behind. The young girl from the other day helped Sally bring out dishes and plates of food from the kitchen and arranged them in the centre of the large table. A mouth- watering joint of what looked like roast beef was positioned in front of Kevin, for him to carve.

I smiled at the attractive waitress who blushed. I found myself checking out her neck for marks, there were none visible, maybe employees were out of bounds.

Sally joined us once everything was in place.

"This looks fantastic Sally, thank you both for inviting us. You must be very busy, it's quite a place you have here," said Colin, accepting a glass of beer from Kevin.

"The boys you met yesterday went back today. In fact you only just missed them. Three of us fitted in a last minute early morning hunt, one of the Dave's missed out - he was feeling a bit washed out this morning. Too much beer if you ask me, he was fine after a lie in.

It was a waste of time anyway, the mountains seem strangely empty, must be the bad weather. Things always pick up as the weather improves. For one thing, people can actually get here." Kevin laughed and started to carve the meat.

"The Beef looks good. Thank you Sally, are you not joining us?" Colin asked.

Sally smiled. "Alas no, I'm afraid I have a stomach problem I inherited from my mother, I find it almost impossible to digest solid foods, so I have a special liquid diet. I've gotten used to it over the years." Sally glanced at me. I tried to concentrate hard - on my food.

"Yes, poor Sally," Kevin added, "I sometimes wonder how we got together. We seem opposites in so many things, I can't imagine not being able to sink my teeth into a good juicy stake, I like my meat so rare, it almost has a pulse."

I almost choked on my beef. "Can I get you some water, Alan," Sally said sweetly.

"No thank you, I'm fine," I spluttered. "Something just went down the wrong way."

It struck me that Kevin had a lot more in common with his wife than he realized.

Ben had already tucked in. "This Beef is great, I must admit I was expecting something more like deer or wild boar from the mountains, not that I'm complaining."

Sally smiled. "Thank you Ben. We get the meat from a local man who has a farm down the mountain; he knows how to look after his animals." She looked pointedly at me.

Kevin laughed. "My wife believes that all animals should lead happy lives, no matter how short."

Ben laughed. "Well, if this is what happy beef tastes like, I think I would have to agree with her." I hadn't seen Ben enjoy a meal like this before, perhaps it was the mountain air and the fact that he could not escape to his lab. The trauma of yesterday had disappeared for the moment and he did look a lot healthier.

Colin asked, "Do you have problems with the wolves? Are there any attacks?"

Kevin laughed. "No you've been listening to rumours or reading those silly papers they print in the town, the wolves have never really been a problem, it's all just old fears and superstitions that we should have put behind us years ago.

It's this big bugger that's rattled people. But I've been close a couple of times lately, I'll kill this thing and show them that it's not magical or mythical. It'll die like anything else."

In that instant several things happened all at the same time:

Colin knocked his water clean across the table and managed to douse Jack, Sally's hand shot out and grasped Jack's arm, even from this distance across the table I could see the hairs standing up (far too many hairs) and Ben shuffled his chair closer to me to try to distance himself from Jack.

"Sorry Jack," Colin said, covering the distance between them in a heartbeat.

Sally's hand still tightly gripped Jack's arm, she was staring intently into his eyes, and she spoke calmly, "Come Jack I'll take you out the back and find you one of Kevin's old shirts, you would freeze in these temperatures if you were to go outside, soaked like that."

Jack was visibly shaking but he allowed Sally to lead him away.

Kevin downed his beer. "God that boy of yours has got a temper. I thought he was going to floor you then Colin. Lucky it was only water you spilled on him, not your beer. Now what were we talking about? Ah yes, that bloody wolf. Thought I might go further afield tomorrow, you're welcome to tag along, if you would like."

I could tell Colin wanted to get out of there fast. "Thanks Kevin, but we want to take a few photographs. We'll be heading home in a couple of days, so we won't be going far from the lodge. If you'll excuse me, I'll go check on Jack and Sally. Jack hasn't been himself lately." Colin left and Ben looked at me hopefully, there was no way he was going to make small talk with this guy. I tried my best. It was easier than I thought. In spite of my initial feelings, I found I actually liked Kevin.

"Sally seems very happy here, how long have you two been married?"

"Yes, Sally loves this place, funny thing really. I've visited this mountain on and off for many years, hunting and fishing with my Dad, since I was small. Sally and I met just over a year ago and I bought her here. It was as though she knew the place better than I did. Sally found the old lodge. It was a bit run down, but not in bad shape really. We managed to get it for a song. I've spent a small fortune making it what you see today. Sally would like us to do the skiing and walking thing and forget about the hunting. More beer?"

Without waiting for an answer he headed out to the bar to refill the jug.

"He really isn't a bad guy, when you take the time to talk to him," I said.

Ben shrugged. "Good or bad he won't last long around Jack if he keeps talking about the wolf like that! I thought Jack was going to rip his head off. Colin was quick off the mark, but Sally seemed to have Jack under control. Strange, he doesn't usually respond well to strangers."

Colin joined Kevin when he returned with the beer, they both sat down.

Colin saw my expression and gave me an update. "Sally has found Jack a shirt and they've gone for a walk, he needed to cool off and the mountain air should do the trick."

"Is that wise," I said forgetting about Kevin, but I needn't have worried.

"Oh your friend will be alright with Sally, she knows the woods like the back of her hand. She even takes walks at night. That used to worry the life out of me, but she always comes back looking so refreshed, it obviously does her a world of good."

I smiled to myself, the thought of anything being more formidable than a vampire and a ware wolf. Colin relaxed a little and we sat and had another beer.

Kevin seemed very interested in Colin, one self-made man to another I supposed. Ben and I could have easily left the table un-noticed. It was about an hour later when Sally and Jack reappeared. We all drained the last of the beer and Colin shook hands with Kevin and kissed Sally lightly on the cheek.

We thanked them for a great lunch and an interesting afternoon. Then Sally walked us to the jeep. I found myself checking Jack's neck. Sally saw me looking and smiled.

"Something else, that you might like to consider Alan, have you ever been bitten by a mosquito, and if so where? Kevin will be gone before first light, when I'm sure he's a safe distance away, I'll come and see you."

Sally waved us off, Jack drove. He was the only one who hadn't indulged in Kevin's plentiful hospitality.

Ben looked puzzled. "What did Sally mean about the mosquito?"

Colin gave me a side-long look. "I think I know that one. Our Sally's a vampire, Alan has been checking necks! Mosquitos can bite you anywhere, just like vampires! Am I right Alan?"

Ben laughed. "I thought as much, that makes sense, but she would have to be bloody hungry to risk chewing on Jack!"

I was astounded. "She's a vampire! Is no one else, even slightly worried by this?

She gives me the creeps. Does no one else see anything wrong with what's going on here?" I felt angry that Ben and Colin seemed not only to accept this, but to think this was all - funny.

Colin shook his head. "Alan until you stop thinking within the realms of monsters and men, them and us, you're going to have serious problems. This is the real world and the lines separating good and bad can sometimes be a bit fuzzy!

We are what we are, as far as I can tell, the only thing in any real danger here is the she-wolf. I would suggest you concentrate on her tonight, we may be running out of time. We need to find her and get her out of here. Before, it's too late.

Now let's get home and contact the others, I'm a little concerned about George and Goldie." Colin's tone was reprimanding, but he added a little more kindly, "I think Sally or should we say Jess, has given you a lot to think about Alan. When you're ready to talk, let me know, but try not to lose sight of the reason we are here.

JACK!    Will you take those corners a little slower please? Remember you have four wheel-drive, not four paws."

It was good to get back to our lodge. Ben had already released Tina2 from the confines of her box. None of us needed any food after the huge lunch. Jack hadn't eaten much, but he was more than happy with a steak, straight from the fridge. The rest of us settled down with coffee and a brandy, in front of a roaring fire.

My mind was racing. I kept going over the things Sally had said, but Colin had been right, I needed to concentrate on why we were here. When we got back to the island I'd contact my mother and arrange to go and see her. As for Natasha, she'd promised to return and I had to trust her.

Tina2 interrupted my thoughts. "I have a call coming in for you Colin. Shall I put it on the screen?"

"Yes thank you Tina."

It was Sophie. "Hi guys, how are things going. Is Jack healing alright? Meg has been worried about infection setting in. She's not used to letting someone else patch any of us up."

Colin laughed. "We're all good. Tell Meg that Jack's fine, as luck would have it we actually had a fairly impressive Doctor to hand."

Sophie nodded, "We were right about Sally - alias Jess, then. I have some more news on that front. Tina has found images of your Doctor friend in different guises, using different names and moving around, quite a bit. So far we can trace her back about 100 years, fascinating really, in the earliest picture she looks about 18 or 19, which means either she has a bloody good plastic surgeon, or you have a vampire in your midst."

Colin laughed. "Yes Alan assures me that the latter is true. She's being very helpful, I think between her local knowledge and Alan's skills - if he can manage to get over himself and put the garlic away, we should be able to find what we're looking for tomorrow. What happens after that, is anyone's guess."

"Poor Alan, your first vampire. It can be a little - unsettling, they have had so much bad press over the years. You do know the garlic thing is a myth, don't you?"

Even Sophie was finding it funny. "Yes she told me. I can't believe that no one else seems even slightly concerned about her."

Sophie looked more serious. "Trust me Alan, there are far worse things out there. I should know, I'm one of them."

Sophie smiled again. "Well, be careful all of you and do remember to keep Ben in front of you, at all times."

Ben groaned. "I thought we were all over that."

"Yes Ben sorry. Seriously guys take care, we don't know what she will do. Don't corner her and remember she has to come here of her own free will, we all have the right to choose.

Oh Alan, I almost forgot, Natasha has been in touch. She's on her way home, I think she'll be back in a couple of days, you may well arrive at the same time. I was going to leave it as a surprise, but I know how worried you've been."

My heart leapt.

Colin had been looking thoughtful. "You haven't mentioned George and Goldie. I've had this niggling feeling that George is worried about something. They are alright aren't they, you would tell me if there was a problem?"

"Honey there is no problem, Goldie will be fine dear, in fact they're both fine. Meg has things under control. There really was nothing to worry about.

We all miss you, so get your finger out, finish the job and come home."

Colin nodded. "Alright, give our love to everyone and we'll see you very soon."

The screen went blank. Colin still looked thoughtful.

"Is there something wrong?" I asked, although with Natasha coming home, suddenly everything felt very right. Even the thought of vampires in the night couldn't dampen my spirits, but I could tell Colin had something on his mind.

He shrugged. "No it's probably nothing, just a feeling. There, I told you Natasha would come home. Let's all get some sleep and tomorrow perhaps we can finish things here and get home where we all belong."

Colin said goodnight, Jack and Ben followed him. I sat starring into the flames. I was beginning to realize, there were in fact very few real monsters in this world, most of us were just doing what we needed to do, to stay alive, Sophie, Jack even Sally.

Had my father, really been like Sally, had he been forced to leave my mother and me, so that we could lead a normal life? Normal! That word again, at every turn I had to re-think my world and the things I thought I had a handle on. How much did my mother know, what if my seeker powers didn't come from my father?

\*\*\*

I turned out the lights and headed for bed. I didn't feel like sleeping, but I needed to try and focus on the she-wolf, we had to find her tomorrow. I wanted to go home.

I lay in bed listening to the wind blowing round the lodge. I tried to imagine the wolves out there in the cold night. I wondered if the she-wolf even knew how different she was. Maybe she was happy with the life she had, would she want the complicated life that the rest of us led. Did she have a choice?

I let my mind drift, be blown around by the wind, carried through the trees, I could see a cave, three large boulders circled the entrance like guardians, the wind howled - no not the wind, I could hear howling but some way off. Closer now, I could make out a pair of large blue eyes watching me. I forced myself forward, telling myself that whatever was in the cave was probably more afraid than I was. That was hard to imagine. Closer now, I could make out the huge white body of the she-wolf. She was huddled against the far wall, alone in the cold.

All at once, it dawned on me, she really was more afraid than I was. How could she understand what was happening to her, how terrifying all this must be. Had she left the pack, or had she been cast out. Either way, we were her only hope. I wanted to tell her that it would be alright, I wanted to put a blanket around her to keep her warm against the night, but most of all, I wanted to be home, with Natasha and Scruffy.

The moment my thoughts turned to Scruffy, I could see the little dog. Not in the dark cave but in front of another cave in broad daylight. I could almost feel the heat of the sun, it was the dragons cave back on the island and Scruffy wasn't alone. Sophie, Maya, Spike, Toby and George stood outside. They all seemed worried or excited, I couldn't tell. There were so many emotions, my head began to swim.

I woke confused. My body still felt warmed by the sun, my visions were mixed and confusing. But I'd seen the she-wolf, Sally would be able to locate the cave in my vision, I was sure of that. Tomorrow, we would find her.

\*\*\*

Ben knocked on my door, it was still dark outside. I grumbled and he entered, he read my thoughts. "Yes I know it's still dark, but Colin wants to be ready to go as soon as Sally gets here." Ben turned to leave before I could open my mouth to complain.

"I think I know where she is," I shouted at his retreating back. He stopped and turned.

"Great, let's find her and get the hell out of here. I need to get back to Tina and my Lab. My body wasn't built for these temperatures. I think my brain is starting to freeze.

Colin is making breakfast, I'll tell him you're on your way."

I dressed quickly and followed my nose to the kitchen, Colin had breakfast well underway. He looked up. "Ben said you think you have a fix on her. Scrambled or poached?"

"What - oh yes, scrambled please. I don't know about a fix, but I saw her and if I describe her surroundings to Sally, I think with her knowledge of the area she'll be able to take us to her. She was alone," I added, remembering how sad and lonely I'd felt.

"That's great Alan, there was something else?" He did it again, how did he know what I was thinking?

"I'm not sure, I saw Scruffy and the others outside George's cave, they may just have been visiting, but I felt - I really don't know what I felt!"

Colin sighed. "I know what you mean, I've felt something too, but Sophie said everything was fine, let's just get home as soon as we can. Eat up, coffee's ready, help yourself. I must just check on Jack. I said he could go out and get his own breakfast, but I don't want him getting carried away. As soon as Sally gets here, we'll head off." Colin put a plate of Scrambled eggs and toast in front of me. A draft of cold air hit me as the door shut behind him.

Ben had already finished his, he helped himself and me to coffee and re- joined me at the table. "After breakfast I'll show you the guns, one is live ammo, the other is a dart gun. They look almost the same, but I can show you how to tell them apart. I think it would be wise if you and Colin carry one each, I don't ever want to touch the bloody things again."

I tried to reassure him, "Don't keep beating yourself up Ben, it really wasn't that bad."

It had been a while, since I'd handled a gun. If I was honest, I didn't fancy the responsibility either. Ben brought both riffles into the kitchen. Ben had been right, it was hard to tell them apart, but he showed me a couple of tell - tale signs and markings.

"I've made the weight the same, so you cannot tell by just picking them up, however even in the dark, the markings on the barrels show up. So as long as you know what you're looking for, you'll not pick up the wrong one. This one is the dart gun - this one takes the real bullets."

Ben handed each one to me in turn, he was right, you couldn't feel a difference in weight and at first glance they looked identical.

"We're taking both. Colin has asked me to load them, so make sure you remember which one is which, there's a big difference between dead and just sleeping it off."

"Alright Ben, but couldn't we just have the dart guns, I'm not sure I like the idea of having to kill anything."

He shook his head. "That's just the problem Ala, whether we like the idea or not, we may not have a choice. The problem is that even though the dart gun is powerful, it takes a few seconds to kick in, and you know as well as I do that a lot can happen in a few seconds."

Colin opened the door, letting in a cold blast of air and a large wet wolf. Jack padded past us, straight into the living room, collapsing unceremoniously in front of the dwindling fire. He proceeding to wash the areas that modesty and a lack of agility, would prevent him doing in his human form. All three of us exchanged glances. Colin noticed the rifles.

"Ah good Ben, you've shown Alan the guns, are you happy you can tell them apart Alan, it could be crucial."

I nodded, "Yes, although I have to say, I would prefer it if they were both dart guns."

"Me too Alan, but we can't take the risk, if things go badly, we may need an instant result. Let's hope not." From in front of the fire Jack started to growl, he stood, his ears pricked listening to something out of my range, but Colin could obviously hear it too.

"Dogs," he said.

A couple of seconds later, I heard several dogs, barking excitedly and getting closer. We all headed for the windows. It was just light enough to see now and coming up the hill was a sledge, pulled by four large dogs and driven by a striking figure. It reminded me of the ice queen from the Lion the witch and the wardrobe, it was snowing hard now, making the scene even more surreal.

Jack stood growling, hackles raised. Colin was obviously impressed. "That woman certainly knows how to make an entrance." The sledge stopped outside the lodge, the figure threw some scraps of meat on the ground for the dogs and strode towards us.

Colin pointed to the fire. "Jack go lie down," he said firmly. Jack grumbled and growled but obeyed and returned to his previous spot, thankfully, not his previous task.

Colin opened the door and Sally swept in. "I thought we might need a better means of transport," she said and then saw Jack in front of the fire. The effect was instant; she seemed mesmerized by his appearance.

It was the first time she'd seen Jack as a wolf. I started to say, be careful, but there was no need. Amazingly, Jack held out a huge paw, she took it and very gently stroked his head. "He is magnificent," she gasped. "He reminds me so much of my father."

It was Ben and Colin's turn to look surprised, in all the rush I'd forgotten to tell them about Sally's mixed heritage. I shrugged and said simply, "Mixed blood!"

Both men just nodded. That explained everything.

Tina2 drifted in from the kitchen. "I have been monitoring the weather as you requested Colin. The storm is passing, however it will return in a few hours. We have a window of opportunity to.........." The little silver sphere stopped in mid-sentence noticing we had a guest, it was the first time I'd witnessed a computer lost for words. She tried to settle herself discretely on the table.

"Ah, your little space ship or no - sorry it was a radio wasn't it? That's, an interesting station, you have it tuned to." Sally smiled her teeth glinted in the last flickering flames from the fire.

Colin had given up on the pretence, "It's alright Tina2. Sally is here to help us. You don't have to pretend any more. How long do you think we have, before the weather closes in again?"

Tina2 glided over to Ben for reassurance. "It is hard to be precise. I would suggest around five hours Colin."

"Thank you Tina. Sally this is Tina2, one of Ben's friends. She is just a small part of a larger computer, highly intelligent and an important member of the team."

"Nice to meet you finally Tina2." Sally stood and bowed slightly towards the little sphere. Tina2 still seemed a little unsure, but she bobbed up and down a couple of times and flashed her green lights shyly in reply.

"She likes you," Ben said with a smile.

Sally seemed fascinated. "How can you tell?"

Ben smiled. "You got the green light." We all laughed.

Tina had been right. Outside the snow seemed to be easing. Colin was keen to get things moving. "All right, that's the introductions over with. Alan you talk to Sally about what you saw in your vision. Ben and I will get the stuff together. Sally, will those dogs be alright with Jack in wolf form?"

Sally turned her attention back to Jack and nodded "They will be a little nervous Colin, but Jack will be the Alfa male. They will do as they are told." She stroked Jack's head admiringly. I sat on the couch, near to the fire, Sally seemed loath to leave Jacks side, but eventually joined me. After I had described the scene from my dream she seemed excited.

"I know where that is, it's not far, only about an hour from here if we take the dog team, but the sled will be crowded with four of us."

Colin agreed. "That's not a problem. Ben I want you to stay here with Tina2. We'll take one of the hand radios, if we get into trouble, we'll need to be able to call you to get help. Tina will be able to track the radio signal if there's a problem. We'll call in every half hour, if you don't hear from us and can't get us on the radio, then you'll need to get the cavalry!"

Ben looked a little relieved at Colin's request. Then suddenly there was a hint of panic in his voice. "Wait, it's alright saying bring the cavalry, but where the hell am I going to find a rescue team out here, I can't just call thunderbirds."

Sally Laughed. "I don't think you'll reach them here Ben. Kevin has gone further down the mountain. You should be able to get him on the radio. Just tell him we're missing. He will know what to do."

Ben relaxed. "Alright, but keep in touch, Sophie is already gunning for me, after I shot Jack. She would literally, have my guts for garters if anything happened to the rest of you."

Colin patted him on the back. "Everything will be fine Ben. Keep the coffee hot and the fire burning and we'll be back before you know it." I envied Ben. We left him putting more wood on the fire, even though the snow had stopped there was a bitter wind, that seemed to pierce even the thickest of clothing. As we approached the sled the dogs began to fidget and whine. Sally spoke to them gently, but firmly, Jack however wasn't so subtle he padded up to the front two dogs and gave a low menacing growl, instantly all four dogs dropped to the ground.

Jack sniffed each dog's nether regions in turn, then satisfied with whatever information he had gleaned from the exercise, took up his place just to the right of the lead dog. The dogs, although still a little edgy, began to jump and bark ready for the off.

Colin and I climbed on board, behind Sally and with a jolt we were away. The fresh snow helped the sled glide easily across the virgin surface, we seemed to be moving very fast along the road and then off into the woods.

Sally shouted above the wind rushing past our ears, "It can get pretty chilly, there are blankets under the seats." I felt a bit of a wimp, but I pulled out a blanket anyway and wrapped it around my shoulders, she was right, it helped.

The sun was high in the sky now, it made everything sparkle as we sped past, but did little to warm the bitter air around us. After a while Colin looked at his watch and took out the small radio from his jacket pocket, it took some effort with his thick gloves. "Better phone home," he shouted, "The kids will be worried."

Everything looked the same in the covering of snow. I wondered how we would find our way back without Sally, if she decided to leave us out here in no man's land, but I figured Jack should be able to find his way.

Colin had to shout at the radio. "Tina can you hear me." I could just make out the reply

"Yes Colin. We are tracking your progress. Ben can hear you. Would you like to speak with him?"

"No need Tina, just so long as he knows we're alright, we will call again in around 30 minutes, but Tina don't let Ben panic if I'm a few minutes late. It isn't easy getting to the radio out here."

"I will do as you ask Colin."

The radio went silent and Colin tucked it away, he managed to lean forward and tap Sally on the shoulder. "How far?" He shouted, above the wind.

Sally turned and smiled. Despite her face being exposed to the elements she seemed unaffected by the cold and wind. "We have made good progress, about 10 or 15 minutes I would guess, I haven't been up here for quite some time."

For a moment Sally seemed to be distracted, perhaps remembering something in her past, and Sally had a lot of past.

She turned back to the dogs and shouted something at them, I couldn't hear what it was, but it seemed to spur them on. We swept on through the winter wonderland, it really was a magical place, but I found myself longing for the warmth and comfort of the island. I imagined walking hand in hand with Natasha, along the golden sands, Scruffy and Spike scampering around us. I let my thoughts wonder until I could almost feel the warmth of the island sun on my face and hear the rush of the waves on the shore. Abruptly, we stopped.

The dogs stood panting, steam rising from them in great clouds. Sally jumped down and threw them some more scraps of meat. I noticed they all looked to Jack for the ok, before tucking in, this didn't surprise me. I was surprised however, when Sally offered Jack a lump of meat too, he took it without ceremony. I found it hard to think of Jack as both animal and human, Sally seemed to accept and understand this without question.

I didn't recognize any of the scenery from my dream. Sally saw my expression and pointed. "I think it's just over that ridge. I didn't want to spook her. We'll have to go on foot from here. It might be best if Jack leads the way, I think she'll let him get close if he's on his own. I know why she has chosen to come here. There are primitive paintings deep in the cave. They seem to depict wolves, mostly on all fours, but a couple standing upright. My father bought me here when I was just a small child. He showed the pictures to me. I think he hoped that it might help me to understand." For a moment Sally looked distant.

Colin nodded. "She's trying to make some sense of what's happening to her, she doesn't know who she is anymore."

Colin knelt by Jack. "Jack, Sally's right, you go first, but go slowly. Try to remember what it was like for you the first time. She's scared and confused."

Jack put his head on one side, as if pondering this. Then he made his way slowly up the slope towards the ridge top. We followed as best we could. The snow was deep here and it was hard going.

The sled dogs seemed eerily quiet as they huddled together in the snow. Every now and then one of them would whimper. I had to admit, I was feeling apprehensive too. We were almost at the top of the ridge, when Colin stopped suddenly. "Shit! I forgot to let Ben know we're here. I don't want him to panic and call in the cavalry, just yet. We should have the guns with us too. I'll be back as soon as I can."

He saw both our expressions and added quickly. "The guns are just a precaution. You two follow Jack, but keep your distance, if anyone can handle this situation right now its Jack. He's the only one who could possibly know what she's going through right now. I'll contact Ben, get the guns, and join you just over this ridge." Colin didn't wait for a reply.

Sally and I exchanged worried glances. Jack had already disappeared from view. "We should see the rocks and the cave entrance from the top," Sally whispered.

It seemed to take a while to cover the last couple of metres, the snow was deeper here and it was hard work. I wasn't as fit as I used to be. I could feel my heart pounding in my chest, I tried hard not to think of the blood pulsing through my veins, I wrapped my scarf tighter around my neck.

Sally had been right. From the top of the ridge you could see the large rocks surrounding the entrance to the cave. Jack was already half way across the clearing. We half slid, half climbed down, so that we were behind the first of the large boulders.

Jack had stopped. He lay down in the snow. "What's he doing?" I whispered. Sally leaned closer. I had to resist the automatic urge I felt, to pull away.

"She's in there, I can smell her. He wants her to come to him."

Sally was right. We didn't have to wait long, the she-wolf appeared and advanced towards Jack, a couple of metres away she stopped, something had distracted her.

Colin slid down the steep bank to join us behind the boulder. For a second it looked like she might turn and run, but Jack whined and rolled over on his side, thumping his tail on the snow covered ground. It worked. The she-wolf's attention was drawn to him; slowly she advanced, until she stood over him. She sniffed him carefully. Jack lay still and for a few seconds the scene was frozen just like the surroundings. Then without warning she bought one of her huge paws down across Jack's nose, I felt Colin tense at my side and for the first time I noticed he had one of the rifles, slung over his shoulder the other at the ready in his hand.

Jack hadn't moved, he lay still on his side. The she-wolf walked around him slowly then she lay down, her nose almost touching his. Jack rolled back to face her and licked her muzzle. What followed would have been recognized by dog owners, all over the world. It was a playful rough and tumble, just two canine friends, having fun in the park.

The playful exuberance went on for a while. I was grateful that the sun was now high above us, it started very slowly to melt the icicles from the tree's, the little droplets of water sparkled like diamonds, as they fell to the ground. The snow we knelt on however still felt bloody cold. Thankfully my legs had gone to sleep. Despite the discomfort the scene acting out in front of us was mesmerizing, touching and uplifting all at the same time. I heard Sally sigh at my side and even Colin had lowered the riffle.

Eventually both animals lay exhausted side by side on the ground. After a few moments rest, a story even more amazing began to unravel before our very eyes. Up until now I'd only witnessed Jack change form a couple of times. Both times I'd found it almost impossible to watch, not least because it happened in an instant. This was different, almost beautiful, a slow dance, a dance of precision and care.

Jack circled the she-wolf slowly, so close he brushed up against her at every turn. Gradually, almost unperceivably his legs began to lengthen, losing some of their shaggy appearance as he walked. For a few seconds she watched him, she seemed transfixed.

Then slowly she joined in the dance, he walked around her and she seemed to grow taller with him, her legs becoming long and slender and her tail shrinking. Jack's tail had disappeared he reached out a now human hand, to take her slender hand in his, they were both upright now. I could start to make out human features on her face. Long white hair flowed over her shoulders. As we watched the stage, blissfully unaware of the world around us- a shot rang out. It cut through the silence, like a knife.

Both performers fell to the snow. In the confusion that followed, almost in slow motion, I watched Colin leap to his feet, raising the riffle and firing simultaneously. I didn't feel Sally move, but saw her cover the distance across the clearing, far faster than humanly possible. It was only then, that I saw Kevin. He was standing on the other side of the clearing, a riffle in one hand, his other hand to his chest. For a split second, I thought he would fire again, but Sally dived head long, taking him with her to the ground. By the time I gathered my wits, Colin had reached the two figures that now lay together in the clearing. I raced to help him lift Jack's, now human form, from the other strange body that lay on the snow beneath him. The pale face and long white hair, framed now, by the red blood stained snow, one of her arms human, the other still covered in hair and bearing the claws of the wolf, her body all though long and slender, still a mass of thick white fur.

Jack groaned. "Thank god. Jack, can you hear me?" Colin sat on the snow cradling Jack's head in his lap, wiping blood, from a gash on the side of his skull. Jack's eyes flickered open, in an instant, he was leaning over the form that lay very still next to him in the snow. He leaned closer, and I realized he was trying to lick the blood from the wound on her head. I didn't know what to do. I was stunned in disbelief. It had all gone wrong, so quickly. Then, Jack's eyes changed and in them instead of tears, I saw savage anger. No slow change this time, in an instant he leapt on all fours towards the cause of his grief, but Sally stood between him and the body of Kevin, laying a few metres away, on the edge of the clearing. Her eyes shone red and the look she gave Jack, undid all the work of the early afternoon sun. Jack froze in mid leap and landed clumsily in the snow in front of her, he stumbled trying to get to his feet. Sally's look softened and she bent down and touched the gash on the wolf's head.

"Jack, this will do no good, I can help her, let me help her, like I helped you?"

The beast in Jack melted away and the man before Sally knelt sobbing in the snow. She helped him to his feet, he was still unsteady. The bullet must have grazed him, but gone on to do more damage.

Colin grabbed my arm. "Alan, go get the blankets from the sled." I ran glad to be given something I could do. I felt so helpless.

Sally called after me. "There's a first aid kit under one of the seats."

I raised my arm, to show I'd heard, but pushed on. Panic made the hill a lot easier to climb this time, the dogs barked and whined, as I approached. I grabbed the things we needed and rushing back, forcing my tired legs through the thick snow.

Jack knelt down next to Sally, she was inspecting the wound on the - woman's head, it was hard to know what to call her. She really was now - half wolf, half human. However, now it was both at the same time.

Colin was walking back from the body of Kevin. I met him half way. "Is he.....?"

Colin shook his head, "No, he's alive. He wouldn't have been, if Sally hadn't stopped Jack, but no. He's just sleeping off the effects of the dart."

"Thank god. I thought you'd killed him, good job you had the right rifle to hand."

Colin looked away and avoided my gaze, it dawned on me that he probably hadn't had time to check which rifle he used.

"How is she?" Colin asked, putting one of the blankets around Jack's bare shoulders. I handed Sally the first aid kit.

It was heart wrenching to see Jack, he looked so desperate. "I killed her," he sobbed, as Colin put an arm around his shoulders.

"No you didn't, you were doing well. She was almost there," Colin looked at Sally. "How is she?"

She shook her head. "She's alive. The bullet grazed both their skulls, they were lucky, but Jack's skull is harder, he was just dazed. Probably a mild concussion, he should be alright. But her - I really don't know. Her heart is fine and her breathing is a little shallow, but not life threatening. I'm sorry. This is out of my league. It's hard to tell whether we need a Doctor or a vet! I mean look at her."

Jack had hold of her hand, her other paw lay across her shaggy stomach. Her face was lovely, framed by her striking snow white hair, but sticking out through the hair were pointed wolves ears. The combined image was more than a little surreal.

Colin had helped Jack to his feet. "We need to get everyone back to the lodge. I can't think straight here, it's too bloody cold and that storm will be closing in soon, if Tina2 is right and she's rarely wrong."

"What about him," I said pointing at Kevin. "We have to get him back too. I'll get him to the sleigh. You bring Jack and the – girl."

"Cara!" Jack said, almost under his breath.

Sally picked up the first aid kit. "Her name is Cara." She looked away, but for a second I thought I saw a tear in her eye. She continued, "You bring Cara. I'll help Allan with Kevin. How long will the tranquilizer take to wear off?"

Colin shook his head. "Several hours, that stuff is pretty strong. When he wakes up he's going to have a sore head and a vivid memory. But we'll worry about that later." Colin went to pick up Cara. Jack pushed him back and lifted her easily from the blood stained snow, Colin draped the other blanket over the limp form in Jack's arms.

Kevin was a big man and a dead weight. I couldn't help thinking that he could so easily have been a real - dead weight.

Luckily Sally was a lot stronger than she looked and between us we man handled him back to the sleigh. By the time we got there, Colin and Jack had settled Cara onto the floor and wrapped her in the blankets. She looked as if she was in a deep sleep. We loaded Kevin up next to her, which didn't leave a lot of space. Matters were not helped, because Jack kept growling under his breath and Colin had to keep himself between the two men. It was a good job Kevin was out cold.

"It's pretty crowded," I said, stating the obvious. "Will the dogs be able to cope?"

Sally shook her head, "No, Jack I need to put you at the head of the team, can you work with the dogs?"

Jack nodded. Leaning over Cara's sleeping form he kissed her lightly on the forehead, jumping down from the sleigh he hit the floor, landing on four paws.

The dogs whined and jostled, but had little choice. Even, they could work out that you should keep on the right side of a wolf, especially when that wolf was running at your side.

It was a squash, but we all fitted on. With Jack's help the sleigh took off easily through the snow. We headed for home in silence, deep in thought, probably thinking the same thing. What the hell, would we do when we got there?

# THE CAVALRY

It seemed to take an age to get back to the lodge.

Snow fell as Tina had said it would and although Jack and the dogs were moving fast, sometimes they seemed to be trying to go in different directions, which made for a bumpy ride. The radio crackled, and a muffled voice could just be heard, inside Colin's pocket.

"Colin. Come in Colin, are you there?"

"Damn, I forgot about Ben – again." Colin managed to take out the radio.

"Yes Ben Sorry. We're on our way back and we have company. Build up the fire and get the coffee going. On second thoughts, get the brandy out."

"Is everything alright, did you find her?"

Colin hesitated. "Yes and no, we'll be back soon Ben. We'll talk then, just pour the brandy!"

Colin put the radio away, before Ben could ask any more questions. The rest of the trip was in silence. The sun was getting low as we eventually pulled up outside the lodge. It was so cold now, that icicles had formed along the edges of the sleigh. Ben rushed out to meet us, he had obviously been concerned. Spotting Jack at the head of the sleigh, his face was a picture. "Bloody hell, what happened out there?"

Colin jumped down "Give us a hand to get these two in Ben. Then we can talk."

Sally jumped down. "I'll see to the dog's, I think we'll all be staying here tonight. I'll be in, in a minute." She released Jack from his straps, he immediately changed and Colin wrapped one of the blankets around his shoulders. He helped to carry Cara into the lodge.

Ben and I were left to struggle with Kevin.

"Shit Alan, what the hell happened," Ben gasped, as we got Kevin through the front door. "And who the hell, is she."

"We ran into a bit of trouble." What an understatement.

Ben looked unsure. "What sort of trouble, why do I get the feeling, this is not good news?"

"Like I said, there was trouble." By now we had managed to get Kevin's large frame inside. It made me realize, just how strong Sally had been, it had taken far less effort out in the snow.

Cara had been placed carefully on the couch. Kevin on the other hand we dropped into a chair near the fire, thankfully he was still out cold.

Colin looked up and spotted Sally in the doorway. "Sally, come in please. Would you take another look at Cara?" Thankfully Jack had gone to get dressed, so we had chance to fill Ben in briefly about the events of the day. Tina2 hovered by his side. Maybe it was just my imagination, but she managed to look as concerned as Ben, as between us we told the story.

Ben gave voice, to the question that we had all had in our minds, since the shooting. "How much did he see?"

"We don't know, but I suspect too much." Colin helped himself to a brandy and sat down heavily, in the other chair. In front of the roaring fire, he looked over at Sally. "How's she doing?"

Sally shook her head. "I have no idea, oh she's breathing and her heart is strong, but other than that. I really don't know. I can see to the wound on her head, it isn't as bad as I at first thought, after that, I'm sorry but I'm out of my league. Is there more of that brandy?"

She saw our expressions and added sharply, "I need a drink."

I recognized that tone, it said, I'm having a bad day, don't mess with me. I poured Sally a brandy, Colin held up his glass for a re-fill. "Well people, we have a few hours before sleeping beauty over there wakes up." Colin nodded towards the snoring Kevin.

"If any one has any bright ideas, I would love to hear them?"

"What the hell was he doing up there. He must have followed us," Sally said, almost to herself.

We all took a swig of brandy and sat in silence watching the flames dance in the hearth. The warmth was slowly creeping back into my body, helped I think, by the brandy. Jack came in and sat down on the floor beside Cara's head, he gently pushed back the hair from her face, revealing one of her ears. Ben noticed this for the first time. "Oh shit." Ben shook his head and took another swig of brandy "I'll go and get coffee. I think it's going to be another long night."

He headed for the kitchen. However, Tina stayed and approached Colin. She bobbed almost apologetically in front of him. "Excuse me Colin, but would you like me to contact the others. They may have some ideas."

"No Tina. Thank you. Not just yet. I need to think for a moment."

The little sphere bobbed again. "As you wish Colin." Tina glided into the kitchen after Ben.

A thought dawned on me. "Sally, could you not just, make him forget?"

Sally joined us by the fire. She shot me a look that even this close to the fire, chilled me to the bone. "I'm a vampire Alan, I can manipulate the mind a little, yes, but it only lasts a few moments, not a life time. What we need here, is a mind changer." She looked sadly at Kevin and added softly, "I have been trying without much success, to change the way he thinks, for a long time now."

Colin jumped up from his seat, almost spilled his brandy. "That's it," he shouted.

We all waited expectantly, at that point Ben bought in a tray of coffee and it wasn't until Colin had been handed his mug that he continued, "We need Maya."

Even Sally looked impressed. "You have a mind changer in your team. Wow! I haven't come across one of them in years. I thought they had been wiped out years ago. At one time they would have been top of every ones - most feared list. Is she any good?"

"She is eight," I said quickly. I suddenly felt protective of the child. "What do you mean 'most feared list' Maya wouldn't hurt anyone." Sally looked amused. "Calm down Alan, I was merely stating a fact. Surely you are not - that naive, you must realize that your Maya, under some circumstances, could be considered a threat as well as an asset."

Naïve, maybe, or perhaps I just didn't want to think about it. But I remembered only too vividly that Maya had already saved our skins, by simply holding someone's hand. The effect she'd had on Captain Hapi had been truly amazing. But that had been a good thing – right?

I felt I needed to make my point. "She is still very young Colin and may not be as powerful without Goldie!"

"Goldie?" Sally questioned.

I wasn't going to even try to explain, that one. I just shrugged. "Sorry Sally, that's another story."

Colin nodded his agreement. "I know Alan and I'm open to suggestions." He sounded a little tetchy. I saw Jack's expression. You didn't have to be able to read minds to work out what was going through his. He would be more than happy to take out one of the problems, in an instant. If only Colin would just say the word. Colin saw that look too. "We all need to keep our heads. This can all be worked out. We don't want or need any more trouble. I need to talk to Meg. Tina."

"Yes Colin. I'm already calling them."

For the first time in what seemed like an age, Colin laughed. "Thank you Tina, of course you are."

***

It wasn't long before we were explaining the situation to the others; they sat in silence as we described in detail the problems of the day. Finally Meg spoke. "I need to see her. I can't say I'm happy about it, but I think Colin is right, Maya, may well be our only option here. As for Cara, if your Doctor there has checked her out and the wound isn't bad, I would suggest that the problem may lie in the mind, and not the body.

Tina, could you scan Cara, so that I can see for myself."

Tina did as she was asked and hovered over Cara. Jack pulled back the blanket. I felt as if I should look the other way, but there would have been no need. What female features Cara had, were just an outline covered in thick white fur, one white paw rested at her side.

There was silence for what seemed like an age. Then Sophie said, "Oh god, that poor girl."

When Meg spoke it was to Jack. "You must stay by her side Jack. She is lost between worlds. When she wakes, if she wakes, you will be the key. Hold her hand, talk to her, in which ever tongue you wish, but don't leave her side." Jack nodded and carefully covered Cara with the blanket.

"Ben, you need to come get us. How soon can you get here?"

Colin spoke before Ben could reply. "The weather has closed in on us here Meg. Give me a moment to check with Tina2. Tina can you give us an update on the weather?"

Tina's lights flashed as she checked. "The worst of the storm will blow through tonight Colin, with winds up to 70k and heavy snow falls, easing to 40 – 50k in the early hours of the

312

morning, with continued light snow fall over the next couple of days."

Ben wasn't deterred. "No problem, Tina and I will fly out first thing in the morning, can you be ready by tomorrow night?" he said confidently.

This time it was Sophie who voiced concerns. "It may still be too rough Ben, we don't want any more accidents this trip. You must not take any chances."

Ben laughed. "We'll be just fine, Colin was only saying the other day, what a great pilot I am and with Tina's help there won't be any problems. She can work out the best and fastest routes. With favourable winds, we can probably, have you back here in about 36 hours."

Colin laughed again. "Did I really say that, either you've been dreaming or I've been having too much of this stuff lately." He indicated the brandy "Seriously Ben, Sophie is right, we might be hold up here for a few days, at least, until this storm passes."

Ben was adamant. "There isn't time, how long can you keep Grizzly Adams out without causing him long term damage? Besides the sooner we get Meg here the better for Cara, wouldn't you agree. Honestly Colin, we can do this. If Sally can get us to the airport in the morning, we'll be back before you know it." Colin looked unconvinced.

Sally joined the discussion. "Ben's right, we can't keep Kevin under for long and Cara is stable at the moment, but your guess is as good as mine as to how long she will stay that way. If she wakes in this state - I'm not sure her mind could take it, let alone her body.

I can get Ben and Tina2 to the airport, in the sleigh. They always keep the runway cleared, in case of emergencies. So they should be able to take off without too much trouble. I know the man in charge, he won't be a problem. I can radio ahead and have them prepare your plane for the flight and tell them to expect your return trip. They will, do as I ask without question."

I believed that, I didn't need to ask how Sally could be so confident about these guys. I suspected they probably spent many lonely nights at the airport, waiting for scheduled visitors and maybe sometimes, they got an unscheduled one.

Sophie had obviously been thinking. "We will make things easier for you. Ben you will have to get fuel on the main land, before heading back, so I'll leave Toby in charge here and take Meg and Maya to the main airport in the small plane. We'll meet you there. That way, you can save a few hours at least."

Colin sighed. "Alright, but let George know what's going on, Toby will be able to call on him, if anything goes wrong."

"What could possibly go wrong honey," Sophie said, with more than a hint of sarcasm. "Besides, George has his hands full at the moment."

I could tell instantly from Sophie and Meg's faces that Sophie hadn't meant to add that last comment. Like me, Colin picked up on it straight away. "What do you mean? You said George and Goldie were alright." I could tell from the tone of Colin's voice, he felt like his usual control, was slipping away fast.

Meg took over the screen. Her voice seemed calm and commanding. "Colin, listen to me. Everything is as it should be here. You know I wouldn't lie to you.

Maya and I will be there shortly and then hopefully, we can all come home.

You should all get some sleep, especially you Ben. Tomorrow will be a long day.

Oh Sally, with everything that's gone on, we haven't been properly introduced. But thank you for repairing Jack, by all accounts, you did a good job. I look forward to the chance to talk further. I believe we would have a great deal - to discuss."

Sally had been keeping her distance from the screen, but Meg had obviously spotted her. "Thank you Meg. I do my best to help, just as I believe you do. Your people think a great deal of you. I look forward to meeting you in person." Sally smiled, the conversation was polite, but there was a hint of tension between the two women.

Colin shook his head. "All right Meg, I trust your judgment in this. Weather permitting Ben will leave at first light. Sophie please be careful and tell Toby I love him and miss him."

Sophie blew Colin a kiss. "Will do honey. We miss you. We'll talk again, when I have delivered Meg and Maya into Ben's safe hands. But for now, Meg is right, get some sleep, goodnight."

The screen went blank, Tina2 settled herself on Bens lap. We sat in silence.

I got to my feet. "We could all do with something to eat. Ben you can give me a hand in the kitchen, Jack! Sally will watch Cara for a moment, you get some more wood. We need to keep our strength up and we all need to keep warm tonight."

As I headed for the kitchen, a thought struck me, not a nice thought. "I'm sorry Sally, I don't know...." I stopped. Unsure of how to put this, thankfully Sally helped me out.

"It's alright Alan. I don't need anything at the moment thank you. Perhaps a little tomato juice, if you have it? That will be fine."

Ben had noticed how uncomfortable I was, and laughed when we were alone in the kitchen. "Let's just hope she doesn't get a little – peckish, in the night Alan. I would make sure your window is bolted." Ben laughed and flapped pretend bat wings, swooping at me. I pushed him away. But a seed had been planted in my mind. Sally couldn't really do the changing into a bat thing, could she? The thought seemed absurd, but so had vampires a short time ago.

I pushed the door too behind us. "Everyone else seems alright with this vampire thing, have you come across them before Ben?"

He smiled. "Yes, and they really aren't that bad you know. Colin has a bit of a soft spot for them. However they are as you may have noticed, definitely not on Meg's Christmas list. Something that happened when she was a child I believe, you'll have to ask her about it. Now what's cooking Alan?"

I realized that was all I was going to get out of Ben. I decided on omelettes. Not very imaginative, but under the circumstances, they would have to do. I knew however that cheese, mushroom and eggs, wasn't going to be at the top of Jack's list of favourite foods, so I found what looked like a leg of lamb in the freezer and set about defrosting it in the microwave. Ben was pretty useful, as long as I told him exactly what I needed him to do and between us we managed to knock up a reasonable meal. I opened a bottle of red wine and sorted out a glass of tomato juice for Sally.

By the time Ben and I bought everything into the living room Jack had built up the fire and filled the basket with wood. Colin and Sally were deep in conversation.

My mind was on George, like Colin I felt there was something we weren't being told. I knew that Meg wouldn't lie to Colin, so we'd just have to take her word that everything was ok. Still I would feel better when we were home and I could see for myself.

We sat down to the meal in relative silence. Sally joined us at the table for a glass of tomato juice and then some red wine. It was only when Jack slipped outside to enjoy his bone that I noticed Kevin was no longer in the chair by the fire.

"What have you done with him," I asked, pointing to the now vacant chair.

Sally answered, "I've made Kevin comfortable in Jack's room. Jack will want to be with Cara tonight, and we decided it was best not to move her. I'll make sure Kevin is safe and secure, I can give him something to keep him asleep tonight but tomorrow, we may have to tie him up.

He's going to be mad as hell when he comes too, and I'm sorry, but he'll want to tell the world what he saw. I know Kevin as well as anyone. He wouldn't be able to keep something like this secret for two minutes. Our only hope of going back to a normal life - of sorts, is your mind changer."

Sally looked thoughtful for a moment. Then she turned to Ben, "Be ready at first light Ben, I'll have the dogs harnessed and set to go. I'll use my radio and call the airport to arrange for your plane to be fuelled and waiting.

For now gentlemen I will say goodnight, it's been a long and eventful day. I'll see you at first light." Sally turned deliberately to look at me, and added with a smile that purposely showed off her amazingly sharp white teeth. "Not before Alan, I promise."

With that she left us.

Colin laughed. "She knows she has you worried, Alan."

I couldn't deny it, she made me feel uncomfortable. "The strange thing is, I quite like her, it's what she is and what she does that have me confused." I sipped my wine thoughtfully, but at the moment Sally was the least of our problems.

"Do you think she will be able to handle Kevin until Meg and Maya get here?"

Colin shrugged. "I hope so. The real question is will Meg and Maya be able sort things out when they arrive?

I think we should all get what sleep we can. Cara seems comfortable where she is."

Cara hadn't moved at all. Jack had returned dressed but I noticed his feet were still bare and wet from the snow. Colin brushed wet hair out of Jack's eyes affectionately and patted his shoulder. "Keep the fire going Jack and try to get some sleep. If she wakes call us."

317

Colin sighed. "I'm afraid there is little we can do until morning. Tina will you get Ben up at first light and if the rest of us are still sleeping, give us all a call too."

Even Tina2 looked sleepy, but with a couple of softly dimed lights pulsing, she said "Of course Colin."

"Thank you Tina. Right I will say goodnight then, and let's just hope tomorrow goes a little better than today."

Colin, Ben and Tina2 went to bed. I sat by the fire for a little longer watching the flames and listening to Jack talking quietly to Cara, I couldn't understand much of what he was saying, but his tone was loving and gentle, he paid no attention to me. The thing he cared about most now lay between worlds, before him, and despite his strength he was unable to help her.

I prayed that Meg would know what to do. Jack had found someone he cared for. Not an easy task for any of us, let alone one who has a habit of changing more than his clothes on a regular basis. It would be too cruel to lose her like this. I turned out the light and left them, illuminated by the flickering light of the fire.

Tina had been right about the weather, the storm was raging outside. Every now and then I thought I heard a howl that wasn't made by the wind. The dogs barked nervously from the safety and warmth of the barn.

Were the wolves calling for Cara, had they realized their loss?

I slipped in and out of sleep, my mind re-living the events of the day. There were so many thoughts crowding my brain, thoughts of my mother and father of Natasha and George. Something was happening on the island, Colin could feel it, I felt it too.

I wasn't sure how much sleep I got, but I was ready to get up as soon as I heard the others starting to stir. Like them, I wanted to get this mess sorted.

Colin was talking to Ben when I walked in and his voice was raised.

"I can hear the wind Ben and it doesn't take a weather expert to see that there has been a lot of snow, although it's pretty dark, it's not hard to tell it's still rough out there. I don't think it's safe."

"I can make it Colin, if Sally can get us to the airport, Tina2 and I will be able to get airborne and once we get above the cloud it will be clear sailing."

There was a noticeable whirring sound from Tina2 and Ben added quickly, "Sorry Tina, Just a figure of speech."

As they argued, Sally came in bringing a blast of cold air and swirling snow with her, confirming what Colin had said about the weather conditions.

"Dogs are ready, it's still rough, but it's getting light, we'll have little trouble finding our way. The plane is being prepared as we speak. It's your call guys?"

To my surprise Colin turned to me.

"What do you think Alan?" I considered for a moment, looking from Jack and the unconscious Cara to Ben, who looked back anxiously. "If Ben say's he can do it, then we should trust his judgment," I said at last, secretly hoping to god, Ben knew what he was doing.

Colin was outnumbered and after a few seconds agreed. "Alright Ben, but for god's sake be careful and don't take any chances with Meg and Maya. I want you all back here in one piece- no matter how long it takes, understand?"

"Yes Colin," Ben beamed. This was his chance to redeem himself.

Sally was keen to get away. "Right, let's get going, Colin keep an eye on Kevin. I have given him something to make him sleep a little longer. He shouldn't wake before I get back, but be ready - just in case."

Colin nodded. "Will do, don't worry. You just take care of our boy here. We're all relying on him now."

Ben looked about six feet tall as he pulled on his coat, gloves and scarf and placed Tina2 in her travel box. "Right, be back before you know it," he said proudly.

He followed Sally out the door, we watched as they mounted the sleigh and Sally shouted at the dogs. They looked relieved to be leaving this place, and bounded forward with vigour. Within seconds they'd disappeared into the windblown snow.

We closed the door. It was going to be a long day.

Colin sighed, "I hope this is the right thing to do, if it doesn't work, we're involving more and more people in this mess."

I was worried too but the way I saw it, we had no choice. "Ben will be all right, he knows what he's doing," I said, then remembering the incident of the other day, added "Most of the time."

Colin shot me one of those looks. "Thanks Alan - I think! Anyway, we'd better not sit here and mope all day. Let's have some breakfast, I think from memory there's still some bacon in the fridge and there are plenty of eggs.

One of us had better check on Kevin. I saw some rope in the wood shed. I think to be on the safe side, we'd better tie him to the bed. Not something I've had to do before, not really my thing. What about you Alan. Were you in the boy scouts, how are your knots?"

"I was in the scouts, but tying people to beds definitely didn't earn you a badge in my day, sorry. I'll leave that one to you thanks Colin."

He laughed. "Ok, you get started on breakfast and I'll join you in a minute."

I was happy to head for the kitchen, it seemed the safest place at the moment, and I knew what I was doing here at least. I was just loading the toast as Colin came back.

"Kevin is still sleeping soundly for the moment. I've secured him as best I can. We'll take it in turns, to keep an eye on him. I didn't think I was hungry but that smells good Alan. I'll make some coffee."

"What about Jack," I asked, as I buttered the toast.

"He was asleep next to Cara when I came through, he's taking this whole thing badly. We'll leave him to rest." Colin placed the coffee on the table and we sat down to eat.

"What about you Alan? This vampire thing has unsettled you."

I tried my best to look calm. "Sally told you, didn't she?"

He nodded. "That she suspected your father might be a vampire? Yes. There are worse things you know. It might mean that he's alive somewhere. Have you thought of that?"

I shook my head. "But a vampire - sneaking around in the night, feeding on people's blood, farming people. Come on Colin. You mean to say you're alright with that?"

"Like I said before Alan, there are worse things, and anyway in my experience, in most cases anyway, the donors are more than willing. Apart from being a little tired they suffer no ill effects, quite the opposite in fact."

I was surprised to hear Colin talk this way. "How can you know that, for sure?"

Colin laughed. "You may find this hard to believe Alan, but many years ago I was in fact a host, or put in your terms a cow, to a vampire like Sally, who needed my help. I have to say, it wasn't an unpleasant experience." For a second he looked distant, as if recalling a long forgotten memory. He smiled, and then realizing I was watching him, added quickly, "As you can see, I lived to tell the tale. However, don't tell Sophie I spoke so fondly of the experience or it might be the death of me after all."

I laughed. "But what about Meg, I got the distinct feeling that she had a problem with Sally." Ben hadn't given much away. I didn't really expect Colin too either, so I was surprised when he continued…

"Ah, you picked up on that. Yes you're right, Meg doesn't like vampires much. The memories of her past encounters have left her with, shall we just say - a different, view point.

You have probably realized that like Sally, Meg has a longer than average past and this distrust, goes back a very, very long way.

When Meg was a child in Africa, her village was terrorized by a neighbouring settlement. They were led by a family of vampires. As I've said before, on the whole vampires behave themselves and try to keep a low profile. However in this world, there are always exceptions to the rule." Colin sipped his coffee.

I waited for him to continue, when he didn't, I was forced to ask. "So what happened?"

Colin smiled. "Let's just say, shall we, that vampires aren't immortal and those that think they are, may find out the hard way  that, as Sophie so elegantly put it ' there are worse things in this world' - more powerful forces than even they could have ever imagine."

Colin started to clear the plates from the table. That was it. That was all I was going to get. I was starting to get used to ending a conversation having more questions in my head, than answers. Again I felt frustrated, the mystery surrounding Meg just seemed to be getting more and more intriguing, as was my own past.

"You really think my father might be still alive somewhere?"  The thought had been running around in my mind, hiding in the shadows, not daring to come out into the light. Now it was here in the open, dazed and uncertain.

Colin came and joined me at the table. "Look Alan, I really don't know. However, I do know that all vampires have an in built sense that helps them recognize the blood lines of their families, it probably saves embarrassing accidents. They are seldom wrong about these things. Sally sensed something in you.

I would be over the moon, if I believed that there was even a slim chance that my father was still a live, vampire or not. By the way, they are not the living dead as suggested by the horror industry; their life span is somewhat longer than ours that is all.

Colin slapped me on the back and laughed. "Cheer up. I have just the job to take your mind off things. Sally will probably bring the dogs back, so can you go out to the barn and clear up any little presents they may have left and put some fresh straw down. Oh and fill up the water bowls. I'll check on Cara and then look in on Kevin again."

Colin left me with a lot to think about. I poured myself another coffee and sat down at the table. It seemed to me that the more answers I got, the more questions I had.

I finished my coffee, put on my hat and coat and pulled my boots on, it was only a short distance to the barn, but I could hear the wind howling around the lodge and the chances were it would still be snowing.

I didn't mind the work, in fact Colin was right, it helped to put my body and mind into something straight forward for a change. Finding a pair of Jack's boots tucked behind a couple of bails of straw made me smile, I wondered how many clothes he lost that way. When I'd finished I bought them back to the house.

As I entered the lodge I was left in no doubt that Kevin had woken up, the man was shouting and cursing loudly. I thought it best not to get involved; instead I joined Jack in the lounge with Cara. "Has she moved at all Jack?" I said leaning closer to check her breathing. Jack looked up, for a second I thought he was going to growl at me to ward me off, but he just shook his head sadly.

Despite the heat in the room, the fire seemed to have gone, from him.

Cara still seemed to be in a deep sleep, she was attractive, in a pale almost translucent sort of way. Her eye lashes and eye brows were the same white of her hair and her skin looked almost transparent. A shiver went through me, seeing the furry pointed ears poking through her hair and remembering the mixed up body that lay beneath the blankets.

I put another log on the fire and settled down in one of the chairs. As I did this, Colin entered looking a little flushed. He stated the obvious. "Well Kevin is awake and I can confirm, he is not a happy bunny."

In spite of the situation I laughed. "Well you did shoot him and tie him to the bed. I suspect we have over stayed our welcome. Did he say anything about what he saw?"

Colin smiled. "Oh Yes, Kevin thinks we're all in this together. We are a pack of werewolves, plotting to take over his mountain."

This didn't surprise me. "Oh Great, is that all?"

Colin laughed. "No that's not all, our host would like to see us all stuffed and mounted on his walls. In fact, he would be quite happy to do the deed himself."

I laughed. "So no chance we can convince him he banged his head and it was all a bad dream then?"

Colin shook his head sadly. He joined me and sat down heavily in the chair opposite "None what so ever."

"Seriously though, does he seem alright? Apart from being pissed off that is?"

"Yes, I left him to cool off. We'll give him half an hour or so, then you can take him something to eat and drink, he'll be really thirsty and hungry by then, perhaps he'll stop shouting long enough to take something. Besides I'm hoping Sally will have returned by then, she may be able to calm him down a bit. It won't be long before he'll need to use the toilet."

I winced. "Oh shit," I hadn't even thought of that. "Well don't look at me for that one, I draw the line at mucking out the dogs. I'll go and make some fresh coffee and sort out a sandwich, or something easy for him to eat." I didn't wait for an answer. I headed for the kitchen, even in there I could still hear Kevin ranting and raving. I tried to concentrate on coffee and food. It wasn't easy.

The thought of what might happen if our plan didn't work, kept fighting its way to the front of my thoughts. By the time I'd prepared a tray for our guest, everything had gone quiet, but somehow that didn't make me feel any better. I took the tray through and offered it to Colin. He wouldn't take it. "I think you might have more success with him than me. I'm sending Jack out for a break. I'll need to watch Cara. Don't untie him, I'm afraid you will have to feed him, be careful he doesn't bite you. God only knows what you might turn into." Colin tried to keep a straight face.

There was no point in arguing. "Very funny," I shouted over my shoulder. I headed for the bedroom. I took a deep breath, it was still quiet. I prayed Kevin had fallen asleep again. The torrent of abuse that hit me, as I entered the room, proved that prayer had gone unanswered. I waited for a few seconds until there seemed to be a lull.

"We thought you might want something to drink and I made you a sandwich," I managed, as Kevin stopped to get his breath. "It's Bacon," I added. As if this would of course make all the difference.

Kevin's arms were securely tied to the solid looking wooden posts at each corner. Kevin was red in the face and in spite of the tirade, was obviously scared to death.

He calmed a little when he recognized me. "You're not one of them," he said in a whisper. It seemed to be a statement, more than a question.

"One of - them," I said, trying to sound as innocent as one can, when confronted with a man you've recently shot with a dart gun and tied to a bed.

"Them!" he repeated. "The wolf men, they're everywhere. I've seen them change, with my own eyes. Your boss is one of - them. What have they done with my wife?"

I didn't know whether to feel insulted or pleased that Kevin didn't believe I was one of 'Them'. I wanted to ask why, but thought better of it. I decided to make the most of the situation and try to keep the conversation light. "No, I'm not a wolf man. In fact until recently I would have said I wasn't even a dog man. More a cat man, actually." This comment, went right over Kevin's head, but he had calmed a little.

I put the tray down. "Look everything is going to be alright. Sally is fine." I pulled up a chair. "Let me give you some water at least, you must be thirsty." I carefully put the cup to Kevin's lips, remembering what Colin had said about him biting, he had been joking, but you never know! Kevin eyed the water with suspicion. I took a sip myself and then offered it again. He drank deeply and I was about to pour him another cup, when another comment Colin had made popped into my head. I decided against too much liquid, at least until Sally returned. Instead I picked up the sandwich. I was prepared to take a bite, to prove its innocence, in fact I would have been happy to, but Kevin didn't seem to need a taster anymore. I held the sandwich so that he could eat.

"I got one of the buggers," Kevin spluttered. "Did I kill it? I would have had them both if that bastard hadn't shot me. He would probably have killed me too, if Sally hadn't pushed me out of the way like that. If anyone has harmed her I'll…."

He took another mouthful of sandwich.

326

I wiped bits of half chewed bread from my face and moved a little further away, hopefully, out of range. He thought Sally had saved his life, which I suppose was true, he probably believed we had taken her hostage. I figured it would be a good idea to keep it that way, at least for now.

I tried to sound confident, not easy under the circumstances. "No-one is dead. Sally is fine, for now, anyway. The guys have her in another room. If your sensible and do as Colin say's, there won't be a problem. As soon as the storm passes, we can get out of here and you and Sally can go free."

Kevin didn't look convinced. "You'll let us go?" he said uncertainly. "After the things we witnessed, out there?"

He didn't believe me and I didn't blame him. "Think about it Kevin, what are you going to tell people? You saw monsters in the woods, werewolves. Who would believe you, you would be a laughing stock, like Dave the other day!"

Kevin looked a little more hopeful. "You're right, folks around here are always coming out with tall stories, wolf men, bogy men, even vampires. Until today, I would have told them to stay off the booze."

I felt sorry for the man, I knew what it was like to have the goal posts suddenly moved, and to lose track of what was fact, and what was fiction! I found myself wondering what he'd heard about vampires, but I thought it best to leave that hornet's nest, well alone.

"Look Kevin, I'll see if I can get Colin to let Sally come in to talk with you, just so you know she's alright. Would that make you feel a little easier?"

This seemed to work and he brightened. "Thank you – Ah - Thank you."

I sighed. The man couldn't even remember my name. No wonder he didn't think I could be - one of them!

The sandwich had obviously helped Kevin; he was sounding a bit more – well like Kevin. He had been plotting.

"Look the three of us could escape, get out the back and raise the alarm. You could come with us and be free. We could get help from the village, and kill these bastards, before they have the chance to kill again."

I couldn't believe it. Kill - again. Until a few hours ago, this man didn't think wolf men existed. Now they'd already been on a killing spree. Sally was right, if we let this man go now, he would make it his business to kill everything that even resembled a wolf. I sighed and tried to look downtrodden, not hard the way I felt at the moment. "It's no good man, don't you think I've tried. How far do you think we would get before they hunted us down? No, when the storm passes, we will be on our way. That will be the end of it. Trust me, it will be as if we'd never been here. You'll see." I crossed my fingers and hoped to god that would be the case.

I gathered up the tray. "I will go and persuade Colin, that you will behave – if you can see Sally. Ok."

Kevin nodded enthusiastically. I closed the door behind me and breathing a sigh of relief. At least, I had left him looking a little happier.

I got back to the living room as Colin was opening the door to Sally. She handed him a large box. "I called in at our place, to tell them we're staying with you for a couple of days, having a bit of a break, whilst it's quiet. I picked up some supplies, more food and another bottle of brandy."

Sally shook the snow from her coat and hat and handed me the bottle of brandy.

"I stayed at the airport until your boy took to the air, no problems. I told the guys that Ben would be returning, with your wife and daughter, for a bit of a holiday.

I said you loved the place so much, you were thinking of buying some land up here and wanted your wife to take a look. They'll call me here when the plane returns and I can go pick them up.

How's Kevin?"

I accepted the brandy. "He's a wake, very much so! He thinks we've been holding you against your will!" I put the brandy on the table, no point putting it away.

Sally laughed. "Bless him, Kevin has always had the ability to see and believe what he wanted. Anything else I should know? "

"He's convinced you saved his life and he's afraid for your safety, he thinks Colin and Ben are werewolves too."

Sally looked bemused. "Ha- not you though, interesting. Well he's right about one thing at least, I did save his life." She looked down at Jack, who was still at Cara's side. "He would have ripped his head off," she added.

I waited for Colin to return from the kitchen, then filled them in on the conversation I'd had with Kevin, even the bit about the escape plan. Colin looked thoughtful for a moment, then, he smiled. "Good thinking Alan, if Kevin thinks that we have Sally at our mercy, he'll be less likely to try anything stupid. Sally perhaps you should go in and see him, take him a brandy, convince him you could be in real danger if he doesn't do as he's told.

He must need to pay a call by now too, we'll have to untie him for that at least, it could be risky though, any ideas?"

Sally shook her head and sighed. "Play the helpless female. Not something that comes naturally to me, but I'll do my best. Colin you and Alan come in with me, we'll play good cop, bad cop. Alan can untie Kevin, whilst Colin stands behind me threatening to rip out my throat, if he tries anything. He already believes you're a wolf Colin, so he should do as he's told. He trusts you Alan, well, as much as anyone. So you can go with him to the bathroom and keep an eye on him. When he comes back, you can leave us alone for a short while, then come and get me. We use these on him, instead of the ropes."

Sally produced a set of handcuffs from her pocket. "Much easier than tying him up all the time, just cuff his hands together, but don't lose that key or we'll need a locksmith."

"Where on earth did you get those?" I asked, and instantly wished, I hadn't. But Sally just laughed.

"Not what you're thinking. I borrowed them from one of the guys at the airport, thought they might be useful."

I felt my face going red.

Colin laughed, "Borrowed."

"Well, all right, took! But what could they expect, leaving them at the back of a locked draw, where anyone could just stumble across them."

Colin looked bemused. "Right, let's do this. Jack, you stay here, but keep your eye on the corridor. If by any chance Kevin manages to get passed us, you stop him, but not – permanently, understand?"

Jack nodded, Sally poured a large brandy for Kevin and I got ready with the cuffs.

Sally hesitated. "It might be a good idea to tie my hands too, it will enforce the hostage idea, tie them in front of me and I can still carry the brandy tumbler."

The whole thing went very well, Kevin seemed so pleased to see Sally alive and well, that he did as he was told, allowing me to handcuff him and escort him to the bathroom and back. In fact, the hardest part of the whole exercise was getting Kevin's ropes untied in the first place; Colin had done such a good job with the knots, probably using every one known to mankind and a few more besides. It would have been easier to cut them off, but bringing a knife into the equation didn't seem like such a good idea. Sally was right; the cuffs were going to be much easier.

I handcuffed one of Kevin's wrists to the bed post and we left Sally and Kevin alone.

Further along the corridor out of earshot Colin whispered, "We can relax and let Sally handle him for a while. We'll give it half an hour, then I'll go back in and tell them their time's up. Kevin will behave, if he thinks we have Sally at our mercy."

As we re-entered the lounge, we both almost jumped out of our skins as the phone rang, without Tina2, we were back to basics.

Colin answered it. "Oh hi honey, yes sorry, I think my mobiles in my coat pocket, I'll dig it out, I don't think it's charged. Yes, I'll do it as soon as I get off the phone."

Colin gestured for me to go and look for his phone. I found it and held it up. He looked relieved. Whilst Colin continued his conversation with Sophie, I hunted around for the phone charger.

"Great, Ben made good time then. No problems? That's good, alright, hopefully this mess will be sorted out soon and we can come home.

No. No change. Jack is watching her. I'll feel better when Meg has had a chance to look her over, I miss you too. Bye honey, give my love to Toby."

Colin replaced the receiver. "As you have probably guessed, that was Sophie. Ben picked Meg and Maya up a few minutes ago. Ben refused to take a break saying Tina2 would keep an eye on him, so they are already on their way back.

Good, you found my mobile. Sophie was worried. She'd been trying to reach us; she was - to put it mildly, just a little annoyed. She had to phone the main lodge to get the number here! But at least we know the cavalry, is on its way."

Colin took my arm and steered me into the kitchen, closing the door behind us. Even with the door closed he spoke in a whisper. "Alan, I'm worried, how long do you think Cara can survive, without water?"

I understood why Colin didn't want Jack to hear us, he was worried enough already. I knew you could survive a few days without food, but water. "I'm not sure, but you're right to be worried, I'm pretty sure, it's not very long. Sally will know. Perhaps you should go and play tough guy again and get her out here, there may be something she can suggest."

Colin agreed. It wasn't long before he returned with Sally.

"Is he still plotting his escape?" I asked.

Sally smiled. "Yes, but even he, can see that there might be a problem with the handcuffs and the fact that you bastards have taken his boots."

"We didn't take his boots," Colin and I both said in unison.

"No but I did!" Sally laughed, showing off those pearly whites.

Colin lowered his voice. "Sally how long can Cara last without water, it's been a while now, is there nothing we can do?"

Sally nodded, "Yes, your right, we need to get some fluids into her. I picked up a medical kit from the airport; it's in the box I gave you, with the supplies. It will contain a saline drip, if need be I'll put her on that, but first we'll try sitting her up and trying to get her to swallow a little water on her own.

Colin if you can get Jack out of the way for a few minutes, Alan can help me with Cara." Sally fished out a small white container with 'do not remove from airport' written in large red letters, from the box of supplies. I hoped the airport didn't find themselves with any security or medical emergencies in the near future, because we seemed to have acquired most of their equipment.

"Sally found a plastic tumbler in the cupboard and filled it with water. Right, Alan, you're with me. Colin can you distract Jack?"

332

Colin shrugged. "I'll take him out to stretch his legs and get some fresh air. You'll have to be quick though, he'll not want to leave Cara for long."

Colin put on his coat and boots. It took a little convincing to get Jack to go, but at last Colin managed.

Sally quickly moved in, checking Cara's pulse and breathing. "Still the same," she said. "Help me sit her up."

I helped Sally lift Cara into a sitting position. My hand touched the thick fur on the girls back, it felt strange. I tried not to think about it. Sally gave me her instructions. "Keep her sitting up. I'm going to try something."

Sally's voice was strong and commanding. I did as I was told and supported Cara, as best I could. Sally knelt and passed me the tumbler of water. "Here, can you manage to hold this too?"

I nodded. "Yes, she isn't very heavy. But I don't understand," I said taking the water.

"What are you going to do?" Sally ignored me and took Cara's hand and paw in hers, then she glanced up at me.

I almost dropped the tumbler. Her eye's shone with an eerie orange glow. When she spoke, her voice was cold and commanding. "When I tell you, put the tumbler to her lips and tip it gently, just a little at a time. Alan - Don't look at me - look at her."

I had no choice but to do as I was told. A strange feeling washed over me, I felt calm almost detached from my body. I watched as if from a dream. Cara opened her beautiful steel blue eyes, but there was no light in them, just a vacant stare.

"Now Alan, give Cara the water." Sally's voice was in my head, in my very soul. She commanded and I, obeyed.

Cara drank, very slowly, a little at a time the contents of the tumbler passed Cara's lips and she obediently swallowed it down. When the last of the water was gone, Cara closed her eyes again. The tumbler was empty. I could think of nothing but water, cool, clear refreshing water. I was so thirsty. All I wanted to do was drink.

Sally stood, and it was as though I'd been released, from some sort of spell. When she spoke again, her voice sounded normal. "You can lay her down again now Alan, it wasn't much, but it will save me having to put her on a drip, for the moment."

"What did you do?' I managed. My head was beginning to feel like it belonged to me again. "You woke her, you got her to drink?"

Sally crossed the room to the fire and tossed another log into the thirsty flames. "I have a little mind control of my own Alan, however it only lasts for a few moments and works only on a weak or willing mind. Sadly I didn't wake Cara, I commanded her unconscious mind. To be honest, I was surprised I got through, I didn't expect it to work."

"Couldn't you tell her to wake up?" I said, trying to resist the urge to run into the kitchen and drink a gallon of water, cool, refreshing water. I tried to clear my head. Weak or willing Sally had said.

Sally sighed. "Not that simple I'm afraid. I have a feeling our wolf girl doesn't know what to wake up, as."

Sally took a seat by the fire.

I wanted to ask more, but Colin and Jack came in out of the cold. Jack shook himself automatically by the door, his hair was dripping wet, he'd already changed and dressed outside, but he left wet foot prints on the floor, as he padded bare foot over to take up his place at Cara's side.

Colin joined us by the fire. Sally smiled and nodded. "She'll be alright for a while."

"Good, Jack had a run. It was actually good to get out in the fresh air. This place is breath-taking. You know, it would be really nice to return here under different circumstances, one day. Now however, I need some food." Colin warmed his hands in front of the fire.

Sally smiled. "You get warm. I'll sort out dinner, then check on Kevin and take him in a tray."

Sally disappeared into the kitchen, I felt I should go and help her, but frankly just at this moment she scared the hell out of me. Instead I sat opposite Colin by the fire, watching the flames dance. We sat in silence, eventually Colin looked up from the flames. "The weather's improving, it's a nice evening, bloody cold though. I will be glad to get home, I think we all will."

A thought struck me. "Did Sophie mention Natasha?"

"No Alan sorry, but I think she was in a hurry to get back to Toby. I wouldn't be at all surprised if Natasha isn't back before us, at this rate." Colin sniffed the air. "Something smells good." I had to agree the smells coming from the kitchen were beginning to make my stomach rumble and it made a nice change not to be the one cooking.

On cue, Sally called us. "Ready boy's, come and get it."

We were both quick to respond. The table was set for two, steak, veg and potatoes with a couple of beers already open and waiting.

"This looks and smells great Sally. Thank you." Colin took a seat.

Sally smiled. "No problem, strange though it may seem, I enjoy cooking. You two tuck in, I've made some biscuits, they're cooling on top of the oven. I'll give this to Jack on my way through and take a tray in to Kevin."

"Should one of us take you in?" Colin asked.

Sally shook her head, " No thanks Colin I've got this one, it won't be hard to convince Kevin you or Jack are just outside the door waiting to pounce."

I remembered Sally's words, 'Weak or willing'.

Sally was looking a little pale. I had a feeling she would be dining - with Kevin this evening.

We took our time over the meal, and then I cleared the plates, whilst Colin made the coffee.

I retrieved the new bottle of brandy from the lounge. Jack was asleep, curled up on the floor in front of the fire. I was surprised he had left Cara's side.

I re-joined Colin at the kitchen table and poured us both a brandy.

"What time do you think Ben will arrive with Meg and Maya?" I asked.

Colin took a large swig of his brandy. "I'm not sure, I would suspect it will be sometime in the morning. I was hoping they might have rung by now."

"Would they be able to use a mobile on the plane?" As soon as I'd asked the question, I realized how stupid it was.

Colin laughed. "It's my bloody plane Alan, I think I'll let them off just this once, that reminds me, where's the mobile?"

"I found the charger and plugged it in, over there by the toaster, it was totally flat." I felt I'd redeemed myself a little.

Colin checked his phone. "Thanks Alan. Shall we take our drinks into the other room by the fire, it's getting a little cold in here?"

He was right. I decided to bring the bottle of brandy with us just in case we needed warming some more.

Jack had moved back to his spot next to Cara.

It wasn't long before Sally joined us.

Colin held up the brandy bottle. "You'll need a glass Sally. How's Kevin doing?" he asked.

Sally shook her head. "Just a minute I'll get that glass." She returned from the kitchen and Colin poured her a large brandy. She joined us by the fire, taking a large swig of her drink, before she answered. "Kevin is sleeping NOW!" Sally said with a sigh.

"I'm surprised he can sleep with all that's happened," I commented.

She smiled. "He may have had just - a little help." Seeing my expression she added, "I slipped something in his drink. With a bit of luck, he should sleep until morning."

Colin looked concerned. "I thought you said it might not be good for his health, to keep knocking him out like that?"

Sally sighed again and took another swig. "Trust me, it would have been far worse for his health if I hadn't knocked him out, he was driving me mad. Much as I love the man, he can be a bloody idiot at times."

I was surprised. "He doesn't suspect anything?"

Sally laughed. "You mean does Kevin suspect that as well as you lot being crazed werewolves, his much loved and trusted wife, could be a 'bloody vampire!' No Alan, I'm pretty sure he might have raised that concern, if he had it."

She hadn't forgiven me for my earlier comment. "Sorry I didn't mean - I just thought it must be difficult that's all, not being able to be - yourself." I was relieved when Colin came to my rescue.

"I'm sure it will be alright Sally - Maya will be able to wipe out the memories Kevin has of the last couple of days, we'll leave, and things will go back to the way they were."

Sally stared into the flames for a while, when she spoke she sounded tired and sad.

"That's just the problem, I'm not sure I want to return to the way we were. The hunting, the killing, you said it Colin, this place is breath taking. I'm happy to share it with the world, but to look - not to take. Why is it that when people find something that's quite perfect the way it is, the first thing they do is try to reshape it, to take away the very things which made it so perfect in the first place?"

Colin sighed. "I'm afraid I can't answer that one. The only way I've found of protecting the rare and the beautiful, is to keep it as far away from people as I can. We searched the world to find inaccessible islands were my family and my – friends, could live in peace and be safe. The park idea you had was a good one, give people camera's instead of guns and you might have a chance, who knows.

Alan tells me you have wolf blood in your veins, as well as vampire, is it possible that Cara is a relative? It might well explain the link you felt with her and why you seemed to be drawn to each other."

Sally considered this for a moment. "Perhaps, father died along long time ago, but when he was alive, well let's just say after mother left us, he liked to run wild in the woods every now and then to - stretch his legs." Sally laughed. "It was so very long ago and until recently, I knew the rumours where just that, there had been no real sightings for a very long time. In fact I didn't believe them, right up until I came across her in the woods. I knew this wolf was different, but even then I wasn't sure. The wolf is strong in her. I felt the conflict within her. Perhaps that's the problem, perhaps our Cara doesn't want to be human? Who would blame her?"

Colin laughed. "I know what you mean. I'll be glad when Meg gets here. If anyone can figure this one out, she can."

"You have a lot of faith in this Meg. What is she?" Sally asked, "And should I be worried? I sensed a little hostility."

I found it strange that Sally had asked what, not who Meg was. I was as eager to hear Colin's response as Sally, probably more so. We both waited whilst Colin poured himself another brandy. He seemed to consider carefully, before answering. "Meg is a very special person," - he was interrupted by Puff - The Magic Dragon, not the actual dragon of course, but the song. I hadn't heard it since my childhood.

"Ah sorry that's my phone," Colin said, fumbling to get his mobile out of his pocket. Sally and I exchanged glances. I could just make out Ben's voice on the other end.

Colin looked relieved. "Ben how are you doing? And where are you?

That's great. No tell Meg there has been no change. Alright, we'll see you soon." Colin placed the phone back in his pocket, he looked a lot happier.

Sally laughed. "I have to ask, Puff -The Magic Dragon?"

Colin looked at me and winked. "It reminds me of a very old and dear friend.

Ben say's they are making good time and should be at the airport around six in the morning, it will be an early start again. So I think I'll turn in." Colin stood to leave.

Sally and I both said in unison, "You were going to tell us about Meg?"

Colin turned at the door with a smile on his face. "Was I?" He closed the door.

Sally sighed. "And I suppose you're not telling either?" she said.

I shrugged. "You probably know as much as I do, Meg is a mystery to me too. All I know is she is respected by everyone who knows her, including me. I don't think you have to worry, you helped Jack. That if nothing else, will earn you brownie points."

Sally didn't look convinced, but there really wasn't anything else I could tell her.

She finished her brandy and stood. "Well I have an early morning pick-up from the airport, so I'll say goodnight Alan."

"Sally wait, please," I said quickly. I wasn't sure how to ask what was on my mind, but as she joined me again by the fire, the words found their way out.

"What made you say - what you said, about my father?" I wasn't sure if I was ready for the answer, but there was a part of me that had to know the truth.

Sally's usually cool look softened. "I really didn't mean to upset you Alan, I might be wrong."

"But wrong - about what?" I insisted, I had gotten this far, there was no going back now.

Sally hesitated.

"Please Sally, I need to know."

She shrugged. "Alright Alan, this is what I know. You have vampire blood in your veins, maybe not enough to turn you to the vampire way, but it's there all the same. If it is not from your mother, then I would have to conclude that it was from your father's side of the family. I don't know if your father is alive or dead. However if he is alive, I would be surprised if your mother hasn't seen or heard from him. Vampires are true to their partners. We may live for a very long time, but we love only one person at a time. If I'm right, your father will love and be true to your mother until the day she dies. That is our way.

Talk with your mother Alan. Now, I really must go to bed. Good night." With that Sally left me to ponder her words. Colin had already gone to his room

I sat staring into the flames. It was the noise I noticed first, a low growl. I looked up and realized that jack was missing, from Cara's side. He was standing at the window looking out into the night. I could hear the dogs barking nervously in the barn. Turning off the light I went to the other window to look out. At first I could see nothing but snow, then slowly as my eyes got used to the light, from a nearly full moon and a sky that looked to be bursting and overflowing with stars, I could just make out a lone wolf.

It was just sitting there watching. Off in the distance I could hear the sound of other wolves, howling forlornly. But this one didn't answer them. He just sat looking at the lodge, as if he were waiting.

Jack's hand was on the door handle, I stopped him. "No Jack! Go back to Cara." I tried my very best to sound stern, as Colin did when he expected to be obeyed. To my surprise Jack did as I said. When he was back in his place, I opened the door and went out on to the porch, shutting the door behind me. The wolf stood its ground, watching me carefully. I wasn't sure what to do next, so I said, "Shoo go away."

The wolf seemed to consider this strange request for a moment, then the call from the distant wolves came again and slowly, reluctantly it seemed, he turned and disappeared into the trees. The dogs seemed to sense that the danger was past and settled down again.

I stood for a moment longer looking up at the thousands of tiny stars littering the cold night sky. It was breath-taking and bloody cold. As I headed back inside to warm myself by the fire, I thought about what I'd just done, 'shoo!' what the hell was that. Somehow I hadn't felt threatened by the wolf. I knew without doubt, that I wasn't the one he was waiting for.

Jack had settled down to sleep and I decided to do the same. I took one last look outside, it had started to snow. I turned in for the night.

I lay awake for a long time, trying to focus my thoughts on Natasha. I wanted to see if she was home, but every time I got close to the island, in my mind's eye, the vision became fuzzy and unclear. It was as if I was looking at the images through distorted glass, I kept losing focus. Something was keeping me out. Whatever it was, I couldn't break through.

My mind drifted, I couldn't forget the things Sally had said, 'Vampire blood in my veins' could that really be true? My thoughts turned to my mother. Before I realized it I was home, drifting through the front door and down the corridor. Nothing had changed.

It was as though I hadn't been away for all these years. One of my old coats still hung on a hook by the door, photographs adorned the walls. Happy, smiling faces looked back at me from the past.

There was a light on in the library, I drifted in. Mother sat in her favourite chair, book in hand, spectacles on the end of her nose. I'd always teased her about them. I'd said they made her look old, like a grandmother, she had replied 'if only.'

She looked older than I remembered, had I been away so long? She looked up from her book. "Hello Alan." I held my breath. She smiled. "You have finally started to find your way. You look well."

"You can see me?" I stammered. Surely this was a dream, this couldn't be real.

Mother put down her book. "Of course dear, it's a gift and one which we obviously share."

Suddenly I felt angry, she knew, she had always known. "Why didn't you tell me? All these years….all this time." I instantly regretted the anger in my voice, she looked so hurt and sad, she was crying.

"Alan, if you knew how many times I've wanted to tell you; but you were never ready, always so angry and confused. I was afraid of what you might become, what you might do. The man I saw in you then was not the man I knew you could be. But you've changed, grown stronger. I think you may have found your purpose in life. Something I'm afraid I never did.

I'm so proud of what you're doing my son, your father is too - I'm sure."

"Is he alive?" I half whispered, not sure if I even wanted an answer.

She smiled. "There are things I need to tell you Alan, but not like this. When you're ready, really ready, come and see me and I'll answer all your questions truthfully. Now I'm losing you son, I'm not as young or strong as I used to be, the connection is growing weaker, but Alan you must know your father and I have always loved you, so very much."

With those words in my head and in my heart, I was back in my room. But there was the lingering smell of perfume, a smell I recognized. My mother had always worn that same perfume, my father had loved it.

342

I lay awake unable to get my mother's words out of my head. She was right; I'd always been angry and bitter. She had hated it when I started to hunt and been upset when I told her how much people paid me to find them something to kill. I'd been a fool.

I got my seeker powers from my mother! It made sense now that I stopped to think about it. My mother had always encouraged me to hunt for things, when keys were lost, even the neighbour's lost dog (which incidentally I found, and it bit me!), she had been testing me, teaching me. I remembered how pleased she was when I went through my vegetarian phase and now I come to think of it, how pissed off my father had been.

I didn't get much sleep. I watched as the moon moved silently across the crowded sky, squeezing its way through the multitude of stars and light finally crept slowly into my room, forcing the shadows back into their hiding places.

I could hear Sally talking in hushed tones to Kevin, next door. I got up and dressed. I looked at my watch, which of course was no help. I guessed it was probably about 5 am.

In the lounge Cara still lay very still, like a pale and lovely sleeping beauty. Jack was nowhere in sight, I was worried, after seeing the wolf outside last night, I hoped he hadn't gone out looking for trouble. We had enough of that already.

Colin greeted me from the kitchen door. "I guess you couldn't sleep either, coffee?"

"Yes please, where's Jack?"

"I sent him out for a run; he needs to stretch his legs. Are you alright? You look like shit." Colin seemed concerned, he handed me a coffee.

I sat down heavily at the kitchen table and shook my head. "I didn't sleep very well.

There was a wolf out there last night watching the house. It ran off when I went outside. Are you sure Jack should be out

343

there on his own?" I took a sip of my coffee and Colin handed me a bacon sandwich. "Here you look as though you need this more than me, I'll make myself another. Don't worry, I checked on the dogs earlier. There were no signs of Wolves. If jack's not back in a few minutes I'll go take a look, but I don't think he'll go far this morning.

What about you Alan. This vampire thing has gotten to you, hasn't it? If you feel you need to talk, I'm here."

I smiled weakly. "Thanks Colin but I'm alright really. Besides, we have other things to think about at the moment, perhaps when this is all over. For now the coffee and bacon sandwich will suffice."

Jack scratched at the door, Colin let him in.

"Human form please Jack and wipe your feet." Colin handed Jack a towel and his clothes as he padded past us into the lodge.

Sally appeared at the door. "Good morning gentlemen.

Good morning – Jack." Sally was distracted for a second as she watched Jack pass. She sighed, then turned back to us and addressed Colin, "Would you make one of those for Kevin please? I gave him a couple of aspirins when he woke this morning. For some reason he seems to have a bit of a thick head," Sally said innocently, adding one of her perfect smiles. "I'm going out to feed the dogs, and then I'll head to the airport.

Oh, I got a call to say your plane will be landing in a couple of hours!"

Sally seemed to notice me for the first time. "Good grief Alan you look like crap." Before I could comment Sally had disappeared out the back door.

Colin grumbled. "Kevin will just have to wait. Thick head or not, this bacon sandwich has my name on it."

344

# CHOICES

$I$ volunteered to take Kevin's sandwich in to him.

Sally had left Kevin handcuffed to the bed. He was sitting up when I entered.

"Good morning Kevin," I said, trying to sound cheery.

"You lot are still here, so I fail to see what's good about it," Kevin grumbled.

Well I walked into that one. In fact Kevin looked how I felt, Knackered! I chose to ignore his comment. "I bought you some breakfast. How did you sleep?" I put the tray down next to the bed. Kevin eyed the sandwich and coffee suspiciously. He wasn't happy. "Too bloody well, someone slipped me something." He pointed at the food. "I'm not touching that, what is it?"

I shrugged. "It's really up to you Kevin, I'm quite happy to eat it for you." I took a small bite to prove my point. "Mmm- it's really good, you must be hungry are you sure I can't persuade you?"

"Alright give it here," he growled, taking the sandwich with his free hand. He took a bite; unfortunately I was in the line of fire again. "Bloody bacon again," he spluttered angrily. The fridge was stocked with good steaks. I suppose the bloody wolves have eaten the best stuff."

I moved a little further away and hoped Kevin couldn't spray that far, someone really should have taught the man not to talk with his mouth full. I knew I shouldn't, but I just couldn't resist, I looked as grave as I could and said, "It's best to keep them well fed. If they get hungry, well, who knows what or who could be next on the menu. We should count ourselves lucky, it's not quite a full moon, that's when the feeding frenzies always occur."

Kevin's face was a picture. He swallowed hard and lowered his voice, "Sally said that's why they were still here, they were waiting for a full moon, oh god!"

I felt quite guilty. The man had gone suddenly very pale. I added hurriedly, "No, I've been told to start packing, we are leaving, I'm sure we'll be on our way very soon.

I'll leave you to enjoy your sandwich and coffee and come back to check if you need the bathroom a little later on."

Kevin thankfully swallowed before asking, "Can I see Sally again soon? She said they were making her get the meals and clean up after them. She's still alright, isn't she? She seemed a little upset last night."

I resisted the temptation of telling the man, that the only person Sally was upset with was him, and settled for saying "Sally is just fine. So long as you do as you're told, you and Sally will be safe, I promise."

I left him alone and headed back to the lounge to wait for Sally's return. Colin was checking on Cara, he looked up as I entered. "I've sent Jack out to chop some more wood for the fire, he's getting fidgety. He's never spent so much time cooped up like this before. How's our Grizzly Adams doing?"

"Not very happy, he thinks we drugged him. The others should be here soon, I'm going to make fresh coffee, can I bring you one?" Colin nodded. I headed out to the kitchen. Jack passed me, carrying an arm full of logs.

The coffee was brewing when I heard the dog's barking excitedly, as they pulled up outside the lodge. A wave of relief swept over me. Meg was here.

Maya was first through the door. She was so excited, she fell in.

"It's snowing! There's snow everywhere, we got to ride in a sleigh and dog's pulled us." She squealed, throwing her arms around Colin, he lifted her up and hugged her.

346

Meg followed with bag in hand. Jack got to his feet and Meg put her arms around him, she brushed his hair away from his face and inspected the scratches still plainly visible. "She gave you quite a greeting there, didn't she lad?" Jack nodded silently and led Meg over to where Cara lay.

"This is my fault," he said solemnly, tears rolling down his face. Meg produced a handkerchief, like all mothers or grandmothers seemed to be able to do, and wiped his face. "No Jack, you didn't do this. This is not your fault. Let's take a look, shall we?

Hello Alan, is that coffee I smell?"

"Hello Meg, it's really good to see you. One coffee, coming right up."

When I returned with the coffee, Sally had joined the group, but Ben was noticeable by his absence.

So I asked, "What happened to Ben?"

"He wanted to refuel the plane and get a return flight plane lodged, so we could be away as soon as we were ready. That's what he said. Really I think he's had enough, and just wants to go home," Meg said, taking the mug I offered. She sat in one of the seats by the fire. She'd only spent a few moments with Cara, something about this worried me, that and the look on her face. Colin joined us, he looked apprehensive. He'd obviously had the same misgivings as me.

"I must see to the dogs," Sally said, heading for the door.

"Can I come?" Maya squealed, jumping up and down again.

Sally smiled, "Of course." She took Maya's hand.

Meg was out of her chair in an instant. "I don't think that's a good idea Maya," she said, glaring at Sally.

Colin put his hand on her arm. "Its fine Meg, really, let Maya go. Sally will take good care of her, won't you Sally?"

Sally smiled. "Maya is safe with me." To Maya she said "You can help me unharness and feed the dogs, then, maybe we could build a snow man."

Maya looked imploringly at Meg. "Can I Meg? Can I - pleeese?"

Meg nodded. "Make sure you keep your hat and gloves on."

Maya half skipped half ran to keep up with Sally. I could hear her asking umpteen questions about the dogs, and just before the door closed behind them, I heard Maya say, "Sally what's a snow man?"

I realized the child had probably never experienced snow before. Meg did not look impressed. "Is that wise Colin? I don't trust her sort."

Colin glanced at me. "But we do Meg," he said pointedly. "Besides, it gives us chance to talk. I want to know what you made of Cara. You only looked at her for a few moments, what was it, what did you sense?"

Meg looked uneasy. "I think we should talk in the kitchen."

Colin looked over at jack, he nodded. We took our coffees into the kitchen and sat around the table. "Alright Meg, let's hear it? What did you sense? Even by your standards that was quick. I've got this awful feeling this is not good news." I shared Colin's concerns, Meg looked troubled.

Meg shrugged. "I don't have all the answers yet, but this much I know, we must not take Cara from this place. She must stay, and she must stay as the wolf. I don't think the wolf side of things will be a problem, if only we can get her changed back."

Colin and I looked at each other in disbelief, but it was Jack who spoke.

He had followed us noiselessly from the lounge and now stood in the doorway.

"No Meg. You must help her. Cara wants to be like me, she can change, and she is almost there. You can teach her, show her how."

Meg stood. "I'm sorry Jack. Come and sit down, you should hear this too."

Jack allowed Meg to guide him to a chair. She sat down again and took her time. She seemed to be searching for the right words. After what seemed like an age, she continued, "Jack Cara is lost between worlds. She doesn't have the strength, or I believe the will, to become human. Perhaps she never did. Nature doesn't always get these things right, it's no one's fault. As far as we know, Cara has never changed completely and maybe she has never had that ability.

But there is another force at work here, a far stronger force!" Meg stopped.

Jack spoke for us all, "I don't understand."

Meg patted Jack's hand. "There is no easy way of saying this honey. I'm sorry, I know you have gotten close to Cara these past few days, but I felt it the moment I touched her.

Cara is carrying young, three if I'm not mistaken. Only a few weeks on, and for now at least they seem healthy, but we need to get her back or she will lose them, and if that happens we may lose her too. Cara is holding on to life and a sense of being, not just for herself but for her little ones."

Suddenly the light came on in my head, "The wolf. There's been this wolf out front watching the lodge, it was just watching and seemed to be waiting for something. It must be waiting for Cara. He knows she's in here! Could he be the father?" I stopped remembering jack. I felt I'd said too much.

Jack had his head in his hands. Colin put his arm around him. "I'm sorry Jack, this could change everything. We must help her and her cubs. This is no longer just about Cara.

What can we do Meg?"

"I'm working on that. I need to help Cara focus on what she really wants. She needs to get that straight in her head. I will need your help Jack. This time at least, Cara was following your lead to become human. If we take it slowly, she may follow your lead to find her way back."

Jack seemed to consider this for a moment, and then he spoke in almost a whisper. "I will help, then, if Cara wishes to stay, I will stay with her!"

Colin stood abruptly and paced up and down the room a couple of times, he seemed to be fighting with his own emotions. When he finally spoke it was to Meg, he ignored Jack.

"If we can get her back, what's to stop all this happening again? If she starts to change again, she will draw attention to herself and her cubs. It's going to get busier up here whatever we manage to do."

I suspected that Colin had chosen to ignore what Jack had said on purpose, I knew there was no way he hadn't heard the comment.

Meg took her time. It was obvious that she had heard Jack and taken him seriously. When at last she spoke, it was to Jack, not to Colin. "If only it was that simple Jack. I think you would find it hard, maybe even impossible, to go back to a life in the pack. Besides, you could end up doing more harm than good. It's been so long, you've seen so much, and your human side has grown. Besides Jack, you belong to a family already."

Colin sat down again and put his arm on Jack's shoulder. "I know how you must feel Jack, but you don't belong here, you can't stay. You leave with us."

Whether Colin had meant it or not, the last words came out sounding like a command.

Jack visibly flinched, then very slowly with a look of determination on his face. He stood and pushing Colin's arm away said quietly, "I will be with Cara."

The kitchen door closed behind him.

Meg shook her head sadly. The three of us sat in an awkward silence. After what seemed like an eternity Meg spoke, "In answer to your question Colin, I think after this experience, Cara will want nothing more than to bring up her pups, and return to the life she knows and is comfortable with. Besides, my guess is even if Cara wanted to she wouldn't be able to change again. That side of her mind seems to have closed a door of sorts, who could blame it."

Meg sighed. "As for Jack, you know you have to let him choose his direction? As with Toby, you must stand back and give him room. At this emotional time, the wrong words could drive him to make decisions based on rebellious and angry feelings. In some ways he is like a child, you need to let him grow."

Colin spoke in hushed tones, but he sounded angry all the same. "It's ridiculous! We couldn't leave Jack here. I wouldn't leave him here! He's like - he's one of the family."

Colin didn't have to say the words, Jack was like a son to him and his pain was obvious.

Meg put her hand on his shoulder. "It's all about free will," she said simply. "There is no wrong or right way! Just the way we choose, let him choose his way Colin! I think given space, Jack will know in his heart what he must do. But it must be his choice."

In a whisper and almost to himself, Colin asked, "And what if his heart tells him he should stay?" The room pulsed with emotion. I could feel all my own fears welling up inside of me, I needed to get out.

I stood hurriedly, almost knocking over my mug. "I'm going out to see how the snowman is coming," I said, grabbing my coat and hat from behind the door. I didn't wait for an answer.

The air outside was cold but fresh, it didn't take any of my seeker powers to find Sally and Maya. I could hear Maya laughing and squealing. I followed the happy sounds it was a relief after the tension of the lodge.

The snowman was looking a little out of sorts, with a very large round body and a rather smaller squished head. Bits of twig made a mouth of sorts and two completely different sized pine cones formed eyes. I realized the focus of play had changed, when a snow ball hit me squarely in the ear!

Maya fell into the snow in a heap of giggles.

"Come on Alan, show us what you're made of," Sally shouted, as another snow ball hit me in the chest. Now that, was a question I could really do with spending some time on, but now wasn't that time! I was getting hammered. The girls were ganging up on me. I dodged another shower of snow. I tried in vain to anticipate Sally's missiles. She moved so quickly, all I saw was a blur, as snow balls rained.

When at last, Sally stopped still for a moment, she looked so young. The years seemed to have dropped a way, the more she laughed, the younger she looked. After making as much effort as I could to return fire, I dropped exhausted and wet to the snow.

Maya squealed. "You squished Angel!"

Now, in my new line of work, and from recent experiences, this was a worrying statement to hear. I looked down expecting - blood and yes maybe even feathers.

Sally laughed. "I showed Maya how to make a snow angel. You just landed on it!"

With that explanation, we all ended up in a heap in the snow laughing.

It happened to be then, that Colin stuck his head out of the front door and shouted, "Come on in, Meg has made some brunch."

Stupid, but I couldn't help feeling guilty for having fun, but I had to admit I felt a lot better and pretty hungry too. I helped Sally to her feet. Out of the corner of my eye I caught sight of the wolf that I had seen the night before. I tried to nod my head in its general direction, without drawing attention.

Sally looked up. "I know, he's been here all the time. He's alone, I don't think he means us any harm."

Maya noticed him too. "Another doggy! Can we stroke him," she said.

Sally grabbed her hand. "No honey, not this one. Come on, time to go in and get warm and dry."

As I closed the door behind us I looked back, he was still there on the edge of the clearing, waiting patiently.

We all sat around the kitchen table, even with the situation the way it was, Meg had managed to rustle up a great lunch. Jack refused to join us, but I did notice he was sitting by the fire, and not at Cara's side. Maybe he was having second thoughts about taking on the role of father.

Meg placed a glass of reddish looking liquid in front of Sally and addressed her with what seemed like an improved tone - "Sally, Colin tells me that you mix up your own nourishing shakes, because of your - stomach problem. You find this sustains you?"

Sally sipped her drink. "I find it stops me from over indulging, on – other things."

"It's a cool colour. Can I try?" Maya said.

Sally smiled. "Please do."

"No!" Was the instant cry, from around the table.

Sally laughed. "Its fine – really, it's just a mix of fruit and vegetable juices."

Maya licked her lips. "Mmmm it tastes yummy, not like vegetables."

Meg raised an eyebrow, but said no more. Instead she filled Sally in on what she suspected. Sally listened carefully.

Sally tried her best to reassure Meg and Colin. "If all goes well with Kevin, I'll be here to keep an eye on Cara and Jack, and I have a better eye than most. I would let you know if

I thought there was a problem." After a couple of moments thought Sally added, "Do you really think Jack might stay? I think he may have a fight on his – paws, if the wolf outside is anything to go by!"

Meg looked pointedly at Colin, who sighed and shook his head. "It's Jack's choice. The important thing is to get Cara back to her old self. Then we need Maya to have a little talk with Kevin. After that, with or without Jack, we will be going home."

"Oh shit! I mean oops," Sally exclaimed. "I'd forgotten about my dear husband, I'd better go and see how he is. Do you need me for anything, right now?"

Meg smiled. She seemed to be warming to Sally, a little. "No, thank you Sally, I have some herbs warming on the stove. When the infusion is ready, we need to get Cara to drink it. I'm hoping Maya will be able to help me with that. What do you think honey?"

Maya had obviously been very hungry, after all that running around in the snow. Thankfully she had taken a rest from her usual chattering, to eat. She finished her mouthful (better manners than Kevin) before answering, "I will try Meg."

Meg started to clear the dishes, I stopped her. "Let me and Maya do that Meg, I want to hear all about Maya's adventures. You have - other things to sort out." I nodded towards Colin, who was still staring at his half eaten lunch.

Meg patted my arm and smiled. "Thanks, you two. I'll just take this mixture off the stove and leave it on the side to cool. Colin, we need to give Sophie and Toby a ring and tell them we've arrived. No need to mention anything else at the moment. Let's just see how things pan out." Colin obediently, followed Meg into the lounge without a word.

With great excitement, Maya started to tell me all about the little plane and the big plane, and how people looked like ants, when you looked out of the window. Honestly - I sort of tuned out, with the odd yes and really, which seemed to be enough for Maya. Then I heard Maya mention something about not having lessons with Meg lately, on account of her having to look after Goldie!

"Maya," I said, trying to get a word in, "Has Goldie been ill?"

Maya seemed to think about this, for just a moment. "She had a tummy ache - I think."

Meg came in from the lounge. "Maya, if you go and join Colin, Sophie and Toby are on the phone, you could say hello, and tell them all about the snow."

Maya rushed past, eager to tell Toby what he was missing. Meg inspected the mixture cooling on the side. She seemed happy with it and tipped it into a glass.

"What is it? It smells familiar," I asked.

Meg smiled. "It should, you've tasted it yourself, not so long ago. It helped you focus your powers. Let's hope it can help Cara focus now. How are you Alan? You seem troubled! Come talk to me." Meg sat down at the table and I joined her.

I sighed. "It's a really long story! And now isn't the time. I'm fine." I tried to sound convincing. In the scheme of things, my worries did seem to pale into insignificance against what was going on in the other room.

"You're all mixed up Alan..." Meg started to say.

I interrupted her. "Huh that's the problem," I said bitterly.

Meg shook her head. She reached for my hand and looked me straight in the eye's. "You have mixed blood in your veins Alan. That has nothing to do with what's in your heart. Don't let yourself get hung up, on the things you have no control over. The past is just that, you cannot change it. The future! Now that's a different matter."

I looked back into those ageless eyes. She knew? Why should that surprise me, Meg seemed to know everything.

Meg stood. "Right, well this potion is ready, let's hope it has the desired effect."

"And if it doesn't work?" I asked. So much was riding on this.

Meg shrugged. "Then we try something else Alan. But we worry about that, when, and if we need to." She led the way into the lounge.

Colin and Maya were just saying their good byes as we joined them. Meg put the glass on the table. "Everything alright back home?" Meg asked Colin, as he put his phone back in his pocket.

"They're all ok and looking forward to us - all coming home." Colin put the emphasis on the all, and looked over at Jack, who was sitting in a chair by the fire, staring distantly at the flames.

Maya yawned. Meg took her by the hand. "I think you should have a little nap young lady, you will need to be wide awake and sharp as a pin later on. Alan, can Maya use your room for an hour or so, she can hardly keep her eyes open."

"Yes, of course Meg. Follow me, I'll show you where it is." I led the way. Maya must have been exhausted, she didn't complain at all, and allowed Meg to tuck her into my bed. She was asleep, even before we closed the door.

As Meg and I reached the door to the lounge, we could hear Colin, talking to Jack. Without a word Meg and I automatically held back in the hallway, to give them a few moments.

Meg coughed loudly before we entered. "Sorry Colin, we really need to get Cara back to her old self, as soon as we can. Jack, are you ready?"

Sally joined us. "Can I help? Kevin is in a foul mood, I've left him to it."

I suddenly remembered that Sally had managed to get Cara to drink some hours before. I relayed what had happened to Meg and Colin.

Meg didn't look as happy with my story as I'd expected, but she nodded at Sally. "That would be helpful Sally, it would save us involving Maya. I'm not sure how this is going to go. We'll need to get Cara out of the lodge, if this works. We could end up with a large, unhappy, confused and anxious wolf on our hands. I don't want her trapped inside, besides I don't want her any more stressed than she needs to be, for her sake, and for her pups!"

Sally thought for a moment. "We can't use the barn, the dogs would panic. How about the wood shed? It's just outside the kitchen door and there's an upper mezzanine floor on one side, for storage. It would be safe to keep an eye on things from up there."

Meg nodded. "That sounds perfect. Show me please."

The two women left. Jack had re-joined Cara and Colin sat by the fire watching him. I sat down in the chair opposite. "Are you alright?" It was a stupid question.

Colin nodded. He spoke in a whisper, "I don't want to lose him Alan, not like this. Not here. This place isn't right for him - she's not right for him. What he's feeling is guilt for what's happened. He wants to take care of her and the pups, ironic really; he wants to do the gentlemanly thing! He won't listen to reason."

He didn't sound angry now, just sad. I tried to reassure him. "Maybe, when Cara is out of the woods - so to speak, Jack will be happy to leave her - in the woods!" That had sounded better in my head, but I pushed on regardless. "I'm pretty sure the wolf, waiting patiently outside, will be the pup's father. He looks more than capable of looking after her, if in fact, she ever needed looking after. I'm sure once Jack sees Cara safely back to her home, he will be more than ready to leave here with the rest of us," I added. To be honest, I was surprised at how desperate I felt at the thought of leaving Jack behind. He'd saved my life on more than one occasion in the past. Everyone slept easier on the island knowing that Jack was out there in the night.

Sally and Meg returned. "The wood shed will be good," Meg said, crossing the floor to stand over Jack. She pushed the hair out of his eyes affectionately. "Alright Jack, if you will carry Cara out there, we've put down some straw and a couple of blankets. Place her carefully on them and we'll join you in a moment." She turned to Colin. "Have you said what you needed to say, just in case."

Colin just nodded.

"Right, well let's see if we can make this work out for the best, shall we?" Meg led the way. Jack had placed Cara on the blankets and knelt by her side. I followed on. I wondered what the best would actually be.

"Alright, Alan you help Sally, just as you did before." Meg stood beside Colin.

In fact, I had no desire to help Sally again. My head still felt a little woolly from the last time. Sally noticed my hesitation. She smiled and whispered "Like I said before Alan, don't look into my eyes and think of something else, maybe someone else, if that helps. Remember, only the weak or willing!"

Meg handed me the potion and Sally took Cara's hand and paw in hers.

I thought of Natasha, that first day when she'd emerged from the waves like a goddess. Just the thought of that image was enough to distract me, when Sally said now Alan! It took me a moment to remember what I was supposed to do, but Cara drank the potion down willingly when I offered it, and we lay her gently back to the floor.

Nothing seemed to happen. "Now what?" I said.

Meg settled herself on to an upturned log. "Now we wait."

I knew I sounded like an impatient child. "How long?" I'm not sure what I was expecting, but whatever it was, I was expecting it to happen instantly.

Meg smiled. "I don't know Alan. The rest is up to Cara." I felt a little disappointed, but as it happened, we didn't have long to wait.

From somewhere outside, quite close, a wolf howled. I shuddered and so did Cara. I was about to say something, but there was no need, Meg had seen it too.

Meg touched Jack gently on his broad shoulder. "Now Jack! But slowly, just as you did before. Take her back with you."

Jack slipped easily out of his clothes and took Cara's human hand in his. Meg indicated for the rest of us to get up onto the mezzanine level. I followed Colin and Sally up the ladder, by the time I peered over the edge, Jack was already on all fours, his body covered in fur. It was hard to see Cara from my position, Jacks body was shielding most of her from me, but something was happening. The blanket was thrown across the floor, Cara seemed to be crouching and the sounds were anything but human.

It was only as Jack started to circle slowly, that I could gradually make out the white wolf in all her glory. Suddenly everything was clear and right. I felt relieved, looking at the white wolf below, confident, powerful. There was no doubt in my mind that Cara was gone for good. She shook herself, as if throwing off the last of her human skin! Then she threw back her head and howled.

The two magnificent animals circled each other slowly, carefully, showing a great deal of respect. The white wolf was only slightly smaller than Jack and it had to be said, they made a hansom pair. It was only then, in the midst of all this, that I

359

remembered Meg. She had been down there somewhere. When I concentrated the seeker part of my mind, I could make her out, standing very still, almost invisible, at the side of the shed. She was only a few feet away from the action, but somehow completely unnoticed.

Both animals howled and a reply came instantly from just outside the open shed door. The white wolf looked up, seeming to recognize the sound. At the same moment, the door to the lodge opened wide and Maya stood yawning in the doorway. The white wolf snarled and her hackles rose making her appear even larger than before, she took a couple of steps towards Maya. Jack moved like lightning, placing himself between Maya and the snarling white wolf.

Again the howl came from outside, and this time, with Jack distracted, the white wolf made her getaway through the open shed door and out into the fast approaching night. She showed no signs of weakness from her ordeal.

After only a moment's hesitation Jack followed her.

Sally was first to the ground. She leapt down, landing easily. Colin was already halfway down the ladder. I considered the jump and thought better of it. It must have been a good 10 feet.

By the time I followed the others out into the snow, the sun had disappeared and been replaced by a bright full moon (the stuff of dreams and now thanks to me-Kevin's nightmares!).

The wolf we had spotted waiting patiently outside, was now rewarded. Both he and the white wolf showed obvious delight at being reunited. The male wolf was not so happy to see Jack approach. The white wolf stood between them and there seemed to be a kind of uncomfortable truce. The big male headed off into the trees and the white wolf followed. After a couple of steps though, she stopped, and turned to wait for Jack.

"Jack no," Colin shouted. At the sound of Colin's voice, the white wolf bounded into the trees and was gone. Jack hesitated, torn between two worlds.

Colin was desperate. "We are your family Jack," he shouted, his words carried by the swirling wind. It had started to snow again and the light from the moon made the flakes sparkle and dance.

Again the howl went up, from deep in the woods. Jack seemed to make up his mind. Perhaps, the call of the wild was simply too strong for him. After one last look back, he too disappeared. The trees closed in behind him and he was gone.

***

"I'm thirsty," Maya said from the doorway. "And the man is shouting again. I don't think he's very happy."

Sally took Maya's hand. "Ok honey, I'll find you a drink, actually I think we could all do with one. I'll see what the man is shouting about." Sally took Maya back inside.

Meg took Colin by the arm. "Let's all get inside in the warm, this isn't over yet! Come on Alan, Sally is right, we could all, do with a drink."

I felt stunned and unsure of what to do. "Shall I bring in Jack's cloths," I asked.

Colin seemed to wake from a dream. He spun round so suddenly I almost fell backwards into the snow.

"Don't touch them!" he shouted. "Leave them," he yelled.

I was taken aback by his sudden outburst.

Meg smiled calmly. "Just leave things as they are for now Alan, let's get in, we've another problem to solve before this night's over."

I looked back at the woods, the wind had dropped and it had stopped snowing, even so it was bitterly cold. I shuddered. Had Jack really chosen this frozen world over the island and us?

.

Maya was sitting at the kitchen table, a glass of milk in one hand, a biscuit in the other. I could hear Meg talking with Colin in the other room.

"Hi Maya, did you have a nice sleep?" I asked, joining her at the table. It seemed like the safest place at present. But I was wrong. Maya made a face.

"The man next door shouts a lot, I don't think he likes the moon much.

"Alan, Meg has taught me it is wrong to change people's minds for them, without their permission." She took another sip of milk. I suddenly wished I was someplace else. I knew what was coming and I had nowhere to run. I felt like a rabbit, starring down the barrel of a loaded gun.

Maya continued thoughtfully, "Sally said that it would be good to change the shouting man's mind and that he wouldn't shout anymore."

Again a pause, but I knew what was coming.

"Isn't that wrong?" she said, looking at me expectantly.

And there it was! Bang, right between the eyes. What could I say? What did I think? It was wrong, wasn't it? How could I explain to Maya, that normally, what we were asking her to do was wrong? But what might happen, if we didn't change Kevin's mind, balanced out that wrong, or did it? Probably not - oh shit!

I laughed nervously, because I didn't know what else to do. "What did Sally say?" I ventured, looking for an escape route.

"Sally thinks I could make the man feel a lot better, about things. What things, do you think he is unhappy about Alan?"

Maya finished her biscuit and looked around. "Has Jack taken the other doggy for a walk?" Maya took another sip of milk, leaving a white moustache on her top lip.

How could someone this young and seemingly innocent have so much power. Sally was probably right, in the wrong hands this little angel could be a demon.

I smiled. "Yes Jack and Cara needed to stretch their legs," I said, hoping that the other question would go away. I was relieved when Colin and Meg re-joined us.

Whatever Meg had said to Colin had obviously worked wonders, he looked a lot better. They sat down with us at the kitchen table. Colin even managed a weak smile. He put his hand on my shoulder. "Sorry Alan, I didn't mean to take things out on you earlier."

I nodded. "No problem Colin, things have been a bit fraught. I think we'll all be pleased when this is all over and we can all go home." I realized too late, that this wasn't the best thing to say under the circumstances.

Colin just nodded.

Meg produced a handkerchief and wiped Maya's mouth. She smiled at the child. "Now my little one, what's going through that busy little mind of yours? If I'm not mistaken you have a question for us," she asked, soothingly.

Had she overheard our conversation? Meg had been in the other room talking with Colin, there was no way she could have heard Maya's small voice from there. Could she really read minds? Or perhaps, she just simply read and understood people. Either way, I was relieved that it would be up to Meg and Colin to explain things now. I was off the hook.

Maya seemed a little overwhelmed by all the attention. Meg patted her hand. "It's alright honey, you need to tell us if something is worrying you. Is it about the angry man and what we need you to do?"

Maya nodded. "What if he likes being angry?" she asked.

Meg laughed. "He can be angry if he wants honey, all we need to do, is get rid of a few bad memories, which could make him very sick. He could hurt the people and animals that live in these mountains, if we don't do something now. Sometimes, when you are sick, you don't realize how sick you are! So someone has to get you to take your medicine, or you may never get better. Together we will make him well and happy again, does that sound ok?"

Maya smiled and nodded. "Yes Meg. Can we ride in the sleigh again?"

Meg looked at Colin, he nodded. "I'm sure we can get Sally to give you another ride tomorrow, before we leave."

Maya looked happy again and the problem seemed to be solved, for the moment.

Meg stood. "Right Maya, let's go and see what we can do for Kevin shall we?" She held out her hand and Maya took it with a smile.

"Can we ask Sally about the sleigh ride please Meg?" Maya asked. The moral dilemma she had been struggling with, replaced easily with the excitement of another ride on the sleigh.

As Meg and Maya left the room, I hung back with Colin. When we were alone I asked "How are you doing?"

"I'm fine, thanks." Colin looked anything but fine. The strain of the past few days had taken their toll and he looked tired and drawn, but he still managed a smile.

"Are you coming to watch Maya in action?" I asked. I had to admit, I was curious to watch Maya work her magic again. I'd witnessed it once before, without really understanding what was going on. I suppose, I still didn't understand how this small child could have such control over people's minds.

Colin shook his head. "No, I don't want to spook Kevin. He'll be far more relaxed if I keep out of the way. But you go ahead. I'm going to give Ben a ring and tell him we'll be leaving in the morning, after breakfast. He'll have to spend the night on the plane. I don't think that will worry him much. If everything works out, I want to spend a little time with the new Kevin tonight, just to make sure that things are back to normal before we head for home."

I nodded. "You don't think there'll be a problem, do you? Meg seems confident it will work."

Colin shook his head. "Meg is confident about a lot of things and she is usually right, but things haven't exactly gone to plan on this trip. I just want to make sure, that's all. A few hours more, won't hurt us."

I agreed and left Colin, making the call to Ben.

I knew Colin just wanted to give Jack time to come to his senses and re-join us. I'd a feeling, Meg had probably calmed Colin, by telling him that's what she believed would happen. I really, really hoped it was true. I had to admit, that as much as I wanted to go home, the thought of leaving jack behind and how we would explain his loss to the others, didn't bare thinking about.

I joined Sally standing at the doorway to Jacks old room, which up until now, had acted as a jail for our un-willing captive. But things seemed to be changing.

Maya was sitting on the edge of the bed, holding Kevin's hand. He had his eyes shut and seemed to be sleeping.

Meg turned to Sally. "You can remove the hand cuffs, they won't be needed anymore."

Sally quickly did as instructed and removed the cuffs from Kevin's wrist and slipped them into her pocket. Meg was busy watching Maya. Something about Sally's eagerness to help drew my attention. I noticed she seemed to hold Kevin's hand in hers, for a few seconds longer than seemed necessary, she seemed to be concentrating. She saw me looking and let Kevin's hand drop to the bed. She smiled, revealing those pearly whites and again she winked at me, before moving away.

Meg spoke softly to Maya. I could hardly make out the words. Apart from her voice the room was silent, I hardly dare breath. It felt as if there was static in the air. Like that feeling you got before a big storm. The hairs on the back of my neck were standing on end.

Maya was silent. She listened intently, to what Meg was saying. Meg's voice was so soothing. I was finding it hard to keep my own eyes open; her voice seemed to be inside my head.

Sally nudged me. I came too, with a jolt.

Sally leaned a little close for comfort and whispered in my ear, "Be careful Alan! There's a lot of power in this room, don't let it draw you in."

I nodded and tried to clear my head, it seemed to be suddenly full of thoughts, of how great a nature reserve and ski resort would be, and what great shots you could get with a camera, instead of a rifle. I decided it was time to leave them to it. Sally followed me out of the room. We both joined Colin in the lounge.

He looked surprisingly relaxed, too relaxed. "I made coffee if anyone's interested. How's it going in there?" Colin said, throwing another log on the already roaring fire and settling himself in one of the fireside chairs.

I poured myself a coffee and chose the sofa, allowing Sally to sit opposite Colin by the fire. Sally laughed. "If the effect on Alan is anything to go by, I think things are going well."

I shook my head, still finding it difficult to concentrate. "If I'd stayed in that room any longer, I think I would have been here in this winter wonderland forever. Trying to conserve the wildlife and take care of the environment. Its powerful stuff - if only we could bottle it."

I sipped my coffee. The air in here felt almost as intense.

Colin's manner was relaxed. His smile could perhaps have persuaded me that Jack had been forgotten. If only he could have taken his eyes from the front door.

I was relieved when Meg and Maya re-joined us. Maya plonked herself next to me on the couch and slipped her small hand into mine. I half expected the thoughts of ski resorts and nature reserves to return, but they didn't. Colin offered Meg his seat "How do you think it went?"

Meg declined the seat, but smiled. "Everything will be fine Colin. I'm going to sort us out some dinner. We've left Kevin to wake naturally. When he does, he will be expecting to join us all for a pleasant evening meal, to discuss the ideas that he and Sally have for the resort, and maybe get some backing from you – Colin, in the process."

Colin laughed. "That is an inspired idea. If we help out with some finance, it will give us an excuse to keep an eye on things. You're amazing Meg, in fact you are both amazing. Well done Maya. Will he remember anything about the last 24 hours - at all?"

Meg nodded. "That's the other clever thing. Kevin will remember not feeling too good, so he has gone for a lie down before dinner. When he wakes, it will be from a dream or nightmare, if you like, of being imprisoned by werewolves. But of course, it will have been a dream, nothing more. He can tell us about it over dinner. If recounting his story doesn't ring any alarm bells, I think we're home and dry."

Sally looked genuinely impressed and relieved. She stood. "Thank you Meg and Maya. Do you know, this could end up saving our marriage. It's strange, it's as if this was all meant to be. Let me help you with the meal."

Meg had a wry smile on her face. "Thanks Sally, we may have to do plenty of vegetables! Funny thing really, Maya seems to think there was already a thought planted in Kevin's mind, before we started. You wouldn't know anything about that, would you?" Meg gave Sally one of her knowing looks.

Sally laughed and tried without much success to look innocent. "I can't think what you mean. Perhaps Maya put it there, without realizing it! What is it?"

Meg shrugged. "Oh never mind. Let's go and get dinner on. I think Kevin will be joining us shortly.

Colin, have you arranged things with Ben?"

Colin nodded. "Yes, he's happy to stay with Tina and the plane tonight. We'll join him after breakfast in the morning."

Meg and Sally headed for the kitchen.

Maya turned to me and asked, "Alan, what's a veg – e – tar – e - n?" She carefully broke up the unfamiliar word.

The tension in the room melted away. Colin and I laughed till we cried. Maya laughed too, although she had no idea why. An explanation would have to wait, for now this was the light relief we all needed. We had only just managed to gather our wits, when Kevin stepped in from the hall way. He looked a little flushed, from his late afternoon nap.

"Hi gents." He noticed Maya and added, "And ladies of course. Look, I'm really sorry about that, I really don't know what came over me. Maybe Something I ate. Sally says I have been eating far too much red meat, maybe she's right."

Colin jumped to his feet and met Kevin halfway across the room. "Not at all Kevin, don't be silly. You have nothing to apologize for. Please take my seat by the fire. Are you feeling better?"

Before Kevin could answer, Sally appeared at the kitchen door. "I thought I heard your voice honey. How are you? You look a little better.

I had a word with Colin and the others and they are happy for us to stay tonight, if you're not up to the drive back."

Kevin smiled. "No honey, I'm fine, no need to make a fuss. I'll take that seat and a stiff drink though, there's a bottle of good whisky in that cupboard." Kevin indicated the tall corner cupboard. Sally went for a glass and Kevin sat by the fire. We waited. It seemed like an age, Kevin continued, "I had the most vivid dream - well nightmare really! It feels as if I've been holed up in that room for ages. How long was I asleep?"

Sally had returned with the glass and poured him a large whisky. "Oh, I would say about an hour honey." She glanced at us for confirmation. Colin checked his watch, so did I (the fact, that my watch was only ever right twice a day, made no difference here). We both agreed with Sally.

Kevin took a large swig from his glass. We waited for him to continue his story.

"From what I can remember, it had something to do with werewolves. I was destined to be the main course! I don't know what you're smiling at Sally, you were down as desert. The whole thing is starting to fade now, but when I woke, it was so dammed real."

Sally laughed. "Oh come on honey, it is a little bit funny. You're the one who is always taking the mickey out of the locals, for their old stories about werewolves and vampires. Some of those tall tales have obviously sunk in."

Kevin laughed. "Well ok then, maybe a bit funny, your right of course."

That laugh sounded so good, we all visibly relaxed a little. For the first time in a long while, things seemed to be working out.

Meg stuck her head around the door. "Alright everyone, time to eat. I hope everyone's hungry. Sally and I have prepared a feast for our last evening in these beautiful mountains.

Ah Kevin, I'm glad to see you're awake. I hope you're feeling well enough to join us. Sally has been telling me all about your plans for the mountain. I would love to hear more."

"Yes, thank you........." Kevin hesitated.

'Meg," Meg said quickly, "That's good, I would love to hear about the nature reserve, over dinner." Meg disappeared back into the kitchen and we all followed her.

Colin was keen to keep the conversation on track. "Yes Kevin, I'm interested to know how you feel we can help. This place has had quite an effect - on all of us."

That at least was true. As we sat down to dinner, it felt as if we were finally getting back on track. Sally and Kevin seemed to grow closer and closer as they talked, about plans for special areas in the mountains. These would be left undisturbed, to preserve their beauty, and be a safe haven for the larger animals.

Colin was only too happy to help support their efforts and provide advice where we could. In return, he would insist on an update on a regular basis, and the chance to visit every now and then. Just to check - on progress.

I couldn't help noticing a smile flash across the faces of Sally and Colin when Kevin passed on the roast meat, and opted instead for heaps of vegetables.

Maybe when he got back to the Lodge, he would at last lay to rest the souls of all the animals that adorned the walls there.

As the evening drew on, I thought for Kevin and Sally at least, the future looked good. The white wolf would have her pups, in the safety of the reserve, with only the inquisitive nature lovers with cameras to worry about. Meg seemed sure the white wolf would be content in that form from now on, I wondered if the same could be said for Jack.

Things were indeed looking brighter! And then there it was again, the dark cloud on the horizon. Going home without Jack! What would we say to the others?

Suddenly I realized that everyone was looking in my direction. "Sorry," I mumbled, "I was miles away, what did you say?"

Kevin smiled. "That's alright lad. Colin was just telling us about his son, Toby, and I was just asking if you had someone waiting for you back home?"

"Yes, yes I do, I have two very special ladies in my life at the moment, my dog Scruffy and my......" I hesitated, girlfriend sounded so lame.

"Natasha," I added quickly, hoping no one had noticed my hesitation.

I immediately felt guilty, not to have included my mother and hoped that if her seeker powers were, as I imagined better than mine, that she wasn't eves dropping at this very moment. I would know, wouldn't I? I felt flushed. My mother could be watching me at any time - oh bugger!!!

Kevin miss read my embarrassment and laughed. "I thought as much, that's where you keep drifting off to, fairly new relationship – eh. Take my advice lad, if she's that good, that you can't stop thinking about her, even when you're on holiday. Put a ring on her finger! The good ones are hard to find and even harder to hang on to."

He leaned over and kissed Sally gently on the cheek, she smiled, but something deep in her eyes made me remember something she'd said, 'sometimes, it is because you love them, that you have to leave them'.

I wondered how long they had together, before Sally's youthful looks caused tongues to wag. Maybe here, away from the city, no one would take much notice.

Nature had a way of dealing some interesting cards. Hopefully Kevin and Sally would have a good few years yet, to enjoy their new project.

Life could be so complicated, even the happiest times, could be tinged with great sadness. Kevin was right, when you found that special someone, you needed to make the most of every moment you had with them.

Perhaps Jack should stay, maybe this was his moment. Cara was the - one.

Maya tried to stifle a yawn. She had been unusually quiet over dinner. She looked all in. Meg stood. "Well young lady, it's well past your bedtime, say goodnight. We'll have an early start in the morning." Maya got down from her chair without complaint, she was obviously very tired. She kissed Colin and me lightly and skipped over to Sally.

"Can I ride in the sleigh again tomorrow Sally? Please, Please."

Sally laughed. "Yes Maya of course, we'll leave the sleigh here tonight, it's too late to take the dogs out now. Kevin can drive us back here in the morning and then you can ride with me in the sleigh to the airport. Does that sound alright?"

Maya jumped up and down with excitement, "Yes, yes! Thank you, Sally. Goodnight. Goodnight, angry man. I'm glad you're feeling better now."

Meg grabbed Maya's hand and led her quickly from the room.

Kevin raised an eyebrow. Sally patted his hand. "Well you weren't feeling well honey, you were a bit - grumpy!"

Kevin looked a little confused. "I must have been a bit out of things, sorry. What's the sleigh doing here?"

Colin shot me a glance, but he needn't have been worried, Sally had it covered. "You never listen honey. I did tell you, I was bringing it over this afternoon - to take our guests out for a real snow experience. I wanted to see if Colin thought it would be a good idea to offer visitors the sleigh ride, rather than the normal 4x4's." Sally beamed. She seemed to be enjoying this.

"Well?" Kevin looked expectantly at Colin.

I couldn't be sure, but I think, Sally may have kicked Colin under the table.

Sally was far better at this than us. I wondered how many lies she'd told over the years, to keep her cover intact.

Colin realized he was up. "Oh, I think it's a great idea, in fact, I'm really excited about the whole project and I'm so glad you have both asked me to be a part of it." Colin relaxed again, a little too soon.

Kevin had remembered something else. "What happened to the other two guys?"

Sally didn't skip a beat. God she was good. "Oh you mean Ben and Jack. Colin asked me to drop them off at the airport this afternoon, when I took Maya and Meg out for a ride in the sleigh.

"Yes," Colin added, "There were checks to do on the plane, for our journey home tomorrow. Need to make sure these storms haven't affected anything. They'll be comfortable tonight. They have everything they need on-board."

Kevin seemed happy with this. Sally was keen to move things along.

"Why don't you gentlemen shift yourselves into the lounge to talk business, so that I can clear these things away. We don't want to be too late driving home tonight. The weather is pretty good at the moment, but up here things can change in a heartbeat?"

Kevin was already on his feet, he kissed Sally on the cheek as he passed. 'That's a great idea honey, I think there maybe another whiskey in the lounge with my name on it. Will you join me Colin? Oh… and Alan of course."

I knew I was an afterthought, but at least this time he'd remembered my name. I declined the invite and opted instead to stay and help Sally clear the dishes. Kevin looked at me as if I were off my head, but made no comment. He was happy to have Colin to himself, probably to talk money. I wondered just how much money Colin had, I had a feeling this little venture wouldn't even put a dent in it.

Sally closed the door behind them. "I was hoping to get sometime alone with you Alan," She said moving closer. I felt the hairs stand up on the back of my neck, it wasn't that I didn't trust her!....no cancel that, it was that I didn't trust her. Sally made me feel uneasy, about her and about myself.

She lowered her voice, "There is something, I would like you to have," Sally said, removing a small red velvet pouch from her pocket. She held it out to me.

I hesitated. "What is it." I didn't like to sound ungrateful, but I'd been warned about taking things from strangers, and you couldn't get much stranger than Sally.

She laughed. "It's alright Alan. Believe it or not, I'm on your side. You could call it - an heirloom. It's very old and very special. Call it a good luck charm, if you like. It can protect the wearer. You may want to keep it, or it sounds like you may have someone special, you would like to give it to!"

I was curious, so I took the pouch and opened it. It held a ring. I removed it and held it up to the light. The large single stone sparkled and shone, its colour - deep, blood red.

"It's beautiful. It must be worth a lot of money. I can't accept this Sally; it belongs to your family." I tried to give it back.

"No Alan, if I'm not mistaken, it belongs to your family. Your father would want you to have it."

I was about to protest, but there was something about the stone, something familiar. "I've seen something like this before. My mother wears a pendant around her neck, a ruby. When I was a child, she used to hold it up for me to watch the light dance within it, she never takes it off."

Sally smiled. "It is in fact a red diamond, very rare! But, it is not money that gives it its worth. It has a power - of sorts. It protects the wearer. Like I said, it's a good luck charm! Kevin was right, you should put a ring on her finger.

Maybe, this is the ring!"

Again this left me with so many questions. "Did you get the ring from my father, you have met him, haven't you Sally. Do you know if he's alive?" The questions, flooded out, I don't think I even took a breath.

Sally calmly started to clear the dishes. "I'm sorry Alan. I don't have the answers you seek. Take the ring, it belongs to your blood line. Keep it safe and if you should feel the time is right, use it. Now, let's get these things put in the dishwasher and tidy the kitchen. I would like to get home, I'm tired and I feel as though I haven't eaten properly in days."

She read the look on my face. "What Alan - you know what I am!"

"But you told Meg..." I started to say, but she interrupted me. "I told Meg - the mixture I take, stops me from over indulging my needs. It doesn't change what I am Alan. Nothing, changes what I am!" Her voice trailed off and the sadness had returned. I felt guilty, after all, who was I to judge her.

Sally made herself busy, I knew that was it. There was no use trying to get her to say more.

I looked at the ring again, it shone blood red. Tiny lights, like stars, glittered in its depths. It was very beautiful. I put it back in its pouch and tucked it into my pocket.

We finished up in the kitchen and Sally and Kevin headed for home in the jeep, promising to be back at seven in the morning, to get us all to the Airport.

I'd been concerned for the dogs out in the barn, but Sally insisted they would be fine until morning. She would feed them then and get them harnessed, so that as promised, Maya could ride to the Airport in style.

After we'd said our goodnights and the sound of the jeep had died away, Meg reappeared. "I thought it best, if I kept out of the way. I didn't want to complicate things. Maya is sleeping soundly. I take it everything went alright, after we left for bed."

Colin looked distracted now that we could drop the pretence. I could see that the worry over Jack had returned. Meg could sense it too.

"He'll come round, give it time Colin," Meg said, joining him by the fireside.

Colin looked into the flames. "We're running out of time Meg! I don't want to leave this place without him."

I could see that he was close to tears.

I said goodnight and left Colin and Meg to talk. I needed to think about the ring, it was burning a hole in my pocket. For some strange reason, I already felt an attachment to the thing, maybe because it seemed to link me to my father in some way. Good or bad, I missed him.

Maya was asleep in my room, so I took Jack's bed. I felt a little uncomfortable, but suddenly so tired. I could have slept on the floor. I took the ring out of its pouch and turned it around and around in my fingers, watching the lights dance, remembering my childhood. I couldn't keep my eyes open any longer. I replaced the ring and pushed it under my pillow.

As I lay in the darkened room, Colin and Meg's voices drifted around me. I couldn't make out what they were saying, but it was somehow soothing. I convinced myself that by morning, Jack would have returned. Kevin and Sally would be happy creating the reserve, and the white wolf would be happy creating a family. End of story.

I drifted off to sleep.

My dreams were mixed up and many, my childhood, the boarding school, mother and father, the ring, and of course Natasha.

I woke to the first, weak but glorious, light of dawn.

I dressed quickly, putting the ring back in my pocket, not sure of the time. My old room was empty, so I packed up my things. I could hear voices in the lounge. I left my bags ready in my room.

Colin looked as if he'd been up all night. I heard Meg's voice in the kitchen. She stuck her head round the door, "Come on you two, breakfast is ready." She looked past me to Colin, "And before you say - you're not hungry, we have a long journey ahead of us and we all need our strength, so come and eat. Besides, Maya has helped with the pancakes and I think she has done a great job."

Colin didn't speak, but took his place at the table, as ordered. There was no need to ask if Jack had turned up yet. Despite this fact, I couldn't help feeling happy, we were going home. The conversation was mostly one sided, Maya was so excited about going in the sleigh again. When Meg insisted she help clear the table, I took the opportunity to talk with Colin. "Did you get any, sleep at all?" I asked, knowing the answer.

"Not much, but I did a lot of thinking. Meg was right. I can't live Jack's life for him. This is something he has to face on his own. Maybe in a month or so, I'll come back with Sophie, just to check they're alright. But for now, George needs me. We must go home.

I'm going to finish packing. Sally and Kevin will be here shortly." Colin thanked Maya for a lovely breakfast and left to pack.

I let him go, even though his last comment worried me.

"Meg, what did Colin mean, when he said - George needed him?"

Meg smiled. "Alan, you must understand, Colin has a lifelong bond with George, he senses George is troubled now. But trust me, I would tell you both, if I thought George was in any danger."

The next half an hour was a rush of packing and checking, but when the knock came at the door, we were all ready to leave. There was no need to ask Sally if everything was alright, the pair were like a couple of kid's, laughing and joking around, in fact Kevin looked ten years younger, as he aimed a snow ball playfully at Maya.

Colin offered to drive the jeep so that Kevin and Sally could take Meg and Maya in the sleigh. As the sleigh set off I could hear Maya squealing with delight.

Colin took a final look around.

"Should we go into the woods a little way, maybe call him, or something?" I suggested, knowing full well what was on Colin's mind.

Colin shook his head. "No, there would be no point. I already checked. His spare clothes are still in the barn. I think I'll leave them there, just in case!"

I nodded. He started the engine and as we drove away I couldn't stop myself from turning around, one more time, just - to make sure. The tree's glistened in the early morning sunlight. The woods were beautiful but now silent.

The drive back to the Airport took longer than I remembered, it seemed like an age, since we arrived and were met, by Grizzly Adams. I could sense Colin's pain, my heart, felt as heavy as the snow all around us. I didn't know what to say, we drove in silence.

I couldn't help, thinking this mission had back fired. Instead of bringing something back, we were in fact, leaving a big part of ourselves behind. But this was a beautiful place. With the help of Sally and Kevin, and of course, financial support from Colin, it would stay that way. Without intending to, we had created another sanctuary. Only, this one was a little colder.

The sleigh had already pulled up as we parked outside the airport. Sally had put down some meat for the dogs. Colin handed Kevin the keys. "Thanks Kevin, you have a great spot here, I look forward to visiting again soon, to see how things are going. We'll let the lawyers handle the paper work."

Kevin shook Colin's hand warmly. "Thank you. Your visit has had more of an impact on us here than you could ever possibly know." He gave Sally an affectionate hug."

In fact we did know. Hopefully far more than Kevin ever would! But it didn't matter, they were happy. He said goodbye again and took the jeep, leaving Sally to follow on in the sleigh. Sally gave us all hugs accept Meg, who had gone ahead.

Maya gave Sally a big kiss. "Thank you Sally, I've had so much fun. I'll miss the snow and you."

Sally smiled. "Everything's going to be fine, you'll see and you're all welcome to visit anytime. I promise I'll keep an eye out for our - mutual friends."

Colin thanked her and we waved her off. The farewell was cut short. Meg came rushing out of the Airport building. "I think you should all come and hear this," she said urgently. We followed her in. "This gentleman is Blake. He opened the airport this morning and he has had a bit of a shock. Tell my friend's, what you told me Blake."

Blake seemed a little surprised by the audience, but happy to repeat his tale nonetheless. "Well I'd just opened up, not even had time to put the kettle on. When, bold as you like, a bloody great wolf strolled in the front doors. Well I was up and over that counter in a flash, thought my day had come. When I got up courage to look, the dam thing was disappearing out onto the runway, calm as you like. Bloody thing took the custard creams on its way through - never seen anything like it. I don't ever want to see it again either. No one's going to believe me at the lodge, and that's a fact!"

"Oh I wouldn't be so sure." I couldn't prevent the smile, spreading across my face. Colin hadn't waited for the end of the story, as soon as Blake had mentioned a wolf he was out and onto the runway, heading for the plane.

Luckily this morning, Blake was security, passport control and Steward - so he was happy just to wave us all off and finish in his other role as tea boy. He had after all, had quite a shock this morning. He was, of course, the first aider on call as well, so he recommended a drop of duty free brandy in the tea, just to help settle his nerves!

Ben met us as we entered the aircraft. He nodded towards Colin who was already halfway down the plane. I could just make out the shape of Jack. He was naked and crouching on the floor.

Ben looked pale and obviously shaken. "Tell Colin to take care, Jack's not – himselves," he said in a whisper.

Meg settled Maya into a front seat and then got Ben to sit down too. It was only then, I noticed the blood. Ben was holding his left arm to his chest. Blood was seeping through his fingers, soaking his shirt and dripping onto the floor.

"First aid Kit Alan," Meg said calmly. I was rooted to the spot. I didn't move.

"In the cabin at the front - cupboard marked clearly First Aid, NOW Alan!" This time the urgency in Meg's voice got through to me. I found the box and returned as quickly as I could.

Ben was obviously shaken. "He came past me like a bloody steam train. I tried to put a blanket around him. He nearly took my head off and I mean that literally!!" Ben said as Meg dressed a nasty looking gouge on his forearm.

Meg called Maya over. "Maya honey, I need you to put pressure on this cut for me and look after Ben for a moment, whilst me and Alan go and help Colin with Jack. Can you do that for me?" Maya didn't speak, but she nodded and took over.

I'd already had a run in with a wolf, having – a bad day. Toby had bitten me. This was different, this was Jack. I could tell by Meg's expression, suggesting I sit this one out to help Maya, wasn't an option. Meg grabbed a blanket and thrust it into my arms. "Bring this and keep behind me Alan. It's the influence of the wild. It produces a natural and healthy fear of man. Colin and I have witnessed this before. Jack was just a pup then. We just need to calm him down."

I didn't feel to calm myself, armed with nothing but a pink blanket. But I followed Meg closely down the aisle. Jack was crouched growling and snarling on the cabin floor, he was in human form, naked. He was also bleeding from several nasty looking scratches to his arms and upper body. Colin was talking softly to him, telling him it was going to be alright. Meg touched Colin's shoulder. "His body is human, his mind is still wolf. Talk to the animal," she whispered.

Colin nodded. Although his mouth stopped moving, I could still hear a strange language in my head. Muffled sounds, on the edge of my hearing and nothing I could really understand. Meg began to chant softly.

I stood totally helpless, lost in a world I didn't understand. Colin reached out and took the blanket from me, he walked forward slowly and crouching by Jack's side, he wrapped it around his shoulders. Jack didn't resist, instead he looked up, his eyes welling with tears, and said in a voice so full of pain that I had to turn and walk away before my own tears fell.

"She doesn't need me!"

\*\*\*

I joined Maya and Ben at the front of the plane.

"How's the patient doing Maya?" I asked, trying to sound as cheerful as I could.

Maya looked up at me calmly. "Can we go home now?"

I smiled. "Yes Maya, we can - all go home now." A thought suddenly dawned. "Ben, where's Tina2?" I hadn't seen her since we boarded the plane.

"Oh yes, good thing you mentioned her, I locked her up front and asked her to do some complicated equations. I had to get her out of the way, she wouldn't have understood, she would have perceived Jack as a threat. She can come out now that all the fuss has died down."

Ben went to get up. Colin put his hand on his shoulder. "You stay where you are, Meg is getting Jack into some clothes and settling him down, then she'll come and see to that arm. Thank you Ben, you handled this well. Tina will help me get us into the air. You relax. you look as if you're in good hands." Colin patted Maya on the head.

"Well," he said, with a smile, "Let's all go home."

That sounded so good. It wasn't long before Meg joined us.

"Is Jack, our Jack again?" Maya asked, giving voice to all of our concerns.

Meg stroked her hair. "Yes honey, Jack is our Jack. He was just a little confused and upset, he's sleeping now. Well let's get Ben stitched up, shall we."

Ben groaned. "It's not that bad, I think it will be fine with a bandage," he protested.

"Don't be a baby," Meg scolded playfully, "I'll give you a jab, you won't feel a thing and it will be over before you know it. Maya, you can pass me what I need out of the first aid box. Alan, Jack is sleeping back there, would you go and keep an eye on him. I don't think he will wake for a while, but just in case, he needs to know he's with his family!"

I nodded, I felt honoured to be included in this strange family group. I left Ben arguing a case, he was bound to lose.

Jack was tucked up in one of the beds. I made myself comfortable in the seat which gave me the best view, without being so close I might wake him. I felt relieved, that we were all on our way home - together.

From what Jack had said, Colin had been right, Jack didn't belong here with the white wolf. I hoped, for his sake, that he would find that special someone. I took the pouch out of my pocket and removed the ring. I placed it on my little finger and as the diamond caught the light, the red became more vibrant. It seemed to come alive. Tiny sparkling stars danced deep in its heart. Maybe it was just the plane's engines starting up, but the ring seemed to pulsate. I looked up. Jack was watching me intently from his bed. I don't know why, but I felt guilty. I quickly removed the ring and placed it back in my pocket. Jack closed his eyes.

The plane climbed, banked to the left and then settled on its course home. Colin came and sat in the seat opposite, he saw my expression. "It's alright Tina2 is taking care of things and Ben is keeping her company. Meg said it would take his mind off his war wound.

Jack still sleeping?"

I nodded and he smiled.

"Good, it's been hard on him, these past few days, it's been hard, on all of us. Meg tells me Natasha's back, that's great news. Let's hope she at least, has found some answers. What about you Alan. Did you get any answers out of our sally?"

I sighed. "No, not really, just more questions. It'll be good to get back home. I can't wait to see Natasha. What about George and Goldie? You said something earlier about George needing you. Is everything alright, has Meg said, anymore?"

He shrugged. "All she will say is 'things are just as they should be'. I know Meg would tell me if something was really wrong. But still - there is something! Anyway, we'll be home soon. I tell you one thing, the only snow I want to see for a long, long while, will be decorating a Christmas card.

Look Alan, when we get back, why don't you take some time off. I've a rather nice resort hotel, on a small Island in the Maldives. Use the plane. Take Natasha, it would give you two a chance to catch up. Maybe invite your mother."

I obviously didn't look convinced. I had an instant vision of Natasha and my mother discussing my finer and not so finer points. It was un-settling to say the least.

Colin laughed, it was a relaxed laugh. It sounded good, he looked better than I'd seen him look in days. "Ok Alan how's this? Take Natasha for a couple of weeks, and then invite your mother to join you both there. I'm sure they would both like to meet each other. They are guaranteed, to have at least – one thing in common!"

It was my turn to laugh. "I'm sure they would. Seriously though, it's a great offer Colin. Thank you. I will ask Natasha when we get back."

"Of course Alan, take your time, when you're ready the trip is on me. Oh, I almost forgot, Meg told me to tell you there's coffee."

I thanked him again, I could smell the coffee and something else, fresh baked scones of course. How did she do it? Meg could conjure up good food, anywhere, any time.

"Butter and jam?" Meg asked, handing me a mug of coffee.

I nodded and took the mug and a seat next to Maya. She was busy eating, she beamed at me. Meg handed me a plate. "You'd better be quick Alan; Maya is on her second already."

I thanked her. Meg took some up front for Ben and re-joined me as I was polishing off the last of the crumbs from my plate. She sat in the opposite seats and beckoned me to join her. I sat down next to Meg. I could feel the ring burning a hole in my pocket, but I chose not to mention it, not just yet.

Meg put her hand on mine. "How are you doing Alan, looking forward to seeing Natasha?"

I sighed, there was no point in lying to Meg, she would see straight through me. "I'm not sure how to tell her - you know - about the vampire thing! I should tell her shouldn't I?"

Meg smiled. "As usual Alan, that decision is yours to make, but I will say this, a lasting relationship is built on truth and trust. If you want this relationship to stand the test of time, my advice, would be hold nothing back. You're both special people Alan, good people." She squeezed my hand.

I felt reassured, I knew Meg disliked vampires. She had made that very clear, yet she seemed to still like me, maybe everything would be alright. I started to feel a little better.

She continued, "The future won't be easy, you both have your own demons to face, but by facing them as one, you will grow - together, become stronger. We will all be glad to get home."

"Thanks Meg, it's funny, I already think of the island as my home. I don't think I've ever felt this attached, to a place before. But since we've been away, something seems strange. I can't focus, I've tried to find out how things are, but it's as though something is keeping me out."

"Ah yes that would be George!" Meg said as if this explained everything.

I waited expecting her to continue, when she didn't, I was forced to ask. "I don't understand Meg, why?"

Meg laughed. "You shouldn't take it personally, it isn't just you Alan. George is just looking after things whilst we're gone, he'll have thrown a protective cloak over the island, to keep out prying eyes. It would be foolish to assume, that we are the only ones with the power to see further than the end of our nose!"

Of course she was right. I was beginning to realize, that this world held more secrets than I could have ever dreamed possible. It seemed that for most of my life, I'd been walking around with my eyes and my mind half closed.

"Colin has suggested I take some time off, when we get back, meet up with my mother. Apparently he has a nice hotel on an island in the Maldives we could stay at." Meg nodded. "He said to take Natasha," I added.

Meg burst out laughing. "That's Colin to a tee!! Sorry honey, I wasn't making fun of your situation, but really!! You, Natasha and your mother, on a small island in the middle of nowhere - no dear, trust me, that's just not going to work out!"

I laughed too. "I must admit, I had my doubts too."

She smiled. "Alan, you need to talk to your mother, but more importantly, you need to listen. Keep an open mind. I think now, you're beginning, to understand that things are not always as they seem. Go home Alan, meet your mother. She'll feel more comfortable there. She'll find it easier to tell you the things you need to know.

When you have your answers, by all means take Natasha to the Maldives. You will both love it. Colin bought the island to protect a beach, where for many years Turtles have visited to lay their eggs. One half of the Island is a sanctuary and research area, the other has a fabulous eco hotel. The whole thing was a wedding present for Sophie, it is without doubt one of the most romantic places on this beautiful earth. Make the most of it - with Natasha."

I thanked her. I decided to go up front and see how Ben and Tina2 were doing. As it was, I wished I had stayed where I was. I walked straight into an argument. You would think, it would probably be difficult to have a heated conversation with a computer, but Ben was giving it a good go!

Ben's voice was raised. "You would have over reacted Tina."

"I, do not over react. I am programmed to protect you Ben. I cannot do that if you lock me out!" Tina2's voice sounded even, but definitely a little louder than usual.

"I didn't need protecting. I had things under control," Ben said, trying to pull his sleeve down further over his bandaged arm.

"I can see that. You had me doing pointless equations. You could have been killed."

Machine or not, Tina really did sound pretty angry. The little sphere turned, I resisted the temptation to step back. The voice changed instantly and became smooth and calm again, "Hello Alan, it is good to see you again."

I nodded at Ben and smiled Tina's way. "Hello Tina, it's good to see you too. Is everything alright?"

"Yes Alan, thank you for asking," she purred.

Ben indicated for me to sit next to him. I'd never sat at the controls of a plane before and even though the atmosphere was, a little strained, I couldn't help feeling like an excited child. There were dials and flashing light's everywhere.

Tina2 settled herself into a space, made for her on the panel, between me and Ben.

Ben looked slightly embarrassed. He smiled sheepishly. "Sorry about that Alan. Just a little… misunderstanding." He was quick to change the subject. "How's everyone doing back there?" He nodded towards the rear of the cabin.

I felt mesmerized by the lights. "Pretty normal considering, isn't there something you should be doing," I asked.

Ben laughed. "Like what? Once we're in the air, this thing practically fly's itself. I was about to contact base, to give them an update on our present position, although to be perfectly honest, Tina will be monitoring us every step of the way. But a little birdie told me, there could be someone there that you might like to say hi to!"

By the smirk on his face, I knew exactly who he meant and I couldn't hide my excitement. "Could we get them on the radio?"

Ben looked smug. "We can do better than that can't we Tina2? Would you contact base for us please."

Tina2's lights blinked but nothing happened. Ben looked perplexed. "Tina," he repeated a little louder. Tina2 blinked again. "Sorry Ben," she said smoothly, "Did you need me, for something. I thought you had things, under control!"

I stifled a laugh, Ben didn't look amused. "Ok Tina, I get the point. I'm sorry," he said.

Tina2 whirred into action and the small monitor was produced, from her depths. "Thank you, Ben. I am connecting to base now." The little sphere beeped.

I held my breath, would she be there? The screen cleared and Natasha smiled back at me. God how I'd missed that smile.

"Alan, it's great to see you, oh and Ben of course."

Ben laughed. "Oh don't mind me, I know when I'm playing gooseberry, but I think Alan might pee himself, if I leave him up here alone," Ben teased.

But he was right. Natasha laughed. Suddenly I felt like a tongue tied teenager, I didn't know what to say.

Natasha on the other hand seemed relaxed. "It's good to see you Alan. I hear things have been difficult, I'm sorry I wasn't there to help out."

"Not your fault," I managed, eventually finding my tongue. "How about you, did you find your answers?" Her smile faded a little.

"I was close Alan, I know it!" She sighed and I felt sorry I'd asked, now was not the time. I wanted to put my arms around her.

She brightened again. "What about you Alan? I hear from Sophie that you met your first vampire, how cool! I've heard about them, from Meg - mainly, not her favourite people of course. I've never met one myself. What was she like?"

She seemed excited at the prospect of meeting a vampire, hopefully a good sign!

I glanced at Ben, he shrugged. Now wasn't the time for that little bombshell either! I laughed nervously. "It's hard to know where to start. This trip has been a rollercoaster from start to finish. I promise to tell you every detail when we get back."

Before I could say anything else, Sophie appeared on the screen.

"Hi Guys. I'm presuming everything is in order now. What time should we expect you Ben?"

Ben straightened in his seat. "Hi Sophie, there was a - small problem, but all sorted now. With this tail wind we shouldn't have to re-fuel, so ETA should be around 10 am your time."

Sophie looked relieved, she smiled. "That's great. It will be good to have everyone home again. I imagine Colin and Jack are taking it easy with Meg and Maya. They are alright, aren't they Ben? Colin did say he had something he needed to tell me, about Jack."

Ben shifted uneasily in his seat. I could see he wasn't sure what to say. I decided it was best to leave all the explanations till we got home, so I put on what I hoped was my reassuring voice. "All present and correct Sophie, as Ben said, we had a couple of problems but things are good now. We couldn't bring home the white wolf, but we've made life a little safer for her and her cubs. The mountains and forest will be a better place, for the rest of the wildlife too. So all in all, a job well done, I think."

Sophie laughed. "Give us a call when you're nearing the island and we'll all come meet you. Alan, tell Meg everything is going well. She will know what I mean. Oh and say hi to Maya from Toby, he was furious, that she was able to come and help you. Secretly I think he has been worried about her, and all though he would hate me for saying it, he's missed her! We'll see you all tomorrow, safe journey."

With that the screen went blank. I stared at it, for a couple of moments then glanced at Ben. "A small problem!" I exclaimed, shaking my head. "Bloody hell Ben, I would hate to see a big one!"

Ben grunted. "I don't intend to see any more big or small, I don't care if Colin is the boss. I'm not leaving my lab again, for anyone – ever."

I left Ben to kiss and make up with Tina2, well makeup anyway and joined Meg and Maya. They were now playing snap, something I felt much more at home with. I gave Meg, Sophie's message. She just smiled and nodded, but made no comment. I knew there was no point in asking what it meant.

The rest of the journey was thankfully uneventful, Jack slept most of the time. Colin and Ben took turns up front and Meg kept food and drink coming at regular intervals. I had several long conversations with Maya, well, when I say conversations, mostly I listened. Now she had found her voice, she was making up for lost time. But I actually enjoyed hearing her chatter away excitedly, about the snow and the sleigh and Sally. She had really liked Sally.

It was whilst Maya was having a nap, and Meg was off somewhere putting together another of her fabulous snacks, that Jack joined us at the front of the plane. He stood awkwardly in the isle for a moment, and then sat down next to Ben.

In almost a whisper, Jack said, "Sorry Ben." It sounded heart felt, he got up to leave. Ben stood. "Wait Jack, I'm glad you're coming home with us. I always feel safer when you're around - keeping an eye on things."

Jack nodded and slowly mad his way, back down the plane.

Ben looked across at me and shrugged. "Well I owed him one. After all, I did shoot him. We must be even now, wouldn't you say?"

I smiled and nodded, in this strange world what was a bullet wound or the odd tooth or claw mark between friends?

\*\*\*

I managed a couple of hours sleep, but I was restless. I couldn't wait to see Natasha again, but at the same time, I felt anxious. We had to talk. I wasn't comfortable with the vampire thing. How would Natasha react?

Even though we flew straight through, the flight seemed longer going home. Eventually we were instructed to fasten our seat belts for the landing.

Meg pointed out the island to Maya and I looked out of the window at our small sanctuary. From this height it did seem small. Who could imagine the great wonders it held and the safety it provided, for all of us.

As the plane taxied to a halt, I spotted the two jeeps coming to meet us. Toby was driving one. As the door was opened and the steps put in place Spike was the first to greet us, well greet Colin at least. He flew up the steps and into Colin's arms, yapping happily and wagging his tail madly.

I looked down the steps and smiled. Scruffy, who had only recently conquered her fear of the house steps, was now courageously tackling the steep steps of the plane. One at a time, it took so much concentration she didn't even bark. I met her half way and as I scooped her up into my arms, she licked my face.

"Have you got a kiss for me too?" Natasha wrapped her arms around us both, and kissed me gently on the lips. Our eyes met and suddenly nothing else mattered, I had everything I needed, here in this moment. We were home. Scruffy licked Natasha's face too and she laughed. "Well, I didn't specify who - I wanted the kiss from, I suppose."

Toby hugged his father then looked past him, for Maya. She was alighting with Meg. He seemed unsure of how to greet her. Maya on the other hand, had no such worries. She ran at Toby and jumped, wrapping her arms around his neck and squealing. "I missed you. I have so much to tell you - it was snowing – there was a sleigh and dogs and everything!"

Toby looked a little embarrassed, but never the less, happy.

Sophie called out to Jack, who was standing at the top of the steps looking dejected, "Jack come down here now! It's not your fault you know, it sounds as if things have turned out pretty well in the end, besides we already have a new wolf, we need to keep an eye on." Sophie glanced at Toby, who groaned.

"Oh Mum, just because you can't keep up."

I saw Colin trying to catch Sophie's eye. Jack had reached the bottom steps now. Toby shook off Maya and ran to meet him. "Jack, mum say's I can come out with you."

Sophie coughed loudly and Toby corrected himself "If it's ok with you and Dad that is. Please say it is, I want to learn everything. Dad, it's ok - isn't it?"

Colin nodded. "I think it would be alright, every now and then, when you haven't got home work. If Jack can put up with you, that is. What do you say Jack. It's your call?"

Jack never smiled much anyway, but in the past few days, the light seemed to have disappeared from his eyes. But all at once, it seemed to return. The sparkle was back, Jack was home. "I should take a look around the island now, to check on things!" Jack said.

Toby looked at Colin. "Can I Dad please."

Colin laughed. "All right, sod off both of you, but don't think I don't know it's just a ploy to get out of unloading the plane. Don't be too long either. I want everyone round the table together at lunch. Ok?"

"Ok Dad," Toby shouted back over his shoulder as Clothes flew in all directions. Man and boy raced each other, disappearing on all fours into the bush. Sophie shouted after them, "Toby, remember to stay away from George and Goldie. They don't need you hassling them at the moment."

Meg started to pick up clothes. "How is everything going out there, has George managed to get his head round - things yet?"

Colin interrupted her, "Alright you two, we're home now, what's been going on. What things? And don't you dare say NOTHING!"

Sophie took his arm. "You were right of course dear, we were a little worried for a while there. Goldie seemed pretty sick. George was beside himself. We all talked and decided there was nothing you could do. We thought food poisoning, or exposure to a virus, or something. After all, she had been locked away for some time. However Meg soon got to the bottom of things."

Ben joined us. "What's going on?"

Colin shushed him. "That's what we're trying to find out. Well Meg. What is it, will she be ok?" Colin looked worried.

Meg laughed. "Like I told you Colin, it really was nothing - Goldie wasn't sick, well not in the way you mean."

I could tell Colin's patients was starting to desert him, it had been a long and stressful few days. "What other way is there, she is either sick, or she isn't!"

All three women laughed.

Meg beamed. "Well it turns out, dragons get morning sickness. Just like humans.

Who would have guessed."

\*\*\*

We sat on the veranda, looking out over the island. Natasha had her head on my shoulder. Colin and Sophie had gone to see George and Goldie. Apparently dragon's pregnancies are long, about 13 months. We were all excited.

Jack and Toby were off exploring the island.

Meg and Maya were playing with the Kittens, well cats really. They were growing so fast and showed no signs of stopping.

Ben, well he would be safely tucked up in his lab with Tina.

The day was warm. The late afternoon sun danced over the distant water. The sound of bird song, drifted up to us from the forest below and the two dogs, dozed lazily at our feet.

There was so much we would need to talk about, so much we needed to find out about each other. The journey had only just begun. But now, we could make it together.

There was the fabulous ring, still burning a hole in my pocket, a promised visit to see my mother and maybe a holiday on Turtle Island with Natasha.

But here and now - this was all we needed, this was enough.

Tomorrow there would be questions and hopefully some answers, journeys and new adventures.

But well, that would be - another story.

CPSIA information can be obtained at www.ICGtesting.com
Printed in the USA
BVOW08s2027270716

457062BV00001B/1/P